T0051879

DARK DEBTS

KAREN HALL

SIMON & SCHUSTER PAPERBACKS

NEW YORK LONDON TORONTO SYDNEY NEW DELHI

Simon & Schuster Paperbacks
An Imprint of Simon & Schuster Inc.
1230 Avenue of the Americas
New York, NY 10020

This book is a work of fiction. Any references to historical events, real people, or real places are used fictitiously. Other names, characters, places, and events are products of the author's imagination, and any resemblance to actual events or places or persons, living or dead, is entirely coincidental.

Copyright © 1996 by Karen Hall, Inc.
Revised edition copyright © 2017 by Karen Hall

All rights reserved, including the right to reproduce this book or portions thereof in any form whatsoever. For information, address Simon & Schuster Paperbacks Subsidiary Rights Department, 1230 Avenue of the Americas, New York, NY 10020.

First Simon & Schuster Paperbacks edition September 2017

SIMON & SCHUSTER PAPERBACKS and colophon are registered trademarks of Simon & Schuster, Inc.

For information about special discounts for bulk purchases, please contact Simon & Schuster Special Sales at 1-866-506-1949 or business@simonandschuster.com.

The Simon & Schuster Speakers Bureau can bring authors to your live event. For more information or to book an event, contact the Simon & Schuster Speakers Bureau at 1-866-248-3049 or visit our website at www.simonspeakers.com.

Interior design by Ruth Lee-Mui

Manufactured in the United States of America

10 9 8 7 6 5 4 3 2 1

Library of Congress Cataloging-in-Publication Data is available.

ISBN 978-1-5011-0411-4
ISBN 978-1-5011-0412-1 (pbk)
ISBN 978-1-5011-0413-8 (ebook)

For the guy in the flannel shirt

If only it were all so simple! If only there were evil people somewhere insidiously committing evil deeds, and it were necessary only to separate them from the rest of us and destroy them. But the line dividing good and evil cuts through the heart of every human being. And who is willing to destroy a piece of his own heart?

—Aleksandr Solzhenitsyn,
The Gulag Archipelago

Too few dark debts are ever paid . . .

—Gary Gilmore,
untitled poem

—

PROLOGUE

Manhattan, 1995

Michael sat on the witness stand, feeling like a six-year-old who'd just been informed that the nurse would be back momentarily with his shot. He watched the defense attorney pace and think. Scott Bender. Court appointed, in the middle of his Andy Warhol fifteen minutes and milking them for all they were worth. Michael had developed a strong dislike for the guy somewhere around "nice to meet you," for no concrete reason. His haughty attitude, perhaps, with no evidence of money or breeding to back it up. Michael had come from the social class to which Bender aspired, and then he'd opted for a life that meant giving it all up. Which was probably his reason for resenting Bender—the way someone on an eternal diet resents fat people walking around with ice-cream cones.

"Father Kinney"—Michael was addressed as "Father" every third question, lest the jurors lose track and begin to think of him as an insurance salesman in a Roman collar. "Father . . ." Bender repeated, for the sake of the truly dull. "Is Bishop Roger Wilbourne your immediate superior?"

"No, he's not."

"And who is?"

"Frank Worland. The Jesuit provincial."

"Can you explain to us how that chain of command works?"

If the jurors were having trouble remembering his occupation, Michael doubted they'd be able to follow the intricate inner workings of the Jesuit hierarchy. Nor could he understand what difference it made to the matter at hand. But he explained. Provinces. Regions. Rectors. Provincials. Father General. Rome. The delicate balance of Jesuitdom. Forever and ever, amen.

"So if you wanted to do something, say, out of the ordinary," Bender asked, "you'd need permission from your provincial?"

"That's correct."

"And that provincial would be Frank Worland?"

"Yes."

Michael could see Frank glaring from his seat in the third row. Up until this insanity, he and Frank had been friends. Not particularly intimate, but close enough for the occasional dinner or game of racquetball. Those days were over, he knew. Their tense conversation from the night before was still churning in Michael's head like cerebral indigestion.

"Michael, if you go through with this, there will be consequences. And you're not going to like them."

"I don't have a choice."

"There's a very simple way out of this."

"I don't consider lying simple."

"No one is asking you to lie. All you have to do is plead confidentiality."

"Frank, nothing that happened was told to me in confidence. Quite the contrary, as you well know."

"But the judge needn't know it. And the defense has no way to disprove you."

"Well, at least you're not asking me to lie."

"All you're going to do is buy the Church another round of bad publicity. Is that your goal?"

"I don't have a goal! I was subpoenaed."

"And so," Bender continued, "was Frank Worland the superior from whom you needed permission to become involved with my client's . . . situation?"

"No. For that I needed permission from the bishop."

Michael hadn't even told Frank about it, which was part of Frank's anger. But, as Michael had tried to explain, he'd gone into this mess thinking he was doing a small favor for an old friend. He would certainly have mentioned it to Frank had he known it was headed toward a triple homicide.

"And permission from the bishop was never granted, is that correct?"

"That is correct."

"So you made a decision to act without the authorization of either your provincial or the bishop, did you not?"

"Yes."

"And why was that?"

Michael took a moment to search for a diplomatic way to put it. "I felt the situation was . . . critical."

Bender nodded. Michael braced himself for the question he'd been dreading, which he assumed would come next. It didn't. Instead Bender returned to the defense table to check his notes.

Michael took the opportunity to scan the crowd. The courtroom was packed for the third straight day. People had been lining up in the mornings to get a good seat. The first two days had been pretty boring, but their persistence was about to pay off. Today they were going to get their money's worth.

Oh, hell.

That woman. The editor from the *New Yorker*. God had not taken him up on his offer: anything he owned, or would come to own in this lifetime, in exchange for her having some other pressing engagement today. It was bad enough to have to make a public fool of himself without her sitting fifteen feet away. What was her name? Tess something. Tess McSomething. Pretty name. To say nothing of its owner. She was wearing an emerald-green jacket, and her red hair hung loosely around her shoulders. It had been tied back every other time he'd seen her. He'd met her in the hallway the first day of the trial. She had introduced herself and asked him to do an interview for the article she was writing about the trial. He'd said he'd think about it. Yesterday she'd left two messages, which he hadn't returned. Now she caught his eye and smiled. He didn't return that, either.

Bender had reemerged from his legal pad.

"Father, we were talking earlier about this magazine that you edit. What kinds of articles would we find in this magazine?"

There was something subtly patronizing in Bender's voice. Michael wasn't entirely sure of its source, but had a feeling it was something along the lines of "I spend my life fighting for truth and justice, and you spend yours in complete devotion to a fairy tale." There was probably a little bit of "and you're a eunuch to boot" thrown in there. Michael was used to that subtext by now, but it had never stopped bothering him.

"We publish scholarly articles," Michael answered, trying hard not to repay the condescension. "Articles written by priests. Sociologists. Religious historians."

"So this is a serious magazine? People take it seriously?"

"I certainly hope so."

"You don't print articles on things like the Virgin Mary appearing on someone's garage door?"

"If we did, it would be under the category of psychosis and religious hallucinations, and it would be written by a Jesuit psychologist."

Bender nodded and Michael took a breath. It was hard to remember that he and this jerk were sympathetic to the same cause.

"Father, would you describe yourself as a cynical person?"

"I'm a priest. I'm obviously selectively skeptical at best."

"Do you believe in UFOs or alien abductions?"

"No."

"Crop circles?

"No."

"Spontaneous human combustion?"

"No," Michael said, finally losing his patience. "And I don't believe in Santa Claus or the Easter Bunny or weeping statues or milk shakes that cure cancer and I think that Elvis is really dead. If you're asking me if I'm gullible or easily misled, the answer is no. I am not."

"Well, that's certainly direct and to the point," Bender said. "You'd never make it as an attorney."

There were snickers from the crowd and Bender's illusion of dignity was restored.

"Okay. Let's go back in time, to the day before you met Danny Ingram."

Michael wished he could go back to that day, so he could turn and run in the opposite direction. Sitting at the defendant's table, Danny had his eyes locked on Michael. He looked exhausted, and much younger than his fifteen years.

"On that day," Bender continued, "did Father Michael Kinney, the nongullible serious-Jesuit-magazine editor, believe in the Devil?"

A hush fell. Michael heard someone stop midcough.

"No. I did not."

"And if we move forward from there to the day Danny was arrested . . . On that day, did you believe in the Devil?"

Michael didn't answer immediately, allowing himself one last moment of respectability. He could already see his picture on the front page of tomorrow's *New York Post*. He snuck a furtive glance at Tess McWhatever. She was taking notes.

"Father?"

"Yes," Michael said. "On that day I did."

Rustling. Mumbling. At least there was no laughter. No audible laughter, anyway.

"And did your encounter with my client play a part in your change of opinion?"

"Yes."

"In fact, it was your encounter with my client that was entirely responsible for your change of opinion, isn't that correct?"

"Yes. That's correct."

Bender smiled and nodded. This was his idea of a good time.

"Okay, Father. Let's go back to the day you met my client. I want to ask you a few questions about that day."

Michael waited while Bender checked his notes again. He glanced over at the *New Yorker* woman. She was writing and did not look up.

When the elevator door opened on the second floor of the Jesuit residence, Michael was accosted by the sound of a cocktail party coming from the lounge next to the dining room. There was always a cocktail hour before dinner, but it was usually limited to about seven regulars. From the sound of it, there had to be at least fifty people in the front room now. They spilled out into the hall.

Michael headed for his room. Whatever it was, he wanted no part of it.

Halfway down the hall, Larry Lantieri came out of his room, drink in hand. Michael knew why. Larry claimed he'd taken an extra vow: never to drink cheap scotch.

"Mikey," he said, raising his glass in a toast.

"What is that?" Michael asked, nodding toward the noise.

Larry smiled. "Frank's birthday party. Didn't you get an invitation?"

Strangers with wine glasses were making their way down the hall, examining a row of framed magazine covers. Michael looked to Larry for an explanation.

"He removed cloister until ten o'clock so everyone could admire his kingdom. But don't think you can hide in your room, unless you're dreaming of a small parish in Siberia."

Michael ignored that and headed for his room.

"Where are you going?" Larry called behind him.

"To check my messages, change my clothes, and hang myself from the showerhead."

He closed the door before Larry could offer a rebuttal.

He was pleasantly surprised to see only one message on the answering machine. He hit the Play button and started divesting himself of his clerical garb.

"Hi. It's Tess McLaren. Again. The reason I've been calling is that I've decided I'm not the one who should be writing this article. I've been reading some of your stuff, and . . . well, if they end up defrocking you for this, you can come to work for me anytime . . ."

The phone rang just as the message ended. Michael answered it, with some trepidation. He was greatly relieved to hear his grandfather's voice on the other end.

"So how'd it go?"

"I'll send you the *National Enquirer* clippings. I'm sure you'll be proud."

"I am proud. You did the right thing."

"Then why do I feel like crap?"

"The right thing doesn't have to feel good. It only has to be right."

Michael sighed. "Listen, can I call you back in a little while? I have to go to a public lynching."

"Call me when you can. I want the sordid details."

"You can have them now: I no longer have any credibility as a journalist. I no longer have a relationship with my provincial. I wouldn't place big money on getting a hug from the bishop anytime soon. And the jury is still going to vote to convict. But I did the right thing. God is impressed."

"Send me the papers."

"I'll make you a scrapbook."

Michael hung up. He wasn't about to relive the day's events, not even for Vincent. He stared through the blinds at the dirty windows of the building next door. The air was filled with the usual rush-hour din of taxi horns and sirens of gridlocked emergency vehicles. This time of day the city always depressed him.

Shedding the clerics would help. Like most Jesuits, he hated wearing them, and he certainly couldn't lose himself in the party crowd with them on.

He was halfway out of his shirt when there was a knock at his door. Someone wanting a trial update, or Larry coming to drag him to the party? The possibilities were equally repugnant.

"It's open," he called, making no attempt to sound hospitable.

"Are you sure?" A female voice.

What the hell?

He pulled his shirt back on. "Relatively," he said, mostly to himself. He was on his way to the door when it opened and there she stood. Still wearing the green jacket. And a short skirt. And legs that were a near occasion of sin. Not good.

"Hi," Tess said, smiling.

"How did you . . . ?" He stopped, searching for the rest of the question.

"How did I what?"

He tried to put it together. Had she somehow been invited to the party? Or had she just dropped by to visit? Either way, how had she found him?

"I asked someone which room was yours," she said, answering his question. "Why? Is there a rule against girls in the dorm?"

"Even if there were, I'm not a big fan of rules, as you know if you were paying attention in court."

"Apparently you're not a big fan of returning phone calls, either."

"Do you show up at the doorstep of everyone who doesn't return your phone calls?"

"No." She let it go at that, but punctuated it with an indecipherable smile.

"I haven't been avoiding you any more than I've been avoiding anyone else," he said. "I'm a little preoccupied right now."

"I know. I'm sorry. But if we're going to do this thing, the clock is ticking."

"Do what thing?"

"The article. Didn't you get my last message?"

"Yeah. Something about me being defrocked and coming to work with you. I'm pretty sure I can sue you for sexual harassment."

She laughed. She even laughed like a woman with a brain.

"So do you have to go to that party? Because if you don't, the *New Yorker* will buy you dinner and/or a drink and we can talk about the article."

"I don't think it's a good idea."

"The article, or dinner with me?"

He didn't answer. In truth, he liked the idea of writing the article. Almost as much as he liked the idea of having dinner with her. But both were minefields, and he was in no shape to negotiate either of them.

"I just don't want to make a decision tonight."

"Fair enough."

"For the record, I plan to remain frocked."

He didn't have to wonder if she understood. It was interesting to see a stunned look on her face. He doubted it was a frequent occurrence.

"I stand advised," she said, recovering.

"I realize I'm being incredibly presumptuous, but I'd rather be presumptuous now than uncomfortable later."

"So what you're saying is that you're particular about which rules you break."

She went on before he had a chance to respond. "Since you're laying down the ground rules, does that mean you're saying yes to the article?"

"I'm saying maybe. I want to sleep on it."

She nodded. "Good enough. You can call me in the morning."

"Okay."

Just when he thought he was safe, she added, "Are you always this skittish around women?"

"Only the ones who follow me home."

"I don't follow many people home. You should be flattered."

"I stand advised," he said.

She smiled, and then she was gone.

He woke up at precisely three a.m., from a hazy dream about her. Nothing dangerous, but it was all the sign he needed. He'd call her tomorrow and politely decline her offer. He didn't need to set a new record for how much trouble he could get into at one time. And he knew well the slippery slope that started with a simple "So *why* are you celibate?" Very bad time to be venturing toward that cliff. And besides, there was nothing to be gained from writing the article.

Or was there? He was torn between the idea of letting it all die and the idea of explaining himself to the rest of the world. He was never going to accomplish that by testifying at the trial. It would never change anything that mattered.

What matters?

That used to be such an easy question to answer. But the thing (*The what? The brush with Evil?*) had done something to him. Nothing he could define. He just knew that he had not survived the confrontation—whatever it was—unscathed. The events were over, but something bigger was not.

Someday, at some unexpected hour, it would return. And next time, Michael somehow knew, he wasn't going to walk away so easily.

Next time, in fact, he might not walk away at all.

BOOK ONE

Fate is not an eagle, it creeps like a rat.

—Elizabeth Bowen, *The House in Paris*

THE RAT

ONE

Los Angeles, 1996

Randa couldn't move. She could feel her weight in the chair and it was the only thing keeping her upright. How long was she going to have to stay here? It was three o'clock in the morning and she had to be at work by nine. Or did she? Was this a legitimate excuse to take the day off? Did she have a right to mourn? And would everyone see it as mourning, or merely as the final chapter in a neurotic obsession?

She had felt uncomfortable at the paper ever since last summer. She knew a lot of people had bought the self-serving pile of crap Cam had spread around, in which she came off as a psychopath.

"How long did you say you've known Mr. Landry?" It came from the older one: a doughy, middle-aged man wearing a shirt the color of Dijon mustard. Neither of them looked anything like she would have expected a detective to look.

I don't know a Mr. Landry. Mr. Landry is someone's political science teacher. I know Cam.

"Seven years. Or eight." Then she added, "I haven't seen him in a year." She didn't know whether that was relevant or not. It was certainly relevant to her.

They had made her identify the body. A granite-faced man from the coroner's office had lifted the sheet, while a uniformed cop had supported her by the elbow in case she collapsed. Apparently a fifteen-story fall onto the concrete sidewalk had yielded all sorts of ugliness. She'd have to take their word for it. All she had seen were Cam's eyes. Truth be told, they were all she had ever noticed when she looked at Cam. She noticed everyone's eyes, but Cam's were unlike any she'd ever seen. An ephemeral blue, the color of jeans that have faded just right. But it wasn't the color that gave them their haunting quality, it was the depth. A depth that knew no context, like the light inside a prism. Somewhere near the bottom, a crystal base of hope managed to send a trace of itself to the surface. Along the way it was clouded over by layers of pain and sadness and bitter defeat. That was what she had always seen in Cam's eyes. The hope and the bitterness, locked in mortal combat. Even now, she knew something inside her would be forever scarred by the outcome of that battle.

She glanced at her reflection in the dirty glass partition. Her eyes seemed to be sinking into her face. They looked, as her mother would have put it, like "two little pee holes in the snow." She tucked a strand of thick blond hair behind her ear, as if that would help. Was thirty-five supposed to look this old? Had she looked so old this morning? God, why was she worrying about how she looked at a time like this?

She braced herself as an angry wave of pain washed over her.

How can this be real? How can Cam be dead? He's outrun it for so long.

Outrun what? What part of her was talking, and what was it talking about? She'd noticed lately (in the last year, maybe?) that there seemed to be a voice inside her head that would blow through, make some grand pronouncement, and then disappear without the slightest desire to explain itself.

"We've been trying to locate a relative to notify. Do you happen to know of anyone?" It came from the younger detective. His light brown hair had a waxy texture that made him look like a Ken doll.

Randa shook her head. "They're all dead."

"No aunts, uncles, anything?"

"Not that I know of."

She wondered if she should mention Jack. It wouldn't do them any good, but it would give them something to chase and might therefore get her out of here sooner.

"There's a brother somewhere, but you won't be able to find him. Cam has been trying for years."

The younger one clicked his ballpoint. "You know his name?"

"Jack. It's probably a nickname, though. They all had fancy names."

"They all who?"

"Cam and his brothers. There were four of them. "

"And all the brothers are dead, except for this Jack?

"Yes."

I'm not holding out on you. I don't want to keep the corpse for a souvenir.

"So where does this Jack live?"

"Somewhere around Atlanta, the last anyone heard from him. But that was ten years ago."

"And there's absolutely no one else?"

It seemed he wasn't going to let go of this until she told him something new. She tried to think. Who would have been called if she hadn't shown up? The answer slammed into her head. She took a deep breath.

"He has a girlfriend. Nora Dixon."

A lying bitch from some back corner of Hell who'd better not show her sorry ass in here until long after I'm gone, unless you want to add a homicide to your caseload.

"I don't know why she wasn't there," Randa continued. "I thought they were living together."

She must have met someone who could do her career more good.

"Wait a minute." The younger one again. "If she's his girlfriend, who are you?"

"Good question," Randa said before she could censor it. She immediately hated herself for the venom she could hear in her voice. How could she be mad at Cam *now*?

"What does that mean?"

"I'm sorry," she said, not sure why she was apologizing. "We used to be friends."

"Why'd you stop?"

She looked up in time to see Detective Ken Doll wink. Wonderful. Now he was going to flirt with her. Just what she needed.

"I don't see how that's relevant."

"Whoa." He made a show of looking around the room. "Are we in court already? Time flies."

Very cute. David Letterman is quaking in his Nikes.

"What time did you say he called you?" The older one showed no sign of noticing the sparring.

"Around one o'clock."

"Can you be more specific?" he asked.

"One oh nine? Or nineteen?" Randa said. "I remember a nine on the digital clock."

"You remember a niiiiiiine? What part of the South are y'all from?"

The part where men talk to women the way you're talking to me, which is why I left.

"Georgia." She gave him the iciest look she could muster. *Say "peach," I dare you.*

"Georgia," he repeated, in a tone that implied there was something remarkable about being from Georgia. He let it go at that. He seemed not to be picking up on her unequivocal lack of interest.

The other detective raised an eyebrow. "Did you know Mr. Landry from Georgia?"

"No. We met here. That was just . . . a coincidence." She trailed off as she heard her father's voice in her head. *"Coincidence is a fool's defense."* Why she thought she needed to defend herself was another question.

Memories of Cam were starting to emerge, shooting at her like darts. She was surprised at what was coming back. No great moments. A barrage of banality. Stopping to get directions from an old guy in a Shriners hat. An unknown folk singer playing the back room of the guitar store. Late-night dinners in funky little coffee shops. The one with a full bar. Cam's favorite. Following Cam through cramped, musty bookstores while he piled her arms with books she couldn't live a meaningful life without reading. Petty arguments that had turned vicious and personal, only to wind their way back to civility and dissolve in a change of subject or a joke. Sitting here now, she couldn't remember any big events. Had there even been any? Instead, she just felt the time. All the mundane, directionless time that makes up a friendship.

A friendship? Was that what it had been? A friendship that had been hanging over her head like the sword of Damocles for more years than she cared to acknowledge. Did Cam's death mean the sword had been sheathed? Or was she now stuck with it forever?

"So when he called you, he didn't say anything that indicated . . ."

"That he was about to jump out the window? No. And I don't know why he'd call me to come over if he was planning to kill himself before I could get there."

"Are you saying you don't think he jumped?"

"You said his door was locked from the inside. Obviously he jumped.

I'm just saying that if you're waiting for *me* to make sense of it, we're going to be here a long time."

"Had he been depressed lately?"

"I don't know. Like I said, I hadn't seen him for a long time."

If he'd been breathing, he'd been depressed lately. She'd never seen him go longer than a week without falling into a major funk. She had learned to stop worrying about it. Who could blame him? It was a wonder he could tie his shoes.

"So why did he call you tonight?"

HOW many times are we going to go through this?

"I don't know. He said he needed to talk to me. And he said something about being in some kind of trouble. He didn't say what the trouble was, he didn't explain why he was calling *me* specifically, and he didn't say he might kill himself if I got stuck in traffic."

The older detective nodded and wrote something down, completely unfazed by her impatience. He stared at his memo pad. This was how it had been going for the last hour. He'd ask a few questions, make a few notes, and then stare at the pad. If there was any logic to it, Randa didn't know what it was.

Why was this taking so long? Why couldn't they just chalk it up as another suicide in the big city and be done with it? Surely they had better things to do. Wasn't Hollywood, all myths aside, the crime capital of the planet?

The older detective was looking at her as if she'd missed a major point, and she realized he'd just made some proclamation.

"I'm sorry, what?"

"A couple of hours ago, someone robbed a liquor store a few blocks away from Mr. Landry's apartment building."

Was that the big news flash? She knew the liquor store he was talking about. It was on the corner of Sunset and Vista, with a wide front door angled for easy access (and getaway) from both streets. She and Cam had joked that the owner should just put out a sign that read PLEASE ROB ME. ("My brothers would have used that place as an ATM," he'd said.) But what did it have to do with Cam's death?

" . . . witnesses described the robber as a white male in his late thirties, about six-three, salt-and-pepper hair, wearing a nice suede jacket, an odd shade of green. He asked the cashier to throw in a bottle of Chinaco tequila. Not exactly your standard profile." He smiled a little. "Your run-of-the-mill liquor-store robber will usually settle for Cuervo Gold."

Randa stared at him. Cam had a tequila fetish that was no secret to anyone who knew him or had read his books. And she had given him a sage-green suede jacket two Christmases ago. But surely the detective wasn't implying . . .

"I noticed an unopened bottle of Chinaco on Mr. Landry's desk and it rang a bell. Far-fetched, I know, but I swung by and had some of the witnesses take a look at Mr. Landry's driver's license, and what do you know? Bingo."

It was all Randa could do not to laugh.

"That's the most asinine thing I've ever heard. It's . . . comical."

"Yeah, well, I've got a nineteen-year-old stock boy over at the county morgue with a bullet wound in his chest, and he ain't laughing."

"Well, if you think Cam had anything to do with it, you're out of your mind." The incredulity in her voice raised it an octave.

"What makes you so sure?" the younger one asked, in his best serious detective voice.

"In the first place, Cam had more integrity, more *humanity*, than anyone I've ever known . . ." For the first time, she choked up. "And he hated guns. He would never have touched a gun, much less shot someone. And then there's the fact that he'd just signed a book deal with a two-hundred-thousand-dollar advance, which would pretty much alleviate the need to rob a liquor store." She was practically yelling at them, which was a waste of adrenaline. This whole thing was from *The Twilight Zone.*

"Two hundred thousand dollars?" It was the older one who spoke, but the younger one's jaw had dropped open with the sudden knowledge that he was in the wrong business. The older one recovered and continued.

"How do you know that if you haven't talked to him in a year?"

Because all my so-called friends sent me every clipping they could get their hands on, just in case I'd missed it.

"I read it in *Publishers Weekly.*"

The older detective nodded, momentarily appeased. "Well. Be that as it may . . ." He stared at his desk for a moment, then looked back at Randa.

"The neighbors told us some interesting things about Mr. Landry's family history, which I assume you know."

So there it was. Randa had figured they'd end up here eventually.

"That's exactly why I know this is crazy."

"Why's that?"

"Because it is. Look, I've known Cam for a long time and I know him . . . *knew* him . . . well."

"You hadn't seen him in a year."

"I don't think he had a soul transplant in that time."

Then why did he do what he did to you? And why did it catch you so off guard, if you knew him so well? And what was that phone call about? What about what he said . . . "I'm in trouble that I didn't know existed." He certainly knew that liquor stores existed. But what about the witnesses? Could they have been that mistaken? Impossible. No one else on earth looked like Cam.

"Maybe he just had you fooled." Detective Ken again. His arrogance was now enhanced by a patronizing sneer. Randa abandoned all efforts to hide her contempt.

"I don't fool that easily."

They locked eyes, and Randa did not look away as another man approached the desk. She could hear him talking to the older detective as he rustled something out of a brown paper bag.

"Back closet . . . under a pile of clothes . . ." She looked up. The older detective was holding a plastic bag. Inside, marked with a small cream-colored tag, she saw the gun. Her entire body locked with disbelief. The man was still talking.

" . . . Forensics dusted it, we're waiting . . . Ballistics said send it over, they're not busy. I said there's no rush, the guy's dead . . ."

"Rush anyway."

Randa stared at the gun. Were they saying it came from Cam's apartment? Captain Arrogance could barely contain his glee.

"Well, what do you know? Looks like you fool easier than you think."

It was nearly dawn by the time Randa got home. She sat on her sofa in a stupor as the sun rose and the room lit up around her. She could only think; she couldn't feel. Her emotions were locked in the bottleneck of information—Cam's death, the police, the guy at the morgue, the gun—it was too much. It numbed her.

She had finished filing her column by six o'clock and had settled back to zone out in front of a true-crime miniseries that had sounded promising in its reviews. She'd given it fifteen minutes before deciding that the critics were all imbecilic and turning it off. She'd flipped through the latest *Rolling Stone*, but couldn't bring herself to care about Bruce Springsteen's horse farm. All she could do was replay this strange night in her head over and over, searching for any part of an answer.

It had been one of those nights that reminded Randa that she'd inherited her mother's nerves. She had been consumed by a feeling of lurking doom. It had made no sense. Looking back on it now, it was as if she'd spent the night waiting for the phone call, as if some deep, hidden part of her had known it was coming.

She had been sleeping on the edge of the bed with her head near the nightstand, and the phone had scared the hell out of her. She hated middle-of-the-night phone calls. A wrong number or someone was dead—too wide a spectrum to prepare for on a moment's notice with a pounding heart.

"Hello!" She'd answered in a tone that demanded a quick explanation.

"Randa?"

She'd recognized the voice immediately. For a millisecond she had considered hanging up on him, but then she'd asked herself who she thought she was kidding.

"Cam?"

"I have to talk to you. It's really important. I know it's late, but I have to talk to someone and you're the only person I know who might believe this."

"Believe what?"

"I can't do it on the phone. Randa, it's crazy, it's . . . Look, you always said you'd do anything for me."

"That was a long time and many erroneous perceptions ago."

"I know. We can talk about that, too. You don't know . . . you can't believe the things you don't know."

"Hell, I can't believe the things I *do* know."

"Dammit, Randa!" It was so loud and so out of character, she'd almost dropped the receiver. "I'm in trouble! I'm in trouble that I didn't even know existed! Now are you going to come help me, or are you just going to send a nice wreath to the funeral?"

"Okay, calm down. I'll be over as soon as I can."

"No! Not here!"

"All right. I'll meet you at Ray's?"

"That works. But hurry."

"Okay. Bye."

"Randa!"

"What?"

The line was silent as he thought. "Nothing. Just hurry."

Ray's was the coffee shop where Cam all but lived. He ate there at least once a day, sometimes three times. His loyalty had mostly to do with the place's proximity to his apartment. Cam lived in Hollywood, in an area Randa had always referred to as "the hills above Hell." She had tried repeatedly to talk him into moving to a better neighborhood, but he said he couldn't write in an antiseptic environment. She had offered that there was a wide range between antiseptic and "likely to be shot in the underground parking garage," but he'd never listened.

It was a little after two in the morning when she got to Ray's. It wasn't the first time she'd been there at that hour, so the clientele did not catch her off guard. Homeless people, rock-and-roll types, prostitutes of both genders taking a break from trolling, and an eclectic assortment of insomniacs. The "denizens of the deep," Ray called them, with a certain amount of affection.

Ray was in his early fifties, short and round with dark features and several visible tattoos. Where he had ever come up with the money to open a coffee shop was a mystery, as he was no businessman whatsoever. Half the regulars had running tabs that they never paid, and whenever someone approached the cash register holding a bill, Ray seemed pleasantly surprised. Randa was convinced he was in the witness protection program. But he was friendly to her, and extremely fond of Cam.

Cam was nowhere to be found, and his car wasn't in the lot. Ray was sitting on a stool at the counter, poring over a racing form.

"Ray?"

"Hey, Randa! Where the hell have you been?"

"I've been around."

"You ain't been around here."

"No." The last thing on earth she wanted to do was explain it to Ray. "I'm looking for Cam. Have you seen him?"

"Not since breakfast."

"Breakfast?"

"Noon. *His* breakfast. So does this mean he finally unloaded that spook?"

Ray called any woman with dark hair and heavy makeup a spook. Randa had tried before to explain the racial undertones, but Ray wasn't interested.

"I have no idea. I haven't seen him in a long time."

"Yeah, I know. I always ask him about you."

He must love that.

She wondered what Cam had said. She moved away? She got hit by a train? Or had he told Ray the truth? Had the two of them had a good laugh and a moment of male bonding at her expense?

She ordered a cup of coffee and stepped away to use her cell phone. She'd never taken Cam off her speed dial. The call rang twice before it was picked up by an answering machine and she heard Cam's voice telling her to leave a message.

"Cam? It's Randa. I'm at Ray's and you're not. Are you there?" She gave it a moment, but he didn't pick up. "I guess you're on your way. I'm giving it ten minutes and then I'm leaving." *Yeah, talk tough. You'll sit here until Hell freezes over.*

She hung up and went back to the dining room. She could see a cup of coffee sitting at "their" table, where Ray had put it. There was also a Coke for Cam, and a chocolate chip roll. Ray had never been an ally in her effort to get Cam to eat better. Still, it was a thoughtful gesture.

She sat down and tried to collect herself. She wanted to be as stoic as possible by the time Cam arrived. Over the past year she had dreaded the inevitability of coming face-to-face with him, because she had no idea how to act. Part of her still felt the same way about him as she'd always felt, and another part wanted him to die slowly and painfully at the hands of skilled torturers. She tried to will herself to stay calm. She would listen to what he had to say and react to that, and only that.

What was this about? And how did it involve her? No matter what trouble Cam was in, he had throngs of friends he could have called. People who lived closer, people who stayed up later, people he hadn't spent the last year trying to pretend he'd never met. Not to mention Lady Macbeth. Where was her lying ass?

Half an hour and two cups of coffee later, Randa was sick of waiting. Cam could have walked here three times since she'd left the message. It was obnoxious enough to have called her here in the first place. Now he was taking his time getting here, leaving her to cool her heels among the night crawlers?

As soon as Ray's back was turned, she put some money on the table and left to drive up the hill to Cam's place.

She remembered the drive well. It was only then that she had started to wonder if Cam really was in some kind of trouble. Up to that point, she'd been telling herself not to panic. Given Cam's flair for hyperbole, he could make misplacing a credit card sound like a matter of life and death. But he *had* sounded different. She'd told herself that he'd felt awkward because of the nasty way they'd parted. *Hell, he* should *feel awkward.* If he was suddenly willing to call her, knowing it would mean having to face her fury . . . something might really be wrong.

But what?

She'd just begun to hypothesize when she'd turned onto Cam's street, into a sea of flashing lights.

TWO

Barton, Georgia, 1996

Jack reached over and turned off the alarm clock the second it started to buzz. He'd awakened at four a.m. with a sense of foreboding so strong it felt like someone was sitting on his chest. He was used to vague, intangible fear. He'd lived with it his entire adult life. Fear left over from when there was a reason for it, the way an amputee still feels pain from a missing limb. But this was different. It was as if he'd been jarred awake by a loud noise, but he couldn't remember hearing anything.

And then he'd had the most ridiculous urge to call Cam. Where the hell had that come from? He hadn't seen or talked to Cam in almost a decade. He rarely thought of his brother, and when he did, he still felt an anger bordering on rage. Why would he think of calling Cam? What did he think he'd say? "Hey, asshole, it's the Ghost of Christmas Past. How's your cushy life?"

As soon as he'd sent those thoughts packing, his mind began to bombard him with memories of things completely forgotten about. Vignettes from his childhood, random and meaningless. Like fishing trips with his mother's twin brother, Uncle Ryland, the only member of the extended family who had ever acknowledged their existence. Ryland had adored the boys, and they'd adored him, even if he was a certified loon. It was Uncle Ryland who had taken them to the Rotary Club–sponsored Huck Finn Day at Lake Allatoona, the one summer they'd managed to attend that much-heralded event. It was one of his few pleasant childhood memories. Their mother had dressed the four of them in matching overalls and different-colored plaid shirts, borrowed from Ryland's kids (cousins they'd never met), and they had passed themselves off as a normal family. Tallen caught the biggest fish of the day and got his picture in the paper. Probably the only time in his life Tallen had his picture in the paper without breaking a law. There was something about Tallen and fish. Ryland used to say that all that boy had to do was *call* them.

Their father had been unimpressed. Said fish liked Tallen because they had so much in common—their main thought in life was how to keep from being caught. He also said Tallen wasn't any better at it than the fish were. He always seemed to have even more contempt for Tallen than for the rest of them, which was saying something. Jack's theory was that it was because Tallen so obviously worshiped Will. Will Landry was not comfortable with anyone's affection, and made it a point to punish those who bestowed it.

It suddenly dawned on Jack why he was thinking about them. He'd had that dream again. It had been worse than usual, in some way he couldn't remember. It would come back to him, though. The bad stuff always did.

The phone rang. It had to be Rick, the guy who owned the temp company through which Jack usually worked. Rick was the only person who had this number; the only reason Jack owned a phone (let alone an answering machine) was to find out whatever he needed to know about his next job. The machine picked up. He cringed at the sound of his own voice, as always, and waited for Rick's.

"Yeah . . . Jack . . . This guy called here looking for you . . . I told him I'd check with you and call him back. He sounded kinda . . . official . . ."

Jack picked up the receiver.

"I don't care if he sounded like the president, Rick! How many times do we have to have this conversation?"

"Well, he said it was important."

"What do you think he's going to say? 'This is an asshole reporter'?"

"I just thought . . . I mean, do reporters still call you?"

Jack sighed. No use explaining to Rick why that wasn't the point. "This year is the tenth anniversary," he said with forced patience. "Reporters love crap like that."

"Oh. God. Sorry. I didn't think of that."

"Well, start thinking. And don't give anyone my phone number. Anyone. Ever. No exceptions."

Rick apologized again and hung up.

Jack wrenched himself out of bed. The day was off to a lovely start.

He headed for the bathroom, hoping there was a bottle of aspirin in the medicine cabinet. He should keep a record, he supposed. Did he always wake up with a headache after the dream? If the headaches got any worse, he'd have to go back to the pain clinic in Atlanta, and they'd ask him about things like that.

There were two aspirin left in the bottle. He swallowed them without water. He closed the cabinet and glanced at his face in the mirror. He looked like he hadn't slept at all. Felt like it, too. At least he didn't have to be anywhere early. The job he'd been working had finished yesterday, and he didn't start a new one until Monday. He might pick up something for today if he went and stood in front of the Western Auto with all the other day-labor candidates. He didn't have to worry about getting there early. The black and Hispanic guys might sit out there for hours, but the minute a white guy showed up—even him—half the town would remember odd jobs that couldn't wait. Blond hair was all the résumé he needed.

He really didn't care whether he worked today or not. It had been a good month, and it wasn't like he needed to save for anything. Maybe he'd go down to the coffee shop. Maybe a decent breakfast and half a pot of black coffee would be enough of a bribe for his headache. Besides, the thought of being around other people was not as repulsive to him this morning as it usually was.

Half an hour later he was dressed and headed down Route 36, hands in his pockets, his work boots crunching the loose gravel on the side of the road. The early-morning sky was a dull gray, and the fine mist that was falling felt good on his face. If it turned into a steady rain, he'd have a guilt-free excuse for not working.

"Men in the Rain." A poem Ethan had written when they were in school. Something about walking along beneath John Deere hats . . . dirt disturbed . . . a final destination . . . Their mother had taped it to the door of the refrigerator. (Lucy had always gone out of her way to encourage their artistic pursuits. Anything to keep them inside, out of trouble.) He remembered the title because the rest of them had given Ethan a hard time about it, had made all sorts of insinuations about Ethan's sexual preferences. (Tallen, home during one of his brief bouts with freedom, had said, "Go steal a car, Ethan. You'd *love* reform school.") What a joke. There had never been a shred of real doubt about any of them, as far as that went. Even Cam was a raging heterosexual.

Why the hell couldn't he get his mind off his family today? Most of the time he didn't think about them at all. He stuck militantly to the safe subjects: what should he eat, what should he read, where was he working tomorrow? Lately, more and more of the other stuff was slipping through the cracks. Was he getting careless? Or was it somehow safer now? He couldn't figure why it would be.

The dream was coming more often, too. He used to have it about three times a year. He'd already had it twice this month. He couldn't remember when it had started. Was it after Ethan died? Or his father? Or Tallen? Hard to remember; he got the funerals mixed up. Not something he felt great about, but it was the truth.

Whenever it had started, he'd been having the dream for years. Some things about it varied, others remained doggedly consistent. It was always dark. He was always walking down some lonesome stretch of two-lane. Desolate. The sky more purple than black. Angry mountains in the distance. The whole scene always looked like one of those gloomy landscapes Tallen used to paint. Jack would walk along, not knowing where he was headed or why, and suddenly he'd come upon some colossal, gruesome accident. There were always red lights flashing everywhere. Sometimes he would see dozens of cars piled on top of each other, smashed and twisted, shards of glass and metal covering the ground like confetti. Other times, there would be no cars. Just the bodies. Bodies lying everywhere. Horrible-looking bodies—bloody, with limbs broken or missing, some of them decapitated. And no one seemed to be helping them. He'd walk through the carnage, recognizing people from his past—old friends, teachers, distant relatives. At the end of the line, he'd always find them—Ethan, Tallen, his father, and later, his mother. All badly mangled, reaching out for him, calling him, as if he could do something. He'd stare at them, and more than fear or horror or anything like that, the strongest feeling he'd have was always his wonder that he wasn't with them. Cam was never with them, either, but that made sense. Cam had never been with them.

Even after it had become familiar, the dream would cling to him for days, like a filmy coat of something old and sour. He was sure the dream was symbolic as hell, and that it recurred because he didn't know what it meant. Sooner or later, his subconscious would get the message that he didn't give a crap what it meant and would leave him the hell alone.

The coffee shop was not terribly crowded. He sat at the counter, where he was least likely to draw attention to himself.

"I knew you were gonna be here today." Sherry, the new waitress, was already pouring him a cup of coffee. She was an energetic redhead in her midtwenties. Pretty, in a JCPenney sort of way, but she talked too damned much.

"Why?"

"I don't know. Maybe I'm psychic." She fished her guest-check pad out of her apron pocket. "Let's see if I can guess. Two eggs, scrambled, bacon, wheat toast."

"Over easy, sausage, Sunbeam. Don't hang out your shingle just yet."

"You did that to be ornery."

"And a side of grits."

"I knew that."

She left to take the order to the kitchen. Jack watched her go, almost smiling to himself. She had only been working there for a couple of months. He guessed she was new in town. It was the only possible explanation for the fact that she flirted with him. He responded mechanically. On those rare occasions when someone tried to engage him in conversation, his basic rule was to go along with it. Easier to stay invisible if he just went with the flow.

Jack poured cream into his coffee and watched as it turned a smooth caramel color. From an unseen radio Reba McEntire was wailing about whatever man had done her wrong this week, over which floated the usual country small talk: "Whatch'all know good? How's your mama 'n' 'em?" From somewhere else he could hear his mother's voice. *"Jackson Landry, please write the word 'once' and show me where there's a* t *at the end of it. There aren't many things in life that I can control, but I will not have my boys talking like a bunch of ignorant country hicks."*

Sherry returned from the kitchen and went down the counter collecting saltshakers. She came back with a handful and stood in front of Jack to refill them.

"So is it gonna rain?"

"You're the psychic, you tell me."

"Smart-ass." She smiled as she said it. A plump, dark-haired waitress brushed by Sherry and nudged her with an elbow.

"I gotta talk to you." The woman disappeared into the kitchen without waiting for an answer.

"That's Darlene. She usually works the dinner shift."

Jack nodded, although he didn't know why she felt the need to explain it to him.

"She probably broke up with her boyfriend for the fifth time this week. Sonny Reynolds, you know him?"

Jack shook his head no, which he would have done even if he had known the guy.

"He's a prison guard over in Jackson." She leaned down and lowered her voice. "It must not take brains; he ain't got the sense God gave a june bug."

Jack stared into his coffee cup, lest his eyes yield any clue that he didn't need to be told about prison guards. Sherry prattled on.

"I know she's no beauty queen or nothin', but she could sure do better than that ignoramus."

The door to the kitchen opened and Darlene stuck her head out.

"Sherry." She gave Sherry a look that meant business and disappeared again. Sherry looked at Jack and rolled her eyes. She screwed the top on a saltshaker and, with an exasperated sigh, headed into the kitchen.

Jack took the opportunity to survey the breakfast crowd. The usual eclectic mix. Lawyers. Farmers. A couple of housewives and their kids. The janitors from the courthouse. He knew most of them by name—the lawyers and the janitors. He'd gone to school with them. The coffee shop divided into the same cliques the high school had. He'd felt so alienated from them all back then. He hadn't known anything.

He then spied his least favorite coffee shop regular—the priest from the postage stamp–size Catholic church at the north end of town—seated a couple of stools away. As usual, "Father" was dressed in jeans and a plaid shirt over a thermal undershirt, sleeves rolled just right, like he thought he was a lumberjack. The guy never wore his collar, and Jack wouldn't have known who he was except that it was impossible to move to Barton without being the buzz of the coffee shop for a few days. The previous priest had died three or four months ago—of a heart attack, a stroke, liver cancer, or AIDS, depending on which rumor one chose to believe. Father Casual had made his appearance a few weeks later. Jack had heard he'd transferred from New York City and figured he must have screwed up royally to have been exiled to rural Georgia.

Jack rarely had the emotional energy to hate someone on sight, but he'd made an exception for Father. It was partly the clothes. It was also the John Lennon glasses and too much hair for a guy who looked to be in his late forties. And it had to do with Jack's aversion to religion in general, although the Protestant ministers didn't inspire the loathing in him that this guy did.

It might have something to do with the way the guy always stared at him. Once he had tried to strike up a conversation, but Jack had warded it off with "Look, I don't know whether you're trying to save me or seduce me, but the answer is no either way."

The door to the kitchen opened and Sherry returned, no longer smiling. She put the plate of food down in front of him.

"Can I get you anything else?" she asked. The perkiness was gone from her voice.

"No, thanks."

She tore his check out of her pad and laid it on the counter in front of him. He watched her as she went back to refilling saltshakers. She was spilling a lot more than she had been before. She glanced up and their eyes met. She quickly turned and busied herself checking coffee filters. Jack watched her with growing anxiety. A hazy suspicion was trying to form, but he pushed it away.

Suddenly Sherry was in front of him again. She crossed her arms and sighed as if she was disgusted.

"This is so dumb."

"What?"

"Darlene telling me how to run my life."

Jack relaxed a little. This was just some tiff between a couple of waitresses. He reached for his coffee cup and Sherry dropped the bombshell.

"She thinks I shouldn't talk to you."

Jack felt the muscles in his stomach contract as his dark fears were confirmed. Something in Sherry's eyes triggered an old anger. He caught it, turned it off.

"Fine." His voice was calm and quiet. "Don't talk to me, then."

"So is it true? What she said?"

"I don't know what she said."

"You know. About your family."

"What about them?" He'd be damned if he was going to make this easy for her.

"You know."

He stared at her, unflinching. She looked around to make sure no one was listening, then looked back at him and spoke quietly.

"She said you had a brother who was executed."

It had been a while since Jack had heard those words. They went through him like a cold wind. He didn't answer.

"She said it was a few years ago."

Ten. A decade. Another lifetime.

"She said it was in Alabama."

"Well, Darlene is handier than the *World Book Encyclopedia*, isn't she?" His voice was calm and steady, but it was an effort.

"He musta done something terrible."

Jack stood up and dropped more than enough money on the counter.

"You mean she left that out? Get her to fill you in. I'm sure it'd make her day."

Heading back down the road, he told himself it was his own fault. He never should have let himself get drawn into that. He could hear Tallen's voice from long ago: *"Why do you talk to them? They don't care about us. They're just looking for gossip. We're their entertainment."*

No matter where they'd lived, the Landrys had always been the family in town whose name was never spoken without the word *those* in front of it. Actually, Will Landry's name was usually spoken alone, in a tone that said all anyone needed to know. And most people felt sorry for Lucy, for all she'd had to endure. But the boys were *those Landrys*. A blight on the community. The kids everyone warned their kids to stay away from.

Jack couldn't even remember, really, how he and his brothers had first come to be disenfranchised youth. He remembered the earliest deeds, but not the compulsions. Maybe it was as simple as the fact that "juvenile delinquent" was an identity within their reach, and a negative identity was better than none at all. Or maybe it was because they'd inherited Lucy's pride, and they simply couldn't stand the way people looked at them. Maybe they'd provoked people's ire to be spared their pity.

This notoriety had not been easily won. In rural Georgia, adolescent wildness was given a wide berth before it was looked on as anything other than good-old-boy-in-training behavior. Smoking and drinking and poaching a deer or two were hardly enough to raise any eyebrows. Drugs were a right step in the wrong direction—a step that all of them had taken as often as they could afford to. Upon realizing that the Landry brothers hurting *themselves* was not going to keep anyone up nights, they began to go that necessary extra mile. They hot-wired cars for joyrides, leaving them wherever they happened to get bored. They vandalized property. (Turning over the Coke machine in the basement of the courthouse was one of their favorite pastimes.) They committed all sorts of petty thefts and burglaries. Nothing hard-core in those early days. They'd left themselves room to grow.

None of this, of course, applied to Saint Cam. It wasn't like he openly sided against them, or ratted on them when he knew something. He mostly stayed in his room and ignored them. But whenever he'd have occasion to meet their eyes, he'd give them a look that left no doubt as to the degree of his scorn. They'd made his path difficult, and he made sure they knew he hated them for it. Meanwhile, he studied hard, kept his nose clean, and walked around with his put-upon attitude, as if nothing short of some great cosmic blunder could have landed him in a house with these people.

The truth was, Cam knew better than that, he just chose to ignore it. He was too bright and too close to the source to be able to write them all off the way the rest of the world did. He couldn't look at them and say "white trash, lowlife, end of story." He knew damned well that wasn't the end of the story. It wasn't even the beginning.

Jack himself wasn't really sure where it began. Maybe it had to do with the polarity of his parents: Lucy, a sensitive and delicate beauty from an old Savannah family that no longer had any money, but whose remaining forty acres allowed them to keep thinking of themselves as landed gentry. (They'd all disowned her when she'd married Will.) And

Will Landry, a lone hellcat of a man whose only parent had been a mentally unbalanced daughter of sharecroppers; he'd never known anything but poverty and rejection—a fact he did not accept quietly. The two of them had been attracted to each other because of their vast differences, and then spent the rest of their lives trying to kill each other for them.

The boys had grown up caught in the middle. Lucy did everything to encourage the artistic inclinations they all seemed to have inherited from her—Cam's prose, Ethan's poetry, Tallen's painting, Jack's love of reading. Will thwarted her efforts at every turn; he was violently opposed to anything that made his sons look unmanly. He'd never managed to beat the art out of them (though God knows he'd tried), but he'd successfully trained them to sabotage their own efforts. All of them except Cam.

As far as Jack was able to figure, the difference was that Cam had used his talent to pull himself out, and the rest of them had clung to art as a source of comfort in the prison they thought they had no hope of escaping. *Was it really that simple?* he wondered, thinking about it now. Did it all boil down to the fact that Cam had felt hope and the rest of them hadn't? And, if so, where had that hope come from? Was it something a person was born with, like blue eyes? Had the rest of them just been born without it? Where was the justice in that?

He chuckled to himself. Justice. What in God's name was it going to take for him to stop considering the possibility that somewhere, somehow, the world was fair and life made sense? The truth didn't have to be fair. The truth could be that Cam had been born with a chance and the rest of them hadn't. Cam wouldn't have liked that theory much; it would have deprived him of the right to feel superior.

Well, none of that mattered now. The accident waiting to happen they'd called a family had exploded. Jack and Cam had been the surviving debris, hurled in opposite directions, landing intact, but not whole. Now Jack spent his days going through the motions of living, never really sure why he bothered. And somewhere out there, Cam was busy turning his life into a quest for vindication. Maybe he'd even gotten it. Well . . . fine. Good for him.

The drizzle had turned into a steady rain, and Jack could feel the wet chambray of his work shirt sticking to his back. He'd be drenched by the time he got home. What the hell. This day had never had any intention of being on his side.

Suddenly it flashed back to him. The thing that had been different about the dream last night. He didn't know why it had left him so upset, but he knew what was different. Last night, for the first time, Cam's body had been lying there, too.

THREE

Randa managed to get a couple of hours of sleep before it was time to go to work. She woke with a fuzzy knowledge that something horrible had happened, but she couldn't remember what it was. When she did remember, she had a moment of hope that it had been a nightmare. She saw the jeans and blouse she'd worn draped over the chair and that hope dissolved, leaving her with only the crushing reality.

Cam was gone. Even more gone than he had already been. She wondered how many years it would take before she wouldn't even remember what he'd looked like, or the sound of his voice. Or the tiny scar on his chin she'd never asked him about. Or the way he crinkled his nose when she said something that annoyed him. Or the way he stared at his hands when he lied.

She wished, like she'd wished a year ago, she'd had a chance to say good-bye. The man from the coroner's office had told her they wouldn't release Cam's body until after they had spent a reasonable amount of time trying to find Jack, so Randa knew there was no funeral planned. There would probably be some sort of a memorial service that she could go to if she made an issue of it, but whenever she imagined it, she could see herself alone in a corner, watching people console Nora. No thanks.

She decided to go to work, since the alternative was sitting around in her apartment making herself crazy. She showered and dressed in layers of black—black leggings, black boots, black oversized turtleneck sweater. The contrast between the dark clothes and her crop of shoulder-length wheat-colored hair might compensate for something. She stared in the mirror at her pale, sleep-deprived skin and exhausted eyes and decided any energy spent on makeup would be wasted. She brushed some peach-colored blush over her cheekbones and said to hell with it.

She dialed the paper and asked to speak to Roger Eglee, the managing editor. She had to start somewhere, and Roger was a friend. At least, he seemed to be. She no longer put her faith in things like that. "Okay," Roger said as soon as he picked up the phone, "what creative excuse have you come up with for missing the staff meeting?"

"It's pretty creative," she answered in a flat voice. "Cam's dead."

"*What?*"

"He killed himself. Last night."

"Oh my God." In addition to writing a column for the paper, Cam was also one of Roger's poker buddies, although he'd been quick to side with Randa when everything had blown up. "Oh, my God. Randa. I can't believe it. What happened?"

She proceeded to tell him the whole story, including the part about the police station and the liquor store, which sounded even more preposterous as she recounted it. She asked him to spread it around the office before she got there so she wouldn't have to go through telling it again. Told him she'd be in soon, then hung up before he could argue with her about it.

Half an hour later, Randa parked her five-year-old Volvo behind the ratty two-story building that housed the *Chronicle*'s offices and printing presses. The building was on the east end of Sunset, in a neighborhood where Randa definitely had to get in her car and drive if she wanted anything other than a greasy burrito for lunch. But she had always liked the old building. It wouldn't have made sense for the paper to be in some spanking-clean, architecturally barren building on Ventura Boulevard. Creativity thrived in an underdog environment, and this old firetrap certainly provided that.

They were an odd bunch, the people who wrote for the *Chronicle*. Like most members of the alternative press, they thought of themselves as "real" writers. They tolerated rival journalists (barely), but looked down on their peers who sold out for the big bucks and bigger compromises of Hollywood. (The *Chronicle* writers thought of the screenwriters as whores, the screenwriters thought of the *Chronicle* writers as permanent adolescents, and neither group was entirely wrong.) For Randa's part, the job provided her with two things she craved: freedom and respect. She knew she wasn't likely to find either anywhere else.

There was an eerie feeling in the air as she made her way through the newsroom. There was no music blaring, no laughter coming from the offices, none of the raucous atmosphere that usually prevailed. Randa could see people looking at her out of the corners of their eyes. She stared straight ahead and walked quickly to the relative security of her tiny, cluttered office.

The call to Roger hadn't ended up buying her much. The minute she sat down at her desk, her office was filled with people who wanted all the gory details. She'd given them a few perfunctory answers, but made it clear she didn't enjoy talking about it. Finally the vultures cleared out, and she was left with a couple of Cam's actual friends. Barely an improvement, all things considered.

Keith Heller, the paper's film critic, sat in a corner and stared at the wall. Ever since Randa and Cam had parted, Keith had been actively avoiding her, wasting little energy on subtlety. He had adopted Nora's version of the story like it was the latest software upgrade. (According to Nora, Randa's only reason for being attracted to Cam was some bizarre fetish for the criminal history of his family. Randa supposed that made her a first cousin to those crazy women who married their death row inmate pen pals. A wimpy cousin, though, who didn't have the guts to go for the real thing.) In truth, Keith had never liked her anyway, and now he had something concrete to pin it on. She was sure he was currently unhappy about the fact that the pseudo-wake had ended up in her office. It made her grateful for Roger, who was sitting on the corner of her desk, picking the eraser off a pencil and shaking his head over and over.

"I just can't believe it," he said for the dozenth time. He looked ill; but then, Roger was a man who, under the best of circumstances, looked like he was on his way to a CAT scan. "This must be awful for you," he said to Randa.

She nodded, a bit embarrassed. Since Keith considered her grief to be psychotic, it wasn't a topic she wanted brought up for discussion.

Keith looked at Roger as if Randa weren't in the room. "I must have left him ten messages this week. I should have gone over there. I just never would have thought . . ."

"No one would have," Roger assured him.

"I don't get it." Keith shook his head. "Why now? His career was taking off, he had finally gotten into a decent relationship—"

"Excuse me?" Randa interjected.

Keith shrugged. "His words, not mine."

Randa winced. *You vindictive ass.*

Roger jumped in to help. "Do you have any idea why he would have called Randa out of the blue?" Randa appreciated the diplomatic acknowledgment of her existence.

"No." Keith looked at her, finally. "He hadn't mentioned you in a long time."

It was another shot. Roger didn't notice this time. He was lost in his own thoughts. "This whole liquor store thing is from Jupiter."

Keith nodded. "The cops had some candy-ass case they wanted off the books, they found out a little about Cam and they just used him."

"They said they found the gun in his apartment," Randa offered. She wasn't trying to incriminate Cam, but an explanation would be a nice thing to live with.

"They did?" Keith's tone was mocking. "Well, that clinches it. The LAPD certainly wouldn't lie."

Randa told herself that Keith was extremely upset about Cam and held her tongue.

George Maynard appeared in the doorway. George was the paper's insufferably conceited music critic, whom Cam had always described as "the most obnoxious person I know whom I like anyway." Randa agreed with the first half of that.

"What the *hell* is going on? Is it true?"

Roger nodded glumly. "Yeah."

"Christ. I don't believe it." George removed his wire-rimmed glasses in a gesture that seemed calculated. He and Cam had never been particularly close, but there was no way he was going to miss the melodrama. It fascinated Randa, the way people vied for custody of the friendship of anyone who died young or tragically. George, putting in his bid, came into the office and pulled up a chair. "So . . . what? Does anybody believe this?"

"No one believes he robbed a liquor store," Roger answered. "I mean, come on."

"Well, maybe he did." George had an endearing habit of switching positions the minute anyone agreed with him. "Maybe it was, like, Attack of the Runaway Gene Pool."

"George." Roger gave him a look of contempt. George ignored it and turned to Randa. "Somebody said you were there."

"No. I mean, I was, but . . . I got there right after . . ." She didn't know how to finish, so she didn't.

"What were you doing there?" George asked, as if he were conducting a Senate hearing.

"She says he called her," Keith answered.

"He *did* call me," Randa said, trying to stay calm.

Keith shrugged. "Maybe it was someone else, you were half-asleep and you thought it was Cam."

"Dammit!" She picked up a binder from her desk and hurled it at the wall, where it crashed and sent paper flying. The guys were all too stunned to move.

"He called me! I'm sorry you don't like the narrative, but that's what happened!"

Roger was motioning for her to calm down. "Randa, everybody is just—"

"Don't!" Randa stopped him. "Whatever happened last night, none of you were in it! And how I felt about Cam and why I felt it was nobody's damned business a year ago and it's nobody's damned business now!" She left, slamming the door behind her as hard as she could.

She sat in her car and took deep breaths. Now she'd done it. It might have felt good for five minutes, but those five minutes were not going to come cheaply. Keith was already after her scalp. Well, to hell with it. If she got fired she could go find herself a job with a salary she could tell someone with a straight face.

Truth be told, she had no idea what the fallout from this was going to be. She had no history of outbursts. To the contrary, she usually chewed her nails and internalized and planted the seeds of future ulcers.

Randa didn't know what to do with herself. She didn't want to go home and be alone, but being around other people had certainly not turned out well. She decided to drive. Driving always made her feel better. It was a way to have a connection to the world without having to participate. She especially loved to drive in LA, where the landscapes changed vividly from one neighborhood to the next. The lost souls wandering down Hollywood Boulevard. Overdressed agents lunching with disgruntled clients at the outdoor cafés on Sunset Plaza, all of them happy enough to see and be seen; breathing carbon monoxide was a small price to pay. Tanned, muscular guys in tight jeans strolling down Santa Monica Boulevard with their arms around each other. Beverly Hills housewives dressed in their Chanel suits, on their way to lunch at the Beverly Wilshire before the Ferragamo trunk show at Saks. The Santa Monica promenade, with its bizarre mix: yuppies; beach bums; panhandlers; an occasional schizophrenic preaching fervently to a nonexistent congregation.

She drove aimlessly for about an hour, then paid a guy in a red vest three dollars for the privilege of parking at the Santa Monica pier, where she could stare out at the ocean. She did that until she was bored, then leaned her head back on the headrest, closed her eyes, and made a conscious decision to let herself remember.

Cam had come into her life eight years ago. More precisely, she had come into his. She had happened upon a book he'd written during one of her book-buying sprees. She had seen it on the "Staff Picks" shelf at Book Soup and had been intrigued by his name. *Cameron Landry* seemed far too poetic for a mystery writer. When she read on the jacket flap that he was also from Georgia, she decided to give it a shot. The book had startled her with its complexity and insight. She was also drawn to its darkness—its bleak themes and haunted characters. Randa had been attracted to darkness from an early age. Maybe it was just from having grown up in the South, where people clung to morbid fascinations and superstitions as if they were consolation prizes from the Civil War. (A just God would never have tolerated Sherman's rampage, so there had to be powerful dark forces at work that protected Yankees and other agents of evil.) Or maybe it was growing up in her family, where everyone practically worshiped at the altars of depression and morbidity. (The only song Randa could ever remember her mother singing to her was "Put My Little Shoes Away"—a song about a child who knew he was dying.) Whatever the reason, something about the darkness soothed her like a lullaby, and she sought refuge in it by whatever safe means she could find.

The darkness in Randa's soul had been quick to respond to the darkness in Cameron Landry's prose. She immediately bought his other three books and read them, then pestered everyone at the paper until they let her write an article about him. She scheduled an interview through his literary agent, then ferreted out every article ever written about him and every interview he'd ever done. The reviews of his books were consistently effusive. People who cared about such things compared him to Ross Macdonald, Raymond Chandler, Dashiell Hammett. A reviewer in one of the magazines for mystery buffs swore that Landry would leave them all in the dust before it was over.

Very little had been written about the man himself. He'd grown up in several small towns in rural Georgia, the youngest of four brothers in a working-class family. He'd read a lot, he was good in English, a teacher had encouraged him, he'd decided to become a writer, and so on. No indication of where that dark vision had been born.

As she continued to search the computer indexes for anything more enlightening, she came across another Landry, one whose name had an even more poetic lilt: Tallen Landry. She didn't know if the name belonged to a man or a woman, but she loved the sound of it. When she saw it the second time, she decided to detour and find out. She typed the name into the computer and brought up the first citation. It was an article from *Texas Monthly* entitled "The Impact of Capital Punishment on the Families of Death Row Inmates." It had been written by an SMU sociology professor, a Dr. Karl Wiedergott, who had interviewed fifty families of condemned men and women and compiled a study about their emotional and physiological reactions. Near the end of the article, Tallen Landry was identified as a convicted murderer who had been executed in Alabama. (What an irony, she thought, for a murderer to have such a lovely name.) The professor had interviewed some family friends, but said that members of the immediate family had refused to talk with anyone. Randa was about to exit the article when something in the next paragraph caught her eye. Tallen Landry was more specifically identified as the second of four sons from a working-class family in rural Georgia. Randa stared at the paper, amazed. Surely it was a coincidence? *Landry* wasn't a particularly unusual name, and Georgia was not a small state. Still, if there was any connection at all, it would certainly shed some light on the workings of Cameron Landry's mind.

A week later, at the appointed time, she sat at a table at Musso & Frank Grill, poring over her notes and nervously chewing the ice from her water glass. She was surprised to see the maître d' showing a tall guy in a brown leather jacket and black Ray-Bans over to her table. She had certainly not expected him to be on time. He smiled warmly and offered his hand (*"Hi, I'm Cam Landry. I'm not late, am I?"*), then slid into the booth across from her. He didn't look anything like she'd expected, although she didn't know what she had expected. His hair was very dark brown, almost black, just long enough to look artistically unkempt. It had a lot of gray in it for a man his age (which, from the articles she'd read, she knew to be thirty-one). His face was perfectly shaped, with sharp features, and his skin looked as if it had never seen the light of day. And then he took off his sunglasses and she saw those eyes, and all other physical attributes were rendered unimportant.

When they started to talk, she was amazed at how they found an instant rhythm, and it seemed to have nothing to do with their common heritage. By the time the food came, they were finishing each other's sentences.

The one thing he didn't want to talk about was the content of his work. Whenever Randa tried to get into the material in any depth, Cam would quickly and adroitly change the subject. No wonder the articles she'd found had not gone beneath the surface.

After dinner they ordered margaritas and swapped war stories from their careers. When it started to get late and he still hadn't mentioned his family, she finally asked about them. He shrugged. "They're all dead."

"Well, who were they when they were alive?"

He shook his head. "A sorry bunch of people. Don't waste your time."

"A lot of great writers have come from sorry bunches of people."

"Yeah, well . . ." He looked away. "Actually, my mother was okay." He seemed to be saying it to himself. "She just . . ."

"What?"

"She thought she was very selfless, and maybe she was . . . but she put all her effort into maintaining her dignity in a horrible situation instead of trying to get *out* of the horrible situation, you know?" He looked away again. The energy had definitely shifted. Randa decided to go for it.

"By any chance, are you related to Tallen Landry?"

He didn't move, but she could see the muscles in his jaw go tense. Finally, without turning back to her, he said, "How did you know that?"

"I came across an article. I saw that you were both from Georgia and both had three brothers, so I thought there might be a chance . . ."

After a long moment he turned and looked at her again. He didn't appear angry. Maybe a little defeated. "I don't suppose it would do any good to ask you not to mention it."

Randa didn't answer. God, this stroke of luck, this great angle, and he wanted her to just ignore it. She didn't know him. She didn't owe him anything. So why did she feel she couldn't betray an unspoken loyalty?

He picked up his sunglasses. "I know, it's a ridiculous thing for me to ask. You're obviously very good at your job." Before she could figure out what to say, he was gone. She watched him go, knowing it would do no good to call him back.

For days after that she'd found herself missing him. How she could miss someone she didn't know was a mystery to her, but she did. She'd almost managed to clear it from her mind when, about a month after their dinner, she was surprised to get a phone call from him at her office.

"What happened to the article?" he asked, without any preamble.

"I scrapped it."

"Why?"

"I didn't think I could write it honestly if I didn't go into your background, and I didn't think I could sleep well if I did." He didn't say anything, so she added, "I'm sure you've been through enough."

"You don't even know me." He sounded incredulous, and impressed.

She thought about it and decided to risk him thinking she was nuts. "I know, but I feel like I do. I know it sounds crazy, but the minute you sat in that booth, I thought, 'Oh yeah, there's Cam.' I can't explain it, it was weird."

"I know. I felt the same way. It wasn't like we just met, it was like we were . . . reunited. I almost said something about it, but I was afraid you'd think I was coming on to you."

She might as well go for broke. "Maybe I wouldn't have minded that."

"Yeah, but my wife probably would have."

Damn. Of course he was married. She felt like a fool. But then, he hadn't exactly mentioned it at dinner.

"Are you still there?" he asked.

"Yes."

"Listen, let's get together again. I'll give you the real interview."

"Why?"

"I don't know. I guess I trust you not to turn it into a three-ring circus. And it's probably time for me to stop hiding from it. Maybe that's why you came along."

They had met for dinner a few days later, and he'd told her the story. (*"In broad strokes, okay? I can't go through it in detail, I just can't."*) It was fascinating, if relentlessly disturbing. Cam told it without much emotion; she guessed it was a self-preservation instinct. He told her about his father, Will Landry, a violent drunk who had brutalized the family. His mother, Lucy, a classic martyr/enabler who was more terrified of Will than of what he was doing to the rest of them. His brothers, marauding delinquents who had terrorized the neighborhoods in which they had lived. Each of them, however, had been artistically gifted in one way or another. He told her about Ethan, who was almost as talented a poet as he was a cat burglar. Tallen, who had grown up in reform schools and graduated to prisons; painted mesmerizing, melancholy landscapes that screamed of loneliness. He had been the most sensitive, and therefore the most troubled. (The rest of Tallen's story, Cam had said, she could read in the papers.) And then there was Jack, his oldest brother, who had always been a complete mystery to Cam. It was partly because of the age difference, but mostly because Jack had hated Cam too much to reveal anything to him. Jack was the only one who hadn't done anything artistic, although he'd been a voracious reader. Jack had never *done* much of anything, but he seemed to have turned observing into an art form of its own.

Ethan and Will had both died the same year. Ethan had drowned (Cam supplied no details) and Will had committed suicide a few months later. Lucy had also killed herself, on the anniversary of Tallen's execution. Jack still lived in Georgia, as far as Cam knew. Cam hadn't seen him since Lucy's funeral. They had gotten into a bitter argument just as Cam was leaving, and he'd said some things he now regretted. Later he had written Jack a long, apologetic letter. It had come back marked MOVED NO FORWARDING ADDRESS. He had tried to find Jack a couple of times, with no luck. He knew Jack didn't want to be found and figured he'd never see his brother again. It didn't bother him, or so he claimed.

Cam wouldn't offer much about how he had managed to escape unscathed. He attributed it to the age difference (five years) between him and the next oldest, Ethan, or the fact that Will had been kinder to Cam than he had to the others, probably because Will knew it was his last chance to have a decent relationship with a son. Cam said he remembered realizing at a very early age that his family was crazy and declaring, "I'll be in my room until I'm eighteen, then I'm out of here." He had kept that promise and had not done a lot of looking back.

The article about Cam had turned out to be one of the best things Randa had ever written. It caused a bit of a stir for a while, but Cam kept reassuring her he was not sorry he'd given her the interview. He said it had been very "freeing." It had also bought him a lot of free publicity, but he didn't seem to think like that, as far as she could tell.

Not long after her article appeared, Cam's marriage had broken up. She never knew if there was any connection because he never wanted to talk about it. He just kept saying that it had been coming for a long time. Randa never even met Cam's wife. All she knew was that her name was Terri and she was or wanted to be an artist. Through a couple of cryptic comments he'd made, she also suspected that Terri had never been very faithful (although, by his own admission, neither had Cam) and that she had some kind of chemical dependency. All in all, it sounded like Cam was better off without her.

When Cam and Terri broke up, Randa was living with Evan, a

screenwriter who made a fortune writing movies that were never made. The first time Randa had asked Evan if he loved her, he'd said he didn't know what love meant. When he was still saying it two years later, she moved out. The irony was that she wasn't sure she loved him, either, but she wanted the option.

Next she'd taken up with David, a studio musician who'd fascinated her because he was brooding and mysterious. When it had finally become apparent to her that he was merely brooding, she decided to chalk up another waste of time and move on. David hadn't minded much. It gave him something new to brood about.

While Randa was with David, Cam went through a country singer, a publicist, a freelance photographer, and, for the sake of cliché, a flight attendant. Not necessarily in that order and not necessarily one at a time.

Through all this, Randa and Cam remained fast friends. They got together at least once a week to share their successes and bemoan their losses, or to critique movies they'd seen or books they'd read, or to vent about the state of the world in general. They also took each other to any events their mates didn't want to go to, since they both always seemed to hook up with people with whom they had little in common. Their mates were always required to live with this arrangement, and only the most insecure of them had ever felt threatened by it.

Randa wasn't sure when she had realized she was in love with Cam. There wasn't any specific moment, just a sort of growing awareness; she'd admitted it to herself so gradually that at some point it simply became a given that she was in love with Cam, that she had been in love with Cam since the night she'd met him. It didn't really matter *when* she'd known it, because there was nothing to be done about it. Cam had never shown even the slightest glimmer of being romantically interested in her, and there was no way in hell she was going to make a fool of herself by saying or doing anything to call his attention to the fact. As long as they were friends, he'd be in her life. She wasn't about to give him a chance to reject her.

When Randa and David broke up, three days before her thirty-third birthday, Cam took her out to dinner, to "mourn or celebrate, whichever you want." They'd gone to an Italian restaurant on Melrose whose only distinction was that it was possibly the darkest restaurant in the greater Los Angeles area. Randa always complained that every restaurant in LA was lit like a Kmart, and Cam wanted to prove to her that she hadn't been going to the right places. They'd sat on the same side of a large red-leather booth and picked at whitefish while Randa complained about her lousy luck with men.

"You don't have bad luck," Cam informed her. "You have bad taste."

"Gee, that cuts deep, coming from someone whose entire romantic history combined couldn't produce the IQ of an Irish setter."

"We're not talking about me." He was swirling the ice cubes around in his margarita; he seemed oddly serious. "Do you think you ever really loved this jerk?"

Randa didn't have to think. "No. I loved the idea of being in love with a tortured artiste. I figured that out months ago."

"Then why didn't you break up with him months ago?"

"I don't know. I guess I didn't feel like going through all the drama. Not to mention having to find another apartment."

Randa was still living in the apartment she shared with David, sleeping on the couch. Not a comfortable arrangement on any level.

"Why don't you buy a condo in my building? There's one for sale right below me."

"Right. All I need is to move into your lovely, crime-infested neighborhood."

"We could see each other more often."

"Translated: I could feed your cat when you go out of town."

He smiled. "You're such a cynic." He put his fork down and stared at her for a moment, suddenly quite serious. "You know, you really look pretty tonight."

She smiled back. He was just trying to make her feel better, but she appreciated it. "Thanks. I guess self-pity becomes me. Enough of my stupid life. How are you?"

"Oh, you know. My usual cheery self."

"How's Patty?" Patty was Cam's latest girlfriend. She was a waitress at a health-food restaurant (which didn't explain where Cam had met her) who fervently believed there wasn't a problem on the planet that couldn't be cured by the right combination of herbs. Randa and David had gone out with them a couple of times. Randa was still trying to be open-minded.

"I don't know," Cam answered. "I guess you'd have to ask Richard."

"Who's Richard?"

"The New Age weight trainer she dumped me for."

"Oh no." Randa could not possibly bring herself to say she was sorry. "Are you serious?"

Cam nodded. "She doesn't know if she loves him, but she thinks they have karmic debts to settle. And he's going to teach her how to have an out-of-body experience."

"Cam, Patty has never had an in-body experience."

Cam smiled. "Yeah, she is a little bit out there."

"Like Pluto."

They sat in silence for a moment, then Cam got that serious expression on his face again. "Do you realize this is the first time since we've known each other that we've both been single at the same time?"

Randa hadn't thought about it. "Yeah, I guess it is."

Cam picked up his fork, then put it down again. He looked at Randa, then shifted to face her. When he spoke, his voice was different, almost tentative. "Have you ever wondered what we'd be like . . . you know, as a couple?"

Randa had to remind herself to breathe. "Yeah, I've wondered. But I thought you . . ."

"What?"

"I thought you didn't think of me, you know, like that."

"I thought *you* didn't think of *me* like that."

They both smiled at the irony.

"So what do you think? How would we be?"

"I think . . . we'd be great." Randa said it in a quiet voice, wondering if that was the answer he had expected. Cam smiled, and reached down and took her hand. She didn't have the presence of mind to feel awkward about it.

"See, I think the reason I keep getting into these stupid relationships is that I don't care who I'm with if I can't be with you." He smiled self-consciously. "I never said anything because I was afraid of what your reaction would be."

Randa heard the words, but she kept waiting for the punch line. This couldn't possibly be real.

"Cam," she managed to say, "tell me this isn't a joke."

"Of course it's not a joke." He reached up and pushed a strand of hair away from her face; she felt the back of his hand brush her cheek. He kissed her, before she even had time to wonder if he was going to. Then he smiled and said, "God, I've been wanting to do that for so long."

"Me too," she whispered, afraid saying it out loud might jinx something. She could have happily died on the spot. Many times since then, she'd wished she had.

The scene in Randa's mind vanished suddenly, as if the film had snapped in the projector. She couldn't bear to think any further than that. The tears she'd been holding back broke through and slid down her face; they felt like an invasion, but she couldn't bring herself to wipe them away.

She sat in her car for a long time, watching the ocean, trying to lose herself in the waves that rolled onto the sand one after another, effortlessly, as if this were any normal day.

Nick Varella answered the door with a scotch in his hand, very obviously not his first of the day. He had two days' growth of beard and his dark hair looked as if he'd just been in a strong wind. Randa had heard about Nick for years, but had never met him or even seen him before. He was the best friend Cam had, but not in a conventional way. They only got together about four times a year, but Randa knew that Cam told Nick things he never told anyone else. (Probably because whenever they met the main objective was to see who could consume the largest amount of alcohol in the shortest amount of time.) Even though their careers were roughly parallel—Nick's science-fiction novels were as respected in that genre as Cam's crime novels were in theirs—Cam considered Nick a mentor. Or maybe a surrogate brother. At any rate, Randa had heard about Nick until she felt she knew him. At least, she had until he answered the door and she was faced with having to explain her presence.

"I'm sorry to bother you. I'm Randa Phillips." She saw no reason to beat around the bush.

"Oh. Wow. Hi." He was staring at her, his eyebrows arched in a way she couldn't interpret. Maybe it just had to do with being thrown a curve when he was too drunk to handle it. Or maybe no one ever dropped in on him; he was a notorious hermit. She could hear loud music coming from the back of the house, and it suddenly occurred to her he might not be alone. That possibility hadn't entered her mind when she'd decided to go see him. *God, can't you ever think anything through?*

"I wondered if I could . . ." What? She hadn't really thought about what she'd say. She tried again. "I know you don't know me and this is a bad time, but I have to talk to someone."

He just kept staring at her. She suddenly felt very foolish.

"I'm sorry, this was a stupid idea." She turned to leave, but he grabbed her elbow.

"No. Don't go. I'm just . . . I'm not very good at spontaneity." He held up the drink by way of explanation. "I'm also not thinking all that clearly, thank God." He finally smiled. "Wanna join me?"

She managed a nod. He opened the door wider and motioned her inside. He led her down a narrow hall into a room that, judging by the advanced degree of clutter, was where he spent most of his time. The music was coming from an elaborate stereo system against the back wall. It was loud, angry heavy metal; raspy voices screaming unintelligible lyrics. Nick went straight to the makeshift bar and started tossing ice cubes into a glass. "What can I pour you, given I don't have anything dainty?"

"Do you have any tequila?"

"Now, what do you think?" He had already picked up a bottle of Cuervo Gold. "You're not expecting me to mix it with anything that would require concentration, I hope."

"Straight is fine." The music was already wearing on her nerves. Nick poured the glass half-full and handed it to her. He lifted his glass in a semi-toast.

"Well . . . Life sucks." With that he downed half a glass of scotch. Randa sipped the tequila. The slow burn felt great; she followed it with a healthy slug.

"I've always wanted to meet you." It would have sounded dumb even if she hadn't had to shout.

"Yeah. I wanted to meet you, too. Just not bad enough to go to one of Cam's parties. He probably told you I can't be in a room with more than three people. With special dispensation for strip joints." He polished off the rest of the scotch with ease. "Guess I'll have to add funeral parlors to the list."

She couldn't decide whether she liked him or not, but straining to hear made it hard to think. She pointed to the stereo.

"Could you maybe turn the music down a little?"

"Why?"

"So we won't have to shout."

"It's good for you." She'd had this exact conversation with Cam, more times than she could count. She wasn't in the mood for it.

"I'm really not up to fighting with anything."

He shrugged and went over to the stereo. "This is very controlling behavior," he said as he lowered the volume. Randa burst into tears. Nick immediately turned the stereo off, came over, and put his arms around her.

"I'm sorry. I was kidding. I'm really sorry."

"Cam used to say that." It came out in a choked whisper.

"I know," Nick said, rocking her gently. "That's where I got it." Now that she was close enough to tell, his eyes were none too dry, either.

They sat in a booth in a tiny Spanish restaurant on Alameda and shared a pitcher of something that was supposed to be sangria. Randa felt pretty sure it was actually cheap burgundy someone had poured into a pitcher along with a can of fruit cocktail, but if it would anesthetize her, she didn't care.

"I thought . . . maybe you could shed some light on it."

"You're going to be disappointed."

"Well, I hadn't seen him in a year; you surely know more than I do. Had he been more depressed than usual? Had he called you up and said, 'Guess what, Nick, I just robbed a liquor store'?"

"I haven't . . . hadn't . . . seen him in a couple of weeks, so I don't know what his most recent frame of mind has been . . . had been . . ." He sighed. "Christ." He stared at his wine glass for a long moment. He finally continued.

"He certainly didn't call me and tell me he robbed a liquor store, not that he would have. But . . ." He bit his bottom lip and shook his head.

"What?"

"Nothing. It's just . . ." He looked up, directly into her eyes, as if he'd made some sort of decision. "I wasn't terribly surprised when I heard that."

Randa stared at him, shocked. "You weren't?"

"Cam had been acting very strange. I think he just . . ." He stopped; seemed to change direction. "A couple of months ago, he ditched Nora, out of the clear blue sky."

Randa listened, trying not to have any opinion that would show on her face.

"He didn't tell her why, and he didn't even tell anyone else that it had happened. I only found out because I ran into her at the Beverly Center." He smiled. "Oh, yeah. I make an exception for that, too. But only on weekdays, and never when there are sales."

Randa smiled and forced back all the questions she wanted to ask.

How did she look? Devastated, I hope?

Nick fished a square of peach out of his glass with his spoon, popped it in his mouth, and went on. "Anyway, I asked Cam about it; he just said he had to be alone. I never could get any more out of him than that, but you know Cam. They come, they go . . ."

Randa winced a little. Nick caught himself.

"I'm sorry. I didn't . . ." He seemed genuinely embarrassed. "See, I don't put you in that category, so I'm not careful."

"What category do you put me in?" Randa asked, genuinely interested.

"I don't know if I could name it," he said, speaking slowly, as if stalling for time. "There's one thing; I don't know if this will help you. Cam used to say something to me, over the years, every time I'd ask him why the two of you weren't together, if he was so crazy about you. He'd always say he couldn't be in a romantic relationship with you, and I'd ask why, and he'd say, 'I love her too much.'"

Randa felt her brow furrow. "What does that mean?"

Nick looked at her. He seemed to be playing this conversation like a game of chess.

"He never would tell me what it meant. Except for one night . . . It was very late, we'd all been over at Roger's, playing poker. Cam and I went back to his apartment to see how much drunker we could possibly get, I guess. Anyway, it was about three in the morning and we were both several sheets to the wind, and Cam started talking about you. I don't know why. I think it was right after you guys had started to . . . date." He smiled. "I'll be a gentleman."

He paused to take a sip from his wine glass and seemed to weigh the decision to tell her these things one more time. He looked back at Randa. "Cam told me he truly believed there was some kind of a curse on his family. Not like spells and witches and all that, but some real thing that was like this black cloud of bad luck. And he was convinced that if he got very involved with you, it would infect you and ruin your life."

Randa stared at him. "That's crazy."

Nick nodded. "I know. I never said this was going to make sense. I just said I'd tell you.

"Anyway," he continued, before Randa could figure out what to say, "that's just a digression. Although it may have been the beginning, and I just didn't see it."

"The beginning of what?"

"Like I said, Cam had gotten really weird. Even for him."

"Weird how?"

"First, he started calling me all the time. Three or four times a day. Only me, from what I can tell. And he was saying all these bizarre things."

"Like?"

"Like, he was having these nightmares, but he was convinced they weren't dreams. He said he thought he was 'going somewhere' in his sleep."

Randa frowned, trying to follow. "What does that mean?"

"I don't know. *He* didn't know. But he just became more and more insistent that these dreams were more than dreams, and he thought they were going to end up hurting him somehow. I guess he got sick of trying to convince me; he finally stopped talking about it. But then he started to get very paranoid. When we would go somewhere, anywhere, even during the day, he'd always look around, like he was afraid someone was following us. I'd ask him why he was doing that, and he'd either deny he was doing it or just say 'no reason.'

"He'd call me late at night, and he'd just talk forever about nothing, or he'd try to get me into some long, complicated argument. I always felt he was trying to keep me from hanging up. Or he'd show up at night, unannounced, and stay until very, very late, and then sleep on the couch. He'd claim he was too drunk to drive." He stopped, looked at her. "Does that sound like Cam to you?"

Randa shook her head. It didn't. "What do you think all that was about?"

"I don't know. But I haven't even gotten to the best part." He picked up his wine glass and emptied it. He refilled both their glasses with the last of the alleged sangria. Finally he was ready to resume. He looked at her.

"A couple of weeks ago, he told me he had seen Tallen."

Randa stared at him. The restaurant suddenly seemed eerily quiet.

"He *what*?"

"That's what he said. He was adamant about it."

Randa was still struggling to understand. "You mean, he saw someone in a crowd who looked like Tallen?"

Nick shook his head. "No. Tallen. In his apartment. He woke up one night and there was Tallen. He swore it. He saw Tallen, they talked, Tallen told him things . . . We never got to *what* Tallen told him. By that time, I had stopped him, I just couldn't listen to it. I told him I was worried about him and I thought he should stop drinking and find a better shrink. He got furious and stormed out of my house." Nick was quiet for a moment; he looked pained. When he spoke, his voice was different. "That was the last time I saw him."

Randa didn't know what to say, what to do with any of this. Nick shook his head a little, as if coming out of a trance.

"So," he continued, "all in all, the liquor store thing just didn't shock me."

"You think he was . . ." Randa couldn't bring herself to say any of the possible words.

Nick was nodding. "There's that tiny line between eccentric and insane . . . Somehow, when nobody was paying attention, he just crossed over." He looked away, and spoke as if he were talking to himself. "Let's face it. How long could anyone expect him to keep it up—walking around, pretending to be normal, pretending he lived on the same planet with everyone else, like they . . . like *we* had *any* way to comprehend what he'd been through, what he had to live with . . ." He paused for a moment and shook his head. "In my humble opinion," he continued quietly, "the question we should all be asking ourselves is not 'How could this happen?' but 'Why did it take so long?'"

Randa sat back in the booth, dazed, trying to take it in and wondering how much a pack of cigarettes went for these days. Nick motioned to the waiter to bring them another pitcher of fake sangria.

• • •

The door to Cam's apartment looked perfectly normal. Randa had expected there to be police tape, or at least some kind of note. She opened the door with the key she had never returned (not that he'd ever asked her to) and stepped inside. She closed the door behind her and locked it.

Nothing had changed. It looked exactly the same as the last time she'd seen it. She was sure that if she looked hard enough, she'd see signs of Nora's having passed through, but she didn't plan to look that hard.

She had decided to come here halfway through the second pitcher of sangria. She told herself she wanted to pick up the things that were hers, but she knew the real reason had little to do with two Pyrex casserole dishes and a spare hair dryer. Now that she was here, she realized that all she really wanted was some sort of closure. She had lived without it for the last year, but she couldn't go on without it for the rest of her life.

She did have one real quest. There were a couple of scrapbooks—the last remaining vestiges of Cam's family, except for Jack, assuming he was still alive. Randa didn't know what she'd do with them, but she knew she'd make sure they were kept safe. She didn't know why that felt so important, but it did. Just the thought that generations of people had been whittled down to two tattered books of yellowed paper and faded black-and-white photos. The books seemed sacred to her; they were the only remaining evidence that any of these people had ever lived.

Randa looked around, trying to remember where Cam had kept the scrapbooks. She checked the hall closets, but all they contained were clothes and boxes of old magazines. She would have to check the bedroom, something she'd hoped to avoid at all costs—she was sure she would find the scrapbooks there.

The bedroom looked the same, too. The door to one of the closets was open, and there were clothes strewn on the floor in front of it, where the cops had plowed through. They'd obviously found the gun without much trouble. She didn't see any sign of the scrapbooks. Without giving it a lot of thought, she went over and opened the door to the other closet. A couple of shirts hung on a hook inside the door; they brushed her face as the door opened. They smelled like Cam. She hadn't expected this, and the full force of the pain made its way through the wine and the denial. She bent over, as a sob hit her, and let herself sink to the floor, and gave herself up to the misery.

When Randa finally stopped, she felt as if something inside her had given way, like a fever breaking. She wiped her eyes with the sleeve of one of the shirts—a faded red brushed silk, from Traffic at the Beverly Center. She had been with Cam the day he bought it. (*"Randa, what about this red one? It matches my eyes."*) She took a couple of deep breaths and was about to stand when she saw the scrapbooks on the floor next to her. She gathered them in her arms and pulled herself to her feet.

On her way out, she noticed something on the nightstand: a pen and a sheet of paper. The paper was covered with doodles: trees; dollar signs; a skull atop a mound of bones. A couple of phone numbers. One was hers. The other was an 800 number. Unable to resist, she picked up the phone and dialed it.

"Thank you for calling Delta Airlines. All of our agents are busy at this time . . ."

Randa hung up. She looked at the pad again. Cam had written *#178* in the middle of all the pictures and circled it. Randa dialed Delta again. When she got an agent, she was informed that 178 was one of the morning flights from LA to Atlanta.

Why would Cam have been planning a trip to Atlanta? He hadn't been home since his mother's funeral, and he'd always sworn he'd never go there again. She folded the sheet of paper and tucked it into one of the scrapbooks. She could figure it out later.

Halfway to the front door, a sound caused her to stop.

An old man was standing in front of the living room window, staring down at the street. He looked up and saw Randa. His face showed no sign of surprise, or any other emotion.

"It's a long way down, isn't it?" He had a soft voice and a refined Southern accent, as smooth as old scotch. "Me, I'd go with pills. It wouldn't hurt, it wouldn't make a mess, and it wouldn't bother anybody else's life."

Wearing a charcoal-gray suit, white shirt, and maroon tie, all of which looked expensive, he was an attractive man for his age, with a full head of white hair and a neatly trimmed beard. There was a calmness in his eyes that would have been comforting under different circumstances.

"I'm sorry," Randa said, putting the scrapbooks down. "I didn't realize anyone was here." It sounded stupid, but she had to start somewhere.

"I'm Ryland Parker," he said, simply. "Cam's uncle."

Lucy's twin brother. Now she recognized him from the photos she'd seen, although he was much older. She had completely forgotten about him when the cops were asking about Cam's relatives. Actually, it had never dawned on her that he would still be alive.

"Oh, yes. Of course. I'm sorry, I guess the detectives wondered why I didn't tell them about you, but I didn't remember . . ."

"Well, I'm sure Cam didn't talk about me very much. We weren't close."

She wondered how the cops had managed to find him, but there was no polite way to ask.

"I'm an old friend of Cam's," she said. "I was just . . ." *Just what? Just sitting on the floor of his closet, sobbing?*

"What were you planning to do with the books?" His tone wasn't accusatory, but Randa felt guilty just the same.

"Oh. I thought someone in the family should have them. I guess that would be you." She picked up the books and started to hand them to him, but he waved her off.

"No, not me. Jack should have them."

"Well, that's what I thought, I'd try to find a way . . . Do you know where he lives?"

"Yes."

"Then I guess you could take them . . ."

He was shaking his head. "No." He didn't offer an explanation. He turned toward the window again, this time looking straight out, at the lights of the city.

"Cam would have to have a place with a view, wouldn't he? Always *looking* somewhere. Looking in, looking out, looking back. Where did all that looking get him, except looking in a rather unfortunate direction when he finally decided to follow his own gaze."

Randa suddenly remembered what Cam had said about Ryland.

"He makes my mother look sane."

"But," he went on, "he was doing the best he could, all things considered. Like they all did." He looked back at her. "You have to take the books to Jack," he said suddenly.

"Me?"

He nodded. "And tell him about Cam's death. Everything you know about it."

"That's crazy. Why can't you tell him?"

"I doubt he would see me," Ryland said, shaking his head.

"Then leave them at his door with a note. I'm not going to fly three thousand miles to hand two scrapbooks to someone I've never met when you know him and you'll be there anyway . . . that's crazy."

He was suddenly right beside her, staring intently into her eyes. "Listen to me. This is not about the books. It's about getting through Jack Landry's thick skull, and I can't do it."

"What on earth makes you think I could?"

"In the first place, you're the only person left alive who might conceivably want to. And you're a very attractive young lady, and there must be *something* alive in him that would take note of that fact."

Randa was sure she was offended by that last statement, but she couldn't isolate the reason to call him on it. Before she could figure it out, he was talking again.

"I want you to give Jack one message for me. Word for word, please." He was looking her dead in the eye. "Tell him that the thing is real. You have to make him believe that, no matter what it takes."

With that, he turned and headed for the door.

"What thing?"

Let him go, idiot. He's a nutcase.

"He'll know," Ryland said, then turned to look at her again. "If you ever cared about this family, you'll do this." Then he left.

Randa waited, giving him plenty of time to get out of the building. She tried to figure out why he'd been able to upset her so much. So Cam's crazy uncle Ryland was in town for the funeral, and she'd met him and he'd talked nonsense, as crazy people have a tendency to do. So what?

HE'S TELLING THE TRUTH.

The voice. *The* voice. The one that had been drowning the others out for a while now, even though its messages usually made about as much sense as Uncle Ryland.

She headed for the door. She'd track Jack down and mail the books to him. She'd include a note about her conversation with Ryland. That would be that. She'd be done with the Landrys for good; she could move on to another obsession.

She waited for the elevator, unable to get Ryland's face or voice out of her head.

". . . doing the best he could, all things considered . . ."

What was that supposed to mean? Cam had been doing "the best he could," but the best he could was pretty damned impressive.

"Like they all did . . ."

The elevator door opened and she got in and pressed the lobby button, eager to get away.

"If you ever cared about this family . . ."

What? She was supposed to care about them enough to fly clean across the country to deliver a nonsensical message to the surviving member? Assuming she could even find him, why would he listen to her? What did any of this have to do with her?

IF YOU EVER CARED ABOUT THIS FAMILY . . .

I didn't even know them . . .

IF YOU EVER CARED ABOUT CAM . . .

Not fair. Now the damned voice was going to play dirty. Well, what the hell. Everyone else did.

Back home, she sat on her bed and sipped straight tequila and flipped through the scrapbooks. There they were, in time-faded black-and-white photos: Will and Lucy, Jack, Tallen, Ethan, and Cam. She knew who everyone was from having gone through the books with Cam so many times. Randa wondered once more why her heart was so torn by these sad people she'd never met.

She picked up the piece of paper from Cam's nightstand and looked at it again. Asked herself again why Cam would have been going to Atlanta.

"I want you to give Jack one message . . ."

Was that it? Was Cam trying to go to Atlanta to look for Jack? To tell him something? Was Ryland asking her to do something that Cam would ask her to do, if he could?

"If you ever cared about this family . . ."

"Oh, hell," Randa said out loud. She picked up the phone and dialed the Delta number.

FOUR

Jack knocked lightly, rattling the screen door of the trailer. He knew Cathy had seen him come up the walk, but she would take her time about answering the door. She always did.

The storm had moved on and the smell of wet pine filled the crisp night air. Jack looked across the way at the other trailers. The lights were on in almost all of them, and he could hear a radio somewhere, tuned in to a country station. He hated having to think about people living in tin boxes, and wondered why it always took Cathy so long to answer the door. Did she still bother to primp for him? If so, he couldn't imagine why.

The light came on above his head and he heard her slide the lock, then the door opened. She was smiling, the honest smile of a woman who has long since stopped trying to be coy. The lines around her eyes surprised him, once again. In his mind, she was always young.

"I thought it was gettin' to be about time for you to roll in here." Cathy had never put a final *g* on a word in her life. In fact, everything about Cathy belied her intelligence. Jack had always suspected it was all deliberate. Or habit, from having been taught young that smart women lead lonely lives.

He offered his version of a sheepish smile. "Is it okay?"

"Well, I was expectin' Tom Cruise, but I guess I can call and put him off till tomorrow night."

She opened the screen door and he stepped inside. He looked around a little, as he always did, to get his bearings. Everything was neat and as stylish as she could afford for it to be on what she made at the truck stop. There was a half-finished afghan on the sofa that she must have been working on.

"How are you?" she asked.

"Lousy."

"Why?"

"I don't know. I woke up in a foul mood and I can't shake it."

"So I'm the remedy?"

He kissed her on the back of her head—his version of an apology—and walked into the bedroom.

She was the closest thing Jack had to a friend. They had known each other since high school. They had never really dated. Cathy'd had a boyfriend when they met—a genuine creep whom Jack, who loathed the term, couldn't help thinking of as white trash. But even if she'd been available, in those days Jack was spending too much time on the streets or in the juvie courts to have much of a social life anyway.

They had both left school at the end of their junior year. In unrelated incidents, Cathy had dropped out and Jack had been expelled. (He and Ethan had been expelled on the same day. *"Mrs. Landry, it's very clear that your sons are not interested in anything but causing trouble, so let's just stop wasting everybody's time.*") Cathy had married an abusive creep and had stayed with him until Jack had threatened to shoot him if Cathy didn't. (Her motivation for leaving, finally, had been fear for Jack's safety, not her own.)

Cathy and Jack had drifted apart after they left school, and especially after he went to the state prison in Reidsville for ten years, although she had visited him there a few times. When he got out, they would run into each other in town every now and then; they'd make a lot of noise about getting together for dinner or something sometime, but they never quite got around to it. Then Jack had moved to Atlanta, had thought he would have a life there. The Ritz-Carlton Buckhead had just opened, and thanks to a brilliant piece of fiction disguised as a résumé, he got a good job as a waiter in the dining room. Between his deceptively wholesome looks and whatever he'd inherited of his mother's breeding, he had really been able to charm people in those days, and he made a small fortune in tips.

He met a woman, Paula, who worked at the registration desk, and started going out with her. Maybe he even fell in love with her. Back then it was still possible. He'd confessed his entire sordid past to her. When she'd found out about the BA he'd earned by correspondence while he was in prison, she'd encouraged him to go for his master's, to arm himself to fight his past. He'd been in the process of filling out grad school applications when all hell had broken loose with Tallen. He moved back home to be with his mother during the trial. He handed his savings over to the court-appointed attorney to spend on a psychiatrist for the jury to ignore. He never returned to Atlanta; never saw Paula again; never gave another thought to grad school or anything resembling a career.

He and Cathy had become romantically involved (if you could call it that) the day Tallen was sentenced. She'd called him as soon as she heard. Jack had been out of his mind, and she had come to comfort him. He couldn't remember how they'd ended up in bed. (Surely he hadn't been trying to seduce Cathy a few hours after finding out that Tallen had been sentenced to die?) Even if he hadn't instigated it, it seemed heartless and incongruous, thinking about it now. But at the time it had seemed very natural, perfectly in keeping with the desperation he had felt.

Even after that night, Jack and Cathy had never been anything approaching a couple. Jack didn't have the stamina to be in a relationship, and Cathy had never had the stamina to stay out of one. The two of them would get together from time to time, whenever one of them needed the other for anything. That almost always meant sex, since that was the only thing either of them needed that the other could supply.

These days they never wasted time with small talk, so Jack had everything off but his jeans when Cathy came out of the bathroom, still dressed. She went over and sat on the bed and looked at him. "I want to talk to you."

"About what?"

"About us. About this."

Jack looked at her, worried. Surely she knew him well enough to know he wasn't going to talk about "them" and "this." He'd be a streak of light out the door.

"Stop lookin' so petrified. It's not gonna kill you." She patted the bed. "Come here and sit down."

He sat on the end of the bed. She frowned at him.

"Up here," she said, patting the bed right next to her. He didn't move. "Jack, come on. I just need to talk for a minute." She smiled. "You don't even have to speak, you can just nod every now and then." As usual, her voice calmed him a little. He moved up next to her and relaxed, as much as he could. He still dreaded this conversation, whatever it was.

"You're a nervous wreck," she said, starting to massage his shoulders. "Do you see what a nervous wreck you are?"

"I don't think I've ever tried to deny being a nervous wreck, or any other kind of wreck."

"I know you don't deny it, but I'm not sure you really notice it, either. Let me tell you what happens when you come here . . ."

"I know what happens."

"I'm not sure you do. And even if you do, you need to hear it out loud. Do you know how often you show up here?"

He didn't answer. She leaned over and kissed him on the cheek, then continued. "You come here roughly every three months. Unless it's been rainin' a lot, then you come more often. I think that's because when it rains, you're not outside, you're not workin', you don't have any way to let off steam. Because that's what most of this is about. Lettin' off steam. And I'm not sayin' that's bad. I just want to make sure you know what you do and why you do it. It's gonna be important to you later."

"I know what I do and why I do it," he said, trying to be patient. "Why can't you trust me on that?"

"What happens when you start thinkin' about comin' here? How do you feel?"

"Cathy . . ."

"Just tell me, the simplest way you know how."

He thought about it for a minute. He knew she wasn't going to let him out of this. "I feel . . . like I can't stay calm." He looked at her. She was nodding.

"Okay. That's good."

"Great. I passed. Is it over?"

"It's not just about sex, Jack. It's about that volcano you sit on all the time."

"You think I'm unaware of it?"

"I love you to death, Jack. You're my oldest friend, and I'd love to think it could be more than that, but you . . . you know . . . your life is what it is and I think it's a stupid waste, but it *is* your life."

He suddenly knew what she was going to say. He kept quiet and let her say it.

"I've been seein' somebody. I mean, *really* seein' somebody . . . I think we're . . ." She stopped. She shook her head, then looked away, toward the wall. He got her drift. He'd been through lots of boyfriends with Cathy, and while there may have been occasional problems of logistics, it had never altered their relationship.

"Where'd you meet him?" He didn't know why it mattered, but he wasn't ready to say anything else.

She looked back at him. "He's the night manager at Winn-Dixie. He transferred from Columbus about six months ago. I kept seein' him in there . . . One night I had to get a check approved and we started talkin' . . . He asked me out and we just . . ." Her voice trailed off. "God, I hate this . . ."

"Cathy, it's okay," he said quietly.

She was starting to cry. He pulled her to him and held her. She tried to go on.

"I want a life, Jack. I'm tired of being alone, I'm tired of living in a trailer . . ." Jack handed her a tissue from the box by the bed and she dried her eyes. "I know I'm probably just headin' for another disaster—"

"You don't know that. It could be fine." He kissed her cheek, then rubbed a stray tear away with his thumb. "Don't cry. You've told me, it's over, everything's okay."

"I'm worried about you."

"Cathy, I'll be okay. I'm not going to go nuts, I'm not going to . . ." He stopped. "Look, if I didn't know how to take care of myself, I wouldn't be here, would I?"

"But after tonight?"

"I'll come out to the truck stop. You can introduce me to some of your friends."

She smiled a little. "Just . . . be careful."

"I'm always careful. You know that."

Back home, Jack went through the nightly routine like a robot: got undressed, brushed his teeth, set the coffeepot. He got into bed and tried to read, but he couldn't keep his mind focused. It kept going back to everything Cathy had said. Was he that volatile, he wondered, that a prolonged period of celibacy was a threat to society? Maybe, but it didn't matter. It wasn't a theory he planned to test.

It took his mind a while to settle down, but he finally felt himself slipping into unconsciousness and was deeply grateful.

He was walking down a shady residential street. Broad daylight. Up ahead he saw a girl walking toward him. She was in her late teens, pretty, with long blond hair and tan legs in cutoff blue jeans. She smiled and motioned for him to come to her. He went, stood in front of her, and waited to see what she wanted. She looked at him oddly, like she could hear his thoughts and was pausing to listen. And then, without warning, she was kissing him, with a strength that amazed him. He could barely stand up. And then he realized she was pushing him down. He felt his knees give way and he was on the ground and she was on top of him, still kissing him, his face cupped in her strong hands. He kept his eyes closed and tried to just go with it, but he couldn't stop wondering why it didn't feel as good as it should. Something told him to open his eyes; he did, and instantly he knew something was wrong. The girl's hair, hanging down around his face, was not blond anymore. It was gray and coarse. He pushed her away so he could see her face. It wasn't the girl.

She was the most grotesque thing he'd ever seen. Her skin was a transparent, slimy white and covered with open, runny abscesses. Her eyes were blue, but the whites of them were laced with red, and the look in them was pure hatred. She smiled at him; her mouth was full of sores and half her teeth were missing. The ones she had were yellow and pointed, like a vampire's. She looked at him like she owned him.

He tried to push her away, but it was like pushing a brick wall. He tried to roll himself out from under her. She laughed, a howling, mocking laugh. The more he struggled, the louder the laugh became, until the woods were echoing with it. He screamed at her to leave him alone, and she stopped laughing. The silence was almost worse. She looked in his eyes, and he couldn't move. Somehow her gaze had the power to paralyze him. He couldn't do anything but watch as she wrapped her bony hands around his throat and started to squeeze. He tried to move, but he couldn't. He could feel her fingers digging into his throat with a strength that was not human. In seconds, he couldn't breathe at all. She started that laugh again, and as she leaned her head back to howl, he was suddenly able to move. He grabbed her hands, but her grip was like iron. He thrashed, trying desperately to throw her off him. He had to breathe. His chest felt like someone had run a hot knife through it. In a wild attempt that he knew would be his last, he summoned every ounce of strength and shoved himself to the side. Her grip slipped just enough, and he managed to shove her off and roll away. He sat up, gasping for air. He looked around quickly, to see where she was, and realized he was awake.

He sucked air into his lungs in visceral gasps. His eyes scanned the apartment. The late-morning sun was bright and he could see right away there was nothing wrong. He lay back down on the pillow and took deep breaths. His head felt like someone had it in a vise.

The phone rang, making him jump. He glanced at the clock. Christ, had he really slept until eleven? The machine picked up. He heard his own voice; the one that followed the beep was not Rick's.

"Yes, I'm trying to locate a Mr. Jack Landry. This is Bill Warren at the Los Angeles County coroner's office and I need you to return my call at your earliest convenience. The number here is (213) 343—"

Jack turned the machine off, then stared at it in disbelief. There was only one reason he'd be getting a call from the Los Angeles County coroner's office.

Cam is dead.

He didn't move for a long time. Just lay there, staring at the phone.

Cam is dead.

What the hell was he supposed to do about it? When he finally picked up the receiver, it was to call Rick and say he wasn't going to work at all this week, pretending he had the flu. Then he dressed and headed down the road, on the two-mile walk to the liquor store.

He sat in the vacant lot behind the train depot, where he and Ethan and Tallen used to play. He took the pint of Jack Daniel's out of the paper bag and looked at it. He'd felt as nervous buying it as a kid with a fake ID. He hadn't gone near alcohol in ten years, no matter how much he'd needed to escape, but he'd always told himself it would be there if things got bad enough, and that it would be okay as long as he was careful. He twisted the cap and broke the seal, and was halfway amazed that there was no ensuing thunderclap.

He opened the bottle and tilted it, letting half the contents spill onto the ground. He watched the copper pool soak into the dirt until he was satisfied the right amount remained in the bottle—enough to spread a soothing fog over him, but not enough to do any real damage. He put the bottle to his lips, paused for a moment, then tipped his head back and felt the welcome burn slide down his throat. A few minutes and a couple of ounces later, he let himself think about Cam.

What on earth could have happened? It was hard to believe Cam and death could travel the same axis, much less collide. It made him think about nights when he was a kid, lying in bed, fantasizing about smothering Cam with a pillow and letting everyone think Cam had died in his sleep. His plan included comforting his mother with a theory he thought she'd buy—that the angels had decided they just couldn't live without Cam another day. The whiskey dulled the pain in his head, but it was getting back at him in other ways. It stirred the old voices and, as always, brought him closer to the anger. Pictures flashed through his head. His father holding Cam by the hand, waving Cam's report card like it was the goddamned flag. Looking at the rest of them like he wished the ground would open and swallow them.

"At least I've got one son who's gonna amount to something. The rest of you combined ain't worth the breath it'd take to cuss you."

And now the Boy Wonder was gone. Jack suddenly saw clearly what he'd known since the moment he'd heard the message. The LA County coroner would have to move on to plan B. Even if Jack had loved Cam the way he'd loved the others, he wouldn't have been able to do it again. He couldn't do one more funeral.

At least he could comfort himself with the knowledge that it was all but over. There was no one left to die. No one but him. And when he died, there would be no phone call, no stricken faces, not even one ambivalent drunk wrestling with his conscience. Just a quiet end to the chain of misery.

He drained the last of the whiskey. He put the cap back on the bottle, stared at it for a moment, then hurled it at the side of the depot, where it shattered and fell to the ground in a violent spray of a thousand pieces.

FIVE

Driving her rented car down I-75, Randa began to feel it—the almost tangible poignancy she always felt in Atlanta, and had felt ever since she first went there on a second-grade field trip. Memories whirled over her, and she could feel her throat tighten into what she had come to think of as the Atlanta knot.

There was a bank of black clouds on the horizon, and every now and then a streak of lightning would split them. Randa was driving right into the storm, and had to force herself not to look at it as an omen. Thunderstorms were high on the list of reasons she had left Georgia. She reminded herself of all the reassurances she'd heard about a car being the safest place to be, and how statistically slight her chances were of being struck by lightning. Those statistics never calmed her, though, since they had likewise applied to anyone who ever *had* been struck by lightning.

The storm seemed to be stalled somewhere. By the time she was within three exits of Barton, it was still off in the distance. Maybe it would stay wherever it was until after she was safely back in her hotel room.

Barton was a little town about an hour south of Atlanta. It was also the town where Will Landry had finally done his version of settling down, and the town the Landry boys had spent their youths terrorizing. Randa had never been there. It was one of those towns there was no reason to visit. Its biggest claim to fame was the country's oldest still-standing buggy factory. Once a year everyone got decked out in antique clothes and celebrated Buggy Day by riding buggies up and down Main Street. But that event was hardly worth the time it would have taken her to drive down there when she was growing up in Gainesville, two hours north.

Chances were slight that anyone in Barton would know where Jack lived now, but she had to start somewhere, and it seemed like the logical place. (Not that any of this had anything to do with logic.) She took the exit, followed the signs to the downtown area (such as it was), parked in one of the diagonal spaces on Main Street, and surveyed the landscape. Typical small-town Georgia. A little row of shops that hadn't been updated in decades. The lawn in front of the courthouse was dotted with silver historical markers and a large statue in honor of the Confederate war dead. She'd been gone long enough to find it all quaint.

She spotted a small coffee shop, always the best place to go for information in a small town. A sign painted on the window read TILLIE'S GOOD FOOD COFFEE SHOP. Randa left her car unlocked and headed inside. Tillie was not doing a booming business. A few customers, mostly elderly ladies, were beating the dinner rush. As Randa passed them, they stared hard at her, their eyes squinting with the intense mistrust of strangers only rural Southerners can muster. Randa ignored them and made her way to the counter, where a pudgy waitress greeted her with a forced smile.

"Do you need a menu?"

"No. Actually, I'm trying to find someone. I wondered if you could help me."

"I'll try. Who is it?"

"A man named Jack Landry. He grew up here and moved away. He's in his late forties, probably blond . . ."

"Yeah, I know who he is."

Randa stopped, a bit surprised. "You do?"

"He eats here sometimes." She lowered her voice. "Is he in some kinda trouble?" Her tone was not one of concern.

"No, no. Nothing like that." Randa tried to hide her amazement. "Does he live around here?"

"I think he lives in that boardinghouse out on Thirty-Six. That's what I heard."

Randa was too stunned to know what to say. If Jack still lived here, why hadn't Cam been able to find him? Had Cam lied about it? Why would he do that?

"The road that goes past the courthouse is Thirty-Six. Go east, it's about half a mile."

Randa thanked the girl, who had already gone back to filling the napkin dispensers. As she turned and headed for the door, the early diners seemed to be glaring even harder. Evidently they'd overheard. Evidently the Landry reputation had not diminished with time.

The boardinghouse was a run-down Victorian, sitting by itself out on one of the two-lane highways that ran into town. The place had obviously been a nice house at one time. Now it was badly in need of a paint job and a new roof. Randa parked her car on the side of the road. The wind had begun to pick up and the thunder was sounding closer.

She took a moment to breathe deeply, bracing herself. She hadn't expected to have to face him so soon. She wondered what he would look like. She'd only seen photos of him as a child. She'd been intrigued by him since the first time she and Cam had gone through the family albums. Jack stood out because he was cutting up in every photo—sticking his tongue out, rolling his eyes, making devil horns behind someone's back. Looking at the photos, anyone would have picked Jack as the one who would wind up where Tallen had. Randa had made that observation aloud once, but Cam had disagreed. "That's just it. Jack got it all out of his system."

Randa took another look at the dilapidated boardinghouse and told herself that Jack must have gotten a lot of things out of his system. She picked up the shopping bag containing the scrapbooks and headed for the front porch.

There was an elderly woman sitting on the porch swing. She eyed Randa suspiciously as Randa made her way to the front door and knocked.

"He ain't in."

"Excuse me?"

"Mr. Overby. He works during the day, at some bank over in Griffin. His wife is usually here, but she had to go to the store. I don't think there's any rooms available anyway, except that attic room, and nobody in their right mind wants that thing."

"Well, I wasn't looking for a room, actually, I was looking for a boarder."

"A what?"

"Someone who lives here."

"I live here."

"No, I mean . . . I was looking for Jack Landry. Do you know him?"

"Know him? Don't nobody know him." She cocked her head a little, seeing Randa in a new light. "You kin to them?"

"No. I'm a friend of his brother's."

"Which one?"

"Cam."

"Is that the one in California?"

Randa nodded. Her clothes must have given her away.

"That's the only other one still alive, ain't it?"

"Yes." Randa was in no mood to get into it. "Could you tell me which room is Jack's?"

"Basement. It's got a separate entrance back around the other side of the house."

"Thank you." Randa turned to go.

"He ain't there, though." Randa stopped, discouraged. "I seen him go out about an hour ago and he ain't come back."

"Oh. Well . . . I guess I could leave a note."

"Why don't you go on in and wait?"

"Go in?"

"He never locks it. Mr. Overby told me he wouldn't even take a key."

"Well, I can't just go into someone's place."

"Suit yourself. It's comin' up a bad storm."

"Still . . ."

Raindrops were beginning to strike the tin roof. There was a flash of lightning and a crack of thunder that was sharp, though it was still in the distance.

"Lord!" the old woman exclaimed. "That was bad somewhere."

Randa looked at the car. She was debating going back to it when it suddenly started to pour. The old woman was watching her.

"Car's the safest place to be, unless you're sitting under a power line. Or a tree." Randa's car was sitting under both. She was starting to rethink the ethics of going into Jack's apartment. How could he be annoyed with her for wanting to come in out of the rain?

"I'm gonna get myself inside," the old woman said, standing up. "They're worse if it takes them a long time to get here, and this one's been coming all day." She gathered her needlepoint and headed for the door. "I wouldn't stay out here under this tin roof if I were you."

As soon as the screen door slammed behind her, Randa headed for Jack's apartment.

The door was indeed unlocked. Randa made sure no one was watching, then went inside. She closed the door behind her and stood facing it for a moment, savoring the last few seconds of not knowing what the place would look like. She shivered with a chill that was not from the rain, flipped the light switch, and turned around slowly.

She had told herself to be ready for anything, but nothing had prepared her for how utterly bare the place was. The room she had entered served as the bedroom and living room. It was furnished in Early Yard Sale. There was a chair and a coffee table that threatened to match. Behind the sofa was a double bed with an old iron headboard, graced by a nondescript grayish-blue blanket and a couple of pillows in plain white pillowcases. The dresser beside it was bare. There was no television, no radio, not even a window, with the exception of the one in the top half of the door, which was covered by a faded blue curtain. On the nightstand sat a telephone, an answering machine, and a clock. She couldn't imagine why he would need any of them.

She wanted to sit down, but it seemed wildly inappropriate. Not that her being here at all wasn't wildly inappropriate. But the bareness of the apartment made her presence feel like that much more of an intrusion. At least it was dry in here. And clean. That was the other thing that surprised her. Everything was so clean.

A brilliant flash of lightning lit up the room, followed immediately by a sharp crack of thunder. The lights flickered but stayed on. If he'd been working an outdoor job, they would have packed it in and he'd have had time to get home by now. He must have stopped somewhere to get something to eat. Deciding that she had a little time, Randa gave in to the irresistible urge to snoop. She slid one of the closet doors back and looked inside. A few pairs of jeans in various stages of disrepair. Work shirts, work boots, a gray sweatshirt, a pair of khaki pants permanently stained with white paint. Something in a garment bag. The only thing even remotely personal was a tan corduroy shirt that looked as if it had been hung hastily, the sleeves still rolled up. The shelves were empty.

Sliding the closet door back into place, she tried to put it all together. She thought about the cute blond kid in the photographs, always eager to draw attention to himself, always looking so full of life . . . How had that kid ended up in this apartment? It was as if he had sentenced himself to his own prison. But what was his crime?

She had only glanced into the darkened kitchen. Now she turned on the light and looked inside. A small white wooden table, bare. Two chairs. Inside the cabinets were plain white dishes; a couple of pots and a frying pan that had seen some years but were otherwise nondescript. A bottle of Ivory liquid soap on the counter was the only sign any of it was ever used.

She was about to check out the refrigerator when something caught her eye. There was a small hallway that led to the back door. It was obviously a service porch—just enough room for a small washer and dryer. Instead—she moved closer to make sure she wasn't imagining things—there was a desk and chair. It was a nice desk, obviously an antique and made of some rich wood like mahogany or cherry. In front of it was a matching Windsor chair with a worn maroon cushion, and on the desk stood a beautiful Tiffany lamp. It all looked so incongruous, shoved back into this dim corner like a secret hideaway; which, she guessed, was exactly what it was. She felt vindicated. She had been sure there was no way a person could live without giving a single sign of who they were, or where they had come from. The desk definitely spoke to the latter. She was sure it had belonged to Lucy. She gave the drawer a slight tug, somehow convinced it would be locked. It wasn't. She fairly collapsed into the chair and pulled the drawer to her. It was full of all sorts of odds and ends. She reached for the first thing she could find—an old, yellow photo, torn around the edges. She recognized it immediately: it was almost identical to one she'd seen in Cam's photo albums. A picture of Jack, Tallen, and Ethan as kids, dressed in cowboy costumes and posing proudly beside a large, crudely carved pumpkin. In spite of all the holiday trappings, there was something tentative in their faces, as though they were afraid they'd get into trouble for smiling.

She put the picture back. She was dying to go through the entire drawer, but she thought she'd better check the window first and make sure it was safe. She stood up and turned, then froze in place.

He was standing in the kitchen doorway, glaring at her with a mixture of anger and confusion. His hair had darkened with age to a sandy blond and all the mischief was gone from his face. He was wearing dirty jeans and an equally dirty blue work shirt. He was wet from the rain. He folded his arms across his impressive chest and continued to stare at her, waiting silently for an explanation. Randa forced herself to meet his eyes. They were the same shape as Cam's, except they were a strange pale olive color. And they were keenly alert—not the zombie eyes that often accompanied such a physique.

"I'm sorry. I didn't hear you come in." It was the best thing she could come up with under the circumstances.

"I don't generally knock on my own door." His voice was a deeper version of Cam's and flat with restraint. The fact that he wasn't yelling at her was giving Randa the creeps.

"My name is Randa Phillips." She figured the best defense was to pretend there was nothing wrong with what she was doing. Any other option was too embarrassing to even consider. "I'm a friend of Cam's."

"If you're here to deliver the sad news, the coroner beat you to it, so I guess you wasted a trip." There wasn't a trace of emotion in his voice.

"Well, I can at least offer you my condolences; I can see you're devastated."

He nodded toward the drawer. "Were you looking for anything specific?"

"No." She didn't bother to defend herself. "Look, I happened to be in Atlanta visiting my family"—*not that I wouldn't have flown two thousand miles for the pleasure of your charming company*—"and I drove down here to bring you some things I thought you might want."

"I don't want anything of his."

"Fine. But I'm sure *I'm* not the person who should end up with your family albums. I left them on your sofa. Have a nice life." She made a beeline for the door. Faced with the prospect of spending another minute with him, she suddenly felt that the storm seemed a lot less threatening.

For some strange reason, her main thought as she brushed past him was that she hoped he caught a whiff of her perfume.

If she'd caused a disturbance when she'd stopped at Tillie's to ask questions, Randa was about to shut the place down by having dinner there alone. It was packed now, and there was hardly a person in the room who hadn't stared blatantly at her at least twice. Some kept staring, as if thinking if they looked long enough, she'd get up and tell them who she was.

She was still shaken from her encounter with Jack. She didn't know what she had expected. Certainly not open arms, but at least some sort of connection, however brief. She didn't know why she'd expected that, but she had. At least he could have acknowledged the fact that this trip had required some degree of effort, not to mention money. But then, she'd told that lie about being in Atlanta. She wondered how he would have reacted if she'd told him she'd come all this way just to meet him.

She looked up to signal the waitress for her check.

Uh-oh.

There he was. Dressed in clean but paint-spattered jeans and a denim jacket she didn't remember seeing in his closet. He was looking at her. He turned away the minute she met his eyes, and stepped over to the end of the counter, where a sign said TAKE OUT.

Now what? She couldn't bolt. Well, she could, but she'd have to walk within three feet of him to get out the door, which would be extremely uncomfortable. She ordered a cup of coffee and decided to wait. She fished a pen out of her purse and started on a napkin, as if she was making a shopping list. Instead, she made a list of ten albums she'd take to a desert island, and ten singles she'd die before admitting she liked. All the while, she prayed he hadn't ordered anything hot.

You have a right to be here.

Right. She knew damned well she shouldn't be here. It was his territory, and he'd made it clear that she wasn't welcome.

From the corner of her eye, she saw him leave with nothing but a cup of coffee. She doubted he'd walked all this way for that. Well, she'd soon be gone and out of his hair for good. She would pack the Landrys in the back of her mind with all the other embarrassing memories—all those things that present themselves like flash cards during spasms of low self-esteem. This entire episode would be just another card in the deck. Outside, the storm had left the air chilly, reminding her that in places other than LA, it was the middle of winter. She tried to remember what clothes she had packed. She had decided to stay for a few days. She might even call her mother and admit to being in town.

Yeah. Just *what you need, Mom on your heels with: "Cam? Cam . . . isn't he the one whose brother killed all those people?"*

She wasn't sure whether she was truly nostalgic and homesick, or just trying to justify the airfare. Not that it mattered. She'd paid for it out of the Hostility Fund—the money her father had left her. Her rule of thumb was that she spent it only on things she knew he'd disapprove of. This trip would certainly qualify. Irrational, impetuous, and definitely on the wrong side of the political fence.

She turned the corner on the side street where she'd left her car. Jack was leaning against the wall of the Western Auto, sipping his coffee, waiting for her. She walked closer, then stopped. They stared at each other for a moment before he spoke.

"How did he die?" His tone was different. Quiet. Not as icy as before.

"Well . . . they say he killed himself."

"They say?"

"He did kill himself, it's just . . ." She sighed. "There was a lot of weird stuff going on and I'm not sure how much of it was true."

"Such as?"

"Well . . ." How was she supposed to tell him like this? "Do you want to go someplace where we can talk?"

"Aren't we talking?"

"I meant for a while. It's all very complicated."

"Just give me the bare bones." The lack of emotion in his voice made her wonder why he even cared.

"Okay. I hadn't seen him for some time. We had kind of a bitter parting, and—"

"This doesn't sound like bare bones."

Randa glared at him for a moment, then rattled it off. "People who'd seen him right before he died think he was having some sort of nervous breakdown. And the cops think he robbed a liquor store and killed a guy."

For the first time, Jack looked nonplussed. "What?"

"That's as bare as I can make it. If you want the rest, we're at least getting inside the car, because I'm cold."

He thought about it, as if it were a monumental decision. "Okay. Let's go sit down somewhere."

"Is there a bar around here?"

"I don't drink."

"Is there a reason you can't have a Coke and watch *me* drink?"

He stared off down the street. He looked like he might just start walking that way. Instead, he looked back.

"All right." It sounded like some sort of surrender. "There's a bar a couple of miles down the road."

The "bar" was more like a truck stop with a liquor license. It was a brick building with no windows and a neon sign above the door that read COUNTYLINE TAVERN. It looked like the kind of place where if you didn't have a gun going in, they'd give you one at the door.

They found a booth in the back. Other than wanting to be away from the commotion, Jack had shown no signs of having an opinion about the place one way or the other. He was completely focused on wanting to hear the story. By the time Randa had finished with the basics, he was on his third Coke and Randa was on her second bourbon, and wishing she didn't have to drive to Atlanta so she could order about five more. She wondered why he had made such a point of telling her that he didn't drink. It was the only bit of personal information he had offered. He certainly didn't impress her as a proselytizing former alcoholic.

When she'd finished the story in as much detail as he would allow, he repeated it to her, like someone unsure of a set of directions. She answered by rote, and took the opportunity to study his face. It looked softer in the glow of the cheap red patio candle on the table. He had a high forehead, like Cam, and a square jaw. Perfect teeth, which she knew had to have come through the grace of God and not as the result of years of expensive orthodontia. She sensed he had the kind of smile that would change the entire nature of his face, and wondered when was the last time anyone had seen it.

She nodded as he finished recounting the story. He shook his head. "There's no way in hell Cam robbed a liquor store." It was the first sign of any emotion other than anger she'd seen from him. Maybe it was all the sugar and caffeine.

Randa nodded. "I have a hard time with it myself. But if he was . . . crazy . . ."

"I don't care how crazy he was." He polished off the Coke. He didn't volunteer anything else.

Randa stared at her cocktail napkin. She was sick of carrying the conversation, but the silence was cloying.

"So which county is dry?"

"What?"

"I grew up in Georgia. If this is the 'Countyline' Tavern, it's because the next county is dry."

He came very close to smiling. "Henry County. Next door. You think my father would own a house in a dry county?"

Randa was startled. It had never occurred to her that Will Landry had ever *bought* a house. Cam had certainly never mentioned it.

"So . . . what happened to the house?"

He suddenly looked pained, realizing he had disclosed something. He shifted his weight. "It's still there."

"Does it belong to you?"

"Technically."

"But you don't live there?"

"Obviously not."

"How come?" She knew he was hating this, but she couldn't resist.

"Look, are we done?"

"Well, no." She paused and sipped her drink, giving him time to recover from having accidentally stumbled into normal human interaction. "There's one more thing."

"What?"

"Well, when the cops couldn't find you, I guess they called—" She stopped, remembering. "You know, you're living right here where

Cam last saw you, but he told me you had vanished off the face of the earth."

"Did he?" His tone was snide.

"He said he sent you a letter and the post office sent it back, 'moved, no forwarding address.'"

Jack looked vaguely amused by that. He shook his head. "It came back 'return to sender, addressee wants to be left the hell alone.'"

"Why did Cam lie to me?"

"How should I know?"

"Well, it doesn't make any sense."

"Don't expect anything about my family to make any sense." She could see a flash of anger in his eyes, but it seemed to vanish as quickly as it had appeared. When he spoke again, his voice was quiet and he was perfectly composed.

"So . . . what's the rest of it?"

She got the feeling he had been in the company of another person for as long as he could tolerate it.

"When I went to get the scrapbooks, I met your uncle Ryland. He was at Cam's. I guess he came to go through Cam's things and . . . you know, make all the arrangements. But he was weird. I mean, Cam had told me he was a little bit fruity—"

"What paper do you write for?" he asked, cutting her off. His voice was angry and Randa could see the tension in his jaw. She looked at him, puzzled. She hadn't mentioned her career to him once.

"How did you know I was a writer?"

"What paper?"

"The LA *Chronicle*. It's a—"

"I don't know what the hell you're trying to pull. Obviously Cam told you just enough that you can smell a story."

"What are you talking about?"

"Oh, cut the act." He was standing now, pulling money out of his wallet. He threw it on the table. "I don't know how you people sleep at night."

"I don't know *what* you're talking about."

He didn't show any sign of hearing her. He headed for the door. She ran to catch up to him.

"Would you please tell me what is going on?"

He ignored her and kept walking. Annoyed, Randa reached out and grabbed his arm. He stopped and turned, jerking his arm away. He stared down at her with an anger that was almost palpable.

"You shouldn't have relied on Cam for your information. He never knew or cared about anything that went on in the family. That's why I didn't even bother to tell him."

"Tell him what?"

"That Ryland died. He had a heart attack; he's been dead for three years. Nice try, though."

He was out the door before Randa even realized what he had said.

SIX

All he wanted out of life was for nothing else to happen to him. Good, bad, indifferent, it didn't matter. He couldn't deal with one more thing. He lived his life as invisibly as possible. He did nothing to draw attention to himself. No driver's license, no credit cards, no checkbook. He'd even had his phone and utilities listed in the landlord's name and paid his bills in cash. No doctors, no prescription drugs. He didn't want his name in any computer. He just wanted to be left alone. He'd felt that way most of his life. It didn't seem like a lot to ask.

"It doesn't work that way, Jack," Cathy said as he finished giving her that speech for the zillionth time. "Life's not juvie court. It doesn't cut you a deal everyone can live with and then lose your address if you never screw up again. Life is a serial killer. It just keeps comin' back for more."

"I don't have any more to give. You can't get blood out of an onion."

"Turnip," she corrected him.

"Whatever stupid vegetable. You know what I mean." He sighed and leaned back in his chair. Cathy was at the sink, washing a large pot that had been the focus of her attention ever since he'd arrived.

"Let me know when you need me to leave," he said.

"It's okay. How many times do I have to tell you?"

He continued to stare at the yellow Formica on top of her kitchen table and traced a crack with his index finger. No matter how much she denied it, he was sure his presence was making her nervous. Otherwise she would not have declined his offer to help with the dishes.

"Is what's-his-name coming over after work?" It probably sounded pissy, but he was too tired to care.

"His name is Ben and he's at a friend's deer camp in Locust Grove till next week sometime. He'll never know you were here."

"And it doesn't bother you?"

"That you're here?"

He nodded.

She dried her hands with a dish towel and looked at him. "Jack, I wasn't tellin' you not to come to my house anymore. Is that what you thought?"

"We didn't discuss the new rules."

"Do we need to?"

"No, I get it. I'm still welcome in the kitchen."

"So your short reign of bein' a prince about this is over?"

"I'm still a prince. I'm just . . . a tired prince."

"When was the last time you had a decent night's sleep?"

"I think I was in junior high school." He mustered a feeble smile, which she ignored. He ran a hand through his hair and stared at the blackness out the window. "I want a drink like I can't tell you."

"Well, if you don't have the sense to keep your butt out of a bar . . ."

"Where should I have gone? Her hotel room?"

"So is that why you came over here? So I'll make sure you don't drink?"

"I haven't needed a babysitter in a long time, thank you." It was as icy as he'd meant it to be, although he had only himself to blame for bringing up a sore subject. He should never have even told her about the bar, but he'd been in too much of a huff when he got there to be careful.

"I just think you've got enough to worry about without lettin' somebody drag you into a bar."

"She didn't drag me. And I hate to break it to you, but I'd want a drink right now if I'd spent the last two hours in a church."

She turned away from him, back to the sink. He didn't know why he was sniping at her, except that the AA crap annoyed the hell out of him. Still, the last thing he needed was to alienate the one person he could talk to.

"I'm sorry," he said, sighing.

"Okay." She didn't look at him. She was about to scrub the enamel off the sides of the pot, which had never been very dirty to begin with.

"I know what you're doin'. You're takin' it out on me because you're upset about Cam."

"Thank you, Doctor."

"Jack, it's okay if you're upset. I hated my father's guts and I was still a wreck when he died."

"I am *not* upset about Cam." He drew the line at *Good Housekeeping* psychology. Especially when she was right.

"Do you have any aspirin?" The best defense being a change of subject.

"Yeah." She didn't make any move to get it, just stared at him to let him know she saw through the ploy.

"I would get it, but I'm too grief-stricken to move."

"Jack, you're right on that line." She tossed it over her shoulder as she headed for the bathroom.

He smiled. It was a bit left over from high school. In earlier days it was preceded by "You know that line where you stop charmin' people and start pissin' them off?"

He wondered what she'd think if she knew what was *really* eating at him. Randa. Randa's face. The fact that he couldn't get it out of his head.

As angry as he had been to find her sitting at his desk, rummaging through his drawer, the moment she had turned around, something had stirred beneath the anger—feelings so long buried he'd forgotten they existed. He had no idea what had happened. She was certainly not the first pretty woman he'd seen in ten years, and it wasn't like she was cover-of-*Vogue* gorgeous. But there was something in her face—a beauty that was straightforward and unpretentious. And those eyes. Such a deep shade of sable it was impossible to tell where the pupils began. And that mop of blond hair. Back when he had cared about such things, he'd always been a sucker for brown-eyed blondes.

It all went beyond the way she looked, though. He loved the fact that she'd simply refused to offer any bullshit excuses for what she was doing, as if that would be beneath her dignity. In fact, everything about her implied a refreshing authenticity.

Then why did she lie about Ryland? It doesn't fit.

I don't know. When did I claim to have all the answers . . . any *of the answers?*

He'd been able to admire it all from a safe distance until she'd grabbed his arm in the bar, but then he'd felt it in every cell of his body, even though he was furious with her at the time. He wasn't sure now whether that rage had been aimed at her or at himself for not being able to keep her out.

Well, it didn't matter. It was over. She was probably already on her way back to LA to break the bad news to her editor. In his own life, she'd been nothing more than a signal, like the dreams and the headaches and the home movies flashing through his head. All these things were a warning that some strange tide was eating away the seawall, and it was time for some shoring up. Where he was going to get the sandbags was another question.

Cathy returned with a small bottle of aspirin and a Dixie cup full of water.

"I'm only givin' you these if you swallow 'em like a normal human. It makes my skin crawl when you chew 'em."

She put the cup down on the table and handed him the bottle. He shook a few pills into his palm.

"How many are you takin'?"

He looked at her. "I don't know. How many do I have permission to take?"

"I don't understand why you refuse to get a prescription. It couldn't be any worse than livin' on aspirin."

He popped four into his mouth and made a big display of chewing them.

Cathy made a face. "Thank you."

"Spite is my natural reaction to nagging." He handed the bottle back to her.

"No, keep it. You might get hungry later on."

She moved behind him and began to massage his temples, which surprised him, given the tense undercurrent since he'd walked in the door. He closed his eyes, tossing her the olive branch of letting her know it felt good.

"How did you know where it hurts?" he asked.

"I know all your headaches. The press always gets you right here."

She was right, which was amazing, since it had been years since he'd had any problems with the press. But then, Cathy had been through the thick of it, so it probably shouldn't surprise him that she remembered. (The day of Tallen's execution, she had chased a reporter from the

Atlanta Constitution off Lucy's front porch with a baseball bat. Called him a "selfish, insensitive, chickenshit jackass." It made the front page, in a sanitized form.)

He could smell her perfume. She'd always had a knack for finding cheap perfume that didn't smell like cheap perfume. Still, hers paled in comparison to the memory of Randa's, which had been light and crisp and—he'd bet money—French. Reminded him of the perfumes he used to smell on the women at the Ritz-Carlton—the ones who dripped Chanel. It had been off-putting then, the scent of a wall he'd never scale. But without the Chanel and the jewelry and the hair that wouldn't move in a wind tunnel, the effect was different. French perfume on a woman wearing faded jeans and a baggy sweater was an alluring incongruity.

Cathy's voice saved him from his thoughts. "It doesn't make any sense."

"What?"

"That Cam would kill himself. He was always the survivor."

Jack opened his eyes. "You don't think I'm a survivor?"

"I guess that depends on your definition of survivin'."

Jack refused the bait. "I don't know why he killed himself. What difference does it make?"

She shrugged. "I just always thought Cam was safe."

"Yeah, well. Nobody's safe." He hadn't told her about the liquor store thing, not wanting to endure the barrage of theories sure to follow. In fact, he'd only told her about Cam's death at all because it would hit the local paper sooner or later, and she'd be insulted if she hadn't heard it from him first.

She moved away, back to the sink. She leaned against it, facing him. The look on her face made him feel like he was in the crosshairs of a deer rifle.

"Was she pretty?"

Damn. How had he given himself away? He picked up the Dixie cup and drank the water slowly.

"Jack?"

He put the cup down. "Yeah, for a bloodsucking, lying, scheming, self-obsessed journalist who dragged me to a bar, I suppose she was pretty."

He looked at the clock on the wall above the sink. It was almost midnight. "I should go home."

"You've been sayin' that ever since you got here. Why don't you go home?"

He didn't answer. He didn't know how to tell her, and it was getting to the point where he'd have no choice.

"Jack?"

He stared at the table. She sat down in the chair across from him.

"Jack, what is wrong?" Her voice was full of concern that he knew was genuine. He continued to rack his brain for a way to go from *A* to *C* without passing *B*. After a long moment, he looked at her and shook his head. "It's crazy—"

"What?"

"The stupid dreams—" He had told her about the dreams yesterday, although not in any kind of detail. There was no way to describe them that did them justice.

"What about them?"

"They're not just bad dreams. Not like nightmares. They're like—" He shook his head again.

"What?"

"I don't know." There was no use trying to explain. He didn't understand it himself. He might as well get the worst behind him. "Can I stay here tonight?"

She gave him a look that was about what he'd expected. "Jack . . ."

"To *sleep*."

"I can't keep you from havin' bad dreams."

"I know that."

"Then what's the point?"

He couldn't believe she needed to ask. Maybe she just wanted to hear it out loud. Hell, he'd give her that.

"I don't want to be alone."

She looked at him like she was waiting for the punch line; then, realizing there wasn't going to be one, she shifted to thinking out loud.

"All right . . ." she said, weighing it carefully. "As long as you stay on your side of the bed."

"Scout's honor."

"So, Jack . . . what are we solvin'? I mean, what are you gonna do *tomorrow* night?"

"I don't know. How long are they gonna be in the woods?"

"I'm serious."

"So am I." He smiled a little. She didn't return it. "What's wrong?"

She sighed, shook her head a little, finally spoke. "You never once slept here when I asked you to, you know? When *I* needed *you*."

It landed where it was thrown. He waited a couple of respectful seconds, then decided he should at least go through the motions of defending himself.

"Look, you know—"

"Don't, Jack. Save it for somebody who doesn't know it by heart." She got up and left the room.

He sat bolt upright in bed and reached for Cathy in the dark, but he was alone. He could hear the sound of the TV in the other room, and a dog howling in the distance. He took deep breaths and waited for his heartbeat to slow down.

The dream had been the same as last time, only more vivid. He could still see the hag-woman's face. He could still feel her hands around his throat, her thumbnails piercing the skin on his neck. He could remember the putrid smell of her sour breath. He half expected to see her step out of the shadows. He looked around the room, though he didn't know what he was looking for.

He lay back down and closed his eyes, trying to clear his head. He felt foggy and disoriented, as if he'd *left* reality instead of returning to it. Or like he'd come back from someplace far away—farther away than a person's mind could travel in a dream. It didn't make any sense, yet the feeling was strong. He felt drained by it.

The headache was throbbing. He pulled himself to his feet and went to look for the bottle of aspirin Cathy had given him. Cathy glanced up from the TV.

"What's wrong?" He shook his head and headed for the bathroom. "Did you have a bad dream?"

"It didn't kill me. Don't worry about it." He went into the bathroom and closed the door. He didn't care if she knew he was annoyed, even if he had no right to be. To him, it had been implicit in the unspoken deal that she would go to bed when he did, to be there if he woke up. He had offered her a rare glimpse of his vulnerability, and she had opted for Jay Leno.

He popped a couple of aspirin, then turned on the cold water and splashed it on his face until he felt better. He wiped his face on a towel without bothering to take it off the towel rack, then looked in the mirror, as if to check for damage.

What the hell?

On his neck, just where he had felt her thumbnails, were small red crescents, surrounded by a cluster of purple bruises. He blinked hard, then leaned closer to the mirror. They were still there. He touched one of the crescents and could feel a slight indentation.

Suddenly he felt a hand on his back. He gasped and swung around wildly, almost knocking Cathy over. She jumped out of the way. "Jesus, Cathy!"

"I'm sorry. I thought you saw me."

He closed his eyes and winced as a pain shot through his head, sharp and hot. He felt Cathy's hand on his shoulder. Her skin felt cool against his. He shook his head and she pulled her hand away.

"Are you okay?"

He opened his eyes, slowly, and looked at her. "You're not going to believe this."

"What?"

He was surprised she hadn't already noticed. He pointed to his neck.

"What?" she asked again.

Maybe he wasn't pointing to the right place. He turned and looked in the mirror.

Nothing. He put his hand to his neck. "They're gone."

"What's gone?" she insisted impatiently.

He looked at her. What was he supposed to say? *A witch-woman tried to choke me in my dream and it left marks on my neck; they're gone now, but you have to believe me.*

He shook his head. "Nothing."

He moved past her, trying to look annoyed, like it was her fault she didn't see anything. He slammed the door to the bedroom—not hard, just enough to keep her from following him. He made it to the bed before his legs gave way.

What the hell was going on? Had he still been asleep when he saw the marks? Hell, no! He'd been wide awake. Then what had he seen? He must have made the marks himself. He'd somehow pressed his own hands on his neck so hard that even his bitten-down-to-the-quick nails had made the marks. And somehow they'd vanished before Cathy could see them. That had to be it. Might not hold up to a lot of scrutiny, but it was stone solid compared to the alternatives.

He lay down in hopes of calming the pain in his head. It had spread from his temples to the base of his skull, as if someone were tightening a steel band. He definitely had to do something about the damned headaches. They were getting worse, along with the dreams. He felt he was under siege. Maybe Cathy was right. Maybe it was time to break down and trek to Atlanta in search of someone with a couch and a prescription pad. Unloading the family secrets couldn't be any worse than this. (Although he could just imagine his first visit. *Let's see. There were four brothers, three with impressive criminal records, which, by the way, includes me. One brother was executed by the state of Alabama. One supposedly drowned, although I've long suspected that my father killed him. My father killed himself, which was the only good thing he ever did for the world. My brother the token success story just killed himself, but first he had a nervous breakdown and killed someone else. My mother was basically psychotic and delusional by the time she died, and, oh yeah, she killed herself, too. Me, I've never had the guts to kill myself, but I'm working on it. I haven't been to a therapist before now because I didn't think I needed it.*)

The lighted dial on the clock by the bed said 1:10, which meant Cathy would probably be watching the stupid television for at least another twenty minutes. He'd just have to stare at the ceiling and think. Not something he relished, but he didn't have any other choice.

Something moved.

He raised his head and looked in the direction of the movement.

There's something there.

In the corner, by the dresser. It wasn't really a *thing* so much as a *shape*, but it was moving—a constant, fluid motion. Swirling. It was colorless—shades of black, somehow. The darkest parts were a vile black, like wet tar; and yet it was transparent. Looking at it was like staring through gasoline vapors.

Jack closed his eyes tightly, then opened them. It was still there. It was floating now, slowly, across the floor, still swirling within itself. For reasons that made no sense, he had the strange sensation it was *watching* him.

It knows who I am.

It was moving toward him, slowly but steadily. He opened his mouth to call Cathy, but the dry scream lodged in his throat, making it even harder to breathe.

And then it was gone.

Gone. It didn't dissolve. It simply wasn't there anymore. He turned his head enough to make sure the room was empty, although he knew without looking. The air around him was warm.

Oh, God . . . What was it? What was *it?*

His mind grasped furiously for an explanation. There was only one.

It didn't happen.

Of course it happened. Why am I shaking?

You think it was there, but it wasn't. Just like the marks on your neck.

Screw the marks on my neck! There was something in here just now! I saw it!

Right.

I'd swear on my life!

That's just what Mom used to say.

He could feel a mist of cold sweat on his chest and his forehead. He forced himself to stand and reached for his jeans from the back of the chair. He pulled them on. His hands were trembling so, he could barely zip them up.

There was a tap on the door, then Cathy pushed it open. "Jack?"

He couldn't look at her. He kept dressing.

"Jack, what is goin' on?"

"Nothing," he said quietly. He was losing his mind. It was that stark and that simple. Cathy came over and put her arms around him; kissed him on the shoulder, a gesture that was far too intimate for him in his current state. He pulled away from her.

"Sorry," she said, under her breath. She was too used to it to be offended.

I'm losing my mind. Isn't that *just perfect?*

He reached for his shirt.

"Where are you goin'?"

"Home."

"Are you mad at me about somethin'?"

He shook his head and fumbled with the buttons.

"Then why are you goin' home? I thought you wanted to stay here."

He stopped buttoning. "You know what she told me?"

"Who?"

"Cam's friend. She said he had some kind of breakdown . . . he lost his mind."

Her face slowly softened as she began to understand. "Jack . . . you're not losin' your mind. You're just havin' bad dreams."

She put her hand on his arm and gave it a gentle squeeze. He kissed her on the forehead and finished buttoning his shirt on the way out the door.

Back home he turned on the shower and let the hot water pour over his head, as if it could wash away the events of the last forty-eight hours and he could start over somehow.

What was happening to him? The onset of schizophrenia? A brain tumor? Or just a garden-variety nervous breakdown? Was that what had happened to Cam? Did things like that run in families? Would the imaginary sights and sounds turn into a sudden urge to rob a liquor store? Or was he just going to gradually disintegrate until he wound up living on a heating grate in downtown Atlanta, shouting to passersby that aliens were controlling his brain?

Out of the shower, he dried his hair with a towel and made a point of looking (*really* looking) at his face in the mirror. He hadn't cared about his appearance in ten years, just so long as he looked clean-cut enough not to threaten anyone who might want him to paint their house. Now all of a sudden, in the middle of a nervous breakdown, he found himself wondering what he looked like. He didn't look crazy. Did crazy people look crazy when they first started to go crazy?

He made his way to the bed and lay down on top of the covers. He folded the pillow and propped his head on it in an effort to keep from nodding off. He did not want to know what his subconscious had in store for him next.

He knew why he was thinking about his looks. That damned reporter woman. What was there about her that brought back thoughts that hadn't troubled him in years? He couldn't shake the feeling that he was going to see her again. Like they'd made some date he had every intention of keeping. What if they *had* made some arrangement to get together again? Where would they have met? What would they have talked about? Would she have apologized for the Ryland story and begged him to forgive her? Would he have? (He knew the answer to that one, although he'd have made her work for it.) Would he have told her that he'd been hallucinating, and, if so, would he have told her before or after he slept with her? God. What would it be like, after all this time, to sleep with a woman he was actually strongly attracted to? He was, he realized, making the gigantic assumption that *she* was attracted to *him*. It had been a very long time since he'd tried to capitalize on his looks, so he had no idea what, if anything, remained intact. (*Slightly aged but formerly extremely good-looking schizophrenic wishes to hook up with beautiful, understanding single white female, preferably recently deceased brother's ex-girlfriend.*)

He suddenly realized what he was doing and winced. He told himself that it was just easier to fantasize about her than to wonder about what was happening to him. In fact, if she hadn't hit him at a vulnerable time, he probably would never have given her a second thought.

The clock said 3:16. He should probably try to get some sleep, even if it meant risking the dreams. When he lost sleep he just got more depressed, and he needed to keep his head as clear as possible to deal with whatever the hell was going on.

He reached over to turn off the lamp and saw that the red message light was blinking on his answering machine. He thought for sure he'd checked it when he came in, but he must not have. He debated leaving it till morning, since he knew it was Rick with Monday's work schedule. But every once in a while Rick found weekend work for him, and the idea of having something to do tomorrow appealed to him. Anything to keep his mind off his encroaching insanity. He hit the Play button.

For a few seconds there was only static, and Jack had decided it was a hang up and got up to reset the machine when he heard the voice. "*. . . Jack . . . you have to get help . . .*" The line crackled for another second, then the voice returned. "*She was telling you the truth . . .*" Jack felt his legs give way and he collapsed onto the chair. More static, replaced by a dial tone, then the machine's robot voice: "*End of messages.*" He reached for the machine. His hand was shaking so hard it was all he could do to rewind the message. He heard the static again and waited. It went on and on, long after the message should have started. The dial tone cut it off again. "*End of messages.*"

Jack rewound the tape again and hit the Play button. The machine beeped at him. "*End of messages.*"

He pulled the tape out and made sure it had rewound all the way. It had. He snapped it back into the machine and pressed the button, hard, as if that would help. "*End of messages,*" the machine insisted.

Nothing. There's nothing on the damned tape!

Jack put his face in his hands and tried to breathe. His eyes were welling up and his throat had closed so tightly it made his chest hurt. The voice was still echoing in his head. He hadn't heard it for a long time, but he knew it well.

It was Tallen.

SEVEN

Randa stared at Tillie's breakfast menu through unfocused eyes, the result of a hangover that rivaled anything she'd ever done to herself at a freshman mixer, and tried to remember why it had seemed like a good idea to stay and have two and a half more drinks last night after Jack had stormed out.

Could it possibly be because you apparently had an in-depth conversation with a ghost?

I did not have a conversation with a ghost. There are a million logical explanations.

Name one.

Maybe it was someone pretending to be Ryland. Cam had a respectable amount of money and, as far as anyone knew, no locatable next of kin.

The man you saw was the man in Cam's scrapbook, and you know it.

Maybe Ryland isn't really dead. Maybe Jack lied.

Why would he lie?

Well, Cam seems to have lied to me all over the place. Maybe they're a family of pathological liars. They're certainly a family of pathological somethings.

The breakfast crowd had not paid her a lot of attention, with the exception of the occasional scowl she was getting from the little old woman who owned the guesthouse she had checked into upon discovering she was too drunk to drive to Atlanta.

She looked out the window and was just beginning to worry about the possibility of Jack showing up when she saw him, a blur of old denim, making his way up the highway, his hands in his pockets. He was walking briskly, as if he was late for an appointment. Barely checking for traffic, he half ran across the road. He came through the door and headed straight for her booth, sliding into the seat across from her like she'd been waiting for him.

"I called every hotel in town looking for you." This was a long way from what she'd expected; it took a Herculean effort to conceal that fact.

"Why?"

"I want to talk to you."

"You could have fooled me last night."

"Will you just hear me out?"

"Why, certainly. You were so patient with me, the least I can do is return the favor."

"Let me know when you've gotten all this out of your system," he said without emotion. He was untouchable behind the fortress of that blank expression, and he knew it. She wanted to kick him.

"Okay," she said. "What is it?"

"I need to know the truth."

"About what?"

"What you said, about talking to Ryland. I have to know if that really happened."

"How could it have happened? You said Ryland's been dead for years."

"Forget that. Let *me* worry about it."

The redheaded waitress appeared, Bic poised above her guest check.

"What can I get y'all?"

"Coffee. Black," Randa answered mechanically.

"Two," Jack added.

The waitress pocketed the guest check, took Randa's menu (while giving her a stern once-over), and was gone.

"The guy who said he was Ryland. Where did you see him?"

"Cam's living room. He said I should find you and give you the books. I asked him why he couldn't do it himself. He said he couldn't get through your thick skull." She paused for effect, then added, "Whatever could he have meant by that?"

Jack remained stoic. "So what was it that a total stranger was supposed to be able to get through my thick skull?"

"He seemed to think you were in some kind of trouble."

"What kind of trouble?"

"I don't know. He wasn't making a lot of sense. But then, the poor guy's been dead for three years; I guess I shouldn't pick on his syntax."

The waitress returned with two mugs of coffee.

"Are y'all sure you don't want breakfast?" It was aimed at Jack. Randa had a sneaking suspicion the girl had a greater interest in eavesdropping on their conversation than any genuine concern over Jack's nutritional needs. He looked at her, annoyed.

"Hadn't you better stop talking to me, before you get Darlene all upset again?"

Her face turned sheepish, so Randa assumed Jack had hit a nerve. Whatever he'd done, it had worked. She was gone. Jack turned back to Randa.

"How can I know?" he asked.

"Know what?"

"That you're not just trying to trick me into something."

"Oh, come on. Are we going to do that one again?" It came out louder than she'd meant it to, and Randa was drawing stares, but she was too annoyed to care. "Look, if I wanted to write some tabloid exposé on your sacred family, I would have done it a long time ago and I wouldn't have needed you. Cam's followers will have a new messiah by the time I get home, so a story about his childhood wouldn't even be an easy sell, much less a hot property. And in case you haven't noticed, this country has been executing people at far too rapid a rate for anyone to give a damn about Tallen anymore. So if I'm trying to trick you into a story, you tell *me* what the hell story I'm trying to trick you into."

He was quiet for a long moment, staring into his coffee. When he finally spoke, he didn't look up. "Then why are you here?"

"I don't know. The man who said he was Ryland told me that I'd do this if I cared anything about your family."

"Why do you care about my family?"

"Apparently I have a pathological obsession with them, if you want the unsolicited opinion of your late brother's most recent girlfriend."

He looked at her, startled out of his shell. "I thought you were . . . I mean, I assumed . . ."

Randa shook her head. "Nope. My stint as Playmate of the Year was cut down in its prime by one Nora Dixon, formerly my closest and most trustworthy friend."

"Cam ditched you for your best friend?" He seemed mildly amused by that.

"Well, from what I heard, Nora wasn't exactly a passive participant. And I'm the idiot who introduced them, so it's hard to come up with a blameless party in the mix." She didn't know why she was telling him any of this. It was none of his damned business. "I don't have an answer.

My current theory is that I was very bad in another lifetime, and for punishment, God has made me obsess over your family."

He smiled. He actually smiled. It took years off his face, and the hardness was replaced by something close to warmth.

"Well, whatever you did, I must have done something worse. At least you didn't have to grow up with them."

He sounded like Cam when he said it, down to the tiniest inflection. It made Randa wince. She was grateful when he didn't seem to notice.

"I don't get it. If Ryland's still alive, why wouldn't he just come to me?" The smile was gone as quickly as it had appeared.

"Is it possible that Ryland's still alive?"

"I guess so, technically. I didn't go to the funeral. Mainly because he'd been dead for a year before my aunt bothered to tell me."

"Why would she tell you he was dead if it wasn't true?"

"I don't know." He sipped his coffee and stared out the window. "Nothing in my life has ever made sense." He hesitated, then looked back at her.

"The reason I wanted to talk to you"—he paused and took a breath—"I know how crazy this sounds, but last night when I got home, there was a message on my answering machine from Tallen."

Randa stared at him, waiting for him to explain. He didn't. "You're serious?" she finally asked.

"It's not something I'd joke about."

Randa remembered Cam's claim that he'd seen Tallen, and she had to work to suppress a shudder. "Are you sure it was Tallen?" she asked.

"It was Tallen's voice," he said. "You probably wouldn't have any trouble convincing me that I'm losing my mind, but I know Tallen's voice." He choked on the words and stopped, stared down into his coffee cup. "It was him," he said, quietly, to no one.

"Well . . . did he . . ."

Did he what, Randa? Leave a number where he could be reached?

She tried again. "What did the message say?"

"That you were telling me the truth."

So his ghost believed that she saw her ghost. That helped.

"Do you still have the tape?"

"There's nothing on it."

"What do you mean?"

"I rewound it, and there's nothing on it," he said. "Look, it's probably just—my mother was batshit crazy when she died. My father was not even human, and Tallen had to have been at least temporarily insane to do what he did, I don't care what the jury said. And if even Cam could lose it, there's no reason to think I'm somehow exempt." He sighed. "I've been coming unglued lately. I've been having these migraines, one right after another. It keeps me disoriented. And these dreams . . . I can't even describe them. They're unreal. I mean, even for dreams. It's like . . ." He groped for a word.

"Like you're going somewhere in your sleep?"

His face tensed with disbelief and went ashen. "How do you know?" he asked in a tight whisper.

"Cam was having weird dreams, too. That's how he described them to someone."

"That's exactly how it feels," he said, still half-whispering. He put his coffee cup down and shoved it aside.

"Was there something your family referred to as 'the thing'?" Randa asked. "That's what Ryland was saying. He said, 'Tell him that the thing is real.'"

Jack froze. He looked numb, like someone who had heard one too many bits of bad news.

"Are you okay?"

He stood up. "Let's get out of here."

Before she could answer he was up, on his way to the door. Randa signaled the waitress for the check.

She found him outside, pacing in front of her car. Randa wondered what land mine she'd stepped on this time.

"Where are we going?" she asked, bracing herself for whatever came back at her.

"I don't know," he said quietly. "I just . . . couldn't breathe in there." He took a few steps away from the car, stopped, and stared down the road.

Randa had a sudden idea. "Could I see the house?" she asked. He looked back at her.

"The house?"

"Your family's house. Is it near here?"

He nodded. "About five miles down Thirty-Six."

"I'd really love to see it," she said. She was surprised by her brazenness, but none of this felt real anyway. She was sure that any minute she'd wake up, Cam and Nora would be announcing their engagement, and she'd be working on a story about where to find the best soft tacos in the San Fernando Valley.

"Well . . . okay," Jack said. "I guess we could go there."

Randa unlocked the car door quickly, before he changed his mind.

As was usually the case anywhere in Georgia, as soon as they left the town, they were in the boondocks. They rode in silence. Jack stared out the window, but Randa doubted he really saw anything.

The two-lane wound them through the gentle landscape. Rolling hills dotted with grazing cattle; miles of pastures bordered by tall Georgia pines and huge old oak trees. Randa had forgotten how beautiful it was, and how deceptively peaceful.

"What do you know about me?" Jack asked suddenly.

"Not much," Randa said. She wondered why he was asking. He didn't say anything else.

"I know you've done time," she said. "Cam told me."

"I'm sure he did," Jack said. He had no attitude that she could pinpoint.

"He didn't tell me what for."

"Overdue library books," Jack said without smiling. Randa glanced at him. She thought she could detect the tiniest trace of a smirk.

"What was it really?"

"Armed robbery."

Randa was stumped for a response.

How interesting. I've never driven down a deserted country road with an armed robber before.

"Don't worry," he said, breaking the silence. "I gave that up." He pointed at something up ahead. "Turn left at those mailboxes."

She turned. There were pastures on either side of the gravel road, enclosed in barbed-wire fencing. In the pasture on the right, a herd of white-faced Herefords were all lying down, feet tucked neatly under their bellies, watching the car with great indifference.

"Guy down the road owns the cows," Jack offered. "He tends the fence, fertilizes and Bush Hogs the pasture, in return for running his cattle on the land."

"This is your land? All of it?"

"It's not that much. Forty-five acres."

"Where's the house?"

"Other side of those trees. It's about half a mile off the road."

"How on earth did your father afford this?"

"He didn't. Ryland paid for it. My mother had this stupid theory that my father would settle down if they had their own home, so she talked Ryland into buying this place for us. It went cheap. No one around here wanted it."

"Why not?"

"Family who lived here right before we bought it . . . guy went nuts one night and took an ax to his wife and three kids, then shot himself. Nobody was in a big mood to live here after that."

"I'm surprised your mother would."

"What my mother wanted more than anything else was a permanent address. I guess that won out over potential ghosts."

"Did anything weird ever happen?"

"If I ever heard anything go bump in the night, it was generally my father slamming my mother's head against the wall."

The road curved and suddenly the house was in sight.

There was nothing about it that offered any hint of its ugly past. It was the standard white clapboard story-and-a-half farmhouse with a front porch, the roof of which was supported by concrete and brick pillars. The place wasn't immaculate, but it wasn't in a state of disrepair, either. The only thing that would even verge on gothic was the fact that it was so isolated. It was impossible to see the road from the house, and empty fields stretched out beyond it on all sides. Will must have loved that—plenty of room to wreak havoc on Lucy and the kids, and no one within miles to hear anything and call the cops.

"Forgive the obvious question, but why don't you live here?" Randa asked, as they emerged from the car.

"Too many bad memories, I guess. As trite as that must sound."

"Then why don't you sell it?"

"Partly because I don't want to deal with all that."

"What's the other part?"

"I have this fantasy of striking a match to it." He didn't smile when he said it. "Burn it to the ground, just sit here and watch."

"So why haven't you?"

"I guess some other part of me needs proof that it all really happened."

He nodded toward a small barn a few yards away. "I'm going to get something for the ducks." He was gone, disappearing inside. Randa looked around, wondering what ducks he was talking about. He returned with a small red plastic bucket full of dried corn.

"You don't mind walking, do you?"

She shook her head and followed him. It was chilly, but the quiet was intoxicating, worth any discomfort. The sky was gray from the storm front that had not quite moved on, and it gave the place a touch of the ominous atmosphere it deserved. Jack led her up a hill, down a shallow valley, and up over a ridge, beyond which lay a small lake. The silence was broken by a frenzy of quacking from the half dozen mallards on the lake, who had seen them coming. Randa smiled. Ducks always seemed like cartoon animals to her. Cute, but surely not meant to be taken seriously. Jack reached into the bucket and tossed a handful of corn to the shoreline. The ducks waddled out of the water and all dove after the same kernel, not noticing that the ground was yellow-speckled all around them.

Randa watched Jack watching the ducks. No matter how he felt about the house, he and the land suited each other nicely. It was the first place she had seen him look as if he belonged. He seemed almost calm.

He tossed the ducks another handful of corn, then put the bucket down on the ground and sat beside it. She didn't know whether she was supposed to join him or not. She sat, careful not to get too close. He didn't even seem to notice.

"So are you going to tell me what 'the thing' is?" she asked, as gently as possible.

He nodded slightly and stared at the ducks for a moment before speaking. When he did, his tone was matter-of-fact.

"My mother had this theory that there was a curse on our family," he said.

"Was this theory based on anything?"

"A seventy-five-cent fortune-teller she saw at a county fair when she was nineteen years old." He smiled, remembering.

"Do I get to hear the story?" Randa asked.

"Sure, why not? My parents had been married for about a year and they were still living somewhere down near Savannah, where my mother grew up. One night, while my father was out somewhere getting drunk, my mother and her best friend, Bird, decided to go to the fair that was in town. So they went, they rode rides, played bingo, all that stuff. Just as they were leaving, they saw this cheesy fortune-teller's tent, so they decided it would be fun to have their fortunes told. Bird had a brainstorm: she put on my mother's wedding ring. You know, to test the fortune-teller."

He paused for breath, then continued. "So they go in and pay their buck and a half to this old woman, who was wearing what my mother described as a tacky gypsy outfit—as opposed to a classy gypsy outfit, I guess—and the old woman looks in her crystal ball for a few minutes, then she looks at Bird and she says, 'Why are you wearing that ring? You're not married, and you're going to have a lot of trouble before you're ever married.' Now, Bird's kind of impressed with the ring thing, except that she's engaged and getting married in a month. She decides the old woman must have seen her take Mother's ring. Meanwhile, the old woman turns to my mother. She looks at her, she looks into her crystal ball, she looks back at my mother. Then she gets this look on her face like she's just seen a ghost, and she says to my mother, 'You'll have to leave.' My mother says, 'What are you talking about?' The old woman says, 'When I see this, I don't go near it. That's my one rule.' My mother says, 'When you see *what*?' But the old woman just keeps telling her to leave. Well, Mother's not about to leave now. Finally the old woman says, 'You've taken on a debt you don't know about. You'll pay, your children will pay, a lot of people will pay, for a long time.' That's all she would say, and she wouldn't explain what it meant. She just kept saying, 'I don't go near this,' and practically shoved my mother and Bird out of her tent.

"So my mother and Bird decided the old woman was a nutcase. Then, a couple of weeks later, Bird's fiancé got drunk and wrapped his car around a tree. Died instantly. Whereupon my mother decided the fortune-teller was the real McCoy, and there was a curse on our family. Everything that went wrong after that, she blamed on the curse. When we were kids, we believed it. Then we got older and started using it. Told her we had this strange compulsion to get into trouble. We tried hard to resist, but it was just bigger than we were."

"Did she buy it?"

"Of course. It was a hell of a lot easier than believing she was raising a bunch of sociopaths."

"Where did she think this curse came from?"

"That was the big question. She spent the rest of her life trying to figure it out. She imported mediums from five counties and held séances in our house regularly. They consulted Ouija boards, they threw tarot cards, you name it."

"And?"

"Pick a theory. My personal favorite was that my father's father was a direct descendent of Genghis Khan and his spirit was haunting us. Mediums loved the fact that my father was a bastard, and not just metaphorically, because it left them wide open for the evil-ancestors stories."

"What did your mother believe?"

"Whatever was the last story she'd been told. Although I think she liked the Genghis Khan one, too."

"And that's the thing?"

He nodded. "We used to call it Mother's thing, or the curse thing. Then, eventually, just . . . the thing."

"Then that's it. Ryland and Tallen are trying to tell you that there really is a curse."

Jack shook his head. "My family was cursed, all right. It started when my mother married Will Landry, and there was nothing supernatural about it."

"Then how do you explain me seeing Ryland?"

"He's still alive, he's turned on me for some reason, and the family is after Cam's money. They think if they scare the hell out of me, I'll stay away."

"What about the phone call?"

"I imagined it. Or I dreamed it. Who knows? I'm being taken over by the family insanity."

"So you'd rather believe you're losing your mind than entertain the notion of an afterlife?"

"An 'afterlife' is not a pleasant concept to me. This one will have been enough, thank you."

"But a good one, to make up for this one."

He shook his head. "It just seems so stupid to me. The idea that if you survive this quagmire—not that you're going to *survive* it, because there's only one way out of here—but if you endure it, and stay reasonably good-humored about it, surprise, there's all sorts of meaning and order in store for you after you die. What kind of sense does that make?"

"Maybe it's too big to understand," Randa offered.

"Maybe it's nonsense."

Suddenly he stood up. He offered Randa his hand and pulled her to her feet.

"Come on," he said. "I'll show you the house."

Randa hadn't expected that, and wasn't sure that Jack had, either. He seemed to be trying to get out of the conversation more than anything. She followed him without speaking; she didn't want to say anything that would make him change his mind.

He unlocked the back door, pushed it open, and stood back.

"After you."

Randa brushed past him, crossed the threshold, and stood in their house. The back door opened into the kitchen—an old farm kitchen with beadboard walls covered in yellow-white paint that was flaking in random and somehow sinister patterns. The appliances were all several decades old, and the floor was a hideous gray-and-maroon marbled linoleum, rippled by time and curled in the corners. Jack turned on a light, which she knew only from the sound of the switch; the room didn't get any brighter. There was nothing ghostly about the place. The eerie feeling had nothing to do with the threat of diaphanous apparitions or a sudden drop in room temperature. It was something much more insidious. Something blacker.

Evil.

She didn't know what that meant, or if she even believed in such a thing. Still, the word came to her like someone was whispering clearly in her ear.

She looked around the room, taking it all in. Jack seemed to understand (or at least be willing to indulge) her need to do that. He stood in silent patience. He followed her when she moved on.

The living room was even drearier than the kitchen. The same beadboard in a worse state of peeling. The sofa and chairs were covered with dusty sheets. Randa couldn't imagine why Jack would feel the need to protect the furniture, or that there was anything under the sheets worth protecting. The end tables were probably halfway decent antiques, under about twenty coats of black varnish. There were a couple of fringed Victorian lamps and even framed photos on the tables, mostly various school pictures of the boys. (Randa spotted a gap-toothed six-year-old Cam grinning up at her.) Overall, the room looked as if the family had just gone out of town for an unknown period and simply never come back.

There was a hallway on the other side of the room. Randa glanced down it and could see an open door and a little bit of a bedroom that seemed to have similarly depressing decor.

"My parents' room," Jack said, answering her unspoken question. "Our rooms are upstairs."

"It's very . . . dark."

Jack nodded. "It always was, no matter how many lamps you turned on. The rented places were nicer, but my father liked it that way."

"Why?"

"He wasn't exactly a cheery guy. Cam may have mentioned that. I think he was attracted to the house's history, too."

"The man who murdered his family?"

Jack nodded. "His name was Bennett Reece. I think he was Will's hero."

"*Because* he murdered his family?"

Jack nodded. "I think Will admired him for having the guts to do the full job. Anyway . . . have a look around. I'll wait outside." He went out the back door, leaving it open behind him.

Randa was not at all happy about being in the house alone, but she didn't blame him for wanting to be away from all the reminders, and she wasn't about to relinquish this opportunity.

She stood in the doorway of the master bedroom and stared at a double bed with a wrought-iron headboard. She wondered how any woman could lie down and go to sleep beside a man who routinely sent her children to the emergency room. What sickness had bound the two of them? She knew it was too late for questions like that to be answered. It was too late for them to even matter.

When she returned to the living room, Jack was still outside. She could see him in the front yard, walking aimlessly, gazing out at the land. He didn't look her way as she headed for the stairs.

The old wood creaked in protest under her weight. The stairs were sunken in the middle from too many years of use, and the entire stairway, wall included, listed toward the left side of the house. About halfway up the stairs, the beadboard ended, and Randa was amazed to find that the remaining walls were unfinished. The planks were gray-brown and weathered like the side of a barn, and there were cracks between them on the inside walls. At the top of the stairs were three tiny rooms;

all still had small beds and dressers. Twin beds and a small dresser filled the middle room, leaving no space for anything else. Randa assumed this was the room that Jack and Tallen had shared.

She felt a lump rise in her throat as she thought of Cam and Jack, and even the ones she didn't know, living up here in what was barely more than an attic. She thought of them lying in bed, listening to their parents try to kill each other in the rooms below. Cam had told her he was the only one of the four who'd ever ventured downstairs to try to break up the fights. The rest of them had either put their heads under their pillows or climbed out windows and gone off into the night, looking for trouble they could control.

She made her way back down the stairs slowly. She stopped when she saw Jack. He was standing just inside the door, staring at an empty spot in the far corner of the room. He didn't show any sign of noticing her.

"Jack?"

He broke out of his trance and saw her looking at him. "Sorry. I just . . . flashed on something."

"What?" she asked, as she eased down the last two steps.

"The day they killed Tallen," he said in a quiet voice. He breathed deeply, collecting himself before he continued. "He didn't want any of us there, so my mother and Cam and I were sitting here the next morning . . ." He nodded toward the corner. "There used to be a TV over there, and we were watching the news. This sports—"

He stopped; laughed to himself, a bitter laugh. "I almost said sportscaster." He shook his head; took another moment.

"This reporter was interviewing people on the street about the execution . . . and there was this woman . . . she had on this *hat.* I don't know why it matters, but something about that hat just irked the hell out of me. Anyway, the reporter asked her if the execution made her feel like justice had been served, and she said that it did, then she said,

'Some people are just animals, and you kill rabid animals, so what's the difference?'"

He stopped again and took yet another breath, upset by the memory.

"My mother had this antique iron she used as a doorstop. I grabbed it and . . . kind of . . . hurled it through the TV screen." He smiled sadly.

"That couldn't have been good for the TV," Randa said, trying to lighten the mood.

"No, but it sure felt great." He chuckled, looking at the corner again. "Glass flew everywhere. Smoke, sparks, the works. My mother screamed."

"What did Cam do?"

Jack's face clouded over. "Saint Cam was not pleased. He just picked up his suitcase and walked out the door. Went back to LA. I didn't see him again until my mother's funeral a year later." Jack looked out the window, as if he were watching Cam go.

"That seems like a cruel thing to do to your mother. Just walking out, on that day?"

He paused for a second, letting the anger pass.

"My mother," he continued, "was so far gone by that point. Tallen's death was really the last straw." He took a few steps away from Randa, as if he needed the distance. She could see his face go taut with pain. "Have you ever read a detailed account of what happens when someone is electrocuted?" he asked.

"No," Randa answered, without admitting that she'd tried to once and hadn't been able to get through it.

"I read every one I could get my hands on. I hunted for them. It was like a compulsion. I just had to know."

Randa prayed he wasn't going to share any of it with her, but she knew what was coming.

"They shave the person's head, you know, so they can attach the electrodes. And then they have to rub this gel in—something that helps conduct the electricity. The gel has to be rubbed in really well; takes about forty-five minutes. Imagine sitting there for forty-five minutes while someone rubs gel into your head so they can kill you easier. But that's really nothing compared to the rest of it."

Randa wanted desperately not to hear the rest of it, but she sensed he needed to tell her. She braced herself.

"The body reaches a temperature of about nineteen hundred degrees—there have been cases where a body was so hot it melted the electrodes. The skin turns bright red and stretches, almost to the point of breaking. The brain reaches the boiling point of water. The eyes pop out of the sockets and end up resting on the cheeks. Witnesses say there's this loud sound, like bacon frying, and it smells—I don't know, like however it smells when you cook a person. Smoke comes out of the person's head, sometimes flames. And this is all if everything goes *well*. I read about this one where something went wrong and it took twenty minutes and three separate jolts of electricity to kill the guy. He stayed conscious for a while, and in between jolts, he was begging them to hurry. By the time he was finally pronounced dead, the body was so hot they had to wait an hour before they could even touch him to move him out of the room." He stopped for a moment, but he wasn't done. "In one of the articles I read, a doctor described it as 'setting a person on fire from the inside.'"

Randa nodded. She wanted to tell him he was preaching to the choir, but there'd be time for that later.

"Can you *imagine* having all that happen to someone you love? Your brother? Your *child*?"

"No," Randa said quietly. There was no way she could imagine it.

"Well, if it does, there's no way you can *avoid* imagining it." He took a breath, then: "So . . . if you want to know how my mother was . . . that's how she was. The warden might as well have strapped her in next to Tallen. When she finally killed herself, it was just a formality."

Randa didn't know what to say, yet the silence was too sensitive to bear. Jack stared at the floor, unable to meet her eyes. She had a strong urge to go over and put her arms around him, but she couldn't imagine him letting her (or anyone) do that.

"I'm really, really sorry." It sounded ridiculously lame, but she didn't know what else to say. "For what you went through."

He looked at her, frowning. "For what *I* went through?"

"All of you. The whole thing."

He just stared at her, not knowing what to make of it.

"Why don't we go," she suggested. She was uncomfortable under his stare, and he needed to get out of the place, whether he knew it or not. He nodded, looking enormously relieved. He turned and headed back through the kitchen. Randa followed. She reached up and put her hand on his back. She felt him flinch under her touch; she pulled her hand away.

Outside, he locked the door behind them. Then, after staring at her face for a brief moment, he reached for her hand. Randa wouldn't have been any more surprised if he'd slapped her, and she doubted she was doing a good job of hiding that fact. He led her back toward the car, gripping her hand tightly, as if they'd come to some kind of an understanding. When they reached the car, he stopped. He looked at her as if he had something important to say, but didn't speak. Then she noticed that he was leaning closer. Was he . . . was he going to kiss her? She hadn't had time to wonder how she felt about it when he quickly pulled away, and his head jerked in the opposite direction.

"What was that?" he asked.

"What?"

He cocked his head and squinted, as if reacting to a sound. "That!" He looked at her. "You didn't hear that?"

She shook her head. "I didn't hear anything."

He took a few steps toward the house, listening. After a moment, he turned and hurried back to her. "Let's get out of here," he said, and got into the car. Randa, left with no option, followed.

"What is going on?" she asked, slamming her door.

"Nothing. It must have been the wind." He was gone again, back inside his shell. And there was no wind, but Randa knew it would do no good to point that out.

Neither of them spoke on the ride back into town. Randa didn't know what to say, and Jack just stared out the window. He asked if she would drop him off at his place, and she pulled up in front of the boardinghouse and turned the engine off.

"Look, why don't we go out to dinner tonight?" she said, pressing her luck. "We can relax, talk some more." She stopped. A look had come over his face, as if she'd just told him the tumor was inoperable.

"Dinner? You mean, at Tillie's?"

"No. Someplace nice. Someplace with dim lighting and a liquor license."

He looked out the window. "I don't know."

A thought occurred to her. "Is it that you don't have anything to wear?"

He looked at her. "Did you go through my closet, too?"

"That's not an answer," she said, avoiding the accusation.

"Neither is that," he said with a slight smile. "No, it isn't because I don't have anything to wear. You can't belong to my family without owning a suit; there's a funeral every other week."

"Then what is it?"

"You know. I don't do things like that."

"Yeah, it seems to work, too. You're obviously happy."

He looked out the window and didn't answer.

Randa tried again. "One night isn't going to kill you. It'll be good for you. You might even have fun. Or is 'fun' something else you don't do?"

"All right," he said. "Uncle. But I'm not drinking, and you're not getting anything out of me in dim lighting that you wouldn't get out of me at Tillie's."

"We'll see. I'll come back at six to pick you up," she said.

"Whatever," he said, either resigned or feigning resignation. He held the door open but didn't make a move to get out.

Uh-oh . . . he's coming up with an excuse . . .

"*Did* you go through my closet?" he finally said.

"Don't worry. I didn't touch a single skeleton."

"I don't understand why I don't hate you," he said, and got out of the car.

As she soaked in the antique claw-foot tub in her bathroom at the guesthouse, Randa took stock of her life. She'd been valedictorian of her high school class. Graduated magna cum laude (fifteenth in a class of 929) from a college that prided itself on an impossible curriculum and a high suicide rate. She'd moved to Los Angeles to set the world on fire, win a Pulitzer, and marry some fascinating man who adored her—preferably another writer. They'd buy a Greene & Greene bungalow in Pasadena, just off the parade route, and every year they'd throw a New Year's Eve party that people would live in terror of not being invited to. She and Mr. Perfect would both have offices at home, on opposite sides of the house, and they'd write all day. At night they would sit in front of a fire and drink brandy and read poetry aloud, or talk about their work. (Mr. Perfect, of course, would be far too secure to be jealous of her accomplishments.) Eventually, they'd have a couple of gorgeous kids and a politically correct dog, and in between carpooling and trips to the vet, she'd write the Great American Novel.

Now here she was, all these years later, without one thing that even resembled the life she'd dreamed of. Instead, she lived alone in a tiny, overpriced apartment with no air-conditioning and lousy plumbing; she was welded to a low-paying, dead-end job, the politics of which were taking years off her life. Mr. Perfect, who wasn't all that perfect to begin with, had ridden off into the sunset with her best friend and then, just for spite, had invited Randa to his suicide. Now, for reasons unknown to her, she was spending her trust fund on a lovely vacation in Mayberry R.F.D., where she was sitting in a strange tub, in a strange room, in a strange town, thrilled to death because Mr. Perfect's estranged brother—an antisocial day laborer with a prison record—had grudgingly accepted a dinner invitation that she didn't know why she had extended.

"I'm insane," she said to a glass of bad merlot.

At least that was something she and Jack would have in common.

EIGHT

She hadn't heard it. How was that possible? It had been so close, so clear. He'd tried to figure out where it was coming from, but it seemed to be coming from everywhere.

"Jack . . ."

A man's voice in a low, whispering moan. At first it had just called his name. After he'd moved away from her, it had said something else . . .

"I know who you are."

What the hell did that mean? And where had it come from?

Your brain, idiot. Where else could it have come from?

Why couldn't he shake the feeling that she was somehow responsible?

How could she be responsible?

From the moment he'd first seen her, he'd been torn in two. Half of him was drawn to her as if he'd been waiting for her all his life. The other half wanted to turn and run in the opposite direction, as far and as fast as possible.

She's dangerous.

That's ridiculous.

Is it? She could have pushed Cam out that window, for all you know. She could be here for you now.

Oh, for Christ's sake . . .

Losing his mind was so much more lucid than he ever would have guessed. He would have imagined it as all of reality starting to blur and fade until nothing was recognizable. But it wasn't like that at all. Reality remained in place, as relentless as ever. *He* was the only thing blurring and fading, and no one else could see it.

Why did you say you'd go out to dinner? Why didn't you get rid of her while you had the chance?

What do you mean, get rid of her? I don't want to be rid of her.

He was standing in the shower, lost in a spray of hot water and steam. He was afraid to turn the water off—the silence was somehow worse than any noise. In the silence, the voice could return. But he couldn't stay in the shower forever, and he was starting to lose the hot water.

He forced his hand to turn the water off. The spray became a trickle; the last few drops hit the tile in angry little splats, gurgled down the drain, and then the room was quiet. He slid the shower curtain back slowly, wishing he'd brought some kind of weapon into the shower with him.

Do you hear yourself? What are you going to do, stab disembodied voices with a kitchen knife?

Still, he looked around the small room before stepping out. He felt as if he were seeing his bathroom for the first time. Nothing seemed familiar. Had that crack in the tile been there all along? Why had he never noticed all the rust on the chrome of the medicine cabinet? Why did he feel someone was watching him?

He dried off quickly, twice startled by the sound of the towel hitting the sink. He hung the towel over the shower rod to dry. He was compulsively neat. He'd always been compulsive about anything he could control. (There were so few things in that category, they were almost sacred to him.) He shaved quickly, then replaced the razor and shaving cream in the medicine cabinet. The sound of the magnetic catch made him jump, even though he'd expected it.

"Jesus, get a grip," he said out loud. The words dissolved into the air, and didn't prompt any unearthly response.

When they were young, Tallen used to say he could hear a voice.

"What kind of a voice?"

"Just a voice."

"What does it say?"

"I'm not supposed to tell anybody."

"You're so full of shit."

"It's the truth! I swear!"

Around the same time, Tallen started to have night terrors. He'd wake the entire house screaming. He'd be hysterical for half an hour, babbling about some kind of winged monster with red eyes that would fly into his room and hover, staring at him. God himself couldn't have convinced Tallen it was a nightmare. Tallen said the flapping of the wings always woke him up.

This went on for a couple of years, then Tallen had been packed off to reform school, and Jack had no idea what ever became of the red-eyed, wing-flapping monster. After Tallen came home from reform school, he was a different person. When he'd get mad, there would be a look in his eyes that no monster would have messed with.

Jack took a deep breath and headed to the other room to dress. He'd lied about having a suit. He'd given it to Goodwill two days after his mother's funeral. But he had a nice jacket, slacks, tie, the whole deal. He'd bought it all a couple of years ago, when he'd gone with Cathy to her cousin's Christmas party. Jack could still feel the stares he'd gotten that night. He'd actually enjoyed it, in a perverse way. (*Yeah, I clean up pretty nice, don't I, you judgmental bastards?*) He'd made a lot of people uncomfortable that evening. It's one thing to have executed the brother of a lowlife misfit, but another to have executed the brother of a guy in a camel-hair jacket and a designer tie.

He liked making them squirm. That was exactly why he'd stayed in Barton all these years, instead of changing his name and vanishing into the anonymity of some distant city. He wanted to be there every time they looked up—a constant reminder, for whatever small degree of discomfort that might cause them.

He could barely remember how to tie the tie, but it gradually came back to him. After half a dozen attempts, he decided it looked good enough for "dim lighting."

Don't do it. Call her and cancel.

No. She was right, one night out wasn't going to kill him.

What about the voice?

There was no voice.

There was, and you know it.

How?

It doesn't have to make sense to be there.

Like Tallen's voice on the answering machine. Had he imagined that? Had there been something else on the tape? Had he imagined Tallen's voice because that was what he wanted to hear? And if so, why had he imagined a warning? Was his subconscious trying to tell him something? Then what about Cam? Why had he told people he'd seen Tallen? Why would Cam have imagined Tallen? He'd never wanted anything to do with Tallen. And what about Ryland? They'd always been so close; if Ryland were still alive, why wouldn't he come to Jack? Why would he be sending messages from three thousand miles away by a total stranger? And why would Ryland have let Jack go years thinking he was dead? But what was the alternative? That Randa really had a conversation with a ghost? Then why wouldn't the *ghost* of Ryland come to see him? There was no scenario in any of this that made any sense.

He checked the mirror. Not bad. Not bad for a delusional paranoid schizophrenic. He should tell Randa tonight. About the voice. She deserved to know the extent of his insanity, if she was going to get involved with him.

It's not "involved." It's one dinner. She's got a life on the other side of the country. She's going back there any day . . .

There's something in here.

He looked around. Nothing. Why did the room suddenly feel different? Like the air was heavier?

He looked around again. The room was still.

Is it cold in here? Isn't it colder, all of a sudden?

The ticking of the alarm clock broke the silence in a steady rhythm.

Usually it was a calming sound. Now it sounded threatening, like something closing in on him.

"Jack."

The same voice as before. He whirled around, looked in the opposite direction. Nothing.

"Jack."

It wasn't in his head. It was outside.

Where? How?

There was another sound. A scratchy sound, like wind against dry leaves. He looked around.

Do I really hear something?

He held his breath. The sound was growing louder. Deliberate. *Oh, Jesus . . .* The sound formed a word. It took him a moment to make it out.

"Away . . . away . . ."

What does that *mean? Why is it always talking nonsense?*

What "it"? Why do you keep saying "it"? There is no "it."

Oh yeah? Then why can't I move?

Why *couldn't* he move? He was straining, but his limbs didn't seem to be connected to his brain anymore.

"Away . . ."

A woman's voice. A breathy whisper, meant to terrify him. Working beautifully.

"Leave me alone!" he screamed, at nothing.

Another voice. Male. Laughing; a smug laugh. An *evil* laugh. The woman's voice was saying something else. A sentence. He couldn't make it out, but he could hear his name in it.

Get out of here. Get to the door.

His legs began to move, slowly. There was something bearing down on him, trying to stop him. Pressure, like the centrifugal force of a carnival ride.

Do I really feel it? Is any of this happening?

Under the man's laughter, the woman's voice became more distinct. By the time he made it to the door, it was chillingly clear.

"This is the house they built for Jack . . ."

A mocking cadence, like a nursery rhyme.

"Away . . . away . . ."

With a desperate burst of energy, he grabbed the doorknob and flung the door open. Randa was standing there, about to knock. She jumped back and they both gasped.

"Jesus!" Jack said, breathlessly. "Give me some warning."

"That I'm about to knock? How would that work?"

"Oh" was all he could say. He gasped for breath.

"Are you okay?"

"Yeah," he lied. "You just scared me."

He turned and looked back at his apartment. The sounds were gone. Whatever had been there was gone.

"Did you need something?" she asked.

"No," he said, turning back to her quickly.

This is not in my mind. Something is really happening.

"Look . . ." he said.

Maybe dinner's a bad idea. Maybe you should just drive me straight to the psych ward . . .

"What?"

"Nothing." He closed the door. "Let's go."

They sat at a table in the dining room of the Ritz-Carlton Buckhead, where she had made a reservation.

"You're kidding. I used to work there."

"I know. That's one of the few things Cam ever told me about you."

"He told you that? In what context?"

"The context that you're a classic underachiever."

"Yeah, well. He's a classic asshole."

"Not anymore."

"Sorry."

He didn't like being reminded that he'd inherited her from Cam. He couldn't help wondering what would have happened if he'd met her while Cam was still alive. Would she have even looked at him twice, or would she have written him off as Cam's weird hermit *underachieving* brother? She could have done that anyway. What could she possibly see in him? Like everything else in his life right now, it made no sense.

He was grateful she'd brought him here, of all the places they could have gone. The hotel had hardly changed in the ten years he'd been away, and he felt perfectly at home. He'd served enough people dinner here to know how it worked. (He could even order a martini—*"Bombay gin, dry, straight up with an olive*"—with the right attitude: *I do this so often I get tired of hearing myself say it.*) He wished there were still people working here that he knew, so he could have the pleasure of introducing Randa, but no such luck. He'd have to settle for the envy of strangers.

Her face was bathed in the flickering light of the candle in the center of the table. It gave her a soft golden glow. She was talking about her father and his political ambitions, how they had superseded any code of ethics he might have possessed, although she'd never seen any sign that he'd possessed one. And something about him intentionally losing a court-appointed capital case when he was in private practice—in return for which he'd been awarded a well-positioned job in the DA's office. Jack had nodded in all the right places and let her do most of the talking, because it gave him an excuse to stare at her without being obvious.

Dinner was over and they were waiting for coffee. He was amazed at how smoothly it had gone—no awkward moments, no searching for topics of conversation. On the surface, they had absolutely nothing in common, and yet he'd never felt so comfortable around another person. Talking to her was like dancing with a partner whose steps he already knew.

The waiter appeared with their coffees and then was gone.

"Okay," Randa said, "here's something I've always wondered."

"What?"

"Coffee. How did anyone ever come up with the idea for coffee? Who said, 'I know what! Let's take these little beans and dry them in the sun. Then we'll grind them up and pour hot water over them and make a drink. But it'll taste like hell, so we'll mix it with cream and sugar until we can stand to drink it . . . Of course, we'll have to wait for it to cool off first.'"

Jack laughed.

"You like that? I've got a million. Who looked at an artichoke and decided there was anything inside worth the trouble it would take to get to it? And why is it that we put a man on the moon before anyone ever thought of squeeze-bottle ketchup?"

"Are all your existential dilemmas food related?"

"No. I'd like to know what God has against famous musicians in small airplanes. And why people think pushing the elevator button again will make the elevator show up faster."

"You mean it doesn't?" he said, still laughing. He could tell she was enjoying his laughter and didn't want it to stop. Neither did he. It had been a long time since he'd really laughed. It felt good.

"Here's my personal favorite," she said. "Why will people only elect a president who's never had therapy? 'We're sorry, you've explored your emotions, you're disqualified. We only allow a repressed individual with a lot of internalized rage to have his finger on the button.'"

"Okay," he said, surrendering to the urge to chime in. "Here's one I've always wondered about: 'Four out of five dentists surveyed recommend sugarless gum . . .' What did that fifth guy say? 'Rot your teeth out, what the hell do I care?'"

She laughed. Her entire face lit up, and the light in her eyes danced mischievously. On impulse, he reached down and took her hand. It startled her so much, she stopped laughing. She let her eyes meet his, and they sat like that for a moment without speaking.

"Will you tell me now?" she asked, suddenly serious.

"Tell you what?"

"About the armed robbery." Reality came crashing down on him.

"Why?" he asked. "Were we having too much fun?"

"I just can't imagine it, that's all. You just don't seem . . ."

"What?"

"I don't know. Like the armed-robbery type."

"Known a lot of armed robbers, have you?"

"All right. Never mind."

"No, I'll tell you. It's just . . . a stupid story. It's embarrassing."

She leaned closer, which amused him. He hadn't meant he was embarrassed for the *waiter* to hear it.

"My brothers and I used to rob convenience stores . . . recreationally. You know. Some guys play football. Anyway, this was one night, about a year or so after Ethan died. I don't know where Tallen was, but I was alone and I was just driving around, and I found this two-pump gas station and general store out in the middle of nowhere. I was bored . . ."

"And you just happened to have a gun in the car?"

"As fate would have it," he said, smiling. "Nothing major. Something in the Saturday night special family. I stuck it in my pocket and ambled in. There was absolutely nobody there except me and the cashier. I got kind of depressed right away because the cashier was this girl, about my age. Long blond hair. Really cute. But it's kind of hard to flirt with someone and point a gun at her at the same time."

Randa laughed.

"No," he said, becoming serious. "I looked at her and I felt bad because I knew I was going to scare her. But I also knew I wasn't going to hurt her, so I figured she'd be scared for a few minutes and then have a great story to tell for the rest of her life; it wasn't really a bad deal. Anyway, I told her to give me whatever was in the cash register, and she said all the money was in a cash box under the counter. I said fine, I didn't care where it came from. She reached under the counter and came up with a sawed-off shotgun."

Randa's eyes got wide. "What did you do?"

"What could I do? I wasn't going to shoot her, and she sure as hell was going to shoot me."

He laughed, remembering. He'd never told this story to anyone. It wasn't really such a bad story, now that he heard it.

"She made me go to the pay phone and call the cops and tell them to come get me. Made me use my own dime."

"And then?"

He shrugged. "Then I did ten years for it. That part's not funny."

Her smile faded.

"Don't stop smiling," he said. "I love your smile."

She smiled again, and then she leaned in and kissed him. He kissed her back, and when he came up for air, the only thing he could think to say was "You don't know me."

"Well, I'm trying to remedy that."

"I like your remedy."

"I don't want to go back to LA."

"I don't want you to."

But how can I ask you to stay here and watch me sink further and further into God-knows-what?

"What *do* you want to do?" he asked, letting himself temporarily off the hook.

"Honestly?"

"Yes."

"I want to go to the front desk, take out my American Express card, get a nice suite on the twenty-second floor, and stay here tonight. With you."

He couldn't speak.

"Does that scare you to death?" she asked, though he was sure she already knew the answer.

"Yes."

"Okay. What do *you* want?"

"I want you to hurry back with the key."

There was a warm wind blowing, gentle against his face. He and Randa were lying on a blanket on a beach, watching the sunset, a bottle of champagne between them. They took turns drinking from the bottle, giggling. He kissed her.

"AWAY . . ."

He pulled back. The damned voice again.

"AWAY . . ." *The woman's voice; a throaty whisper that traveled on the breeze.*

"AWAY . . ."

He stood up, looking around. Beyond the beach, the sand disappeared into a thick forest. He knew, somehow, that the voice was coming from there.

"AWAY . . . AWAY . . ."

He got up and followed it, determined to confront his tormentor. The woods were dense. The sun was blocked by the trees, and it was as dark as night.

He stopped short as he saw her up ahead. She was sitting on a log, waiting for him. It was the blond girl—the one from before. She was laughing at him now, a hollow, evil laugh.

"This is the house they built for Jack," she said with scornful glee.

"I'm sick of this!" he screamed. "Go play your games with someone else!"

She just kept laughing. His anger amused her. Her laughter infuriated him.

"I mean it!" he yelled. "Get the hell out of my life!"

She stopped laughing, but retained a taunting smirk.

"What life?" she asked. "Your girlfriend? The one who's sleeping with you because she was in love with your brother?"

He reached for the first thing he could find—a thick branch that had fallen off a tree—and started for her. She watched him coming and began laughing again. Her laughter and her lack of fear fueled his anger until he was lost in it. He lifted the branch and brought it down on her head with all his strength. The force of it knocked her off the log. She staggered a couple of steps; he brought the branch down on the back of her head, knocking her to the ground, her face buried in the dirt and pine needles. Consumed by his anger, he continued to pummel her until his fury was spent and he was too tired to go on. He dropped to the ground and gasped for air. He looked at her still form on the ground beside him and didn't feel any remorse. She deserved it for making him think he was crazy all this time. It took him a moment to realize he was covered in blood, and then the enormity of what he had done started to sink in.

Christ. How was he going to explain this to Randa? How was he going to tell her he'd beaten this girl's head to a pulp because she'd been torturing him in a voice that Randa could never hear? Jesus, how was he going to tell Randa that he'd killed someone?

He reached for the girl. He took her by the shoulder and turned her over.

The bloodied, lifeless face in front of him was Randa's.

"Jack!" A voice in the distance. Hands on him. Whose?

"Jack, it's okay! Jack!"

He woke up.

"Jack, it's okay! Jack!"

The fact that she kept calling his name made him realize he was still screaming. He forced himself to stop. "Randa . . ."

She's alive! She's here!

"Jack, it's okay. You just had a bad dream."

He could feel her arms around him. He was still breathing hard and he could barely control his trembling, but he took her face in his hands and looked at her.

"Randa, you're okay . . ."

"I'm fine. You were dreaming."

He pulled her to him and held her as close as he could without hurting her. He rocked her and kissed her on the forehead and said her name over and over. He could feel her arms on his back, hugging him. It was okay.

"Was it one of those dreams?"

"I thought you . . . were hurt."

"Well, I'm not." She kissed him on the cheek. "Here, lie back down." He obeyed. She pulled him close to her and held him. She stroked his cheek with her hand and whispered, "It's okay." There was no way he could explain. It wasn't even the dream that had scared him so badly. It was that feeling, when he was lost in that homicidal fury. It was the familiarity of that feeling. He'd been there before, and not in a dream. But he couldn't tell her that.

He felt her kissing his shoulder.

"I'm okay," he whispered, lying again. "I'm sorry."

"Don't be." She put her head on his shoulder and snuggled closer.

She fell asleep after a few minutes. He stared at the ceiling and waited for the sun to come up.

He dressed in the sitting room, where his clothes were still lying in a pile on the floor. He put on the jacket and stuffed the tie in the pocket, then looked at himself in the mirror over the wet bar. Nothing he could do about shaving, but the hair on his face was so blond it took him days to look unkempt. He didn't know why he was concerned about his appearance, except that he felt so horrible about what he was doing, he didn't want anyone to look at him and suspect anything close to the truth.

There was a MARTA station on Lenox Road, within easy walking distance. He could take the MARTA downtown, then catch a bus back to Barton. Maybe when she woke up and found him gone, she'd be angry enough to give up without a fight.

What if I'm blowing this all out of proportion? What if I'm leaving her for no good reason?

You can't risk it. You can't gamble with her life.

He stuck his head in the door to the bedroom to look at her one more time. The room was darkened by the heavy hotel drapes, and the light from the doorway fell across her like a pale spotlight. Her face was partly covered by her hair, but he could see how peaceful she looked. There was a tiny smile that showed up only on the corners of her lips. Her arm was still bent upward beside her where he'd slipped out from under it.

It came back to him in a rush, the memory of her skin against his, the smell of her hair, the safety he'd felt in her arms. But *his* safety wasn't the issue.

He forced himself to turn away from her, closing the door softly behind him. When he left the suite, he hung the DO NOT DISTURB sign on the door. By the time she woke up, there'd be a safe distance between them.

Making his way down Lenox Road, it was all he could do not to relive the night in his mind. The good part. The part that, up until the nightmare, was easily the best night of his life. Why did she have to show up at the exact moment he was disintegrating? But then, he was a Landry. What else should he expect?

Maybe he should have told her. Maybe he should have let *her* decide whether or not she wanted to be in love with a lunatic. They could just enjoy his sane periods while they lasted, then she could come and visit him in the asylum.

It's too dangerous.

What? He looked around, then realized the voice was clearly internal this time, although it was as obvious and as intrusive as the "outside" voice.

You know who you are.

What is that supposed to mean?

You know what it means.

It was true. He knew. He'd known for a long time. What would happen the first time something triggered one of those lethal moments that crop up in any relationship? The first time he wanted to strangle her for something. *Would* he?

It's not like you don't have it in you.

Yeah, thanks. I'd almost forgotten.

He didn't need to be reminded of the incident that had ruled his every waking moment for the last decade. The night that had, for all intents and purposes, ended his life. Provoked by what? Anything worth throwing his life away? Hardly. One mouth-breathing hillbilly yelling at a TV screen. One drunk, ignorant redneck exercising his constitutional right to free speech.

"Oh, shut that ACLU bitch up and fry the bastard!"

And then an unaccountable lapse of time, until he was suddenly aware of people pulling on him, shouting, and the drunk on the floor, his face a strange purplish red, his eyes bulging, and Jack's hands around his throat. The strength in those hands when people had tried to pry them off. The fury into which his consciousness had dissolved, in that unknown moment when he had unleashed whatever was inside him and then just stood out of its way. And the most frightening part—that even after he'd realized what he was doing, he'd still wanted to kill the guy. And if the others hadn't been there to stop him . . .

I would have.

At Cathy's trailer later, in the early hours before dawn, holding on to her like a drowning man clinging to a buoy.

"Jack, you didn't kill the guy."

"But I would have."

"You don't know that."

He knew it. Knew it then, knew it now. And every minute in between, even though he rarely let himself think about it head-on. He couldn't. It was excruciating. That's what people never realized—what you could never explain to the "they're just animals" crowd. The pain of hurting someone that way. (And the pain that made you *want* to.) He could only imagine what that pain would be like if he'd actually killed the guy . . .

Was that what had happened to Tallen? Had something snapped inside him and called forth some uncontrollable rage? How long could such a thing last? Long enough, after the initial impulse, for Tallen to find the gun, head to Alabama (a two-hour drive even if he was going ninety), park the car, go into the church? (Why a church? And why *that* church, as opposed to all the others he must have driven past? They didn't even *know* any Catholics.) Long enough to climb the stairs to the balcony and (from what witnesses had described) sit there waiting for the right moment—when everyone stood up to sing, unwittingly lining themselves up like beer cans on a fence rail? (Had Tallen specifically waited for them to sing "Joy to the World"? Something in that logic made a strange kind of sense to Jack—not that any of it made any *real* sense.)

If he'd been in some kind of wild fury, why wouldn't he have opened fire on the local Dairy Queen? Or a local church, if it had to be a church? It was Christmas Eve, it wasn't like he had to go far to find a church that was holding services. Why did he drive almost two hundred miles? Was he trying to outrun it somehow, whatever "it" was? Then why did he give up?

No, it wasn't possible. No one could have sustained a blind rage for that length of time. He had to have known what he was doing. Still, that wasn't the way Tallen had described it, the one time they'd talked about it.

Jack had spent the entire year trying to get Tallen to open up about it. The only thing Tallen would ever say was "I'll tell you someday. I don't want to talk about it now." Finally, the night before Tallen's execution, Jack had pressed the point.

"Tal, I need to know what happened."

"No, you don't. How's that gonna change anything?"

"I don't want to spend my life wondering."

"Then don't."

"Oh, for Christ's sake, since when is there something that you can't tell me?"

"Since last Christmas Eve."

"Why? Do you think it would change how I feel about you?"

"I just don't see the point."

"The point is that I'm the one who's gonna have to live with this for the rest of my life, so at least do me the courtesy of telling me what it is that I'm living with!"

Tallen had been quiet for a long time, staring at the floor. Then, finally, he'd sighed—a long sigh, as if he were exhaling something more than air. The macho façade had melted away before Jack's eyes, and when Tallen looked up, Jack had seen a flash of the guy he used to know.

"Okay. If I tell you this, you'd better swear to me you're not gonna tell the ACLU or the Atlanta Constitution *or anybody else. You don't even tell Mom."*

"All right. I swear."

"I haven't told you because . . . I don't remember."

"What do you mean?"

"I don't remember. Driving there, going into the church, any of it. I don't even know where I got the damned gun."

"Are you serious?"

"No, it's a joke. Of course I'm serious. I remember calling Mom that night, looking for you. She said you had to work and you wouldn't get there until after midnight. Cam was there and the two of them were going out to eat, did I want to come? I said yes, just because I knew how much it would piss Cam off. I remember getting into the car and starting to drive to the house. The next thing I remember, I was lying in the church parking lot with a cop pushing my face into the gravel with one hand and pointing a gun at me with the other, saying if I moved, he'd blow me to Hell where I belonged."

"Tallen . . . were you . . ."

"No, I wasn't on anything. And you know I'd tell you if I was."

"Did you tell any of this to the shrink?"

"No."

"Your lawyer?"

"No."

"Why the hell not? Are you crazy? It might have made a difference."

"I know."

Their eyes had locked, and Tallen hadn't taken it any further. He didn't have to. Jack knew. Now it made sense, why Tallen had been so insistent about dropping all his appeals. Tallen didn't want to live, because he didn't want to live with what he had done. Especially since he had no memory of it, because he'd never be able to understand it, and it would never get any easier. Somehow, all of that was conveyed in the look that passed between them. No more was ever said about the crime. They'd spent the rest of their time together reliving some of their escapades, and talking about Lucy and what Jack was going to do about her, and going over the disposition of Tallen's few worldly goods.

Jack had never planned to stop on the way home. He certainly hadn't planned to stop at a bar. He'd made up his mind he wasn't going to drink until after Tallen was dead. But he had underestimated how hard it was going to be to leave Tallen. (*"Tell Mom . . . just tell her I love her. Tell Cam to take care of himself, not that he won't anyway. And, you . . . you just"—his voice cracking—". . . God, Jack . . ."*) That was as far as Tallen could get—as close as he could come to saying good-bye to Jack. The guards had let Tallen hug Jack. Hadn't even told him when to stop. Jack had prayed that they would. It was the most agonizing decision he'd ever made: at what moment to let go of his brother, knowing he'd never touch him—never see him—again. When he'd finally pulled himself away, all he could do was look Tallen in the eye and nod. If he'd tried to say anything, he would have started sobbing and embarrassed them both. He'd managed to mouth a silent "I love you, Tal," and then turned and walked away without looking back.

He'd underestimated how hard that was going to be, even though he'd expected it to be devastating. He hadn't thought about having to walk through that parking lot, through the carnival of TV news crews and cameras and weeping protesters and festive revelers. Tailgate parties. High school kids with six-packs and buckets of fried chicken. They'd come with *dates*, for Christ's sake.

"So, we could go to a movie, or we could go over to Huntsville and have a picnic while they kill that guy."

One comedian was dressed like the Grim Reaper and carried a handmade sign that said BURN, BABY, BURN, with a lightning bolt through it and a happy face in the corner. By the time Jack somehow made it to his car and got out of there (after almost coldcocking a reporter who wouldn't stop shoving a microphone in his face), he'd been in such agony, he couldn't think about anything *but* finding a bar and getting drunk as fast as he could.

Maybe if he hadn't been so upset by the last-minute knowledge that Tallen might have saved himself, but chose not to . . . Maybe if he'd been mentally prepared for the scene in the parking lot . . . Maybe if the jerk in the bar had shot his mouth off *before* Jack had time to get so drunk . . . Maybe if even one element of it had happened differently . . . he might be back at the hotel right now, asleep in Randa's arms.

But it did happen.

Ever since that night, he'd asked himself how much difference there was between his deed and Tallen's. The difference was one of degree and circumstance. Fundamentally, they were the same. Jack had wanted to kill the guy. Had *tried* to. Someone had stopped him; no one had stopped Tallen. Jack was alive and free because a couple of redneck truck drivers had pried him off his victim. But what was the difference between what was in his heart and what was in Tallen's?

Precious little.

Could he live the rest of his life without acting on it again? He'd fought it all these years with rigid control, convinced that the only way to keep from doing something horrible was to keep from doing anything. Cathy had been right; he did sit on a volcano of rage, all the time.

What would happen if his mind slipped into someplace where he wasn't aware of the danger?

You know what would happen.

I don't know for sure.

If Cam couldn't escape it, what makes you think you can?

Jesus. Cam. He'd almost forgotten. When Randa had told him about Cam and the liquor store, he'd immediately written it off as a case of mistaken identity and "his brother was a criminal so he must be, too." But what if it wasn't? What if Cam, who didn't even cheat on his income taxes, really did kill someone? Was it possible?

Look at the facts. Your father probably killed Ethan. He could have killed other people you don't know about, given all the time he spent away from the house. Tallen went nuts and killed five people. Now Cam's friends say he went nuts, the cops say he killed someone. What does logic say will happen next?

It was true. Everyone in his family went insane, sooner or later. The men went insane and killed people. Whether it made sense or not, it was undeniably the pattern.

Up ahead, through the heavy morning fog, he saw the dark stairwell of the MARTA entrance, beckoning him underground. He walked faster, eager to accept the offer. He thought of Randa waking up in the hotel room to find him gone. He hoped she'd be too angry to be hurt. He couldn't stand the thought of causing her pain. Still, it was better than what he might cause her if he stayed.

He would return to his life, just the way it was. Working, eating, sleeping, reading. No human contact. A danger to no one but himself, and free from any ridiculous hope for the future.

You can't hide from it forever.

No, probably not. But he'd hide as long as he could. And if he took anyone down with him in the end, it wasn't going to be Randa.

If you had the guts to kill yourself, you wouldn't have to worry about taking anyone down with you.

It was true. He wasn't sure whether it was because he was gutless (*yes, you chickenshit coward*) or just that he wasn't convinced it was the only answer.

When will *you be convinced? When you're standing next to a corpse?*

Shut up! Just shut the hell up! I need time to think.

You mean rationalize.

He reached the stairs and descended, stopping at a machine to buy a token. In his coat and tie, he blended in easily among the morning commuters. He could be any one of them—an accountant, a salesman, a computer programmer—on his way to the same world as everyone else.

But you're not one of them.

No, he wasn't. He knew that much. He just wasn't sure how far it went in the other direction.

Don't kid yourself. You know.

For a fleeting moment, the voice in his head was Randa's. He felt her hand on his face, heard her whispering, *"It's okay."*

But it wasn't okay. It would never be okay.

The train was coming. He could hear the wind whistling through the tunnel. It slid into view and squealed to a halt. The doors hissed open and Jack climbed on board, flowing with the sea of humanity. He sat and waited for the train to move. Away from her.

"The doors are about to close . . ."

The metallic warning evaporated into the air above the indifferent commuters; the doors closed and the train pulled out.

Jack stared blankly at the people surrounding him. The fact that the train was packed was a mocking irony—a cruel wink from a vindictive God. Wherever Jack was headed, he was going alone.

BOOK TWO

Look around: there is someone else, always someone else.
What he breathes is your suffocation,
what he eats is your hunger.
Dying, he takes with him the purest half of your own death.

—Rosario Castellanos, from "The Other"

THE OTHER

ONE

"Father, can I get you a cup of coffee?"

Michael shook his head. "No, thank you."

"Are you sure?"

"I'm sure." He offered the best smile he could muster. The plump storm-trooper-with-a-heart-of-gold nurse had been offering him coffee about every thirty minutes. He almost never wore the collar for exactly this reason: it made people so solicitous he wanted to strangle them. He'd thought about accepting the coffee just to make her stop asking, but he really didn't want it, and she seemed to be the type who would check to see if he was drinking it and give him grief if he wasn't. She gave up easily this time and headed back to her station. He breathed a small sigh of relief. All he wanted was to be left alone with his thoughts.

He looked at the clock. His grandfather had been in the operating room for two and a half hours now. The doctor had said it would be between five and eight. Michael wondered how it could take so long just to remove one organ. The doctor had explained it all in a vocabulary that meant nothing to Michael, along with:

"The operative death percentage is high. For someone your grandfather's age, as high as thirty percent. And you should keep in mind, it's only a palliative procedure, to prolong life and reduce pain. My best educated guess is that it would give him a couple more months."

That day the words had been horrifying. Today, a couple of months seemed like an extra lifetime.

Vincent was the only "parent" Michael had ever known. His mother and father had died when he was a toddler, and Vincent had raised him until he'd left home to join the Jesuits. After that, Vincent had been an advisor, a mentor, a friend. Michael couldn't imagine his life without Vincent in it. He tried not to. The reality of it would be here soon enough.

"How about a homemade honey bun?" She was back. He smiled again and shook his head.

"I don't think so."

"You need to eat something. You don't have a bit of color in your face."

"I don't think it's from hunger."

She sat down in the chair next to him. "How about a hug from a fat old lady?" She put her arms around him without waiting for a reply. She smelled like a mixture of roses and cheap hand cream. She pulled herself away and looked at him. The pain in her eyes was not forced; it touched him.

"My father was a Methodist minister," she said. "I used to think, everyone cries on his shoulder, but whose does he cry on?"

Michael could only nod.

"Let me know if you change your mind about the honey bun."

"I will," he said through a tight throat. She smiled and was gone. He stood and made his way down the stark hospital corridor. He couldn't stand another minute of fluorescent light.

The tiny chapel was dimly lit, which in and of itself was a great relief. He sat in the back pew. There was no place to kneel, as most of the chapel's visitors were Protestant, but this was his only option. He sat for a while and stared at the cross on the stained-glass window above the altar, wondering what to pray for. For Vincent to survive the operation? Why? To die a slow and torturous death, spending his last days helpless and in unimaginable pain? For Vincent to die now and be spared all that? For God's will? Wouldn't that happen anyway?

For the strength to handle whatever lies ahead.

That was it. All he could really hope for.

And considerably more than I deserve.

All day he'd been thinking about something he and Vincent used to do—an old routine, from as far back as he could remember. Every Friday, as soon as they sat down to dinner, Vincent would announce the date, and then ask Michael, "Where are you today?" Michael would give an assessment, recounting the highlights of the week and working them into the context of his life. Vincent would never comment, except for an occasional nod or smile. Scrutiny was unnecessary. The point was to make Michael take a focused look at the big picture. After he'd moved away from home, Michael had continued the practice mentally, by force of habit. For a long time, it had been a comfort—a psychological deep breath. Lately, it seemed more like a type of self-inflicted torture.

How would he answer that question, if Vincent were to ask him today?

I'm a parish priest—the last thing I ever wanted to be—in rural Georgia—the last place *I ever wanted to be—because I was stupid enough to pick a fight with my provincial* and *a vindictive bishop. And I'm mourning things you don't even know about.*

It had been a year of losses. Vincent would be the greatest loss by far, but there were a slew of close seconds. New York was a huge loss, encompassing many smaller ones. He missed everything about the city—even the things he hadn't particularly liked: the crowds; the subway; the ill-tempered cab drivers. Waking every morning to the familiar sound of the Con Ed "Dig We Must" jackhammers. He missed his work, his friends, and the feeling of having a purpose.

The intensity with which Michael had loved New York was paralleled by the intensity with which he hated Barton, Georgia. He hated the isolation—both the isolation of being the only priest in a tiny parish, and the isolation of being an hour's drive from a decent bookstore. He didn't like the work at all. In fact, it was hard to think of what he did as work: endless—and pointless—committee meetings. Listening for hours on end to people confessing to the exact number of *damn*s and *hell*s they'd uttered that week. And then there was the wide assortment of for-this-I-took-Advanced-Greek paperwork that should have been handled by the staff that the parish couldn't afford. Most of his time this week had been eaten up by a plumbing problem, in the form of a good ol' boy in bib overalls who wanted $3,500 to hook the rectory's septic tank up to the county sewer line. Inflamed by Michael's uncalled-for comment (*"That sounds a little steep"*), Plumber Jim-Bob had accused Michael of trying to "Jew" him down. Delivered with the appropriate "that ain't how we do things 'round here" tone, and followed by:

"Maybe y'all can find a Catholic plumber in this county who'll do the job for free."

(A snort)

"Hell, if y'all find a Catholic plumber in this county, I'll *do the job for free."*

Even when he managed to block out the surroundings, it was impossible to ignore the fact that there was no one to talk to, no one to have dinner with, no one who might drop by unannounced with an existential crisis and a bottle of twelve-year-old scotch.

Supposedly this torment was only going to last for another month, but he didn't have a lot of hope that the next assignment would be any better. The powers that be were just keeping him quiet temporarily until they could find a way to keep him quiet permanently. They knew Michael wasn't going to make a career out of one flaky issue, but he had broken their trust. As one auxiliary bishop had put it, "The last thing we need right now is a loose cannon Jesuit with a fan club."

And then there was Tess. The fact that she wasn't first on his list of losses only proved how brutal the list was. With the clarity of hindsight, he knew now he should never have agreed to work with her. He'd told himself it would be okay because it was a short-term assignment. When the assignment had turned into a friendship, he'd ignored the warning voice in the back of his head in favor of the voice in the foreground—the one that said "nothing will happen." The one that kept saying "nothing will happen" until the morning he woke up in her bed.

When inclined to give himself a break, he remembered there was no coincidence in the timing that connected his fall off the celibacy wagon to the aftermath of the article. The first night he'd stayed at Tess's apartment was the night he'd found out he was being sent to Deep-in-the-Sticks, Georgia.

His last days in New York had not been pleasant. He and Tess had bickered incessantly. She couldn't understand why he felt so guilty about his relationship with her, since he'd told her that he thought celibacy was a stupid and antiquated concept. And the big one: Why couldn't Michael leave the priesthood so they could be together? Couldn't he accomplish anything he wanted just as easily in a secular context? Michael hadn't done a very good job of explaining it to her. These weren't things he could explain on some logical level. He didn't understand them very well himself.

"You know what it is, Michael? You just have zero interest in living in the real world."

"Mine is as real as yours. In fact, mine is more *real than yours."*

"Well, I'm not allowed on your lofty plane, so how is this going to work?"

When he'd left for Georgia, they'd agreed to three months with no contact, to give him some time and space in which to make a decision. Since then, he'd talked to her only once. He'd called her when Vincent was diagnosed. After the initial awkwardness, she'd been sympathetic and concerned about him. She offered to come down for a few days, but he told her it wasn't a good idea. It had taken every ounce of willpower he possessed.

He'd been tempted to tell Vincent about Tess, but he'd decided against it. Vincent considered his grandson the Jesuit to be the greatest accomplishment of his life. In fact, no matter what he decided, Michael knew he could never resign while Vincent was still alive. He'd been coasting on that rationalization for months now, but it wouldn't be available much longer.

God, You know where I am. Please help.

He sighed from somewhere deeper than bone marrow, and willed himself to his feet, to return to the waiting room.

He'd begun to have second thoughts about coffee and a honey bun, but the nurse wasn't at her station. He looked down the hallway and saw her in front of the door to the operating room, talking to someone . . . the doctor . . . why was the doctor in the hallway, when the operation wasn't supposed to be over until . . .

Oh, God, no . . . not yet.

The doctor looked up and saw him . . . said something to the nurse. She looked at him, too, and the look on her face told him everything.

He nodded to them, slightly; reached into his pocket for the vial of holy oil he'd brought with him, just in case. He felt himself shift into autopilot. Things to do. Rituals to hide behind.

It was early afternoon by the time he was done with all the hospital paperwork and necessary phone calls. He'd gone through it in a daze. Even though he'd known the odds, it had never really hit him he might be doing all this today. By the time everything was wrapped up, the doctors and nurses had moved on to other priorities. He left the hospital alone, unceremoniously.

He was already in the parking lot when he heard the nurse behind him.

"Father Kinney!"

He stopped, turned to her. She was hurrying toward him with an envelope in her hand. Surely there weren't more papers to sign.

"I promised your grandfather I'd give you this if . . . if he didn't make it . . ."

"What is it?"

"I don't know. I didn't open it."

He took the envelope and thanked her, then accepted her condolences one last time. He waited until she was gone and he was encased in the relative privacy of his car before he opened the envelope. There was no paper, but something solid at the bottom. He turned it over and a microcassette player spilled out. No note, so he assumed the tape inside would explain itself.

So typical of Vincent. He couldn't leave a note or, God forbid, have an actual conversation. Michael knew what the tape was: Vincent's assurance that he'd have the last word. A few last pearls of wisdom. Advice. Admonitions (for things it was probably too late to avoid). Michael put the recorder back in the envelope and laid it on the passenger seat. He wasn't about to listen to it right now. The drive to Vincent's house already felt like an insurmountable task.

Vincent still owned the house where Michael had grown up. Vincent had designed it himself, in 1945—a year or two before he became the most sought-after architect in the city. He had designed almost a third of the houses in their neighborhood, Branwyn Park, a suburb due north of downtown Atlanta. By now Vincent had restored most of the houses he hadn't built. In fact, anyone who lived in Branwyn Park and had not had their house restored by Vincent Kinney was announcing the fact that they couldn't afford it—not the kind of announcement people who lived in Branwyn Park liked to make. Vincent had also designed several of the buildings prominent on the downtown skyline, a couple of churches, and a gorgeous retreat center in the north Georgia mountains. His name was well-known and highly respected in the state, the region, and even the country, among people who knew anything about architecture.

Vincent's style was clean-lined and no-nonsense. His buildings were an eclectic mix, though all classically inspired. They were variations of his basic prototype, a pared-down Victorian. Vincent's theory was that Victorian houses had beautiful lines, which were betrayed by "curlicues and jelly-bean colors" that kept them from being taken seriously. Vincent always said he built Victorian houses that didn't look as if Jack and Jill should live there.

Vincent's own house was white with black shutters. There were white Brumby rockers on the front porch, and flower boxes filled with red begonias; the overall effect was classic and dignified. Michael used to joke that the house looked as if it had been designed by Calvin Klein. Vincent couldn't decide whether to take it as a compliment or an insult, so he'd just give Michael his best ambiguous "hmph" and change the subject.

Vincent had begun construction of his house in 1945. It had taken almost two years to build because Vincent had to scrutinize every nail that went into it. It was supposed to have been finished by Christmas of 1946, but Vincent had made some last-minute structural changes that had thrown everything off schedule. Having sold their former house, Vincent and his wife, Claire, had found themselves homeless for the month of December. There was an additional problem: Michael's parents (Vincent's son, Matthew, and daughter-in-law, Laura) had planned to come up from Savannah to spend all of December in Vincent and Claire's new house so that Michael—who had just turned one—could spend some time with his grandparents. Vincent had come up with a solution: they would all check into adjoining rooms at a nice downtown hotel. It wouldn't be as comfortable as Christmas in the new house, but in those days, downtown Atlanta was an exciting place to be during the Christmas season. The plan was agreed upon, and on the fifth of December, they'd all checked into a suite on the eleventh floor of the Winecoff Hotel.

At the time, the Winecoff was one of the city's nicest hotels, located in the heart of the shopping/theater/restaurant district. It was right across the street from Davison-Paxon, the largest department store in Atlanta, where the women could shop and Michael could visit with Santa. Michael had always suspected that Vincent had chosen the Winecoff as much for its architecture as for its location. It was a beautiful building: red brick, Beaux Arts–inspired, crowned by a white concrete facing that covered the bricks on the first three and upper two floors. Elegant and simple. Vincent could have designed it himself.

On the afternoon of Friday, December 6, Laura and Claire had taken Michael across the street to the Paramount Theater to see *Song of the South* while the men drove around the city critiquing arches, columns, and patterned masonry. They'd all met back at the hotel for dinner, and then retired to their rooms. The plan was to get up early Saturday and go back to Davison-Paxon so Michael could ride on the four banks of escalators scheduled to begin operating that morning.

Somewhere around 3:45 a.m., the hotel caught fire. With *Titanic*-style arrogance, the Winecoff's builders had declared it fireproof, and therefore had not included sprinklers, fire escapes, or fire doors. The elevator in the center of the hotel was surrounded by an open stairwell that became a funnel, quickly sucking the fire through every floor of the hotel. By the time the flames were extinguished, near dawn, 119 people were dead. Among them were Michael's parents and grandmother.

Vincent had told him the story so many times it was almost as if Michael could remember being there. He'd heard how the five of them had huddled in the corner of Vincent's room, under blankets they'd soaked with water from the bathtub; how the room had filled with smoke and the mattress on the bed had begun to smolder and the water they'd spilled on the floor had begun to boil. He'd heard about the screams of the people who leaped to their deaths, the matching screams of the people who were watching on the streets below.

Vincent and Matthew had made a rope out of bedsheets, hoping they could all climb down to the aerial fire ladders, which only reached to the eighth floor. Vincent had insisted on going first—not because he was trying to save himself, but so that he'd be the sacrificial guinea pig if the sheet rope didn't hold. He had made it safely to a fire ladder, and was climbing down to the street when Claire started down the sheet rope. When she reached the top of the ladder, Michael's mother started down. Laura was three months pregnant with what would have been Michael's younger sibling, and she wasn't strong enough to hold on to the rope. She had fallen, knocking Claire off the ladder on her way down. Vincent had watched it all in helpless horror. Instead of rushing toward the women, though, he'd waited for Matthew and Michael. He had thought they would make it. They were halfway to the fire ladder when there was a huge flashover explosion that sent flames shooting from the windows on all floors. The sheet rope holding Matthew and Michael was burned in two, sending them plummeting toward the ground. As Matthew fell, he tossed Michael toward the hotel's awning. Michael hit it, rolled off, and was caught by Vincent, who had seen what was happening and was waiting. Matthew had fallen onto the hotel marquee and was impaled on one of the wires holding it up; he died instantly. His dying act had saved Michael's life.

Michael had no memory of the fire, yet he'd had nightmares about it all his life; dreams that were so real and so terrifying, he felt as if the memory were locked somewhere deep in the cells of his body. Other than his being an orphan, it was what made him feel most like an outsider—the fact that an event he couldn't remember, except in some dark pocket of his subconscious, had directly determined the entire course of his life.

Somehow Michael managed to survive the drive from the hospital to Vincent's house. He was met at the front door by Barbara Berryhill, Vincent's secretary for almost twenty years. (Vincent, in a typical act of defiance, had hired her just before his seventy-fifth birthday.) Michael had called her from the hospital so that she could get started on all the preparations for the funeral.

Barbara was not given to displays of emotion; at this moment, Michael was deeply grateful for that. Her eyes were a little red, but otherwise she was as composed as ever.

"Hi," she said softly, and stepped aside to let him enter. Her hand on his back was all the consolation she would offer. She knew him well enough to know he wouldn't want anything more. She launched straight into business.

"I spoke with the funeral director. Vincent left him written instructions down to the tiniest detail."

"Good."

"Apparently he also gave a copy to Monsignor Graham."

"Even better."

When they'd discussed the memorial service weeks ago, Michael had told Vincent there was no way on earth he could officiate. He'd promised to do a short eulogy, and right now even that was a daunting thought.

"I think this guy is General Patton come back as a funeral director," Barbara continued. "I'm just going to stay out of his way. He and the monsignor can duke it out for King of the Hill."

Michael nodded. Tom Graham was someone's spinster aunt come back as a priest.

"I've been calling people," Barbara said.

Michael had noticed a portable phone on the coffee table, and a list of names and numbers that he was sure Vincent himself had made. There was also a hand-drawn map, with directions to the church, written in Vincent's flawless draftsman's hand, still steady at ninety-three. Michael knew Barbara was faxing the map to people who needed it. Vincent and Barbara together were a machine of frightening efficiency.

Michael collapsed onto a love seat, took his glasses off, and rubbed his eyes.

"How tacky would it be if I made you call everyone?" he asked.

"It's fine. They'll all think we split the list and they're on my half. Don't worry, I'll spare you everything I can. However . . ." She paused, giving him time to brace himself.

"Why do I suspect I'm about to hear Tom Graham's name again?"

"He's called half a dozen times already."

"I thought he had the instructions."

"Michael, you know how he is. When he comes over here, he makes an ordeal out of deciding where to sit. Now he's got a genuine drama."

"I'm granting you power of attorney."

"I tried that. He said all the decisions have to come from you."

"Okay. Next time he calls, tell him you'll check with me. Then call him back in fifteen minutes and tell him anything you want to."

She smiled. "I applaud your lack of integrity. He also wants you to let him know if you change your mind about saying the Mass."

"I haven't and I'm not going to." These days he felt lousy enough about the Masses he couldn't avoid saying.

"I told him that; he said he has to hear it from you."

"I'll send him a telegram. Is the heat on? It's freezing in here."

"Michael, it's stuffy in here. You're not getting sick, are you?"

"No." He felt fine, physically. At least, no worse than usual, these days. He just felt like he was sitting in a crypt.

The last time you felt like this . . .

Stop it. You've got enough to deal with without adding paranoia to the list.

"All right," Barbara said. "The only thing left is that you have to decide when you want everyone to come over here."

"Here? I don't want anyone to come here."

"I know, but they're going to come anyway. If you give them a time, at least you can get it all over with at once."

She was right. There was no way to avoid the onslaught of casseroles and banana bread.

"What about right after the wake service?" Barbara asked.

"Fine," Michael said. "Just promise me you'll hire a bouncer to get rid of anyone who's still here at ten," he added, "including and especially Monsignor Graham."

"Easily solved. Close the bar at nine forty-five. That'll get rid of everyone, including and especially Monsignor Graham."

Michael nodded his approval.

"Listen," Barbara said, "if there's one thing I have down to a science, it's throwing a party in this house. And Vincent told me it had to be a party. He didn't want a bunch of long-faced people standing around being miserable on his account."

That was Vincent, Michael thought. Running the show from the grave.

"Okay," he said, relenting, "give me my half of the phone list."

"No, no, no. You go lie down. I know you didn't get any sleep last night."

"How do you know that?"

"Because I know you. You spent half the night bargaining with God and the other half convincing yourself it's your fault Vincent got cancer in the first place."

He pulled himself to his feet. "You do know me," he said, patting her on the shoulder as he started away. It was a lie. She didn't know him, not anymore. He didn't even know himself.

TWO

Upstairs, he stretched out on the twin bed in the room that had been his. The bed was far too small to accommodate his six feet three inches with any degree of comfort, but he felt a strong need to be there. He pulled a blanket over himself, but it barely took the edge off the chill. He continued to shiver.

He never felt like he was alone anymore. He felt . . .

Something (someone?) . . .

It was like the intangible heaviness that wakes a person when someone is watching him sleep. Michael couldn't shake the feeling that something was hovering over him.

Why?

Waiting.

For what?

A clear shot.

He turned onto his side and stared out at the room, hoping to distract himself. Vincent had not changed a thing since Michael had moved out. From the ceiling hung model airplanes they had made together. Michael had never had the heart to take them down, even in high school (opting, instead, to make the room off-limits to anyone who might tease him about it). Over his desk was a bulletin board covered with layers of mementos: Ancient baseball cards. A charcoal sketch of himself and Vincent, done by a stringy-haired blond girl, whose face he could still see, on the boardwalk at Myrtle Beach, in the summer of 1951. Ticket stubs from sporting events and concerts. A picture of himself and Donna Padera: St. Pius Senior Prom, 1962. Poor Donna had been convinced the two of them would become "pre-engaged" that night, whatever the hell that meant. (One of those terms teenage girls used to throw around in those days, just to give their boyfriends heart failure.) Instead, he'd broken the news to her that he had decided to become a priest. She hadn't taken it well. She'd thrown her corsage on the floor, stomped on it, called her mother to come get her, and never spoken to him again. Even now, more than three decades later, she refused to speak to him when they occasionally ran into each other, despite the fact that she was married to a radiologist and had three kids in private school. So far, he'd resisted the urge to tell her to grow up, but just barely. He could only imagine how she would react if she knew about Tess. Probably hire someone to have him shot.

You should be thinking about Vincent. (And life and death and resurrection.) Why are you thinking about your neurotic high school girlfriend?

There were a number of réasons—good reasons—not to think about Vincent. The most obvious was that it hurt too much to remind himself that Vincent was gone.

Not gone. You know he's not gone.

All right. But Vincent was somewhere beyond communication, on any level that Michael understood. He couldn't pick up the phone and call Vincent. He couldn't turn around and see Vincent standing there, or reach out and touch him. Any contact he had with Vincent from now on would be subject to scrutiny and suspicion; there had been several moments already when he'd thought he *felt* Vincent around him and immediately told himself he was just making it up out of the need for comfort.

He should be grateful for things he *did* know. Like the fact that Vincent was safe now, and happy. If Vincent Kinney wasn't in whatever constituted Heaven, there was no hope for a soul on the planet. For all his stubbornness and his crotchety demeanor, Vincent was, without a doubt, the best person Michael had ever known. Religious without being pious. Moral without being judgmental or self-righteous. Most of all, Michael had admired Vincent's vehement refusal to claim his own goodness. God only knew (literally) how much money Vincent had given away. He would go out of his way to keep people from finding out. Among other things, he'd built a church and a retreat center with his own money, on the condition that the funds used were identified as gifts from an anonymous benefactor. Vincent had no interest in proving what a saint he was. He did what he did for one reason: to serve God. Vincent had constantly admonished Michael to live a good life with a low profile. *"God knows everything you do. If you need to crow about it, you must be doing it for someone else."*

Michael searched for some way out of the pain.

Vincent is out of pain now. And happy.

What if he isn't? What if he is just gone*?*

You know he's not gone.

How?

You know how.

It was true. In the winter of 1954, when Michael was nine, he'd almost died in this room. A couple of weeks before Christmas he'd become very ill, with what the doctors had finally diagnosed as rheumatic fever. That night, he had a fever of 105 and was in and out of consciousness. The doctor and Vincent were with him; he remembered trying to hear what they were saying, but their voices sounded garbled, like a record set on a slow speed. He couldn't read the looks on their faces, either. Everything was a blur, as if he were underwater. Whatever they were saying, he could tell it wasn't good. Then Father Donahue had arrived, so Michael knew he was in trouble.

The doctor came over to the bed and checked Michael's pulse. Michael could open his eyes for seconds at a time, and his focus was a bit clearer. He could see the grave expressions on all their faces. He saw the doctor look over at Vincent. He saw Vincent read the look, then pass it on to Father Donahue. Father Donahue moved to the bed and uncapped a vial of holy oil. Behind him, Michael could see Vincent put his face in his hands. He could see Vincent's shoulders moving up and down as he wept silently. Then Michael heard Father Donahue speak, in a solemn, hushed tone.

"Per istam sanctam Unctionem, et suam piissimam misericordiam indulgeat tibi Dominus . . ."

Michael didn't feel anything when Father Donahue touched his forehead. Suddenly, he realized he was above everything, looking down. He could see the top of Father Donahue's head. He could see Vincent and the doctor, his own body—even his face. He didn't feel frightened, merely confused. He knew he wasn't asleep and dreaming. On the contrary, he felt keenly alert. He wondered if he was dead, and if so, why he hadn't gone anywhere. He was still wondering what he should do when he heard someone call his name. He looked toward the voice. There, in the corner of the room, stood a beautiful woman in a maroon velvet dress with ivory lace around the collar. She was smiling at him, her eyes full of kindness and love. He recognized her from photos he'd seen. She was his mother.

He opened his mouth to speak but found he couldn't. Instead, she spoke to him.

"It's all right, sweetheart. You're going to be fine." Her voice was gentle and it calmed him immediately. "You're going to be around for many years," she said, "because there's something you have to do."

Then, as suddenly as she'd appeared, she was gone, fading before his eyes. He wanted to run toward her, to stop her from leaving, but he couldn't move. He felt himself being pulled back toward the bed, as if by a strong undertow. He had a sensation of dizziness and for a brief moment lost all sense of being anywhere. Then he felt himself open his eyes and look up at Father Donahue, who looked back at him, surprised.

"Grandpa," he said to Vincent, "I saw my mom."

Ignoring that, Vincent asked him how he felt. Michael kept trying to tell them what had happened, but they wouldn't listen. They were preoccupied with the sudden improvement in his condition. Two days later, he was strong enough to get out of bed, and a week later he was back at school.

No matter how hard Michael tried, he couldn't get a rise out of Vincent. It wasn't that Vincent didn't believe him; it was that Vincent acted like Michael was casually reporting something he'd seen on TV.

"Grandpa, I'm serious. I saw my mom!"

"I believe you."

"But . . . she's dead."

"I know."

"Dead people can't just come back and talk to you."

"Apparently they can."

"What is the thing I'm supposed to do?"

"I don't know. But you will, when the time comes."

"But—"

"Michael, what was the one thing Jesus told every person He cured?"

"Not to sin anymore."

"Besides that?"

"I don't know."

"He told them not to mention it to anyone. Which they all promptly ignored, but that's not the point. Why did He try to keep the miracles quiet?"

"I don't know."

"Because He knew that faith based on magic tricks is a shallow faith. He didn't want them all to get so caught up in the supernatural that they didn't hear what He was saying to them. All you need to worry about is the message. Stop worrying about how the message came to you."

The logic made sense, but Michael had never been able to follow the advice. The vision changed his entire personality. Up to that point, he'd been outgoing and gregarious, and loved running around the neighborhood and hanging out with his friends. Afterward, he felt too removed from them to be very interested. He spent a lot of time alone in his room—reading, writing, thinking. Wondering about the other reality . . . this realm that was out there, somewhere just beyond his reach. Trying to keep himself ready for this mysterious thing he was supposed to do.

Michael had been convinced that Danny Ingram was the thing. He still could be. Maybe he'd blown it. Obviously he'd blown it. A tragedy with that much forewarning should have been averted, and he should have been the one to avert it. He asked himself, for the billionth time, if it would have ended differently if he had taken it more seriously before it was too late. He'd never know the answer, but it didn't really matter. It certainly didn't matter to the Ingrams.

He finally fell into a ragged sleep.

It was almost dark when he woke. He changed clothes and went downstairs. Barbara was on the phone. He could tell by her forced-patient tone that she was talking to Monsignor Graham, even before she looked over and rolled her eyes.

"Mortuary," Michael mouthed, and she nodded.

He left a note in the kitchen, telling her to lock up and turn on the alarm when she went home. He had no intention of being back anytime soon.

He drove slowly through the neighborhood, looking at all Vincent's houses and wondering what to do with himself. He'd lied about the mortuary—he'd already called from the hospital and been told there was no reason for him to go there. Vincent had already picked out and paid for everything. Michael was glad about that. Faith or no faith, rooms full of coffins gave him the creeps.

After weighing the options, he got onto I-85 south and headed downtown. He'd decided that a trip to The Varsity, his favorite fast-food restaurant, would solve both his problems: hunger and the need for a religious experience.

The Varsity, an Atlanta institution, was a glorified hot dog stand on the outskirts of Georgia Tech. Michael wasn't sure exactly how old it was, but everyone in Atlanta acted as if it predated the Civil War. Tradition and atmosphere were probably larger draws than the actual food, although the latter left nothing to be desired. Michael had loved the place all his life. So had Vincent. It had been "their" place. Vincent used to say that when he died and before he went to Heaven he was going to stop by The Varsity for a fried peach pie. Remembering that, Michael smiled to himself and wondered if he was going to The Varsity just to make sure Vincent wasn't there.

He'd managed to hit a rare slow time. He made his way up to the mile-long counter. There was no system for standing in line. The next person to get the attention of one of the surly, red-shirted cashiers, by whatever means, was the next person to be served. Right now that posed no great challenge, but after a Georgia Tech game it was an awesome undertaking, to be risked only by the bravest or most foolhardy.

Michael got a couple of hot dogs and fries and sat in his usual place, an upstairs corner that overlooked Spring Street. He felt somewhat guilty about having an appetite, even though he'd had nothing but coffee in the last forty-eight hours. He was also sad to realize the place wasn't as much of a comfort as he'd thought it would be. He tried to think about all the good times he and Vincent had had here, but he couldn't get his mind off the fact that they'd never come here together again.

The man at the next table was disregarding the NO SMOKING sign, and the smoke from his cigarette was drifting straight into Michael's face. Michael waved it away and looked over. He was planning to ask the guy to put the cigarette out or move, but the words stopped in his throat the minute he got a good look. The man was in his midthirties, wearing an obviously expensive black leather jacket that did nothing to offset some intangible smarminess. He was staring at Michael intently, with a look that said he was *hoping* Michael would say something so he'd have an excuse to vent a lot of pent-up rage. Michael quickly turned his attention back to his food. After a second, he glanced over. The guy was still staring.

Oh, for Pete's sake. Like I need this.

Michael picked up his tray and moved to the other side of the room. When he glanced up a few minutes later, the guy had turned in his chair so he could continue to stare at Michael.

He has that look.

Did he, or was Michael just imagining it? No. It was a real thing, regardless of its meaning. It showed up in the eyes, as if they were glazed over by a film of something very nearly colorless, like the thinnest possible coating of milk. No sign of life underneath. Soulless eyes.

Michael had seen the look before—in fact, had noticed it often in the course of his travels, even though he didn't know what it meant. The first time he'd seen it was when Vincent had shown him the Winecoff Fire scrapbook. One of the clippings showed a photo of a man who had been suspected of starting the fire. The alleged arsonist, a career criminal named Roy "Candy Kid" McCullough, was the son of a well-known murderer who was executed in Georgia in 1933. McCullough had the look so blatantly it seemed as if someone had tampered with the photo. (In fact, Michael had half suspected that this was what had happened, until he got out into the world and noticed the look over and over again.) Michael had always been fascinated by McCullough, since he had no one else to blame for his own parents' deaths. (Certainly more comfortable to blame an ex-con than to blame God.) The rumor was that McCullough had gotten into a heated argument with another participant in a big card game that had been taking place on the third floor. He had stormed out, threatening to get even, and had returned a couple of hours later and set the place on fire. Apparently he had bragged about it to several of his friends, but the authorities had never been able to come up with enough proof to make an arrest. In the meantime, McCullough was convicted of another crime and sentenced to life in prison, and the police let it go at that.

Of the many things he'd read about McCullough, there was one description that had returned, during the Danny Ingram episode, to haunt Michael. It came from a book written by a man who had known McCullough in prison: *"Nobody could be better to you than Candy, if he liked you, and nobody was more dangerous than he was if he hated you. . . . Don't know that I'll ever understand how Candy could be a warm friend one minute and totally heartless the next, void of any basic human emotions."* Michael could never understand such a thing, either, before he met Danny. Now he understood all too well.

The Danny Ingram affair had started simply enough. In the middle of an ordinary day, Michael had received a phone call from Kevin Ingram, an old St. Pius classmate whom Michael barely remembered. Kevin, who now lived on Long Island, had tracked Michael down through the magazine; he needed advice. He was having a horrible time with his oldest son, and the priest at his parish had been very little help and, in fact, was now becoming annoyed by Kevin's continued pleas for assistance.

"What kind of problem is your son having?" Michael had asked.

"I think he's possessed."

Michael had laughed. Not because he didn't believe in possession (though he didn't) but because he thought Kevin was joking. Most parents of fifteen-year-olds were convinced their kids were possessed. When there was no laughter on the other end of the phone, the realization had hit Michael—the guy wasn't kidding.

Michael had asked why Kevin thought such a thing, but Kevin's answers were vague: *"Weird things happen around him. And he's not himself anymore. Plus there's this thing . . . can't describe it, it's a feeling . . . the air in the room gets thick and it bears down on you, like gravity has suddenly doubled or something. I know this doesn't make any sense. You have to come feel it for yourself."*

Michael had agreed to go over to the house and feel it for himself.

The Ingrams lived in a beautiful, solidly upper-middle-class Cape Cod in the suburb of Plandome, on the north shore of Long Island. Kevin was an investment banker and his wife, Maureen, was an attorney in private practice. Their house was decorated in perfectly coordinated fabrics and expensive antiques. A little too heavy on the hunt prints for Michael's personal taste, but it definitely reflected careful attention to detail and two sizable incomes.

Danny was in his room, where, according to his parents, he'd been all day. He'd been told Michael was coming and apparently was not thrilled about it; he'd been in a morose stupor for hours. Still, the way things had been going, Kevin said, they preferred catatonia to the other options.

"What's been going on?" Michael asked.

"A lot of weird stuff," Kevin said. "Things happen . . . lights go on and off . . . the toilet flushes itself . . . one night I was in the den paying bills, and the TV just came on by itself. When I pushed the button, it wouldn't go off. I finally had to unplug it."

"Things fall off shelves," Maureen chimed in. "A couple of times, the gas flame on the stove shot up about a foot high, for no reason."

"What makes you think Danny's responsible for all that?"

"It didn't start happening until a few months ago," Kevin said.

"About the same time Danny started behaving strangely."

"And how has he been behaving?"

"He has these bizarre mood swings," Kevin said. "Before all this, he was a pretty normal kid. A little shy, but nothing to worry about. All of a sudden, he starts flying into these fits of rage, without any warning or provocation."

Maureen nodded. "He throws things, screams—and he uses the vilest language you can possibly imagine."

"The rest of the time, he's just kind of sullen and morose, hardly talks to us anymore," Kevin said. The pain of it was obvious in his voice. "Every now and then he's his old self, but not very often, not anymore." He shook his head, then added: "And there's that feeling, you know, like I told you. Sometimes it's a lot stronger than other times, but it's around all the time."

"Father, I know my kids," Maureen said in a mildly defensive tone. "When Danny was little, he would get ear infections, but he didn't react to the pain, so there was no way to tell. But I always knew. I'd take him to the doctor and tell him Danny had an ear infection, and Danny would be running around like a wild man, and the doctor would stare at me like I was a lunatic . . . until he looked in Danny's ear and saw that I was right. I'm not saying I'm psychic. But I know when something is wrong, and there is something in Danny that is not Danny." There were tears in her eyes and she could barely talk. "I don't care how crazy you think I am, I know I'm right."

"I didn't say I thought you were crazy."

"Well, I know you think it."

"I promise you, I haven't had a thought one way or the other. I'm just listening. The minute I think you're crazy, I'll tell you, okay?"

Maureen nodded and even smiled a little. Kevin reached across the table and squeezed her hand.

"We're both pretty wrung out," he said.

"How long has this been going on?" Michael asked.

"Six months, more or less."

"And you haven't been able to get anyone to do anything?"

Kevin shook his head. "Father Garra came over one night and blessed the house, but Danny started screaming obscenities at him and he got mad and left. I think he writes Danny off as a spoiled, obnoxious rich kid who resents authority."

"Father Garra grew up in Brooklyn, in a very poor family," Maureen added. "I think he was done with us the minute he saw the house."

"Well," Michael said, smiling, "Kevin probably told you that I grew up a spoiled, obnoxious rich kid. And I *still* resent authority."

Maureen and Kevin both laughed, but their eyes were filled with fear.

After talking with them a little longer, Michael met with Danny alone, in Danny's room, the walls of which were covered with posters of heavy-metal bands and pictures of skeletons and winged demons—drawn, apparently, by Danny. The furniture was draped in clothing, mostly jeans and black T-shirts also sporting heavy-metal logos. Danny was a thin, pale-skinned boy with shoulder-length blond hair and watery blue eyes. He sat on the bed and stared into space, answering Michael's questions with shrugs and two-word sentences. None of which was a sign of anything other than youth. He did seem to be more depressed than the average teenager. His eyes had a peculiar unstable quality, as if he couldn't see anything in the room, but saw something else in its place. And the air *did* seem heavy somehow, although Michael couldn't be sure if he really felt it, or just felt it because he'd been told he would.

"Who invited you here?" Danny suddenly asked, in a voice surly beyond his years.

"Your parents."

"And what do you think you're gonna do?"

"I don't know yet."

"Just couldn't pass up the chance to get into a teenage boy's bedroom?"

"Wrong number, pal. But points for keeping up with current events."

"What then? Little girls?"

"Sheep. I grew up in Georgia. Why don't we talk about you for a while?"

Danny stared at him and said nothing.

"You wanna tell me what's going on?" No answer. "Your folks say you've been having a rough time." No answer. "Look, I'm arrogant enough to think I might be able to do something for you, but you're going to have to give me a hint."

"Leave me alone!" Danny screamed. He picked up the lamp by his bed and hurled it across the room; it crashed against the wall and fell to the floor in a thousand pieces. Michael tried to stay calm. Danny was breathing hard and still trying to stare Michael down.

"You already had my attention," Michael said calmly. No response. Just a glare that made Michael grateful there wasn't a second lamp. Whatever was wrong with this kid, it was beyond his area of expertise.

Michael surrendered from the glaring contest, turned, and headed for the door. He was about to open it when he heard Danny speak.

"Father Kinney?"

Michael turned around. What he saw stunned him. Danny had collapsed on the bed; he was sitting slumped over as if exhausted. The murderous glare was gone, replaced by a look of fear and complete helplessness. Danny was barely recognizable as the same kid. He didn't speak again or look up. For a moment, Michael thought he'd imagined hearing his name called.

"Father Kinney," Danny whispered. It was a statement, as if Danny were somehow introducing the thought of Michael to his brain. Absorbing it.

"Yes, Danny?"

Danny still didn't look up.

"Do you really think you can help me?" he asked in a small voice.

Michael couldn't speak for a moment, he was so shocked by the transformation. The kid on the bed was a portrait of humility.

"I'm going to do my best," Michael finally said. Danny nodded. He stared at his hands, which were in his lap, trembling. At that moment, Michael swore to himself that no matter what it took, he was going to find a way to help Danny Ingram.

Kevin and Maureen were waiting for him in the kitchen, eager to have their suspicions solidly confirmed. Michael knew he couldn't do that, but he was not going to be one more priest who wouldn't take them seriously.

"I don't know what's going on," he said to them, "but there's obviously something. What I'd like to do, as soon as possible, is get someone in here who knows a lot more about this kind of thing than I do."

"How long will that take?" Kevin asked, ready for another runaround.

"How's tomorrow?" Michael had no idea how he was going to pull it off, but the outpouring of gratitude and relief that followed was enough to cement his promise.

He'd called his secretary, Linda, on his way back to the office and told her he needed to find someone who had experience with exorcisms.

"Exorcisms?" she asked, in her usual charmingly patronizing tone. (No one on the staff could pour a cup of coffee without an editorial comment from Linda.)

"I'm not joking and I'm pressed for time."

"Where are you?"

"Plandome. Long Island. First thing you'd better do is check and see if there's an official exorcist for the Rockville Centre diocese. I seriously doubt it, but I don't want to get anyone's nose out of joint."

"And if there isn't?"

"I don't know, try the Yellow Pages. Figure it out. I'll be back there in about half an hour."

"I'll find someone by the time you get here."

Linda was true to her word, and when Michael got back to his office there was a list of names and phone numbers waiting. Michael looked at the local names and, flying by instinct, called one Father Robert Curso, a parish priest in the South Bronx. According to Linda's note, he worked at a soup kitchen on 124th Street during the week; there was a number, Michael could probably reach him there. It took a little effort to get in touch with him, since the person who answered the phone at the mission spoke no recognizable language. (Michael tried three and gave up.) He finally got through to Father Curso (*"Call me Bob"*), who had a brusque smoker's voice and sounded like a former drill sergeant. Michael explained who he was and why he was calling, then started a brief summary of the case. Halfway through Michael's spiel, Bob cut him off.

"Has he shown any signs of abnormal strength?"

"Not that I know of."

"Spoken any foreign language he's never studied? Exhibited telepathic ability or aversion to religious symbols?"

"They didn't mention anything like that. Just these minor disturbances and fits of temper."

"So what makes you think he's possessed?"

"I didn't say I thought it," Michael said, losing patience. "*They* think it. Look, if you're not interested, just say so and I'll call someone else, but somebody has got to do something, because *whatever* is wrong with this kid, these people are going through hell and no one is doing a damned thing to help them!"

There was silence on the other end of the phone for a moment, then Bob asked, "How old are you?"

"What the hell does that have to do with anything?"

"Nothing, really. I'm just surprised."

"At what?"

"You got a lot of spunk for a Jesuit."

"What is *that* supposed to mean?" Michael asked, though he knew exactly what it meant. Curso, like most parish priests, thought of himself as in the trenches and therefore superior to the order priests. To him, a priest who belonged to a religious order was someone who sat in an ivory tower and wasted time writing his latest PhD thesis on some obscure, esoteric, and irrelevant subject. Secular priests resented the Jesuits in particular, because they thought the Jesuits considered themselves better than anyone else. Which, of course, they did. (The truest description Michael had ever read was a quote from Denis Diderot: "You may find every imaginable kind of Jesuit, including an atheist, but you will never find one who is humble.")

"Give me the address," Curso said. Michael gave him the address and detailed directions. "What's that," he asked, "forty-five minutes on the expressway?"

"About that."

"Okay. I'll meet you there."

"When?" Michael asked.

"In forty-five minutes."

"Are you kidding? This time of day, it'd take me forty-five minutes to get to the Midtown Tunnel, not counting the forty-five minutes it would take me to get a cab. I was thinking maybe first thing tomorrow morning . . ."

Bob chuckled. "There you go. *Now* you sound like a Jesuit."

"I'll get there as soon as I can," Michael said, and hung up, already hating Bob Curso and wondering what the hell he'd gotten himself into.

At the house, Kevin and Maureen had their lists of incidents and witnesses spread out on the table, ready for Bob's perusal. He ignored it all and asked to see Danny, alone. Michael waited with the Ingrams in the kitchen, telling them what he knew about Bob, which wasn't a lot. Bob hadn't been in Danny's room ten minutes when he returned to the kitchen.

"Father, we've been writing everything down," Maureen said, "in case you have any questions."

"I don't have any questions," Bob said.

"Then . . . you think we're right?" Kevin asked, afraid to hope.

"No," Bob said. "I *know* you're right."

At that moment, Michael concluded that Father Bob was, in the kindest estimate, some sort of occult-obsessed drama junkie. (But then, it probably wasn't easy to find a calm, rational person with a strong exorcism-conducting résumé.) Michael didn't see how Bob could hurt anything, though, and there was still the outside chance that he could help. Kevin and Maureen were so thoroughly convinced Danny was possessed, they'd probably convinced *Danny* that he was possessed. For all Michael knew, the theatrics of an exorcism might be enough to convince Danny he was cured.

The bureaucrats had given them the runaround Bob had expected, and then some. They put Danny through weeks of psychological tests, physiological tests, interviews, and various other forms of torment. When the bishop finally exhausted every stalling method he could think of, he sent Michael and Bob to the cardinal. They did the whole dog-and-pony show and left more than a hundred pages of test results and documented incidents. The cardinal promised to get back to them as soon as possible and reminded them how busy he was.

Bob, who'd been through it all before, was frustrated but not surprised. Michael was dumbfounded. What on earth could it possibly hurt for him and Bob to dress up and throw around a little holy water? "The guys in the red hats don't like to be bothered by thoughts of the supernatural," Bob said. "They're afraid it'll make people think they're not serious politicians."

Another week went by. Danny's fits were becoming more violent and lasting longer. It was clear that if he wasn't already, he would soon be a threat both to himself and to everyone around him. It was also clear Kevin and Maureen weren't planning on doing anything other than waiting. There was no point in suggesting they move on to another potential remedy.

At the end of the week, Michael called the cardinal. It took two days to get him on the phone, for which he did not apologize or offer an explanation. He did explain that he had sent the reports to an independent psychologist for "further evaluation." Dr. Brennan was on vacation for a couple of weeks, but he'd look at them as soon as he got back.

Michael had gone ballistic. "We don't have a couple of weeks! We don't have a couple of *days*! Something has got to happen now!"

He might as well have been talking to concrete. The cardinal just kept repeating his refrain, showing no sign of even hearing Michael, much less taking him seriously.

The next morning, Michael got a call from Maureen. The night before, Danny had attacked Kevin with a fireplace tool, leaving a gash in Kevin's forehead that had taken eleven stitches to close. Danny fled the house. When he returned, in the early hours, he claimed he didn't remember doing it. He'd been in his room ever since, but Maureen was afraid to even be in the house with him. Michael hung up and called the bishop.

"Michael, I have been as clear as I know how to be. There is a very definite way a thing like this is handled, and it's being handled. It will proceed at its own pace."

"Yeah, well my thing's got *its* own pace, and it's not waiting for you! I'm telling you, if we don't do something *right* now, something serious is going to happen! Someone is going to end up dead!"

"Then take him to a psychiatrist."

"He's been to a *hundred* shrinks! If there's one thing that's obvious, it's that he doesn't need another damned shrink!" *And if you'd get off your royal ass long enough to go sit in a room with him, you'd know that . . .*

"The experts will make that determination. Meanwhile, I've heard all I want to hear about it, and I'm sure you have more than enough work at the magazine to keep yourself occupied."

Late that afternoon, Michael and Bob had a long talk over a pitcher of beer. Bob knew what he was going to do. He was going to proceed without the Church's authorization. He wanted, and needed, Michael's help. At that point in his life, other than the occasional dicey article and a bad habit of running his mouth too much, Michael had never been anything but a good soldier. The thought of being involved in an illicit undertaking did not appeal to him. But there was a prospect that was much worse: the way he would feel if he said no and something awful happened. He agreed.

Michael had been naïve enough to assume that "yes" meant "give me the text and I'll read the responses." To Bob, it was a license to begin indoctrination procedures.

They took a cab to Bob's church. Bob led Michael to a classroom just off the fellowship hall. He instructed Michael to have a seat in one of the chairs, then Bob went to the green chalkboard up front. He picked up a new piece of chalk and broke it in half.

"Remember Venn diagrams?" he asked.

"I remember hating them," Michael answered, his mind flashing on connecting circles with shaded areas and letters, and identities like "all attorneys named Sam who drive BMWs."

"This isn't complicated," Bob said, drawing a small circle on the board. "And it will help you to have a mental image."

He drew an *M* inside the circle.

"Mind," he said, as if that was supposed to make sense to Michael. He drew a larger circle around the *M* circle. He labeled that circle *B*.

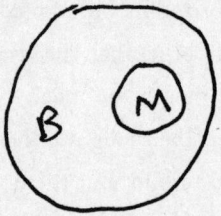

"Body," Bob said. "Home of the mind." He drew another circle, intersecting the *B* circle, and labeled it *W*.

"Will," he said.

"Whose theory are you diagramming?" Michael asked.

"Mine," Bob said. He drew a larger circle around the *W* and *B* circles and labeled it *S*.

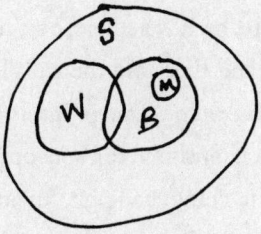

"Soul," Michael said, getting the direction, if not the point. Bob nodded.

"Now," he said, "Father Bob's Crash Course on Possession Theory." He smiled; he was enjoying this.

"Is there going to be a quiz?" Michael asked.

"The final exam is tomorrow morning, and this is the only chance you've got, so pay attention."

Michael smiled and nodded. Bob's face became deadly serious. "Most people think there are four stages to possession." *Most people? Most people would have you committed.* "I see the actual possession stage as a couple of phases, although it's all a continuous process," Bob continued, returning to the board. "The first stage is *infestation*," he said as he wrote the word on the board, then began to draw another diagram.

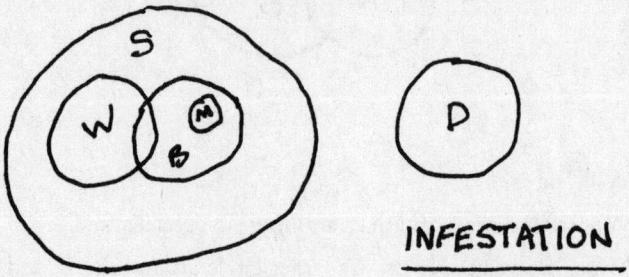

"*D* for demon. Don't worry about what he is or how he came to be there; we don't have the time, and it's not important right now. During the infestation phase, he hovers here, on the periphery, looking for an entry into the body and therefore the will. There are a lot of physical manifestations at this point. Things the Ingrams described: lights turning on and off, toilets flushing, drawers opening and closing. Also, unidentified sounds: scratching, banging, hissing. The demon is stalking its prey. The point is to make the potential victim disoriented, off balance . . ."

Bob went to the board and drew again. "The next stage is *obsession*," he said.

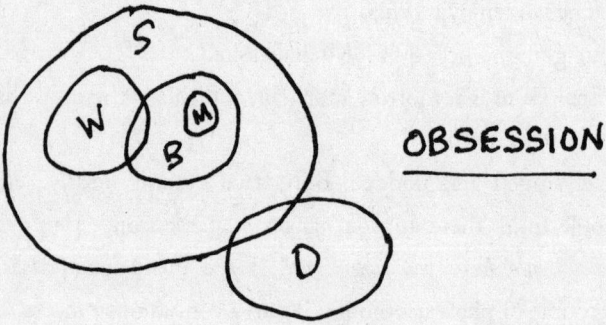

"The victim having been weakened, the demon starts to move in. Invades the soul, weakens the body and the will. Physical manifestations decrease, usually. Most of what is going on at this point is now going on inside. The victim feels agitated, anxious, ill-tempered, has trouble sleeping. People around him will notice a personality change, often a drastic one. The demon's influence starts to manifest itself in the actions of the victim. Danny's mood swings, outbursts. Older victims lose their defenses against old vices or pick up new ones—various addictions, mainly, which weaken the consciousness and consequently the will. All of which helps the demon accomplish its goal—to weaken the victim; mind, body, and soul."

Michael nodded. He couldn't believe he was sitting here with a straight face, listening to a lecture on the operating patterns of demons. Part of him—in fact, the vast majority of him—had never believed any of this, even when he was begging the bishop to let them proceed with the exorcism. There was another part of Michael, though, to which all this hocus-pocus made some kind of sense, even rang true—as if it were something he remembered from another time, another place.

At the board, Bob was drawing again.

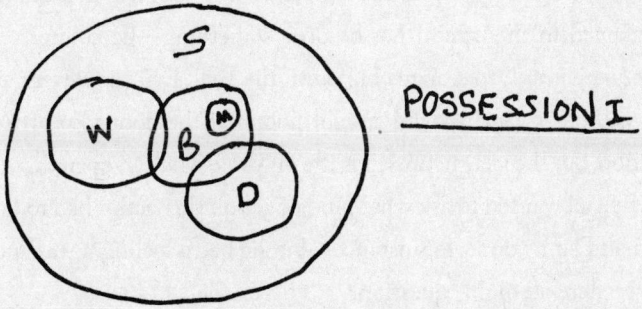

"What I call first-stage possession," Bob explained. "The victim still retains full consciousness at all times, but he is strongly invaded. He might start to hear voices, maybe even see things."

"Like what?"

"Bizarre animals, part human, part goat or pig—demons are very partial to cloven hooves, don't ask me why. Sometimes they're winged. Sometimes they're reptilian. Sometimes there's nothing but a vague black cloud. People who've seen it describe it as blacker than any earthly black."

People who've seen it?

Michael's mind flashed on a commercial he'd seen for some reality-based (*yeah, sure*) mystery show: two men in overalls, with thick Ozark accents, describing the crashed UFO and dead aliens they'd chanced upon in the woods: "*Four were layin' on the grah-yund.*"

Bob was still talking.

" . . . more sounds. Smells. The victim is assaulted in all his senses, even in his dreams. Dreams become violent and deeply disturbing; they cast a pall over the victim's waking hours, as well. The point of all this is to exhaust the victim and weaken his will until the demon finds what is known as an 'entry point.'" He stopped for a moment, giving Michael time to take it all in; then he went on. "We'd be here all night," he said, "if I tried to explain that to you. The simplest way to put it is that the victim is weakened to the extent that he does something—he commits some act, *of his own will*, that aligns him with the Evil. Evil can never gain an entry without an invitation. It might pound at the door to provoke the invitation, but the victim himself is the only one who can open that door."

Michael wanted to ask what kind of action the victim had to take—what had Danny done, for instance—but he had a feeling it was another "we'd be here all night" question.

"Then," Bob said, solemnly, "there's stage two. That's where we are now." He stopped to draw it.

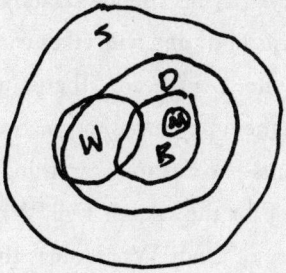

POSSESSION II

Whether this was a lot of medieval hogwash or not, Michael felt an involuntary shiver as he watched Bob extend the "demon" circle to encompass the circles of body, mind, and most of the will.

"Now the demon has full access to the victim's body and will. The victim will suffer blackouts, because the demon can move in and go into business for himself. That's what happened to Danny last night, when he attacked his father."

"He said he didn't remember it," Michael said, putting it together.

"He *didn't* remember it," Bob said. "He could have passed a polygraph saying he didn't do it, because *he* didn't do it."

Michael sat back in his seat. This was starting to make sense, which didn't make him feel better.

"This little sliver"—Bob tapped a crescent-shaped area of the "will" that remained free of the "demon" circle—"we'll come back to that." He began to draw again. "Last diagram," he said.

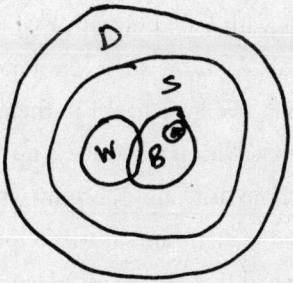

PERFECT POSSESSION

"*Perfect possession.* What we're trying to save Danny from. The demon, having invaded the victim's body and will, takes complete control. Once that happens—" He shook his head. "There's nothing you can do but hope someone locks them up before too many people die. Because that's all the demon wants—to destroy everything in its path. Death for the sake of death. Evil for the sake of Evil. What is it you Jebbies say? 'For the greater glory of God?' Whatever is the exact opposite, that's what the demon wants. To spit in God's face. To destroy humanity, God's creation. To destroy life."

Bob walked back over to Danny's diagram.

"Here's what's vital," he said. He pointed to the "free" sliver of "will." He shaded it in with the chalk, drew an arrow to it, wrote *will* on the board, and underlined it three times.

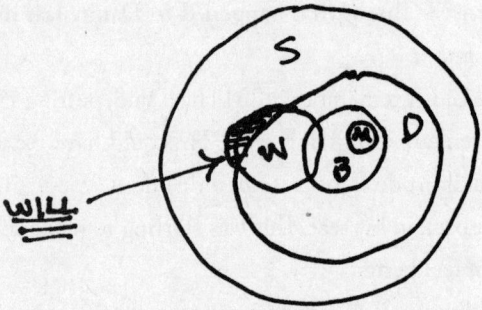

Bob tapped the shaded crescent with his chalk.

"Will," he said. "Will is the heartbeat of the soul. Through will, we can choose to align our souls with Good or with Evil. Danny's will is still alive in there, but it's weak. An exorcism is like a quadruple bypass of the will. We're the surgeons. We have to get in there and make the will strong enough to fight back. Ultimately, there is nothing we can do but strengthen the will. The choice is Danny's. Danny, with his own will, must choose to deny Evil and realign himself with Good. The important thing is, it's through the will that we can save Danny."

He shook his head, disagreeing with himself. "No. *God* can save Danny. We're just there to do a job."

Bob put the chalk down and dusted off his hands. The room was agonizingly quiet. After a moment, Michael spoke.

"I'm still a long way from believing any of this," he said.

Bob nodded, apparently unfazed. "You know the thing the recovery groups say, about taking the action and letting the feelings follow? 'Act as if,' they say."

"Yeah . . ." Michael replied hesitantly, not sure how it applied.

"Just promise me you'll 'act as if' you believe it between now and tomorrow morning. By the time you find out you *do* believe it, it'll be too late for shoring up."

"You sound pretty confident that I'm *going* to find out."

Bob nodded, with a self-satisfied chuckle. "That's the easy part," he said.

Michael let it go. He could tell there was no point in offering an alternative hypothesis.

"We're going to hear each other's confessions," Bob said. "Then I want you to go home." His tone was different; solemn. "Go home and pray. Say Mass. Do whatever you do—just make sure you're as strong as you've ever been when you walk into that room tomorrow morning. Give yourself enough time to sleep, too. Get as much sleep as you need to feel good. In fact, sleep like a baby." He smiled, a sad smile. "It's the last chance you'll ever have."

Michael kept a straight face and nodded, "acting as if" he didn't think Bob was a certified fruitloop. He went home, put himself through the motions of "shoring up" ritual, as promised, and went to sleep. Though he tossed and turned and woke up frequently, he slept more peacefully than he knew. In fact, he slept just as Bob had ordered. Like a baby, he slept unaware of the full extent of lurking danger. Like a baby, he did not suspect any vulnerability in the forces protecting him.

THREE

"God, Father of our Lord, Jesus Christ . . ."

Michael stood over Danny's bed, dressed in his official exorcism attire (though why the demon should care what color stole he had on, Michael couldn't fathom). He had the *Roman Ritual* open in front of him; he listened to Bob's voice and waited for his cue to respond.

Bob was on the other side of the bed, tirelessly reading the text, as he had been for hours now. Danny was lying on the bed, staring at the ceiling, showing no sign of reacting; he seemed to be in some trancelike state. Early on, he'd yawned a few times, but he hadn't moved at all in the past hour. It made the straps restraining his arms seem even more ridiculous than they already had.

" . . . give me strength against this and every unclean spirit tormenting this creature of yours . . ."

Maureen, Kevin, and Danny's younger brother, Chris, were waiting in another part of the house. Michael wondered what Bob was going to tell them once he finally admitted the futility of the alleged exorcism.

" . . . through the same Lord Jesus . . ."

"Amen," Michael answered, hoping Bob wouldn't hear the lack of conviction in his voice. It was obvious to him now that there was nothing tormenting Danny except Danny. Possibly a controlled substance or two. At any rate, if the hocus-pocus placebo were going to work, they'd have seen some sign of it by now.

"I exorcise you, most unclean spirit!" Bob went on. "Invading enemy . . ."

"Oh, give it a rest," Danny said suddenly. Bob looked up. Michael looked up. The voice had come from Danny, but it was not Danny's. "It's too late for this one, Padre," the guttural voice said. "You waited too long."

Something in Danny's eyes made Michael shiver.

"Here you are wasting time, when you could be downtown feeding the schizos. Noble work, isn't it? Keeping wretched people alive so they can live to see another miserable day. I wholeheartedly approve, for what it's worth."

The thing on the bed had a contorted grin on its face that was somehow obscene.

Would you stop! There's no such thing as a demon!

Danny had a grin on his face that was somehow obscene. He didn't even look like himself.

Would you stop! There's no such thing as a demon!

Danny turned his head to look at Michael, as if noticing him for the first time.

"Well, if it isn't Father Rock-and-Roll." He smiled. "Enjoying the show? Don't worry, we'll be done in time for you to get back to Manhattan for the cocktail party."

Michael felt himself stop breathing.

Bob returned to the text. "I exorcise all evil spirits! Every one of you!"

Danny was still staring at Michael, in a way that made Michael feel slimy. He felt a strange pressure weighing down on him. He glanced around. Bob was still reading. There was no one else in the room. There was nothing to explain the feeling.

But how . . . ?

"Too bad you couldn't be at your office today," Danny said to Michael. "Linda, your secretary? No, I'm sorry, your *personal assistant*—wore that red dress. You know. The one with the scoop neck. If she leans over just right—"

Michael looked at Danny, stunned. Danny smiled at what must have been a puzzled look on Michael's face.

He heard his parents talking to Linda on the phone, that's how he knows her name. And every woman in America has a red dress. There's no such thing as a demon . . .

" . . . in the name of our Lord Jesus Christ," Bob said, making the sign of the cross over Danny, "be uprooted and expelled from this creature of God."

Danny didn't react, or take his eyes off Michael.

"She just wears it for spite, you know. She gets off on being leered at by eunuchs. She likes proving what hypocrites you all are."

"He who commands you is He who ordered you thrown down from highest Heaven . . ."

"Last time she wore it, you went home and dreamed about her all night, didn't you?" Danny said, still smiling.

" . . . He who commands you dominated the sea, the winds, and the storms . . ."

"But I know what's under that bullshit altar boy act, and so do you. The liar, the charlatan, the coward—the weak, spoiled twit who wakes up hard in the middle of the night from dreaming about banging his secretary . . ."

"Stop it!" Michael yelled.

"Michael!" Bob's tone left no room for argument. Michael turned his attention back to the text.

" . . . Hear, therefore, and fear, Satan!" Bob's voice was growing louder. "Enemy of the faith!"

Danny raised his voice over Bob's. "But that's just a *dream*, right, Father? You can't help what you *dream*, right? That's out of your hands."

" . . . Source of death! Robber of life!"

"What about after you wake up?" Danny asked. "At first light, in the dark, when you think you're all alone? It's not out of your hands then, is it? Quite the contrary!"

" . . . Twister of justice!" Bob snarled. "Root of evil!"

"With full knowledge and free consent of will . . ." Followed by a chilling cackle as Danny threw his head back and laughed.

MAKE HIM STOP!

"You never quite mention that in confession, do you? You confess your temper and your ego and all your noble sins, but you don't confess the mornings when you take your sheets downstairs and wash them yourself, now do you?"

Michael couldn't breathe. The invisible pressure had intensified until he felt he might suffocate.

"Michael?"

Bob was waiting for a response. Michael stared at the swimming text in front of him. He couldn't force himself to function. His body was paralyzed and his thoughts were scurrying like terrified ants, fleeing in circles. Colliding.

How can he know that? He can't know. But he does. Danny doesn't know. He does. (What does that mean?) I can't breathe. Why did You let him do that?

"Michael!" Bob was firm, trying to bring him back.

Michael squinted, trying to make the words come into focus. After a moment, he shook his head. "I can't," he whispered. He put the book down on the nightstand and left the room. Behind him, he could hear Danny howl with laughter.

By the time Michael had recovered enough to continue, Danny had reverted to his catatonic trance. Eventually he fell into what seemed to be a normal sleep, at which point Bob declared it a day. He told Maureen, Kevin, and Chris not to feel discouraged. (*"The shortest exorcism I've ever heard of lasted three days. It's not as easy as it looks in the movies."*) He promised he and Michael would return first thing in the morning, and left them his beeper number in case anything drastic happened in the night.

On the train back to the city, Michael couldn't stop shaking. He was nauseated, his body ached, and he went back and forth from chills to feeling feverish. He told Bob he was coming down with the flu. Bob shook his head.

"It happens," he said.

"Do you feel like this?"

"Not as bad as times before. Try not to think about it."

"Fine," Michael said. "If I throw up on your feet, try not to think about that."

"Wouldn't be anything new," Bob answered with a familiar smirk.

"Jesus," Michael muttered to himself. Or maybe to Jesus.

"You did fine,"

Michael opened his eyes. "I wasn't having performance anxiety," he said, instantly regretting his choice of words. Bob didn't show any sign of making the connection. For all his purported calmness, he looked ashen, and about ten years older than he had that morning.

"Doesn't take long in a room with it to make you a believer, does it?" Bob asked.

Michael shook his head. "I just—"

"What?"

"I know I believe something right now that I didn't believe when I woke up this morning. I just don't know *what* it is I believe."

"Tell me what you're sure of."

Michael waited a moment before he spoke. "There was *something* in that room." He said it quietly, as if voicing it aloud would make things worse. He didn't even like admitting it to himself, but there was no way around it.

Bob nodded.

"It's in Danny," Michael continued. "It can take him over."

I can't believe it, and it makes no sense to me, but I saw it. I heard it. And besides . . .

Bob waited.

"Everything he said about me is true," Michael said quietly. He hadn't known he was going to say it until it was out.

Are you crazy? You could have told him it was a lie and he would have believed you.

"Don't let it get to you," Bob said. "That's what he wants."

Michael stared at Bob, amazed.

"But . . ."

"No but. Beating yourself up right now isn't going to help Danny."

Bob leaned forward, closer to Michael, unwilling to let him escape. "Tell me how I can help you," he said, in a tone far gentler than anything Michael had heard from him yet.

Michael sighed. "Make it make sense," he said.

Bob nodded, undaunted by what seemed, to Michael, an impossible request. He thought for a moment before he spoke.

"Obviously you believe in the concept of spirit," he said. "You believe in God."

"Yes." That was the only thing he still felt sure of.

"So tell me. If you believe in a *benevolent* spirit, why do you have trouble believing in an *evil* spirit? There's just as much evidence in the universe to support its existence as there is to support the existence of God. The cynic in me thinks there's more."

"I don't know," Michael said, shaking his head. "I mean, I throw words around like everyone else: Satan, Lucifer, Christ casting out demons—but I've always thought of those words as symbols. Metaphors."

Bob started to speak; Michael cut him off.

"Don't crank up your anti-Jesuit spiel. Historically, we've been as into the mystic as anyone else."

"Historically, yeah. Have you looked at a copy of your own magazine lately? It's about as spiritual as an ACLU newsletter."

"Spirituality takes on a lot of forms."

"Yeah, well—when we go back in there tomorrow, try some aromatherapy on it and see how far you get."

Michael didn't know where Bob thought he'd gotten with the *Roman Ritual*, but he let it go.

"All right, you tell me," Michael said. "You really believe in the Devil?"

"I don't believe in a little red guy with horns and a pitchfork."

"What, then?"

"I think it's all very complex, interwoven. I believe there's more than one level of evil. At least two that I'm sure of: the evil of man himself, and something larger. I think of it as capital-*E* Evil. I think it parallels the hierarchy of Heaven. God, saints, angels—Satan, demons, lesser demons—they are all beings. I know that. Whether there's any logic—any *human* logic—in it or not, my experience has reinforced that belief time and again. I don't know what form it all takes. I don't know what Satan looks like any more than I know what God looks like. What I *do* know is that when big-*E* Evil finds a doorway into the human realm and can communicate on a level we understand, it's not some vague, nebulous force. It's right there, in the room, in your face. It's individual. Personal. I swear to you, these things have *personalities*."

He gave Michael a second to digest this, then continued.

"It's like most of life, Michael. You hit a point where it stops making sense, and there's no place left to look for answers."

Michael thought about it. He had no argument for that.

"What did you believe before this morning?" Bob asked. "How did you think of evil?"

"I told you, it was all very abstract," Michael said. "This . . . stuff . . . floating out there, like radioactivity. We could get off course and veer into it; it could corrupt our thinking, pull us farther out, like an undertow. We lose ourselves. We lose God."

"And where did this *stuff* come from?"

Michael shrugged. "Original sin?"

Whatever that means . . .

"Maybe our wrongdoings create some universal cesspool of negative energy."

"Like nuclear waste?"

Michael nodded.

"And why would an all-powerful and benevolent God let that happen?" Bob asked.

"If He gives us free will, He has no choice. There's no way life can be as wonderful as it is unless the ability to *destroy* life is as horrible as *it* is, and if we have free will, we're going to have that ability."

"Natural disaster?"

"God's way of reminding us not to put our hearts and souls into material possessions," Michael said. "Although I doubt He ever accomplishes much more than making people update their homeowners' policies."

"So you had it all figured out. Now what?"

"You know what. Whatever was in that room today . . ." Michael shook his head. "It wasn't some cloud of New Age negative energy. It was . . ."

"What?"

"Old Age Hell," Michael answered, shivering. He wrapped his arms around himself and wished for a stadium blanket. He was freezing.

Bob nodded. "We rational modern people don't like to think about anything we can't understand. Floods and famines and plagues. We think we can *explain* everything, and if we can't, it's because we haven't isolated the right gene just yet; but a little more money, a little more research . . ."

Bob stopped. He seemed to be waiting for Michael to speak, but Michael couldn't make his head stop spinning long enough. Bob went on.

"Now, what's a rational, modern Jesuit to do with the thought that when Jesus talked about demons, He *meant* demons?"

"I don't know," Michael answered. "I don't know how to make myself suddenly believe things I don't believe."

"You mean you don't know how to allow yourself to believe things you don't *like*. You can't deny what you saw and heard in that room today. You know what it was. Evil. Individual, personal, intelligent Evil."

Michael put his face in his hands. *God, help me. I believe it. How can I believe it? What does it mean?*

"The good news," Bob said, "is that the minute you believe that, you become a lot safer. The best thing Satan has going for him is people's refusal to believe in him. You don't arm yourself against something you don't think is there."

Michael looked at Bob. There was something in his eyes. A milder version of something that had been there all day. A vague uncertainty. No. More than that. What, then?

Fear?

A horror of a thought was creeping into the back of Michael's mind. "Safer?" he asked.

Bob nodded.

"But not *safe*?" It wasn't really a question. Michael could already see the answer in Bob's face.

"What are you telling me?" Michael asked. It took everything he had to speak at all. "When I walk into that room, *God* can't protect me?"

"I don't know."

"You don't *know*?"

"People have died during exorcism. *Priests* have died." He sighed. "I've known a few who may as well have. Others don't seem too much worse for wear. I don't know what makes the difference."

"But you're okay."

"So far. Though I wouldn't say I've been the same. No one can go one-on-one with that kind of Evil and come out of it unchanged. I feel it."

"Feel what?"

Bob took a moment, then spoke softly. "It takes something out of you. I can't tell you what that's like. You'll find out soon enough." Bob's voice was filled with pain.

"Why do it, then?" Michael asked.

Bob smiled sadly. "Back when you guys were 'into the mystic,' you would have known the answer to that."

"*What* would I have known?"

"It's all about who you work for," Bob said, ignoring Michael's tone. "God or Satan. Good or Evil. If you love one, you have to hate the other. If you love one, you have to do battle with the other. It doesn't get any simpler than that."

Michael didn't answer. Nothing felt simple to him right now.

Back in his room, Michael got undressed and set the alarm clock for five a.m. He wanted plenty of time to pray before leaving for Long

Island. He was so tired he knew he wouldn't be able to focus for very long tonight.

He got into bed and pulled the blanket around him as if he were four years old and trying to protect himself from the under-the-bed monsters. He could see Danny's face as if it were still in front of him. Not the real face. The other one. The evil one. Contorted. Hideous. Utterly inhuman.

He turned off the light; the room was dark.

Dear God . . .

Dear God, what?

Dear God, why would You create something so vile?

If there really is a Devil, one of two things has to be true: (1) God is not all-powerful, or (2) God is not all-good.

The first thought was merely deeply disturbing. The second thought was too frightening to even go near. Not so much because it was blasphemous, but because it scared the ever-living hell out of him.

Dear God, please give me the—

His head was suddenly full of voices. He couldn't make out any words, but the din kept him from being able to hear his own thoughts. In his mind, he could still see Danny's face, and all the voices seemed to be coming from it. He tried to continue praying, but no words would come to his chaotic mind. He tried again.

Our Father—

More chatter. Louder. Voices. Laughter. He couldn't think. He couldn't remember the words. A line, then. Anything!

Deliver us from evil . . .

He could feel himself trembling. He pulled the blanket closer, but he knew it was useless.

Deliver us from evil . . .

He closed his eyes tightly, but it didn't make Danny's face go away.

DELIVER US FROM EVIL!

"Danny" started to laugh—a depraved cackle, rising above all the voices, so loud in Michael's head he couldn't believe he was doing it to himself. Then Danny stopped laughing and the sounds ended abruptly. Perfect silence. Then:

If He can . . .

Howling laughter.

IF HE CAN!

Rain had begun to fall; Michael could hear it on the fire escape outside his window. Thunder rumbled, somewhere far away.

For the rest of the night, the insane laughter rang in his head.

Michael picked Bob up at seven o'clock the next morning. The traffic wasn't overly miserable, and they made it to Plandome in an hour and fifteen minutes.

When he turned the car onto the Ingrams' street, Michael immediately stopped. The street was filled with police cars. The Ingrams' house was cordoned off by yellow tape and uniformed officers. Two ambulances were parked in front, but their lights were off and no one seemed to be in a hurry. There was a station wagon from the coroner's office.

Bob and Michael looked at each other. They knew.

It took them about five minutes to find an Irish cop who was happy to supply the details. Around five o'clock in the morning, Danny had taken a shotgun he'd stolen from a neighbor's house and shot his parents and brother while they slept. Neighbors had heard the shots and called the police. The Ingrams had been found in their beds, lying in pools of blood, all dead.

When the cops had arrived, Danny was sitting on the front porch, waiting, with a smile on his face. He laughed the whole time they were reading him his rights.

For Michael, the circus was only beginning. Danny's court-appointed attorneys found out about the Ingrams' belief that their son was possessed, and they decided it was as good a defense as they were going to come by. They contacted Bob and Michael, who both agreed to testify. They were both ill (not to mention furious) over what had happened, and they wanted to help any way they could. Bob could corroborate facts, but he wasn't going to be an impeccable witness. He'd performed too many exorcisms; the jury would figure he was obsessed with demons and saw them everywhere he looked. Michael, on the other hand, was a highly educated, levelheaded magazine editor who hadn't even believed in possession until Danny Ingram had made him a believer. He was the defense team's star witness.

When Danny's attorneys made their strategy known, the story became instant national news. The press launched into their feeding-frenzy mode, and Michael couldn't walk out the front door of the residence without tripping over reporters. He waved them off with "No comment" until he felt as if someone should be briefing him on foreign policy.

A week before the trial began, Michael received a call to meet with his provincial. Michael had expected it; he knew those on high would want him to be careful about the way he worded certain things. But he had not been expecting what happened. Frank Worland informed him that he was not to testify at the trial. He was to maintain complete confidentiality about the Church's involvement in the Danny Ingram affair. Michael couldn't believe what he was hearing.

"Frank, even if I agreed, they would subpoena me. What am I supposed to do, lie?"

"You're supposed to maintain confidentiality. How you do that is up to you."

"This is insane!"

"Whether it is or it isn't, Michael, I'm just the messenger. This is coming from higher up."

"Higher up than what? God?"

"All I can tell you is, it's coming from higher up."

"How high?"

"You'd need a passport to go there," Frank said.

Michael was astonished. "What, they don't have enough to worry about?"

"Look at it, Michael. You were denied permission to perform an exorcism on a kid you claim was genuinely possessed. What do you think the press is going to do with that?"

"The press? Frank, three people are dead and a *child* is on trial for something he doesn't even remember, and they're worried about being *embarrassed*?"

"Michael, the credibility of the magazine is at stake. You leave me no choice but to order you, under virtue of obedience—"

"I will testify and then appeal your order."

"There will be severe consequences if you do that."

"Fine."

Michael had taken the witness stand and told the truth, every crumb of it he could remember. Danny got a twenty-five-year sentence, with a chance for parole after fifteen. His attorneys assured Michael that his testimony had a lot to do with keeping Danny from getting a life sentence. Michael was grateful for that much.

The press had the predicted field day. Michael's picture was everywhere, from *Newsweek* to *Christianity Today*, along with sidebar stories on other Satan-related murder cases and surveys on people's beliefs about the Devil. All of which was met by a deafening silence from on high. Michael knew they were waiting for everything to die down, so as not to invite further criticism or more bad publicity.

It was the *New Yorker* article that had sealed Michael's fate. Two days after the article hit the newsstands, Frank Worland received an irate phone call from the bishop. Michael had "disregarded authority, created a scandal, and publicly humiliated him, the cardinal, and, in fact, the entire diocese." Frank was ordered to do something about it immediately. The next thing Michael knew, he was on his way to Butcher Holler.

Before leaving New York, Michael had gone to the prison to visit Danny. The kid in the visitation room was the same lost kid who had asked Michael for help the first day they'd met. Danny could barely talk about his family for crying, but he managed to reconfirm everything he'd said at the trial—that he didn't remember a thing about the night of the crime, and that there were large holes in his memory in the six months before it. He did remember hearing voices in his head. The voices had told him to hurt people, that they deserved it, that it was what God wanted him to do. The voices had become louder and more insistent as time went on. They'd driven him crazy, and he hadn't been able to get them to shut up. He also said he didn't hear the voices anymore. He hadn't heard them since the night of the crime.

Danny Ingram's face haunted Michael's dreams. So did the faces of Kevin, Maureen, and Chris, who had once confided to Michael that he was afraid Danny was going to kill them all in their sleep. Michael had told Chris not to worry. *"No one is going to let it go that far."* At least once a week, Michael woke up in the middle of the night in a cold sweat, with those words pounding in his brain, those faces tearing at his heart.

The Varsity was beginning to fill up with the early dinner crowd, and the noise brought Michael back to the present. Someone behind him dropped a tray and he jumped. He looked up to see the smarmy guy chuckle at him, which sent him spiraling into even more shame. He told himself to knock it off. The next couple of days were going to be difficult enough. He collected his trash and dumped it, then headed outside.

As he walked through the parking lot, Michael had a mental image of the creepy guy pulling a nine-caliber semiautomatic out from behind the leather jacket and blowing him away through the window of The

Varsity. He could see it across the front page of the *Atlanta Constitution*: PRIEST GUNNED DOWN IN VARSITY PARKING LOT.

Michael realized how exposed and vulnerable he felt, and he knew it had to do with Vincent's death. Even though they hadn't been able to spend a lot of time together the last few years, just knowing Vincent was alive in the world had made Michael feel somehow protected. He realized, already, how much of a shield Vincent had been for him. Vincent and the Church. One gone, the other teetering on the brink.

And something vile lurking in the wings.

You're imagining it. You're turning into a theological hypochondriac.

He heard the vague sound of thunder in the distance, even though none of the clouds he could see looked threatening.

Look at the bright side. Maybe you'll be struck by lightning.

As he drove out of the parking lot, the thought came to him that he should go to Emory and pick up a grad school catalogue. Maybe he could talk the Royals into letting him go back to school for a year or two.

The standard Jesuit answer to an emotional crisis: get another doctorate. Learn one more language, everything will fall into place.

What else am I supposed to do?

How about the radical concept of dealing with the actual problem?

I will *deal with the problem. As soon as I can figure out what the hell the problem is!*

You know what the problem is.

No. He knew the symptoms. He had no idea what was really at the bottom of it all. Maybe nothing more than your basic midlife crisis. Maybe he'd become a living cliché. If he were a doctor, he'd be pricing red convertibles.

It was an appealing thought. If this was a midlife crisis, at least it would eventually pass. In his heart, though, he feared that whatever was happening to him was nothing so harmless. And nothing so temporary.

He drove aimlessly around the city for almost an hour. He didn't know what to do with himself. He didn't want to go home until he was sure Barbara was gone. For some reason, he felt compelled to make her believe he was all right, and he didn't have the energy for any more of that today.

Something Danny had said to him that day at the prison was ringing in Michael's head.

"I'm so tired, Father Kinney . . . and there's no rest."

Every time he tried to take his mind off Danny Ingram, it headed for another danger zone. Tess. He kept thinking about the safety he'd felt in her arms. Even if it was an illusion, it was a desperately comforting illusion.

He'd packed a bag to stay with Vincent for a few days after the operation. It was still in the trunk of the car. Delta had a seven o'clock flight to LaGuardia. He could catch it easily. With a little luck, he could be at Tess's door by ten. Ten thirty, the latest.

He told himself he should be ashamed for even thinking such a thing at a time like this.

He told himself that all the way to the airport.

FOUR

Tess looked through the peephole, then unlocked the door and jerked it open.

"I don't believe this," she said.

"I should have called, but I didn't want to give you a chance to say no."

She moved aside to let him in. He closed the door behind him and locked it, as Tess was still too stunned to move. He tossed his bag to the floor.

"I really can't believe this," she said again. "I mean . . ." She didn't try to go on. She was wearing a soft pink bathrobe and had her hair tied loosely back with a strip of white chiffon. She looked more relaxed than he'd ever seen her. Tess usually looked as if she were in charge of a state dinner and no one could find the president.

"Can I hug you," she asked, "or am I supposed to keep a safe distance?"

Michael reached for her and pulled her into his arms. "I didn't fly all the way up here and risk my life in a cab for you to keep a safe distance," he said. He held her tightly, for a long time. The familiar smell of her hair was a welcome comfort.

"Vincent died," he finally whispered.

"Oh, Michael." She held him tighter. "I'm so sorry."

"I knew he was going to die. I just thought he had a little more time," Michael said, trying to explain his emotional state.

"I'm so sorry." She stepped back and looked at him. "I know how much you're going to miss him."

"I already do."

"I know," Tess said, rubbing his arm.

The empathy in her eyes was making it hard for him to keep from crying, and he didn't want to cry.

"I had to tell someone," he explained. "And you were the person I wanted to tell."

"I wish I could do something to make it hurt less."

"You just did," he said, and pulled her to him again.

"And—were you going to stay here?" Her voice had the tentative tone the situation merited, and she pulled away from him.

"If it's okay."

"Of course it's okay," Tess said immediately, but she still sounded hesitant. "It's just . . ."

"What?"

"Well, you know. I mean—am I supposed to make up the sofa bed?"

When he tried to answer, he felt himself start to cry. He pulled Tess back to him and felt the soothing warmth of her skin, the heat of her lips on his neck. He lifted her face and kissed her. It took him no time to lose himself. The guilt vanished as quickly as it would return.

• • •

He awoke to the smell of coffee brewing. The room was light and he was alone. He'd left his glasses on the dresser across the room, and the numbers on the digital clock were a red blur, but there was a strong chance the first one was an eight. He forced himself out of bed and staggered to the bathroom.

He showered, shaved, and dressed, donning his standard jeans and a concession-to-New-York-City oxford cloth shirt, white with blue pinstripes. With his glasses on, he probably looked like a Columbia law professor. He studied himself in the mirror and wondered why, if he really loved being a priest as much as he thought he did, he hated looking like one.

He ventured out and found Tess in the kitchen, cooking breakfast. She was stirring eggs with one hand and pouring orange juice with the other. He watched her, thinking of all the people in the world who took such a scene for granted. For him, it was a forbidden form of poetry.

He pulled a chair back from the small table in the breakfast nook and sat down. "I don't have a lot of time," he said.

"You're eating breakfast anyway. You've lost too much weight." She brought a plate over and put it down in front of him. "Don't they feed you down there?"

"I've become a vegetarian. It's the only thing they don't deep-fry."

Tess sat down across from him with nothing but a cup of coffee. She had no business criticizing *his* eating habits. He didn't know how she stayed alive, as little as she ate. But he wasn't going to get into that one this morning. The air was already thick with undercurrents.

He crossed himself and started to bless the food. Tess frowned.

"Can't you do that in your head?"

He looked at her, surprised by the hostility in her voice.

Tess asked. "You know I was a heathen."

"I knew you were a lapsed Catholic."

"But what? You thought I was a closet Christian?"

Michael couldn't speak. As surprised as he was at the discovery, he was even more surprised at his reaction. Why did he feel like someone had just kicked him in the gut?

Tess smiled. "What, Michael? Is your superior going to be even more disappointed when he finds out you're sleeping with an atheist?"

"You're not even an agnostic?"

He felt like he was ten years old. What the hell difference did it make what Tess believed? Didn't she have a right to believe anything she wanted? Why should it affect his life at all?

"So . . ." He couldn't leave it alone.

"What?"

"So you're one of those people who thinks Jesus was just a better-than-average rabbi?"

"No. I'm one of those people who thinks He probably didn't exist."

He put his fork down and stopped trying to be open-minded.

"Are you serious?" he asked.

"I read a book; this guy made a very intelligent case of Jesus being a composite character."

"What *guy*?"

"A Harvard professor."

"Well, that settles it then. Great. Think how much money we'll save next December."

"Why do you care so much what I believe?"

"I don't understand how you can be in love with me when you hate everything I stand for."

"How can you claim to be in love with me when you work for people who go against everything I believe in?"

"I thought you didn't believe in anything."

"You know what I'm talking about. You are addicted to a Stone Age, misogynistic institution whose rules you don't even believe in! Which, in my book, makes you a hypocrite with no right to look down on me!"

She left the room. He gave her a few minutes to calm down before following her.

He found her sitting on the bed, crying. He leaned in the doorway and waited.

"This is insane," she said. "This isn't about Jesus."

"I know," he said.

She took a breath and dried her eyes with the tissue he'd handed her. Finally she spoke.

"I know you just lost Vincent and I shouldn't be thinking about myself, but I think I've done this limbo thing for about as long as I can stand it."

"I know." He sat beside her and held her until she stopped crying.

"And I'm angry," she said. "Because I just have to sit and wait until you're ready to deliver the verdict."

"I realize that," Michael said. "But this isn't a *job* you're asking me to give up. It's my *life*."

"In exchange for a better one!"

"I didn't vow to do this until something better came along."

"Then why are you even here?"

He had no answer.

"And this is going to delay you making up your mind."

"No, it won't. I think it will help."

At the airport, she let him off at the Delta curb. He kissed her, chasing away the thought that it might be the last time. Neither of them said good-bye as he got out and slammed the door behind him. He didn't look back as she drove away.

FIVE

The wake service lasted for almost two hours, and the wake itself didn't get under way until almost nine thirty. That didn't dissuade anyone from heading to Vincent's house with casserole dishes. The irony, Michael thought, was that what would *really* feel like consolation to him would be for everyone to go home and leave him alone. But since none of them were there for his sake, he knew that he and Barbara would be throwing them out at midnight, bar or no bar.

The gathering was rife with miseries Michael hadn't even anticipated. On top of everything else, Monsignor Graham appointed himself Michael's emotional guardian for the evening and dragged Michael all over the house, introducing people, telling stories that had been only mildly amusing the first dozen times Michael heard them. Now he had

Michael and a couple of other hapless victims trapped in a corner, with no way out short of flagrant rudeness.

Michael scanned the crowd and found Barbara, who was positioned near the kitchen, directing the flow of incoming food. It took him a few minutes of diligent effort to catch her eye, but he finally succeeded. Using his hand to shield the side of his face, he mouthed *"Help."* She nodded, excused herself from the cluster around her, and came over to him. Along the way, she picked up speed and a convincing look of urgency.

"Excuse me," she said, in the general direction of Monsignor Graham. "Michael, your housekeeper's on the phone, she says she has to talk to you. I tried to take a message, but she said it's an emergency."

Bless you, Barbara.

He excused himself and made his way quickly through the crowd and into the sanctuary of the kitchen. Barbara followed.

"I had to get away from Tom Graham for a few minutes," he said.

"I know. You're starting to get that nailed-to-the-cross look."

"Other than him, everything is fine. Thank you."

"You're welcome. And don't get me wrong, I want them out of here as much as you do."

Someone across the room caught Michael's eye. A guy who had just come in the front door and was talking to Graham. A guy in clerics.

"Who's the priest?" he asked.

"Oh, I meant to tell you about him. He was Vincent's new best friend. They spent a lot of time together at the villa. He lives there."

"The Jesuit villa?" Michael asked. Vincent had restored an old estate north of Atlanta for the Jesuits from the region to use as a getaway. Vincent had his own room out there, for when he wanted to escape the city.

"I think he's originally from Chicago," Barbara said. "Do you know him? His name is Gabe—"

"Novak," Michael finished.

"Do you know him?"

Michael nodded. "He makes himself known."

"What do you mean?"

Michael ignored her question. "Vincent spent time with him?" he asked.

"I think they played chess, mostly. And went bass fishing at the lake. Why, what's wrong with him?"

"He's a narrow-minded, abrasive, pre–Vatican II, self-righteous, holier-than-God papist ass."

"So you know him?"

"No."

"Then how do you know—"

"I'll find you some articles he wrote before his superiors wisely gagged him."

"No thanks. I'll take your word for it."

"Is he the minister?"

"I thought you were all ministers."

"Is he the guy who calls the plumber, makes sure there's beer in the refrigerator?"

"That sounds right."

"You see? Any time you have a guy with two PhDs who speaks seven dead languages, and he's handing out towels at a villa, it's because he can't get along with anyone."

"Vincent was very fond of him."

"Vincent could get along with anyone. Gabe Novak is proof." Michael grabbed his jacket from a hook on the wall. "I'm out of here. I'll be back later to help you clean up."

He was out the back door before Barbara could voice an opinion.

• • •

Michael drove around aimlessly for an hour, ending up in downtown Atlanta. He found a parking place on Ellis and walked up the hill to Peachtree. There was a fair amount of traffic; a couple of limos were pulling in and out of the Ritz-Carlton. The glass tower of the Westin Peachtree lit up the sky for seventy-four floors; he could see the glass elevator, currently on its way to the top. The downtown area was putting forth a gallant effort, but between its legitimately respectable crime rate and the equally crippling plague of white paranoia, it was still just an echo of its former self. Michael turned away from the nightlife and walked uphill, stopping directly across Peachtree from the building that had been the Winecoff Hotel. (The builders had been right about one thing. The *building* hadn't burned. Just the furniture, the carpet, the drapes, and the guests.)

The building was dark now, deserted, except for a Chinese restaurant on the first floor. Half the windows were broken out and there was a large FOR SALE sign above the door. In spite of the broken windows and peeling paint, the building was still beautiful. Michael felt some strange affection for it. Like an abused child gravitating to the offender parent, he returned again and again. And now that Vincent was gone, it seemed, somehow, the right place to remember the dead.

He thought about the first night he had stood on this spot. The night Vincent had told him about the fire. Up until then, Vincent had told him that his parents and grandmother had died in a car wreck while out Christmas shopping, and that Michael had survived because they'd left him at home with Vincent. One warm spring evening, a week before what would have been his First Communion, Vincent drove Michael downtown, parked, and led him down the hill to stand where he was now standing. By then the hotel was the Peachtree on Peachtree retirement home. As they stood there and looked at the building, Vincent told Michael the true story for the first time. He said he hadn't wanted to tell him the truth until he felt Michael was old enough to deal with the visions it would inevitably conjure. Michael had been too stunned to feel much of anything at first; he had been embarrassed by his lack of feeling—felt he should be crying or something, and that his reaction would disappoint Vincent. He covered by asking questions: which window had been theirs; how, exactly, had his parents died; how, exactly, had he and Vincent managed to escape. Vincent answered everything, and did not sugarcoat it.

Back home, Vincent had taken out a scrapbook he'd made of newspaper clippings about the fire. He'd been waiting to give them to Michael when the time was right. They sat down together and went through the book. It was overwhelming that night, but Michael had returned to it time and again, and was deeply grateful that Vincent had put the book together. At least he'd had something tangible in front of him—a place to search for answers, even if there were none to be found. He read the names over and over, including several accounts of how his father had saved Michael's life. There was even a picture of Michael—at least, the caption said it was Michael—being carried by a fireman. The baby in the picture was smiling and playing with the fireman's mustache, oblivious to the agony around him. Michael could not connect himself to the photo, no matter how hard he tried.

The tears had come as he and Vincent looked at the book, as Michael read the gruesome details and saw the pictures, and it had all started to become real. Vincent just held Michael in his arms and let Michael cry for as long as he needed to. Vincent cried with him. The night had lived vividly in Michael's memory ever since. It had cemented the bond between them that had never weakened. But it had also created their first rift.

In Vincent's mind, there had been a healing significance to Michael's hearing all this a week before his First Communion. In Michael's mind, the juxtaposition had been jarring.

"Grandpa, how many people were in the hotel?"

"Two hundred and eighty."

"How many died?"

"One hundred and nineteen. God saved me so that I could save you."

"If God saved us, why couldn't He save everybody?"

It was the first time Michael had ever asked Vincent a question that he couldn't answer. Not only couldn't he answer it—he admitted that he didn't know.

Michael, making his first "adult" decision, had refused his First Communion. He couldn't go through with it, given this huge question in his mind that no one could answer. He spent the following year asking Father Donahue over and over. He heard a lot of rambling about God's will and acceptance, but nothing ever made sense. It was just words. Almost a year from the night Vincent told him the real story, he got sick and "saw" his mother, and the questions were answered, on some level that went far beyond words.

Now here he stood again, with a lifetime's accumulation of questions that couldn't be answered.

Okay, run it down. Remove the emotion from it. What's the bottom line?

I'm a priest and I've fallen in love with a woman. (That last part being, in fact, the problem. If I'd fallen in love with another priest or a twelve-year-old boy, the Church would be much less horrified—but I digress.)

What are the options?

Stay a priest and leave Tess. Stay with Tess and leave the priesthood. No troublesome gray areas there.

What are the issues?

Vocation. I've always been so thoroughly convinced I had a divine calling. If it's all dissolving before my eyes, what does that mean? I was deluded? God had the wrong number?

His friend Larry's predictably nonchalant answer: "First of all, if you did have a calling, who said it had to be permanent? You've done a lot of good work here, now you'll go do a lot of good work somewhere else. And secondly, there is the possibility that God is and always has been as silently indifferent to your occupation as He is to most people's."

What about Tess's "real world" accusation? Is it true that I don't want to live in the real world? The temporal world?

What would that look like? Everyday stuff. Mortgage, or at least rent. Bills. Some kind of job. Cocktail parties. Car trouble. Income taxes. Friends over for dinner. Sex. Guilt free.

What was the alternative? Spending the rest of his life as a priest, knowing forever what he'd given up. Dying of old age in some home for senile priests. Alone.

And it's not like everything was perfect until Tess showed up. You've been having problems with the Church for a long time.

There were a lot of things that had been bothering him for years. He'd always minimized their importance, tucked them away in the back of his mind, in a file marked "Things to Worry About Later." Over the years, the file had gotten fatter and fatter. When it became too large to ignore entirely, he'd just stepped over it whenever it got in his way. Lately he'd bundled it with Tess. The Priesthood vs. Tess and All This Other Stuff That's Been Bothering Me Anyway.

When did it start?

The first seeds of doubt had been planted in his mind in 1967, while he was a scholastic at Saint Louis University. He had written a rather blistering antiwar editorial for the *University News*, which had resulted in his being hauled before the university president.

"It is not the university's place to take sides in a political matter."

"It's a moral matter. People are dying in an unjust war."

"Who are you to declare it an unjust war? Has the bishop said it's unjust? Has the pope said it's unjust?"

Michael was then informed that there had been complaints from four members of the board of trustees, not to mention several "routinely generous" alumni. While no one disputed the fact that Michael was quite talented and had been making a valuable contribution to the paper, the president was left with no choice but to remove him from the staff. (Thus establishing a lifelong career pattern—people telling him how talented he was while they were getting rid of him.) Furthermore, anything Michael wrote for publication while he remained a student must first be approved by the president himself.

On the heels of all that came *Humanae Vitae*—Pope Paul VI's encyclical on birth control, which had destroyed, in one fell swoop, Michael's hope (and the hope of all liberal Catholics) for reform on that issue.

Celibacy.

His own personal peccadillo. Hard to analyze it with anything approaching objectivity. Maybe it would have been easier if he'd been a virgin going into seminary. If he hadn't known what he was being asked to give up. But he'd had far too much curiosity (not to mention far too many raging hormones) to commit himself to abstinence and ignorance. He'd just see what it was like, he'd thought. So he wouldn't have to spend the rest of his life not knowing. But "just this once" hadn't worked. Neither had "just a few times" or "just until I enter the novitiate." It had been a battle from the beginning; it was a battle still.

Corruption.

First under this heading was the Church officials' unconscionable pattern of covering up pedophilia—shuffling offenders from one parish to another, exposing new victims to a known threat, with cognizance and without warning. Michael had even heard of cases where bishops had destroyed files on repeat offenders in order to avoid lawsuits and, of course, bad publicity. (Given what had happened to him, Michael had no problem believing it.)

Thanks to all the publicity that the Church had not been able to fend off, buy off, or lie its way out of, pedophilia had become a problem to every priest in the country, guilty or not. At his own parish, a particularly paranoid couple had met with Michael before he'd finished unpacking to inform him that he was never to be in a room with their altar boy son unless one of them was present. None of this had anything to do with the priest Michael had replaced. He knew that from asking, and from having grown up in the South. Southerners had only to hear of something once, from any source of national media, to be convinced they were all its next victims. And his parishioners' fears were exacerbated by the fact that Michael had come to them by way of New York City, which meant there was no limit to the range of perversion he might be importing. He realized, thinking about it now, that his preference for civilian clothes had a lot to do with getting tired of watching strangers size him up everywhere he went. He knew the look and he knew what it was about—people wondering if he was someone with a penchant for adolescent boys. (A couple of times he'd had to bite his tongue to keep from saying, "Don't worry, I've got a girlfriend.")

Whenever he had confronted his superiors with any or all of these issues, the unvarying response was "the Church isn't perfect." Maybe not, but if it didn't at least *aspire* to be, it might as well be a bank. He'd spent all these years telling himself that the bureaucracy and the religion were two different things, but the bureaucracy controlled him: where he lived, what he did, what he could and couldn't publish . . .

And yet.

He loved being a priest. And, in spite of all his disillusionment and all his gripes and frustrations, he loved the Catholic Church. Fiercely.

Maybe blindly?

No. It was impossible, these days, not to ask questions. It went far beyond Church issues. Larry was right. The current theological trend was "let's find a way to salvage something from all this, given the fact that we sophisticated intellectuals know it can't possibly be true." Since it was no longer respectable to believe in Jesus's divinity, scholars had to convince themselves and everyone else that it really didn't matter. To Michael, this was sheer insanity—to say that it made no difference whether Jesus was God come down to live on earth or simply the greatest hoax ever perpetuated on civilization! And then there were people like Tess, who were convinced Jesus's entire existence was a fabrication. Which would mean the gospels were all a very elaborate fraud. Not to mention damned good fiction.

Even the people who agreed with him kept his head spinning with their constant commentaries and analysis and insights and new theories and new versions of old theories. All of them convinced they'd happened upon the angle that was going to make sense of the whole mess once and for all. There were more versions of Jesus these days than there were of Barbie. Historical Jesus. Eschatological Jesus. Mythological Jesus. Political Rebel Jesus. New Age Jesus. Jesus Seminar Jesus. Twelve-Step Jesus. Apocryphal Jesus, who made clay birds fly and killed a playmate and brought him back to life. Jesus a.k.a. Joshua and/or Jeshua, who was channeling new holy books and starting new cults all over the place in order to explain (to the select few who happened to be in the right bookstore staring at the right shelf at the right time) where it had all gone astray.

We can never know—really know—anything.

And still, people are expected to devise a moral code and make life-altering decisions, based on what they suspect or guess or hope to be true. What sense does that make?

That was the main reason Tess's proclamation had upset him. If she thought Jesus never lived—and even if he lived as a mere mortal—then she thought Michael's whole life was a lie. Then *who* did she think she was in love with?

They needed to talk about it. Really talk, with no clock ticking.

But what if she talks you into something you end up regretting? Your brain goes out the window the minute you get in a room with her. (Some rooms more than others.)

If my faith is so flimsy that I can be talked out of it, I have bigger problems than Tess.

He heard a noise and looked toward it. A member of Atlanta's large homeless community was making his way up the street with a shopping cart full of meaningless possessions. The guy was barely recognizable as human. He looked like he hadn't had a bath in decades, and there was a wild, glazed stare in his eyes that led Michael to believe he was high on something other than life.

Oh, great.

The guy stopped his cart against a bus bench (downwind, mercifully) and looked at Michael. "You got a cigarette?"

"I don't smoke," Michael said. "And I left my wallet at home," he added, fending off the next question.

And I don't have a MARTA token or the time and I don't know the bus schedule and even if I had any money, I wouldn't give it to you because I'd be afraid I was subsidizing your addictions, which is why I send checks to organizations that would be happy to help you if you went there.

The guy turned his crazy gaze away, across the street.

"You'd never know it burned, would you?" the bum asked, staring at the hotel.

Michael looked at him, surprised.

"It was a sight," he continued, eyes fixed on the building. "Flames comin' outta the windows, people jumpin', like it was rainin' bodies."

Michael stared at the guy, trying to put it together. It was difficult to tell his age under the dirt and beard and ravages of alcohol, but even if the guy was old enough to have been alive in 1946, he certainly would not have been old enough at the time to remember it in any detail, much less talk about it like it was a week ago.

The bum pointed to Ellis Street. "There was bodies piled up on that street, musta been a dozen. People knockin' each other off ladders. This one woman jumped and her arm got caught on the cable that held up the sign with the name of the hotel. She just hung there like meat on a hook. 'Nother guy fell on the cable, 'bout cut his head off."

In addition to the fact that he shouldn't possibly have been able to remember the fire that well, there was something else about the guy that gave Michael a bad feeling. Even as he described the horror in vivid detail, his eyes were dead. If anything, he seemed to be trying to suppress a chuckle. And there was something familiar about his voice. Michael couldn't place it, but it wasn't a comforting familiarity. More like something from an old nightmare.

The bum looked back at Michael. The dead eyes came alive for a second, and the face looked a little more human. Then, without warning, the bum broke into a rotten-toothed grin, which turned into a laugh—a brittle, cackling laugh. Michael felt himself jump, startled. He was too confused to move, even though he was starting to get nervous. This guy's insanity was not necessarily harmless. Still, Michael stood transfixed, for reasons he couldn't understand.

The bum stopped laughing but continued to stare at Michael. It was a chilling stare. Penetrating. Michael felt like the creep was looking into his soul.

It's the look. AGAIN?

"I don't have to tell you about the fire, do I?" the bum asked. Michael couldn't speak. How could this lunatic know?

Because you were standing here staring at the building with a forlorn look on your face? It doesn't take a Rhodes Scholar.

"Well . . ." Michael said, his voice trailing off. He didn't want to divulge anything to this creep and his stroke-of-luck intuition. What he wanted was to get the hell out of there, but somehow he didn't like the idea of turning his back on the guy. And what was he supposed to say to announce his departure? *"Have a nice evening"*?

"Hey, don't let me hang you up," the bum said. "I just run my mouth, I got nothin' else to do."

Michael nodded, again unsettled by the guy's clairvoyance.

Michael wondered what Bob Curso would do. Bob spent his days in un-air-conditioned buildings in the Bronx with guys like this. How did he find some common plane for even the most basic communication? He wished Bob were here, except if Bob were here, he'd be laughing his head off at his friend the pampered Jesuit. (*"You guys are gonna get to Heaven and be pissed off that they don't serve two liqueurs after dinner."*)

Still, Michael told himself, there was more going on than his aversion to two years' worth of BO. This guy was bad news.

Evil.

The derelict obviously had no intention of leaving, so Michael was going to have to either walk to his car backward, or turn his back and pray. He decided on the latter.

"Well . . . good night," Michael said. The bum just nodded, apparently unfazed. Michael turned and started down the hill, walking as fast as he could without looking as nervous as he was. He listened for the sound of footsteps behind him. None. Thank God.

Now that he felt relatively safe, Michael chided himself for his paranoia, not to mention his lack of compassion. The bum was just a guy who'd fried his brain with drugs or alcohol, for reasons that would probably tear at Michael's heart if he knew them. Or else he was at the mercy of screwed-up brain chemicals, which certainly wasn't his fault.

Would your hero Jesus be hurrying down the hill, greatly relieved to make a getaway?

"Hey!"

Michael stopped and turned back to look at the bum.

"Bring your wallet next time, Father!" he yelled.

Michael froze. He wasn't wearing anything even remotely clerical.

"What makes you think I'm a priest?" Michael asked.

He smiled again. "Isn't the better question, what makes *you* think you are?"

Michael tried again to place the voice. Did this guy know him? Had they crossed paths somewhere along the way? He strained to remember, but nothing came to him. He turned around again and headed for his car. Behind him, the bum broke into an insane, piercing cackle.

Around three o'clock in the morning, Michael sat bolt upright, trembling in the dark, gasping for air. In the middle of the dream it had come to him, splitting his consciousness like lightning from Hell.

He knew where he had heard that voice.

SIX

Jesus.

How?

How could the voice he'd heard come from Danny, six months ago in Long Island, turn up in a homeless wino in downtown Atlanta?

It wasn't the same voice. It was just similar.

No. He knew all about the fire. He knew all about you. He knew you were a priest!

There has to be some logical explanation.

Something was wrong. Now. In the room. Everything looked normal, but there was a heaviness. He recognized it: a milder version of what he'd felt in Danny's room.

It's in here.

He turned on the light. The feeling remained. He shivered, then realized that the room was cold. Not ordinary cold. Icy, but stuffy at the same time. He was having trouble breathing. The air was too thick. There was an odd smell, like a smoldering candle.

It's getting stronger.

The air was closing in on him, squeezing from all sides. He tried to move; his body was paralyzed. The air squeezed tighter. He felt as if he were in a pressure chamber. It had never been this strong with Danny.

"Get . . . out . . . of . . . here . . ." he managed to whisper. But the only response was that the pressure became more intense. Michael could almost hear it laugh. He searched his mind for the words Bob Curso had used.

"I . . . command . . . you . . ." He was barely able to force the words out of his mouth, much less sound commanding.

God, help me. It's going to kill me.

" . . . in . . . the . . . name . . . of . . . Jesus . . . Christ . . ." There was a loud sound, like wind through a tunnel. He felt the air reverse direction. The squeezing became pulling. A sucking motion. For a few seconds, he felt he was being pulled apart.

Then it was gone.

The sudden absence of pressure almost threw him to the floor. He steadied himself, then looked around, checking the corners. But he knew it was gone. The air was warm again.

His first impulse was to tell himself he'd imagined it. Or maybe it was something physiological. He'd worked himself into a state because of the bum. He'd convinced himself the demon was after him, and had given himself an anxiety attack.

But he knew better. The same way he'd known during Danny's exorcism. It wasn't in his mind. It was on the outside. A presence. With a will and a fury of its own.

With a trembling hand, he picked up the phone and dialed Bob's private number. Held his breath until he heard Bob answer.

"Hello?" Groggy. Annoyed.

"Bob, it's Michael Kinney. I'm sorry to—"

"Hello?" Bob insisted, angrier.

Michael yelled into the phone. "Bob, it's Michael—" The line went dead. Michael cursed the phone company and hit the Redial button. A ring. Another ring. A clicking sound. A sickeningly sweet voice: "*The number you have dialed is not in service at this time. Please check the number and dial again.*"

Michael hung up; he tried again, dialing the number carefully. He heard two rings, another clicking sound, and then loud static—crackling, popping, white noise in the background. A final try yielded the same. He gave up.

He put on his sweats and hurried to Vincent's study. He searched the bookshelves and pulled down all the books he'd accumulated during the Ingram case. He stacked them on Vincent's desk, then began a frantic search of the chapter headings, looking for any reference to a demon stalking a priest who'd participated in an unsuccessful exorcism. Nothing. At the bottom of the stack, he started again, this time combing the indexes. *POSSESSION. In the Bible, Catholic views of, Characteristics of, History of, Legal aspects of, Medical treatment of. See also: Multiple personality disorder; Exorcism. EXORCISM. Characteristics of, Duration of, History of. See also: Possession.*

A noise in the room. Tapping. He jumped half a mile and slammed the book shut; looked up to see Barbara standing in the doorway, tapping on the door. Dressed in black.

Oh, hell. Vincent's funeral.

"Sorry I scared you."

"It's okay," he said, trying to catch his breath.

"What are you doing?"

"Nothing," he said, too quickly. She came over; looked at the stack of books.

Don't read the titles.

She leaned over and read the titles. "Demons? Again?"

"Barbara, I don't want to hear it."

"Hear what?"

"Anything. Sarcasm. Jokes. Good-natured ribbing. Just leave it alone."

"I didn't say anything."

"Don't even *think* anything. I'd love to be cynical and sophisticated and smug, but I don't have that luxury anymore!"

"Michael, I don't care if you believe in the tooth fairy. I just came to tell you the limo will be here in half an hour."

He nodded. "I'll be ready," he said, and left her.

The church was packed and people were standing in the aisles, which didn't surprise Michael. What *did* surprise him was the absence of Gabe Novak. He thanked God profusely for that, and for the fact that Novak and Vincent had not been the fast friends that Barbara, for some reason, had mistakenly declared them to be.

When Tom Graham had finally concluded his lengthy eulogy, Michael took his place at the podium. Looked at the notes and decided to skip the intro. Anyone who didn't know who he was could ask somebody later.

"When I was about thirteen years old—" His voice was shaky. He cleared his throat and tried again. "—I went through a brief cynical phase and I stopped going to Mass. I'm not sure how I had it worked out in my mind, because I still wanted to be a priest. I guess I was going to find a way to do it without the Church. An ongoing struggle . . ."

Chuckles from people in the crowd who knew of his recent troubles, which gave him a moment to take a breath and steady himself. He still felt weak from the . . . (*What? Demonic attack?*)

"Vincent sat me down one day and asked me what I thought I was doing. I said, 'Grandpa, there's nothing at that church but a bunch of hypocrites.' Vincent looked at me and nodded and said, 'Well, there's always room for one more.'"

(Laughter.)

Okay . . . take a breath . . . keep reading . . .

"If you knew Vincent at all, you knew that side of him. It wasn't my favorite side. Especially when I was thirteen."

He could feel his throat starting to constrict. He forced himself past it, kept reading.

"Vincent's cancer was diagnosed a little over four months ago. I'd gone with him to the doctor, just because I happened to be in town. Neither of us had expected the news to be as grave as it was. We drove home in silence. I was in shock, I think. Vincent was his usual stoic self. About ten minutes into the drive, he asked me if I minded taking him to Marietta. I asked, 'What's in Marietta?' He said his favorite computer store was there, and he wanted to go by and see if they had a color printer that had just come out. I thought he'd flipped—the news had been too much for him and he'd gone into some kind of bizarre denial. I said, 'Vincent, you know, the doctor said—' 'I heard the doctor,' he said. 'That's why I want to go right now. They may have to order it.'"

(More laughter. Nods of recognition.)

Okay. Home stretch.

He opened his mouth to speak again, but was surprised to find that no sound came out. He tried again, and this time his throat began to tighten, as if someone were choking him. He couldn't breathe. At the same time, he could feel the presence again. The oppressive weight of it. He could see the alarmed looks in the faces of the gathered mourners and he wanted to assure them he was okay, but he wasn't. He struggled again to draw a breath. Suddenly Tom Graham was in front of him. In his face, whispering.

"St. Michael the archangel, defend us in battle, be our protection against the wickedness and snares of the Devil . . ."

Michael tried to join him, but whatever had taken control of him would not let him speak, or even form the words. He bowed his head and let Graham finish. He managed to mouth an "amen" at the end. Graham whispered, "Can you go on?" Michael shook his head no. "Then sit down." Michael nodded and obeyed. Graham took over. The congregants assumed Michael was too choked up to continue.

With the pressure off him, Michael was able to draw small breaths, and then larger ones. He was breathing normally by the time Graham finished the eulogy, but went through the rest of the Mass in a daze, trying to understand what was happening to him. And trying to understand Tom Graham's actions. Why had he chosen the St. Michael prayer? How had he known Michael was in the grip of something demonic?

Michael spent the afternoon in Vincent's study, packing books into boxes. He could hear Barbara knocking around in another part of the house, and was grateful for her presence. He dreaded nightfall. He was halfway thinking about going back to Barton for the night.

He heard Barbara's voice from down the hall.

"Michael, I'm on my way to see you. I'm five feet from the door. Don't jump out of your skin."

"Thank you," he said as she appeared in the doorway. Things had warmed up between them in the course of the day. She'd probably written off his rant this morning as anxiety about the funeral. He hadn't had any problem selling "panic attack" to explain his episode at the Mass.

"I need you to sign some papers," she said. "Something about putting all of Vincent's money into one trust fund, and they need to do it before the will is read, don't ask me why. All I know is, I was swarmed by suits at the funeral." She laid the papers on the desk. "All the places are marked with tabs."

Michael made his way through the maze of boxes.

"Do you know who Edna Foley is?" Barbara asked.

"No. Should I?"

"I don't know. She lives in Jonesboro, and Vincent has been sending her a check for fifteen hundred dollars every week for almost ten years. I've never had access to his private account before, so this is the first I've heard of it."

"Me too."

"I can't find a phone number for her, so the only thing I know is to drive to Jonesboro and ask her who she is."

"Give me her address and I'll do it."

"You? Don't be silly."

"I want to. I need a break anyway. I wouldn't mind the drive." *Anything to get my mind off whatever happened to me this morning.*

"Well . . . okay." She handed him the address. "Will you be okay if I go home?"

"Please."

"Are you sure you're okay?"

"Yes.

She gave him a quick hug, which he tried his best to return, and then she was gone.

The temperature had dropped considerably since the funeral. Even in a wool sweater and blazer, Michael was chilly. He turned the collar of the jacket up as he climbed the three steps to the unadorned front stoop and rang the doorbell. Hearing nothing, he followed it with a knock. He waited. The glass on the front door was covered with a lace curtain, so he couldn't see inside. The neighborhood was decidedly working class—small one-story houses; a few side porches full of outdoor furniture and hanging baskets. Rocking chairs and painted antique milk cans. People trying to inject a soul into rental property.

He knocked again. He was about to give up when he heard a sound; the door opened and he was confronted by a middle-aged black woman wearing a white uniform and an expression that was anything but welcoming.

"Hi," he said. "I'm looking for an Edna Foley."

"Uh-huh," she said. She folded her arms across her chest and didn't say anything else.

"Does she live here?" he asked.

"Depends on what you're sellin'."

"I'm not selling. My grandfather just passed away and I'm trying to figure out why he's been sending checks to a woman named Edna Foley, at this address."

"Who's your grandfather?"

"Vincent Kinney."

An undefined look replaced the scowl. "Well . . ."

She unlocked the screen door and opened it. She motioned him inside.

"I'm Edna Foley," she said. Michael hoped the surprise didn't show on his face. "I got somethin' on the stove," she explained, and headed to the kitchen.

He followed, assuming that was what she'd intended. He stopped at the doorway of the small kitchen. Edna was at the stove, stirring a pot of something that looked like navy-bean soup. It smelled wonderful, but somehow he had the feeling she wasn't going to invite him to stay for dinner.

"Mr. Kinney died," she said, to herself. She shook her head. "That's the last news I needed to hear."

"I'm not exactly thrilled about it myself."

"Well, I'll work till the end of the month, then it's gonna be your problem what to do with her."

"With who?"

She didn't seem to hear him. "I said from the start, I just do my work and cash my check," she huffed. "I don't wanna be mixed up in nothin' . . ."

"Listen," Michael said, interrupting, "let's start at the beginning. Why was Vincent sending you money?"

"It's my salary, plus some extra to pay the rent. He said it was easier for me to do that than him." She picked up a large saltshaker and shook it liberally into the pot. "And if you think I don't earn it, you stay here a couple of days."

"I don't doubt that you earn it. I just need to know what it's for."

"I cook and clean and do the laundry and buy the groceries. And I do 'bout everything for her. She can't do much for herself anymore."

"Who?" Michael asked, restraining himself.

Edna stopped stirring and looked at him; she seemed to put it together. "You don't know?"

"No. Whatever is going on here, I don't know anything about it."

"Well," she said. She shook her head. "I don't know much myself. Just what Mr. Kinney told me when he hired me. He said he was a friend of the family and he wanted to get her out of that county hospital. I don't blame him. I've seen that hole."

"Does this woman have a name?"

"Rebecca. I usually call her Becky or Miss Becky, but he called her Rebecca. When he talked to me, I mean. He didn't never talk to her. He wouldn't even let me tell her he was payin' her keep. He sent some priest over here to tell her the rent was bein' donated by somebody anonymous, and to this day she thinks I'm a volunteer from the Red Cross. I told her they had a program for shut-ins and—"

"Let me get this straight," Michael said, cutting her off. "This woman—Rebecca—was in a county institution. My grandfather took her out—"

"The priest took her out. Mr. Kinney said she wouldn't accept nothing if she knew it was from him."

"Okay. He had a priest take her out. He hired you and he's been paying you and paying her rent for ten years. Is that it?"

"That's it."

"And Vincent didn't tell you why he was doing this?"

"Just what I told you."

"What about the priest? Do you remember his name?"

"Yeah. It was Father something."

"That's very helpful," Michael said, matching her sarcasm. "Do you remember what he looked like?"

"Yeah. Like a white man in black clothes. It was ten years ago."

"Was he from around here?"

"I don't know. I told you, I just do my job. I don't ask questions."

"And that's absolutely all you know?"

"That's it."

"Then why do I have the feeling there's more?"

Edna bristled. "Who are you? Matlock?"

"I'm the person who's got your paycheck in his back pocket," he said. It got her attention.

"All right."

"What?"

"I didn't hear this from him. She told me this, years ago, back when she used to talk a lot more than she does now. And she didn't know how much she was tellin' me, 'cause she didn't know I knew Mr. Kinney. But if there's one thing I can do in this world, it's put two and two together, you know what I mean?"

Michael nodded. He had no idea what she meant.

"She told me she got pregnant when she was thirteen, and she had to run away from home," Edna continued. "She's been on her own ever since. So I asked about the baby's daddy and she got all upset and said she didn't want to talk about it. So I figured it must have been Mr. Kinney."

WHAT?!

He struggled to keep his composure. "Why?"

"Why else would he be payin' her rent and payin' for me?"

Damned good question.

"Maybe he's a friend of hers. Or a friend of the family, like he said."

"Then why would he tell me not to mention his name to her? And why didn't he never come to visit?"

Two more damned good questions.

No way! Not Vincent!

"Like I said," Edna continued, "she didn't want to talk about the father. She said she didn't even want to think about it."

"How old is she?"

Edna shrugged. "I don't know. Old."

Was Vincent fourteen when it happened? Or was he twenty-five? It makes a hell of a lot of difference! Assuming any of this is true.

It can't be true!

"What happened to the child?" he asked with forced steadiness.

"What do you mean?"

"Is he still alive? Do you know where he is?"

Edna shook her head. "She said he killed hisself, years ago."

Jesus. Did Vincent know? Did he ever meet his son?

Edna returned her attention to the soup. "Now, that's all I know."

Why didn't he tell me? How could he keep it a secret all these years?

"Everything's paid for till the end of the month," she added. "You better call County and warn them she's comin' back."

"No," Michael said, almost automatically. "Vincent wouldn't want that."

Vincent knew he was dying. He knew I'd end up here. Why didn't he tell me?

"Don't worry," he said. "I'll set something up . . ." Robot voice. He couldn't force an inflection. "So you'll keep getting checks for as long as she's alive. A trust fund or something."

She stopped stirring the soup and looked at him.

"You mean it?"

Michael nodded. "Just keep doing what you're doing."

Suddenly Edna saw him in a new light. "Bless your heart! 'Cause I ain't in *no* mood to be job huntin' right now."

Maybe it's not true. This is all based on Edna's math. No one involved has said that it's true.

"Could I talk to her?" he asked, trying not to sound like his life depended on it.

Edna shook her head. "She's takin' her nap, and if I wake her up she'll make my life hell for a month. Besides, it wouldn't do no good. She don't hardly talk to me, and I know she ain't gonna talk to no stranger. And if I told her who you was, she'd throw your tail out and mine right behind it."

"Then maybe I could come back later. You could set it up."

"What am I supposed to say?"

"I'm your Red Cross supervisor and I need to talk to her to make sure you're doing a good job."

"Uh-huh. And why does my Red Cross supervisor need to talk about something that happened sixty-some years ago?"

She was right. It needed work. They exchanged phone numbers and she started to walk him out.

He stopped in the living room, having noticed a crucifix hanging on the wall by the door. Impossible not to notice it; it was at least a foot high. A severe-looking cross, made of some kind of dark wood. It sported a full-color Jesus wearing a crown of vicious black thorns, eyes rolled heavenward in agony, blood everywhere the "artist" could find an excuse to paint blood.

"Is she Catholic?" Michael asked. He already knew the answer. No Protestant on earth would have that thing hanging in the living room.

"Hmph," Edna said, rolling her eyes. "She makes the pope look like a Presbyterian."

"Really?" Michael said, though he didn't know why it would matter.

"I tried to get her to put it in her room," Edna said, making no effort to conceal her distaste, "but she said it had to go by the door. I don't know, maybe they got some rule that it's gotta be by the door. I hang my dust rag over it when I'm in here watching my stories. She'd have a hissy fit if she knew that."

It felt somehow very odd to Michael that Edna didn't even know he was Catholic, much less that he was a priest. He just nodded and let it go, gave her the paycheck, and left. He'd call tomorrow and start working on wearing her down.

Barton was only another fifteen minutes along I-75, and Michael felt obligated to put in an appearance at the church. A priest from the nearest town had been covering for him, but he was starting to feel guilty about not having checked in.

He drove on autopilot and replayed the conversation with Edna, trying to make some sense of it. Too many holes. No place to look for answers, unless he could talk to Rebecca. Even then, Edna didn't make her sound like someone who'd be at all forthcoming. But if he hadn't inherited another thing from Vincent, Michael certainly possessed Vincent's tenacity. He had complete faith in his ability to break through to whatever information remained available.

He reached Barton and pulled into the church's small parking lot. It was empty except for an ancient Buick owned by his ancient volunteer secretary, Annie Poteet. Annie put in four hours a day, five days a week, if her rheumatism wasn't bothering her and she didn't get a better offer.

The fact that she was holding down the fort did not comfort him, since Annie generally caused more problems than she solved.

He opened the door to find the rectory filled with flower arrangements and sympathy cards from parishioners, which caught him off guard. It hadn't dawned on him that they'd have any reaction to his grandfather's death. He stopped to take it in, and to fend off another wave of guilt.

Annie fairly leaped from her chair the minute she saw him and made a tremendous fuss over him, calling him "Father" about fifteen times in three sentences. Then she went to work giving him the rundown on each flower arrangement and planted basket: who'd sent what, which of the town's two florists was responsible for each, and a couple of editorial comments about flowers that did not properly reflect the income brackets of the families from which they'd come. From there, she moved on to other late-breaking developments.

"The toilets are backed up again," she said, in a tone that said *this is the blow that's gonna sink us.* "I called the plumber and he said he's on his way, but you know how they are. He said we're just going to keep having this problem if we don't hook up to the county. I know you think it's too expensive, I'm just repeating what he told me. And Father Hennessey called and said he can take the two morning Masses on Sunday, but not the five o'clock because he's got the five o'clock at his own church—"

Annie continued, rattling off a list of problems that went on for ten minutes. Michael flipped through a stack of mail and hoped she'd take the hint, but she just prattled on. He heard about half of it.

"—and that charismatic group, whatever they call themselves, wants to know when you can come to one of their meetings."

"Twelve years after I'm dead," Michael said, handing her a stack of bills.

Annie stared blankly at him. Decoding sarcasm wasn't in her job description. Michael tried again.

"Tell them I appreciate the invitation and I'd go to war for their right to exist, but I'm wholeheartedly uninterested in participating."

Not knowing what to do with that, Annie mumbled something about needing to water the flowers and left the room.

Michael went upstairs and threw some clothes into what used to be his gym bag. (He could still remember the look he'd gotten from Annie when he'd asked her if there was a racquetball court in Barton.) When he came back downstairs, the plumber was there. He and Annie were intensely bemoaning the rectory's bleak plumbing prognosis. Michael snuck out the back door, unnoticed.

Before heading back to Atlanta, he decided to duck into Tillie's Good Food Coffee Shop. He needed caffeine if he was going to survive the drive home. He went to the takeout counter and ordered a large coffee from the perky redheaded waitress.

He looked around to make sure he wasn't snubbing any parishioners. The place was packed with the usual dinner crowd, but he didn't see anyone from his flock. He was thankful for that. He was completely out of "everything is fine" energy.

The waitress returned to tell him a new pot was brewing and would be ready in a few minutes. He paid her, then sat at the counter, stared at the napkin holder, and resumed his attempt to make some sense out of Edna's story.

Why hadn't Vincent told him? How could he have kept such a huge secret all those years?

The same way you kept your secret from him.

It's not the same thing.

It's pretty damned close.

What else didn't Vincent tell me? Was all that saintliness just an act?

No. He spent all those years tracking her down. That means something, doesn't it? At least he felt guilty.

The irony of it. The two of them suffering in silence, each determined not to disillusion the other. Faking the intimacy they were actually shutting out. It was sad. Sad, and stupid.

He emerged from his reverie to notice someone sitting down on the only empty stool, the one beside him. He glanced over, then wished he hadn't. It was the weird guy. Michael turned away from him without speaking. He'd made that mistake before, and the hermit had decided Michael was trying to pick him up. But then, he'd probably brought that on himself by spending too much time staring at the guy, trying to figure him out. Michael had heard enough coffee shop gossip to know he lived alone in a boardinghouse and worked as a day laborer. Michael had seen him standing in front of Western Auto, looking out of place among the blacks and Hispanics competing for unskilled employment. It wasn't just his ethnicity that made him stand out. There was also the look on his face—a look of sharp, angry intelligence. There was something in that look that called out to Michael. Maybe just the fact that he saw the same look every day, every time he looked in the mirror.

The waitress finally appeared with Michael's coffee. She was gone again before he could ask her for cream. He saw a small pitcher on the counter, an arm's reach in front of the weird guy.

"I'm not making a pass," he said as he leaned over the guy. "I need the cream."

The guy shoved the pitcher over; then, to Michael's surprise, he handed him a spoon.

"Need this?"

"Thanks." Michael was careful not to say anything else, although he did detect a subtle change in the energy. At least the guy wasn't sending the usual death vibes. As had always been the case, Michael felt a strange compulsion to talk to him. Even now, when he knew what a waste of time it was.

Michael stirred his coffee, then handed the spoon back. On impulse, he leaned over and spoke quietly.

"For the record, I'm not gay and I'm not interested in saving you. I don't believe in that."

"Which?"

Michael was amazed. He hadn't expected a response, let alone a response that invited further conversation.

"Saving people," he said, trying to hide his shock.

"You don't think people can be saved?"

"Not by other people."

"Then what's your job?"

"These days, I'm not very sure."

The guy was completely thrown by that and didn't speak. Michael felt a sense of victory far beyond the accomplishment.

Michael picked up his coffee and left. Quickly, while he still had the advantage.

At Vincent's house, he found a note from Barbara lying on the kitchen counter.

Michael—

You got calls from every Jesuit in North America. They all send condolences, they all want you to call them back, a guy named Larry said to tell you that you're a jerk for not calling him. Let me know what you found out about Edna Foley. I'm around if you need me.

Michael crumpled the note and tossed it into the trash. He didn't even look at the phone list. It would still be there in the morning.

He went into the den and poured himself a couple of fingers of Maker's Mark. He stared at the phone for a few minutes, then finally picked it up and dialed Tess's number. The machine answered on the first ring.

"Hi. I'm not here. Leave a message after the beep."

"It's Jesus," he said. "There's some talk going around that you don't think I exist, so I thought I'd call and set the record straight. I've heard a few other things about you, but we can get into all that later."

He started to hang up, then remembered something.

"Thanks for the wreath, it was lovely. I'm about to drink heavily and go to sleep. I'll call you tomorrow. I love you."

He sipped the bourbon and flipped through an issue of *Commonweal* until he realized he couldn't care less about the future of Northern Ireland or the interpretation of the Catholic vote in the '92 election. It was hard to believe he'd ever care about anything like that again. Such musings were a luxury for people to whom life made some degree of sense.

He put the magazine down. He was going to have to find some way to pass the time. He noticed something in the pile of junk that had been accumulating on the coffee table: the tape recorder Vincent had left him. He'd put it there when he came home from the hospital and hadn't thought about it since. He was going to have to listen to it sooner or later, but the thought of hearing Vincent's voice was not inviting. Especially tonight.

But . . .

But what if the tape was a confession, of sorts? Was that how Vincent had decided to tell him about Rebecca? Michael picked up the recorder, rewound the tape, and let it play. He braced himself.

"Well . . . if you're listening to this, it means I've moved on to the Big Time. Pour yourself a stiff drink, if you haven't already."

Michael smiled at that, even though the sound of Vincent's voice stung like an icy wind; it was frail, and groggy with pain medication.

"Michael . . . you've been the joy of my life, and I can leave here knowing I did at least one thing right. It might be the only thing. I'm proud of you. I'm proud of what you've done, and I'm proud of what I know you'll go on to do. God got Himself a priceless ally the day you signed up."

Michael stopped the tape. He took a few deep breaths, then started it again.

"I have to tell you . . . bad things, Michael. Horrible, dreadful things. I didn't want you to ever have to hear this story, but there's no way to avoid it now . . . because . . . things are happening . . . I thought it was all over, but I saw something this morning . . ." A pause. A sigh. *"I don't know how to tell you this . . . I don't want you to hate me, but you should."* Another sigh. *"Let's start with something easy. You're in Barton because of me. I know you're too smart to think that the shortage of priests is so extreme that they have to start pulling Jesuits out of the order, so you must think you're there because Bishop Wilbourne was being a vindictive SOB. Not that he isn't, but that's not the reason. You're there because I wanted you there. I called the archbishop and cashed in a few chips. He talked to Frank Worland and they worked it out. I know how unhappy you are there, and I'm sorry about that. Michael . . . I hope you can find it in your heart to forgive me after you hear this . . ."*

There was a sound in the background. Banging. Rattling. A woman's voice.

"Okay . . . well. My chariot has arrived. I'll have to finish this later. . . ."

There was the sound of Vincent turning off the recorder, and then the tape went dead. Michael stared at it in disbelief. The sounds must have been the nurse coming to take Vincent into the operating room. Michael had stayed with him until about fifteen minutes before that, when Vincent had asked to have some time alone. Michael had thought Vincent wanted to pray; now he realized Vincent had wanted to make the tape.

He rewound the tape and listened to all of it again. The second listening told him no more than the first. He turned it off again, and resisted the urge to fling the machine across the room.

Great. Terrific. Thank you, God. Things weren't quite strange enough.

Whatever Vincent had been about to disclose, it was more than the fact that he'd had an illegitimate son more than sixty years ago. Vincent was not prone to dramatics. If Vincent said the news was dreadful, then the news *was* dreadful. But what? And how the hell was Michael supposed to find out now?

Rebecca was the only person who might have the answers, but how was he going to get them from her? If she wouldn't let Edna talk about Vincent, what would make her agree to talk to Vincent's grandson? He had a strong feeling Rebecca wasn't someone who'd respond to calm reasoning.

He closed his eyes and tried to think. Almost immediately, he saw Edna's face in his mind, heard her voice: "*. . . she makes the pope look like a Presbyterian.*"

Of course!

He opened the closet and started searching for a clean black shirt.

Edna opened the door and stopped midbreath when she got a look at Michael. Her eyes were fixed on the Roman collar. Finally she found her voice.

"Did you rent that?" she asked.

"No."

"You mean . . . that's what you was, when you was here before?"

"Open the door."

She did. She watched him enter, still trying to recover. Probably rehashing their earlier conversation, wondering if she'd used any profanity.

"Is she awake?"

"Yeah. But I ain't supposed to disturb her."

"You don't have to," Michael said. He headed for the hallway. In front of him were two closed doors.

"Which one?" he asked.

"Don't ask me," Edna said. "I didn't even see you come in the house."

She waved both hands at him, dismissing it all, then disappeared into the kitchen.

Michael knocked on the first door. No answer. He moved to the other door and knocked. Still no answer, but he could hear the faint sound of music on the other side. He turned the knob; the door was unlocked. He pushed it open slowly.

He was immediately aware of the flickering light, which came from dozens of votive candles placed around the room. His eyes were drawn to an antique dresser against the back wall, the top of which was covered with more candles and statues of every saint known to man. Above the dresser hung a dime store painting of the Crucifixion in a gold plastic frame. He detected the familiar scent of incense, though he couldn't tell where it was coming from.

Rebecca was sitting in a wheelchair to the left of him, facing an old mahogany vanity table upon which she'd fashioned a shrine to the Blessed Mother that made Lourdes look subtle. She was speaking in a low, steady mumble. He recognized the rhythm before he saw the pearl rosary in her hands. Her eyes were closed.

Michael took a moment to survey the rest of the room. It was too much to take in at once: the antique bed with a canopy and spool posts, which he remembered as having once been in a guest room at Vincent's house; a curio cabinet filled with icons, rosaries, relics, an entire shelf of crucifixes; by the bed, a hideous statue of St. Michael—a good three feet tall, ceramic, painted in vivid jewel tones, with gold wings that glittered in the candlelight. St. Michael was standing with one foot on top of a red-and-black-winged Satan, who was lying on his back and staring up in horror at the saint's lance, which was pointed straight between his horns. All of it was made even creepier by the music, which was coming from a stereo on the dresser. Monks. Gregorian chant.

"Magnificat anima mea Dominum . . ."

Michael closed the door, purposefully making noise. It startled Rebecca; she turned to look at him.

"I knocked," he said. "I guess you didn't hear me."

"You scared me," she said simply. Her voice was soft, childlike.

"I'm sorry."

"Do I know you?" she asked. She looked to be in her late seventies, but her voice sounded like that of a twelve-year-old.

"No, you don't," Michael said. He took a moment to refresh his memory on the lie he'd concocted on the drive down. "I'm Father Riley," he continued, borrowing his mother's maiden name. "I'm new here." *Vague enough to pass muster.* "I was asked to stop by and check in on you."

He smiled and waited, hoping her response would provide some information he could work with. He got his wish.

"Do you work with Father Graham?"

Michael felt his breath catch in his throat. "Tom Graham?" he asked.

"Yes."

Jesus. Graham? Vincent told Tom Graham about this, but he didn't tell me*?*

He took a breath. "Yes, I work with Tom," he said, trying to sound matter-of-fact. "He knew I was going to be in the neighborhood and he asked me to stop by."

"He hasn't been here in so long, I thought he'd forgotten me," she said. Her tone was plaintive.

"He hasn't forgotten you. He's been very busy. And he's slowing down a little, I think. Cutting back. That's why he thought you and I should get to know each other."

She nodded, but was staring at him like she didn't quite believe it. "You look familiar," she said.

"I don't know why," Michael said, suddenly remembering he bore a striking resemblance to photos he'd seen of Vincent as a young man—which was how Rebecca would remember him. "May I sit?" he asked, hoping to distract her.

She nodded. "I'm sorry. I don't get much company. I forget my manners."

Michael sat in a rocking chair next to her. "You like Gregorian chant?" he asked, nodding toward the stereo.

"No," she said.

She laid the rosary down on the dresser; it hit the wood with a brittle staccato rattle that for some reason made Michael shiver. Rebecca didn't seem to notice.

"I play it because the Devil doesn't like it."

Michael didn't flinch. He'd been a parish priest just long enough to have developed a good poker face.

"Really?" he asked, with no patronizing tone whatsoever. Rebecca nodded. "How do you know that?" he asked.

"Jesus told me."

"I see," Michael said. "Has He . . . been here recently?"

"He's always here. You know that."

"Yes, but . . . how did He tell you that?"

"In my head."

"Oh," he said, nodding as if it made perfect sense.

He took a moment to study her face. Her eyes were a clear, pale green; her white hair was tied in a loose bun at the nape of her neck. Even behind the wrinkles and the weariness, it was easy to see that she had once been a beauty.

"You look so familiar," she said. Something in her tone made him feel terribly guilty. Since she wasn't the shrew Edna had made her out to be, Michael wondered how much it could hurt if he leveled with her. Besides, if he told her who he was, it would take a lot less time to get the information he needed.

"Rebecca," he said calmly, as if speaking to a frightened child, "I wasn't honest with you. My name isn't Riley. That was my mother's name." He gave her a second to take that in, then continued. "I'm Father Kinney. Michael Kinney. I'm Vincent Kinney's grandson."

In less than a second, the expression on Rebecca's face changed to pure terror.

"Edna!" she screamed. "Edna!" She reached for a bell that was sitting on the vanity and started to ring it with all her might.

"Wait," Michael said, trying to grab the bell. Rebecca threw it at the door and screamed louder. "Edna!"

"Calm down," Michael said. He put his hand on her shoulder, trying to reassure her.

"Don't touch me!" she screamed. "Don't touch me! Get out of my house!"

"Rebecca, I'm not—"

"Edna!" she screamed again. The door opened and Edna flew in. She hurried to Rebecca.

"What did you do?" she asked, flinging a look at Michael.

"Nothing, she just—

"Get him out of here! Get him out!" Rebecca was completely hysterical, having trouble catching her breath.

"You heard her!" Edna said, loud enough to drown out Rebecca and the music. "Get out!"

Michael wanted to argue, but he was worried about Rebecca. Edna was opening a prescription bottle she'd snatched off the vanity. "Should I call someone?" Michael asked.

"No!" Edna shouted. "Just get out!" Michael didn't move.

"GET OUT!" Rebecca screamed with every ounce of her strength.

With a parting look at Edna, Michael turned and left. He ran to the car, got in, and peeled away.

• • •

It was a little after ten o'clock when he rang the doorbell at the rectory at Sacred Heart. He waited. He heard shuffling, then the door opened. "Michael?" Graham was wearing a navy silk smoking jacket and bifocals and had a paperback in his hand.

"We have to talk," Michael said.

"Of course." Graham nodded, as if this were no unusual request. "Come in."

Michael followed him down the hall to his study. The light was on. Graham sat behind his desk and motioned for Michael to sit on the sofa.

"Have you read this?" Graham asked, holding up the paperback. Michael shook his head without looking at it.

"It's fascinating. A collection of essays from doctors analyzing the Crucifixion. The one I was just reading is by a member of the faculty of the medical school at Duke University. He's talking about this rare phenomenon called hematidrosis, caused when severe anxiety is followed by sudden calm. Evidently the abrupt restriction of the dilated capillaries forces blood into the sweat glands, which results in a person actually sweating blood—"

"Tom," Michael interrupted, "I'm not here to talk about the Crucifixion and sweat glands."

"I'm sorry," Graham said, putting the book down and adopting his best grandfatherly pose. "Of course you aren't. I was presuming you wouldn't mind a brief distraction."

"I already have a hell of a distraction. I just left Rebecca's house." He realized he had no idea what her last name was, but the look on Graham's face told him he didn't need it.

"Oh," Graham said quietly.

"Obviously you've known about this for a long time." Graham didn't reply. "Would you mind telling me what the hell is going on?"

"I don't think I'm the person to answer that question."

"No, but you're the person who's alive." It was an unnecessarily sharp reply, but Michael didn't care.

"And that is very much to the point," Graham said, in a paternal tone.

"Meaning what?"

"Your grandfather is dead. Why dig up his past?"

"What am I supposed to do, keep paying this woman's room and board and ignore the fact that no one will tell me who the hell she is?"

"Michael, if Vincent had wanted you to know, he would have told you."

"He tried to," Michael said. "He was explaining it on a tape that he was making right before the operation, but he didn't get very far before they came to get him."

"Maybe he changed his mind."

"He didn't change his mind! He died! And stop talking to me like I'm a ten-year-old!"

"I'm sorry," Graham said in the same syrupy tone. "I didn't realize I was doing that." Michael counted to ten and waited for visions of homicide to pass.

"Look," he said, forcing himself to stay calm, "Vincent left me this tape with a long, incoherent preamble about some horrible thing he did. I went to try to get the rest of the story from Rebecca, and she became foaming-at-the-mouth hysterical the minute I told her who I was. You're the only person who can tell me what the hell is going on, and I deserve to know!"

Graham waited a moment, letting Michael's anger hang in the air and dissolve into a cold silence. Then he spoke calmly and evenly.

"Michael, I have complete confidence that everything you need to know will be made known to you, but it can't be through me."

The look on Graham's face told Michael the rest. Whatever it was, Vincent had told Graham under the seal of confession.

"Fine," Michael said, his cool voice matching Graham's. He stood up. Graham didn't.

"Then I guess there's no point in asking you why Vincent might have pulled strings to get me to Barton?" Michael asked, unable to resist one final attempt. Graham just stared at him, having already answered the question.

"All right," Michael said. "Good night." He headed for the door in a huff.

"Michael? When was the last time you made a retreat?"

Michael could feel his blood pressure rising. He stared at Graham, unable to think of an answer that wasn't objectively sinful.

"You don't have to answer," Graham continued. "Just something to think about."

Right. My entire life is imploding, my future is a train wreck waiting to happen, the only relative I had in the world just died and left behind some horrible secret that you won't tell me, but a couple of weeks in the woods with the Spiritual Exercises ought to fix me right up.

"Tom," Michael said, relenting, "things have been happening to me . . . like at the funeral, when I couldn't speak. You knew. You said the St. Michael prayer. Who is going to help me if you don't?"

Graham didn't reply. He opened a drawer in his desk, and took something out. He walked over to Michael and handed him a business card.

"Call this person," he said.

"Who is it? The retreat director who could save my misguided life?"

"Just take it and call the number."

Michael took the card and stuffed it in his pocket, though he didn't know why.

He was in his car before he took the card out of his pocket. He would have torn it up on the spot, except he couldn't help wondering who Tom Graham thought might be wily enough to save even Michael.

He turned on the map light, held the card under it, and read it.

CHARLOTTE DUNNING

210 Shorter Avenue

Rome, Georgia 30125

(706) 555-9212

The first surprise was that it was a woman. He'd been convinced Graham had in mind some wizened priest who'd come out of retirement long enough to whip Michael into shape. It was hard to believe that Graham even *knew* a woman.

Below the name, in the left corner, was a job description that left Michael equally puzzled: *Author/Lecturer.* Really? Graham thought a lecture would do it? A lecture on what? His eyes finally registered the word in the right-hand corner: across from Charlotte Dunning's job description was a more specific title. He stared in disbelief. All by itself, chilling in its simplicity:

Demonologist

SEVEN

Michael called Charlotte Dunning shortly after sunrise. She told him she'd been expecting his call for "years," offering no explanation. She said she had a full schedule for the day, but could see him anytime after five p.m. At 5:05 he was sitting in her living room. He hadn't expected Laura Ashley and needlepoint, but Charlotte Dunning's living room was like something from a childhood nightmare. The walls were adorned with an assortment of African tribal masks and other less recognizable but equally sinister items. Grimacing gargoyles peered out from every nook and cranny; tables and shelves displayed everything from statues of winged demons to a collection of genuine Haitian voodoo dolls. Michael expected a Santeria priestess to step out of the shadows at any moment.

Charlotte herself seemed reasonably normal. She was in her

midsixties, with weathered skin and silver-gray hair, wore faded jeans and a Duke sweatshirt. She chain-smoked without apology as she rummaged through an oak filing cabinet on the other side of the room. Michael sat on her sofa with a cup of coffee that would kill a horse and a copy of her latest book, *Hell on Earth: Real-Life Encounters with the Demonic.* Under normal circumstances he would have been interested, but he couldn't concentrate on anything right now except to wonder why Tom had sent him here. (He'd posed that question immediately upon crossing the threshold, but Charlotte had just laughed and said, "Patience, Father. The Baptists tell me we've got at least three more years until the Rapture.")

She closed the file drawer she'd been searching through and opened another one.

"My father's filing system," she said. "Sheesh. He died ten years ago and I have yet to figure it out. From what I can tell, the alphabet was in no way involved." She smiled. "I know I could refile it all, but I seldom need any of it. I keep it around mostly out of sentiment."

"Was your father . . . in the demon business, too?" Michael asked. She laughed.

"You're uncomfortable with the term 'demonologist,' Father?"

"I'm not uncomfortable. I'm just not sure what it means."

"It's not complicated. A person who studies demons."

"Does that mean you believe in demons?"

"If I didn't, I'd be wasting time studying them, wouldn't I?"

"You could study other people's beliefs," he said, trying to sound as condescending as she had.

"That's true," she admitted. "That's how my father became a demonologist, actually. He began his career as an anthropologist. He went all over the world, studying various cultures' concepts of evil, until he started to realize there was a lot more to it than just legends and superstitions."

"What happened to convince him?"

"The same thing that happened to all the near-death scholars. He kept hearing identical stories from people all over the world who'd never laid eyes on each other."

"I had a near-death experience when I was a kid and I didn't see a tunnel or a light or any of that." Which had nothing to do with anything, but Michael felt the need to announce it.

"Did you see anything unusual at all?"

"Yes," he said. If she wanted details, she was going to have to fish for them.

"Did it have a dramatic impact on your life?" she asked.

"Yes."

"Then you saw exactly what you needed to see, didn't you?" He hated her.

She laughed. "Jesus is a very economical guy. He doesn't waste special effects on people who don't need them."

He loved it. The demonologist was going to explain Jesus to him. "Did He tell you that Himself?" he asked.

She nodded. "He makes an appearance in one of my bathroom tiles on the thirteenth of every month."

Michael laughed in spite of himself. Charlotte laughed, too.

"I knew I could win you over," she said.

"One laugh doesn't prove anything. I'm not that easy."

"We'll see."

"So tell me. What are the universal demon stories?"

"Everything you described in your *New Yorker* article. The voice, the presence, the smell, the ESP—that's all textbook stuff."

"Yeah. I've read a few of those textbooks myself."

"Here it is," she said, pulling a folder out of the drawer. "Filed under *G*, for reasons known only to a dead man." She opened the folder and looked at the contents as she made her way to the sofa.

"I know the story very well," she said. "I just wanted to have the details in front of me, in case you needed them."

She sat in an upholstered chair across from him and placed the closed folder in her lap.

"Did you know Vincent?" Michael asked.

She nodded. "I met him through my father, initially. Tom hooked the two of them up when Vincent started having problems. It was strictly professional at first, but they became friends. After my father died, Vincent and I kept in touch. We'd have dinner about once a year."

"What kind of problems was Vincent having?"

"This was eons ago. Before you were born. First it was a series of physical ailments. Nightmares, headaches, anxiety attacks. Then it moved into sensory assaults. Smells, sounds."

"And Tom told him a demon was causing it?"

"No, actually it was Vincent who told Tom what was causing it."

"Why did he think—?"

"We'll get to that," she said. She reached for her cigarettes; took one out, lit it, stuffed the matchbook under the cellophane, and tossed the pack back on the coffee table.

"Tom tells me you and Vincent were very close," she said.

"Yes."

"I can understand that. Vincent was a real character."

Michael nodded, not sure how to take it.

"I feel for you," Charlotte said. "None of this is going to be easy for you to hear."

"I want to know the truth."

Charlotte nodded. She took another drag on the cigarette, then continued.

"A few months after the sounds and smells and whatnot, Vincent started having these . . . spells, I guess you'd say. He'd black out and wake up somewhere else hours later, with no memory of the intervening time. And he wasn't waking up in church, if you get my drift."

"Where was he waking up?"

"Bars—speakeasies, I guess—brothels . . . places like that. He didn't tell anyone. Just kept hoping it would stop. Then one night he woke up in a room with a prostitute who was cowering in a corner with a recently acquired black eye and a bleeding lip, and there was no one there but the two of them." She paused to let him digest this.

"*Vincent?*" Michael asked.

She nodded, tapping ashes into an ashtray. "That was what prompted him to go to Tom."

"No way," Michael said. Still, in the back of his mind he could hear Vincent's voice from the tape. *"I have to tell you . . . bad things . . ."*

"My father and Tom worked with him," Charlotte said. "Blessings. Prayers. Never a full-scale exorcism. He didn't need it. He threw himself into the Church so completely, it was obvious his choice had been made and his mind wasn't going to change. But your father—he was never very religious, you know."

Michael nodded. His father had apparently been an avowed agnostic—a major source of agony for Vincent.

"So," Charlotte went on, "that left the entire family vulnerable, and the demon damn near wiped you out."

"Wait a minute," Michael said. "You think a *demon* was responsible for the Winecoff fire?"

"I can't prove it, obviously. But yes. I do."

"That fire was set by an arsonist."

Charlotte chuckled.

"What?" Michael asked, annoyed.

"You know the Eskimo story?"

"What Eskimo story?"

"It's an old joke. A guy goes up to the priest after Mass and says, 'This God thing is a bunch of crap. I just got back from Alaska and while I was there, I got stranded in a snowstorm, and I got down on my knees and begged God to help me, and He didn't do a damned thing.' The priest says, 'Then how is it that you're standing here talking to me now?' The guy says, 'Well, luckily for me, this Eskimo just happened to be walking by.'"

She stopped to give Michael time to digest it, then continued.

"God works through people. The Devil works through people. We're all soldiers, for one side or the other. Didn't St. Ignatius teach you that?"

"But you're saying all those people died because of Vincent's demon?"

"What do you think? The Devil's gonna make sure he doesn't hurt any innocent bystanders?"

Michael had no answer, but it still sounded insane.

"Tell me something," Charlotte said. "How much do you know about Vincent's childhood?"

"Not a lot."

"What, exactly?"

Michael thought about it. "I know his mother died when he was born. His father was a mortician. Owned a couple of funeral homes. They had a fair amount of money. His father wanted Vincent to take over the business."

She chuckled. "Yeah. You could say that."

"What's funny?"

"Your grandfather grew up in Charleston, South Carolina," she said, ignoring his question.

"Yes."

"Have you ever been there?"

"No."

"Beautiful place. All those antebellum homes and huge old trees with Spanish moss hanging down. So peaceful looking, you'd never suspect the things that go on . . ."

"What do you mean?"

"They don't mention it in the Chamber of Commerce brochures, but Charleston has a long history as a hotbed of Satanism. There are cults there now that go back to the *Mayflower*, and beyond. Transgenerational cults, passed down in families for centuries."

Michael nodded as if he believed her. He had some vague memory of Vincent talking about Charleston and Satanic cults and Freemasonry and other related issues. Vincent had always been paranoid about cults and secret societies—convinced they were highly organized and poised to take over the world. It was a side of Vincent that Michael hadn't liked very much. A pocket of unsophisticated weirdness.

"Do you know anything about Satanists?" she asked.

"I saw *Rosemary's Baby*."

Charlotte didn't smile.

He tried again. "I know as much as the average person, I guess. They've been getting a lot of press lately—"

Charlotte rolled her eyes. "Let me give you a clue," she said. "One way to tell a die-hard Satanist is that you'll never see him on *Oprah* with the word 'Satanist' superimposed on his chest while he chats it up with the housewives."

She stubbed out her latest cigarette, reached for another. She lit it, took a slow drag.

"The word 'Satanist' is misleading to begin with. There are all kinds of Satanists."

Michael shifted in his seat, annoyed by the digression. Charlotte plowed ahead, unfazed.

"You've got your self-styled individual weirdos. You usually hear about them when they get arrested. That 'Night Stalker' character, for example. They make it up as they go along and then blame the Devil.

Not that the Devil isn't involved. But Satanism, like Christianity, was always meant to be a group activity.

"Then you've got the dabblers. People who think it's cute. I've seen more than a few heavy-metal teenagers who've conjured up something they don't know what to do with. I'd be willing to bet that's what happened to your Danny Ingram."

"How did you—"

"*New York Times*. You look better than your picture, by the way."

Thanks?

"Then you've got your pop Satanists," she continued. "The Anton LeVey crowd. They're basically dabblers with enough money for robes. They think they're bad, but they're mostly silly.

"The gang to worry about are the traditional Satanists. You'll rarely hear about them, and very little has been written. But they're out there. They've been out there for a long time. They're very quiet and very careful. They have to be, or they'd all be in jail."

"So you're one of those people who believes they're out there in organized droves, killing people and throwing them into portable incinerators?" Michael asked. Vincent had been one of those people, too. They'd had several fierce arguments about it.

"Michael, I've been studying this stuff for decades. And things are becoming clearer lately. The baby boomers are starting to remember, and a lot of them are starting to talk."

"Yes, about their 'recovered' memories that they've discovered with the help of expensive therapists."

"You asked me to tell you what I know."

"I meant what you know about Vincent."

"I *am* talking about Vincent."

Michael chuckled. "What? Are you going to tell me Vincent was a transgenerational Satanist?"

"Not exactly." Her face didn't change.

"What does that mean?"

"Your great-grandfather, Andrew Kinney, was a transgenerational Satanist. He was the high priest of a Satanic cult."

Michael stared at her. She might as well have said his great-grandfather was a hyena.

"That's absolutely insane."

"Why?"

"For one thing, Andrew Kinney was a militant Catholic. Vincent told me he went to Mass every day of his life."

Charlotte nodded. "They do that. They go out of their way to look like pillars of society. It diverts suspicion. I've even heard of *priests* who were Satan worshipers. The cults love infiltrating the Church, because then they can steal relics and consecrated hosts and defile them in every way imaginable."

Michael didn't know what to say. It was all too incredible to take in.

"Vincent was raised in the cult," Charlotte continued. "He received the standard treatment of children raised in Satanic cults—he was ritually abused, emotionally blackmailed, made to participate in all sorts of atrocities, and then they convinced him he'd be killed if he told anyone. Meanwhile, he was being groomed to take Andrew's place. If it makes you feel any better, he hated it from day one. He went along because he had no choice. He thought they'd kill him if he resisted. He was probably right."

Michael shook his head. "It's just not possible."

"Michael, why are you sitting in my living room?"

"What do you mean?"

"Who sent you to me?"

Michael thought about it. She was right. Tom Graham was not only Vincent's friend. He was also Vincent's confessor. There was nothing about Vincent that Tom wouldn't know, which was why Michael had gone to Tom in the first place.

"Monsignor has been known to embellish the truth," Michael offered.

"I didn't hear the story from Tom, for the same reason you didn't."

Of course not. She had to have heard it from Vincent. *Jesus* . . . He sat back, bracing himself. "What else did Vincent tell you? Is Rebecca a part of all this?"

"Yes."

"How?"

"Rebecca lived in Charleston. I don't know whether Vincent knew her before it all happened or not. They were in such different social classes that I seriously doubt it. She was one of about thirteen children; her parents were sharecroppers. She was apparently very beautiful, but fragile. And she was only thirteen when it happened."

"When *what* happened?"

"Rebecca was abducted by a couple of the men from the cult. They took her into the woods behind Andrew's house. Andrew had built a barn way back in the woods, which was where they held all their rituals. The two men locked her in a room of the barn and waited until around three in the morning, when they all convened for the ritual. There's a specific ceremony for the purpose of consecrating to Satan the heir to the throne—to Andrew's throne, so that meant Vincent. They do all the usual stuff. Black Mass, animal sacrifices, they drink and eat things you don't even want to know about. The rest of the ritual involves a mock wedding between the chosen heir and an unwilling virgin. In this case, Rebecca. Drugs and alcohol are often involved, and between that and the ritual itself it's a very frenzied thing. At the end of which, the marriage is consummated."

It took Michael a moment to recover enough to speak. "You're telling me . . . that Vincent raped a thirteen-year-old girl?"

"Well, he was only seventeen himself, if that makes any difference."

"Hell, no, it doesn't make any difference."

"Then yes. That's what I'm telling you."

Michael looked at her. She was dead serious. She was real. He wasn't going to wake up, and no one was going to tell him this was someone's idea of a sick joke.

He stood up. "I need some air," he said, and made his way out the front door.

After a moment, Charlotte came out onto the porch and sat on the stoop beside him.

"I realize this is horrible for you," she said, "but there's more. You need to know why Tom sent you here."

"I don't care."

"You'd better care, Michael. This is all a lot more personal to you than you realize."

"It feels pretty damned personal."

"I mean, there are consequences for you. More than just having to live with the knowledge of what happened."

He looked at her. She went on.

"Rebecca got pregnant—"

"I figured that much."

"—and Vincent helped her escape the cult and the two of them ran away. Vincent wanted to marry her and try to start a decent life. But she ran away from him the first chance she got. It took him years to find her again. Meanwhile, he married your grandmother, settled down, tried to leave it all behind him. Except he didn't have that luxury. And neither do you."

"He ran away with Rebecca?"

"Yes."

"So he could have run away before that."

"Michael, he was right about the danger involved. These people don't kid around. But there was finally something that scared him more than what they might do to him."

"Which was?"

"He knew what they'd do to the baby when it was born."

He looked at her. "They'd kill it?"

She nodded. "As a sacrifice to Satan. They probably would have made Rebecca kill it, as these things go. And then they would cut it open, take out its heart—"

"Stop," Michael said.

"—chop it up, and eat it."

"Stop."

"The reason Vincent knew they'd do that is he'd seen them do it before. He'd been forced to participate—"

Michael stood up. "I can't hear any more of this—"

"You have to hear it. You have to know that you're in danger."

"What are you talking about?"

"The reason Vincent knew what was happening to him is he'd seen Andrew do it before. He'd seen the consequences."

"Of what?"

"Andrew's cult had a ritual where they would conjure a demon and attach it to someone. The demon's job was to destroy the bloodline."

"Oh, please," Michael said, turning to walk away.

"Michael, think about it. Do you think it's just a coincidence that you ended up involved in the Danny Ingram thing? He was trying to get you then. He wanted you when you were unprepared—before you knew the story. You saved yourself by calling Father Curso in, because as long as he was the exorcist, you were sheltered. But he's not going to give up."

"I have to go," Michael said. She was still saying something to him as he made his way to his car, but he didn't hear her. He refused to hear another word.

He tried to take a shortcut and ended up lost on a country road that might have worked had he wanted to get to Atlanta by way of Egypt.

The fuel tank and his nerves were both on empty by the time he finally saw the light of a two-pump gas station and convenience store.

When he got out to pump gas, he could hear the sound of the interstate, so he figured he should be able to find it without compromising his manhood and asking for directions. He listened to the ticking of the pump and tried to calm down.

Why was he having such a hard time believing what was happening to him? He was a priest, for God's sake; it wasn't like the Devil was a new concept. And as for Andrew Kinney and his cult—look at Nazi Germany. If people could throw women and children into gas chambers and then skin them and use their skin for lampshades, why was it unthinkable that they'd kill a baby and chop up its heart and eat it? People were capable of doing inconceivably despicable things, and in an organized and ritualized manner.

But Vincent . . . not Vincent, not even Vincent as a teenager . . .

He heard a noise and looked up to see a lanky kid in a blue uniform with RUSTY stitched on the pocket. He had matching coffee and tobacco stains down the front of the shirt and looked like he hadn't drawn a breath through his nose since the third grade.

"Need me to check under the hood?" he asked.

"I've got it, thanks."

The kid looked disappointed but didn't argue. Didn't leave, either. He stood there, staring at Michael.

"You're Ricky Reynolds's cousin, ain't you?"

"No."

"I know you from somewhere."

"I don't think so."

"You kin to any of them Reynolds?"

"No."

"You know who I'm talkin' about?"

"Yeah," Michael lied. "But I'm not related to them."

"Oh."

"Listen, am I anywhere close to I-Seventy-Five?"

The kid grinned like he'd just laid down a royal flush. "Depends on what you call close, I reckon."

A comedian. Thanks, God.

"Are you kin to Jackie Brumfield?" the kid asked.

"No," Michael said, starting to get testy. "I'm not kin to anyone left on the planet."

"I must have you mixed up with somebody else, then."

"Evidently."

Now crawl back into the swamp and leave me alone.

The kid leaned toward Michael and spoke in a voice that was suddenly lower, deeper than before.

"People don't always turn out to be who they look like they are, right?"

"I don't know."

The kid grinned. "I think you know," he said. "I think you know 'bout as well as anybody."

He gave a rattling chuckle and walked away.

It landed on Michael like someone had spit on him from a nearby window. For a moment, he was too stunned to move. Then he moved fast. Shoving the gas nozzle back into its niche in the pump, he took off after the kid. He'd be damned if he was going to let another of these encounters go unchallenged. The kid was walking fast now. Michael quickened his pace, but so did the kid, who reached the men's room and disappeared inside. A few steps later, Michael grabbed the doorknob and found it locked. He pounded on the door with his fist. "Open this door! Now!"

An elderly attendant was passing by, staring at Michael.

"You need the key?" he asked.

Michael looked up. "Yes. Thank you."

The old man shuffled over, reached into his pocket, and came out with a key attached to a lime-green rabbit's foot. He handed it to Michael.

"Just bring it inside when you're done."

Michael nodded, took the key, gave the old man a few seconds to shuffle off, then unlocked the door and pushed it open.

The room was dark. He found the light switch and turned it on. A single small room. A toilet. A sink. An empty towel dispenser. No window. No other door. No Rusty.

With the most normal stance he could fake, Michael returned the key to the old man and was informed there was no employee by the name of Rusty or fitting his description. The only people working were the old man and his son, who was in his midforties. They had both watched Michael fill his tank. Alone.

The minute he got home, Michael called Bob Curso. He got his machine.

"Bob, it's Michael Kinney . . ."

There was a loud snap, followed by a lot of static. "I have a bad connection," Michael said. "I don't know if you can hear." The static got worse. "Damn," Michael said. He hung up and tried again. Bob's outgoing message was perfectly clear, but as soon as Michael started to speak, the static returned. "Bob, I need to talk to you," he said. "Call me." He left Vincent's number, but seriously doubted Bob would be able to understand it over all the noise. Michael put his face in his hands. He couldn't think.

Danny.

A voice in his head. Not his own.

What do you mean, Danny?

The voice was silent. Michael thought about it. There were a couple of things he'd like to ask Danny, but he knew from experience that getting Danny on the phone required something just short of an act of

Congress. He felt compelled, just the same. At least it would give him the illusion that he was doing something. He hunted for the number, found it, dialed. He talked to three Officer Somebodys, a Coordinating Officer Somebody, the prison chaplain, and, finally, the assistant warden, who assured him that Inmate Ingram would be allowed to return Michael's call within the hour. Ten minutes later, the phone rang.

They exchanged amenities for a couple of minutes, then Michael's tone shifted.

"Listen, Danny. I need your help with something."

"Sure, anything."

"Okay." Michael sighed, not sure how to proceed. "When this all started . . . you know, the way you described it to me . . . when you first began to hear the voice."

"Yeah?"

"Did you . . . was there anything before that? Something that might have triggered it?"

"What do you mean?"

"Well, you know—when I was reading about all this stuff, during the trial, I remember reading about how . . . how demons attach themselves to people."

There. He'd voiced the preposterous.

"Uh-huh." Danny's tone was as flat as if he were responding to a perfectly normal statement. But then, Michael reminded himself, Danny would be the last person to laugh.

"I need to know if there was anything you did. Anything that might have brought this thing on."

Silence on the other end. Michael had never asked before, because it wouldn't have made any difference. He wasn't sure what difference it made now, except to give credence to Charlotte's story.

"Danny?" Michael prompted.

"Yeah?"

"I'm not asking because of anything that has to do with you."

"Then what's it got to do with?"

"I'll tell you all about it when I understand it better. Just tell me, was there anything? Ouija board? Séance?"

"Okay, there was something." Danny's voice was softer.

"What?"

A pause, then: "This friend of mine had this book. He bought it at some weird bookstore in Chelsea. Anyway, it had these—spells—you know, like black magic—"

"Rituals?"

"Yeah. Like devil worship." Danny didn't go on.

"And?"

"A bunch of us . . . four guys, counting me, and a couple of girls . . . we got together one night at midnight and, you know, acted out one of the rituals. It was just supposed to be a joke, though. I mean, we were giggling all through it."

Rituals. Again. "How soon after that did you start to hear the voice?"

"Pretty soon. A couple of days."

Rituals as a doorway. That made some sort of sense. If there was one thing on earth he knew he believed in, it was the power of ritual. He didn't understand the mechanics, but he'd felt it, time and again. And if one person could conjure Jesus, what would stop another from conjuring Satan? But this wasn't a Satanic high priest. This was a bunch of kids playing around.

"Why didn't any of this come up at the trial?" Michael asked, more to fill in the dead space than because it mattered.

Danny sighed. "I don't know. I just . . . I knew I wasn't going to get off anyway, and I didn't want to sound so . . . stupid. Besides, I might have gotten the rest of them in trouble."

The rest of them. What about the rest of them?

"Here's what I don't understand, though," Danny went on. "If that's what caused it, how come nothing happened to anybody else?"

The answer shot through Michael.

Because Danny was the one with a connection to me.

"You know?" Danny's voice sounded cloudy.

Michael didn't answer.

"Father?"

"Yeah. I'm here." Michael fought to regain his composure. "Okay. There's just one more thing. When you were hearing this voice . . . and it was telling you things . . ."

"Yeah?"

"Did the voice ever say anything about me? Specifically?" A long pause. Michael could feel all his muscles tighten.

"It didn't say your name or anything. But I think maybe."

The room was suddenly filled with an odor. Putrid. Like someone had just smashed a carton of rotten eggs. Michael covered the phone receiver to stifle his gagging. He looked around, though he already knew he wouldn't see anything.

"Danny . . ." He forced himself to remain calm. "I need to know." Michael could feel the air bearing down on him, just like before. He shoved a window open, but it didn't help.

"I think it told me not to hurt you."

Michael had his nose against the window screen, fighting for fresh air.

"Not to hurt me?" That was as far as possible from what he'd expected.

"It said, 'Don't ever hurt the priest.'"

"That doesn't make any sense," Michael said, more to himself than to Danny.

"Well, then it said something else. It said, 'He's mine.'"

The line went dead. The message delivered, the smell began to fade.

EIGHT

He'd gone to bed around two a.m. He knew he wouldn't be able to sleep, but he was so exhausted he needed to at least lie down. He stared at the ceiling and took stock.

Okay. There's a demon after me. It sounds insane, but that doesn't change the fact that it's also true. "His body isn't in the tomb" probably sounded pretty insane to the first person who heard it, too.

Unless no one ever heard it . . .

Shut up!!

No one ever heard it . . . No one ever said it!

"Stop!" he said out loud, embarrassing himself. He rolled over and went back to reliving the conversation with Charlotte, trying to fit all the insanity into some sort of context. He wondered if this information might explain a lot of things that had always puzzled him—chiefly, the fact that he'd always felt like a bad person without knowing why. He'd always felt that something was fundamentally wrong with him. At the same time, he'd always liked himself, which made him feel guilty for liking a bad person.

What was the truth? Never mind what had been summoned and attached to him; what was in his blood? What was there in Andrew that had made him such a vile person? Whatever it was, had any of it filtered down to Michael? Did that explain his restlessness? His anger? His pervasive sense of disquiet? Did it explain his inability to function from a place of serenity and kindness and charity? His tendency to put up walls, even with the people he loved?

In a very real way, Vincent had been Michael's spiritual lifeline. Michael had told himself there was enough goodness in Vincent for both of them. He'd told himself that, ultimately, the blood that ran in his veins was Vincent's, so all the negativity must be superficial garbage that he'd eventually work his way out from under. Now he realized that Vincent's blood was not going to save him. He couldn't even be sure he'd ever known Vincent. Hell, for all Michael knew, Vincent could have still been meeting in the woods with fellow Satan worshipers, doing God only knew what horrible things. The exterior Vincent could have been a façade, just like Andrew Kinney, the friendly town mortician and devout Catholic. Or maybe Vincent had just hidden in the Church, building a fortress out of icons and rituals and charitable works. Maybe his goodness had been nothing more than a torch to ward off the circling wolves.

The fire. Was Charlotte right about the fire? He knew Vincent had harbored a lot of guilt about it, but he'd always thought it was because it had been Vincent's idea for them to stay at the hotel. Had Vincent known he was responsible in an even more direct way? Had there been a supernatural component to the fire? Michael remembered quotes from arson investigators he'd read in the newspaper clippings: "*. . . the flammable materials in the hallway (carpet, wainscoting, a folding mattress left* *out on the third floor) absolutely would not account for the effects produced by this fire . . . the speed with which the blaze spread has baffled officials."* Maybe the fire had spread unnaturally because it was an unnatural fire. Because it had supernatural help.

Michael continued to pummel himself with unanswerable questions until finally, sometime in the hours before dawn, he fell into a haunted sleep.

He dreamed he was running through a thick forest. Briars were scratching his arms, his legs, his face. He knew he was being chased by something odious, and that he had to escape it at all costs.

He saw a cave up ahead and ran into it, seeking shelter and a place to rest. He found neither. Inside the cave were sinister-looking men in black robes, standing in a circle around a small fire. The leader looked at Michael and his mouth formed a smile, but it was devoid of any warmth or humanity.

"Welcome home," he said.

Another man, who'd had his back to Michael, turned around. It was Vincent. He smiled, too, but his eyes were cold and dead.

"I told them you'd be here," he said.

Michael opened his mouth to scream, but no sound came out. The men all started to howl with laughter. Michael turned and ran out of the cave. He ran back through the forest, stumbling and picking himself up over and over. Ahead he could see a light. It was a brilliant green. He couldn't tell what it was, but he felt compelled to run to it anyway. By the time he got close, he was out of breath. He collapsed into the light. When he was able to look up, he found himself in a large meadow. The soft spring grass was dotted with orange and yellow poppies.

A lone Georgia pine stood in the middle of the field. There was a guy leaning against the tree. He was wearing jeans, a flannel shirt, and work boots. His shoulder-length hair was a reddish gold and slightly windblown. His eyes were a strange gray-blue, startlingly clear, and fixed on Michael in a gaze that was unsettling in its intensity. There was something beyond ethereal about him. A sense of calm, and a transcendent sadness his slight smile couldn't mask.

"Hi," he said.

"Do I know you?" Michael asked.

The smile turned into a bemused expression. "That's a tough call," he said.

Michael searched his memory, but nothing came to him, even though the face in front of him was vaguely familiar.

"Michael . . ." the guy said.

And then Michael knew. He couldn't breathe. He opened his mouth to speak, but nothing would come out.

"All right," Michael said. He took a breath, then unleashed the mental floodwaters: "All right. If it's really you, then I don't know how long you'll be here and I don't want to waste the time being paralyzed by the scope of it . . . I have too many questions."

"What questions?"

"I don't know where to start."

"Start with one."

Michael racked his brain. Which one? Is this real? Is this more than a dream?

"Yes."

"Are you . . . here . . . because of what is happening to me?"

"Yes."

"What do I have to do to make it stop?"

No answer this time. The guy just stared into Michael's eyes, as if that would communicate some message. Michael tried again.

"I need help. I'm lost."

"You shouldn't be."

Suddenly he was gone, fading like a whisper. Michael felt a cool breeze blow by his face. And then nothing.

He woke, trembling. Aching. Smothering in an unbearable sense of loss.

He lay awake for hours, waiting for the sun to come up. Trying desperately, without success, to remember the guy's face. His steady voice. His strange demeanor. The look in his eyes. Warm, but demanding as hell. A thousand times more frightening than anything in the dark forest.

When he went down to breakfast, Barbara was sitting at the table, reading the paper.

"Good morning," she said, glancing up at him. "You look like hell."

"Good. That's what I was going for."

"Did you sleep at all?"

"Yes."

"You don't look like it."

Well, maybe that's because my great-grandfather was a Satan worshiper and Vincent was a teenage Satanic ritual rapist; there's a demon with a vendetta against me; and I spent five minutes in a dream with Jesus, got scolded, and woke up wanting to throw myself off a cliff!

"What are we doing today?" he asked, hoping to change the subject.

"This morning we're going through the rest of the stuff in Vincent's office. I want to get it all sorted before we call Saint Vincent de Paul to pick it up. And for the record, I look a lot better than you do early in the morning."

"That's the beauty of my life. I don't have to look good for anyone early in the morning." He got a mug out of the cabinet and headed for the coffeepot. "Tell me this isn't some weird esoteric decaffeinated crap."

"It's high octane. It'll keep you going until at least lunchtime."

He filled the mug with as much coffee as it would hold. He looked out the window. The sky was a pale pewter and he could hear thunder rumbling in the distance. It had been storming off and on all week. Even one thunderstorm would have been strange for this time of year.

Barbara suddenly put the paper down and looked at him. "Michael, are you not sleeping because of Vincent, or is it more than that?"

"Isn't that enough?

"It would be. But whatever is radiating from you feels like more than grief."

He didn't respond, hoping she'd let it go. She didn't.

"Who is Tess?"

Oh, crap.

"What?"

"Someone named Tess sent a very nice wreath. I know everyone in Vincent's life, and there is no Tess."

He sighed. "Would you also like to know when I stopped beating my wife?"

"Michael, is there a woman in New York?"

"There are a lot of women in New York."

"Yes, but how many of them are you sleeping with?"

Michael almost dropped his coffee mug. "Barbara!"

"Well, at least I got your attention."

"Jesus." Michael put his coffee down on the counter and tried to imagine the path of least resistance.

"If you're trying to figure out how to get out of this," she said, "I offer the suggestion that the truth is a wonderful fallback position."

"All right." He took a breath, then: "Yes. There is a woman in New York." It hardly seemed to matter, at this point, what she or anyone else thought of him.

Barbara looked shocked. "Oh, my God. Really?"

"What do you mean 'really'? You knew it."

"I was hoping you would say she was your secretary and calm me down."

He could see the disappointment in her face and it pained him.

"We're in the process of breaking up," he offered. "If that makes you feel any better."

"Really?"

"I think so," he said, unable to lie.

Barbara gave it a respectful nanosecond of silence, then lobbed the next round.

"Was she the first?"

"Second. But the other was before first vows, so she doesn't count."

"That's a relief, I guess."

"Barbara, I'm not cavalier about my vows. I should have seen this coming and avoided it, but I didn't."

"What about God?"

"What about Him?"

"You two aren't breaking up, are you?"

He shook his head. "I don't know. Maybe we'll just agree to see other people."

Barbara nodded and tried to smile. She wiped a tear.

"I'm sorry," he said.

"Me too," she managed to whisper.

An hour later he stood in the living room and wondered what to do with himself. He didn't want to spend the morning sorting through Vincent's possessions. That had been hard enough before he'd known about Vincent's past. Now he couldn't even stand the thought of going into Vincent's study. He couldn't think of anywhere he *could* stand the thought of being right now.

Barbara wandered in, carrying the newspaper and still reading it. She had calmed down from discovering his fall from grace, but her voice was slightly cold as she addressed him. There was a wall between them now.

"Michael, do you know a guy in Barton named Jackson Landry?"

Michael shook his head. "Why?"

"You really should read this."

"What?"

"It's an article about this weird family. It's just bizarre. These parents had four sons. One drowned under suspicious circumstances. One was a psycho who opened fire on a Christmas Eve service and killed five people. He was eventually executed. The youngest son became a successful novelist; then, last week, for no known reason, he robbed a liquor store and killed the clerk, then threw himself out a fifteenth-story window. And the parents both committed suicide. The father blew his brains out about a year after the first son died, and the mother slit her wrists on the anniversary of the other son's execution."

Michael didn't know how to respond, since he had only heard about every third word. He sipped coffee and pretended to be contemplating it.

"This Jackson Landry is the oldest son, who seems to have remained unscathed so far. Wonder what his secret is." She shook her head. "I can't believe you haven't heard of these people. I'd think they'd be the talk of the town."

"They might be. I'm not exactly up on the local gossip."

"Oh, wow," she said, still reading. "You're going to love this. The guy who wrote this story interviewed the mother right after her son's Christmas Eve killing spree. She told him the family had a curse on it and was being haunted by a demon."

"Really?"

"She said the reason it happened on Christmas Eve was that Satan was pissed off about people celebrating Jesus's birthday."

"Are you serious?" he asked. Now she had his attention.

"Well, she didn't say 'pissed off.' She said 'angry.'"

"Where did she come up with this theory?"

"A fortune-teller told her she had, quote, 'inherited a horrible debt.' And she also had a recurring dream that she was surrounded by a bunch of men in long black robes and the leader told her he had conjured a demon and attached it to her husband's bloodline and they were all going to die. I love how she puts it off on the husband—"

Michael took the paper out of Barbara's hands.

"Hey, I wasn't finished—"

"Why is this story being printed now?" he asked.

"Because the novelist-son-who-shot-the-liquor-store-cashier-and-then-jumped-out-a-window thing just happened a few days ago. I remember seeing a little blurb about it. 'Georgia-Born Novelist Robs Liquor Store, Kills Self.' It didn't seem like much of—"

"When did you see that?"

"I don't know. A few days ago."

"Before Vincent died?"

She thought about it. "Oh, yeah. It was the *day* Vincent died. I was sitting here reading the paper and waiting for you to call."

Michael heard Vincent's voice on the tape: "*. . . I saw something this morning. . .*" And Vincent had been reading the paper when Michael had arrived at the hospital that morning. Was it the story of the novelist he'd seen? Was it just that he was obsessed with another demon-infested family? Possibly. But on the tape, he'd made it sound like whatever he'd seen was connected to the horrible thing he'd done. How could Vincent have had any connection to the novelist-turned-murderer and the family from hell?

"Oh, my God," Michael said as the answer dawned on him.

"What?"

Michael went to the kitchen, found the piece of paper with Edna Foley's phone number, picked up the phone, and dialed. Barbara was not far behind.

"Who are you calling?" she asked.

"In a minute," he said, waving her off. The phone rang twice, then Edna picked it up. "Hello?"

"Edna, it's Father Kinney. I'm sorry to bother you. I need to know Rebecca's last name."

Edna snorted. "You got a lot of nerve calling here. She been sick ever since you left. They put her in the hospital last night, said she's in a coma. And if she dies, I consider you owe me a job."

"If you want to keep the one you have, you'd better tell me her name."

"It's Landry," Edna said. "L-A-N—"

"I know how it's spelled," he said quietly.

Jesus God, I was right.

"Edna, do you know the name of the baby?"

"What baby?"

"Rebecca's baby. The one you told me about."

"Why are you asking me?"

Michael decided to take a shot. "Because I read the article."

Silence on the other end of the phone. Beside him, Barbara was whispering.

"You found Edna Foley? Why didn't you tell me? Who is she?"

Michael ignored Barbara and continued to drill Edna. "The father of the Landry family was Rebecca's son, wasn't he?"

Still no answer.

"Wasn't he, Edna?" Michael pressed.

"I don't have to answer that."

You just did.

He hung up. "Oh, my God," he said again.

"Michael, would you please tell me what is going on?" Barbara asked.

Vincent must have wanted me in Barton because this Jackson Landry was there. His last living grandson from the demonic side of the family. The only one who hasn't spilled any blood. Yet.

"Michael?" Barbara asked again.

"What the hell did he think I could do?" Michael asked out loud.

"What did *who* think?"

"Barbara, just . . . I can't," he said. He handed the newspaper back to her and went back to his room. His mind was racing, pasting the story together.

Vincent's illegitimate son, conceived during a Black Mass, became the father of the family from hell . . . He had four sons of his own . . . two killed themselves, one was executed . . . Two sons took other people's lives . . . One son left . . . Vincent's other grandson, what a thought . . . Only the two of us left . . . the two of us and the demon.

Outside it had begun to rain hard. Hail was beating on the window like the cracking of hundreds of tiny whips. A loud clap of thunder made the house shudder; Michael shuddered with it.

The smell returned. Stronger than before. Michael gagged so hard he had to hold on to the bedpost. With his free hand, he fished a handkerchief out of the duffel bag and held it to his nose. It helped enough that he could draw small breaths.

"Get . . . out of . . . here," he managed to say.

I was invited.

The bum's voice. Danny's demon voice. Michael couldn't tell whether it was in his head or actually in the room.

"I . . . command . . . you . . ."

Oh, do you?

Michael's sides were aching from trying to breathe in the foul air. He searched the duffel bag for a crucifix. And then, as suddenly as it had appeared, the smell was gone. The voice was gone. Even the sound of the hail was gone. The room was still.

Michael dropped to his knees, leaned his arms on the bed.

Jesus. I can't do this. He's right. *I can't fight him. And You know that. What do You expect me to do?*

Silence.

Look, if this is about Good and Evil, You'd better find someone else for this side of the fence.

Silence.

What do you WANT?

Silence.

Stone-cold, infuriating, silence.

BOOK THREE

They are what saves the world: who choose to grow

Thin to a starting point beyond this squalor.

—Mary Oliver, "On Winter's Margin"

THE CHOICE

ONE

"What are you in such a funk about?" Randa's mother asked. Randa had lost count of how many times Jane had asked some version of that question since she'd arrived. Three times since they'd sat down to dinner, and this was her third night home. But Jane would keep asking until Randa gave her an answer she could sink her fangs into.

"I told you, Mom. I'm just tired."

"Well, if you're gonna fly across the country to sit and mope, I don't need any more surprises."

Don't worry.

Randa speared a broccoli floret and let most of the Velveeta drip off before she put it in her mouth.

"You oughta be on your knees, thanking God you're still alive," Jane said.

What is this *about?*

"You think I don't read the papers?" Jane asked, her charm bracelet clinking against the Corelle ware. "I know you think I'm dumb, but I do read the papers."

"Mom, I don't think you're dumb."

"I read what happened to your boyfriend."

Oh, hell.

There must have been something in the *Atlanta Constitution* about Cam, Randa realized. Why hadn't she thought of that? Because apparently she was incapable of rational thought these days. If she'd thought, she'd still be in LA. If she'd thought, she wouldn't have spent the night with yet another Landry. If she'd thought, she wouldn't have been surprised to wake up and discover he'd walked out on her. And if she'd thought, she certainly wouldn't have decided that the cure for her latest broken heart was to come running to a woman who made her want to throw herself into a concrete mixer just to get some relief.

"I *told* you," Jane said. "Back when you were telling me how wonderful he was and he wasn't like the rest of his family. I said, 'Randa, he's trash. You can dress trash up and put perfume on it and give it all the money in the world, it's still gonna be trash.'"

"Well, Mom, he's dead now, so you can relax."

"And so is that poor store clerk. You think he didn't have a family that loved him? Why don't you feel sorry for *his* family, if you want to feel sorry for somebody's family?"

"What makes you think I don't?"

"Hmph."

Randa got up and headed for her room. The only thing that had changed since high school was that her father wasn't there to yell at the two of them about their inability to get along.

"You can get mad at me all you want," Jane called behind her.

Randa sat on her bed and stared at her suitcase. She'd left everything packed in case she needed to flee at a moment's notice. She could even leave right now. She wondered if the relief of leaving would be worth hearing about it for the rest of her life and decided probably not. And besides, it wasn't like she had somewhere to go.

She had two choices, as she saw them. She could get on a plane and go back to LA, return to her lousy job (assuming Keith hadn't successfully lobbied to have her fired by now), and when people asked where she'd been, she could say she'd gone to Santa Barbara for a few days of rest. And that would be the end of the entire sorry Landry saga. Three or four or twenty years from now, she might even stop feeling like a fool.

Or she could go back to Barton. She could knock on his door and demand an explanation. If she sounded angry enough, her groveling might even disguise itself as self-righteous indignation—a display of strength and courage. And he might offer an explanation that resembled the truth. That way, when she went home to get on with her life, she'd have one more piece of the puzzle with which to torment herself.

One scenario sounded about as appealing as the other.

"Randa?" Jane knocked on the door. "You're missing a good movie." Randa didn't answer, hoping Jane would think she was asleep. "It's a true story about that teacher who got fired for hanging the Ten Commandments in her classroom." Well, good. Now she could spend a relaxing evening arguing with Jane about the Establishment Clause.

"No, thanks. I have a headache."

"Well, you might as well have it out here. At least you won't be bored. You know who plays in it? That woman who played on that show you used to like . . ."

Randa relented, since she knew from prior experience that resistance was futile. She lay on the sofa and pretended to watch the movie while Jane provided political color commentary. (*"Pretty soon the government's gonna make it so you can't even pray in church."*)

"Mom?" Randa asked, her voice rising over a tampon commercial, "why do you believe in God?"

"What kind of a question is that?"

A direct one. The unpardonable sin . . .

"I just wondered."

"Well . . . because I've read the Bible," Jane said, as if nothing could be simpler or more obvious.

"How do you know it's true?" Randa asked.

"Because," Jane said firmly, "I just do." She furrowed her eyebrows and fixed her gaze on the television screen.

"That's not a reason," Randa said.

"Randa, don't you come into my house with your California atheist shit."

"I just asked a question."

"Well, I gave you my answer and you didn't like it."

Randa opened her mouth to speak again; she was cut off by a harsh "Shhhh!" Jane picked up the remote control and turned the volume up a couple of notches.

Randa set her alarm clock for five a.m. When it rang, she got up, wrote a note to Jane saying she'd decided to take an earlier flight, and drove off into the dark. She headed for the airport, but when she got to the exit, she could not make herself turn. She kept driving. She stopped in McDonough for gas and in Griffin for a peach milk shake. Neither pause weakened her resolve, now that it had a life of its own. It was a little past nine o'clock when she drove into Barton.

She didn't give herself time to think about what she was doing. She parked in front of the boardinghouse, walked determinedly straight to his door, and knocked. She prayed to anyone who might be listening that he was there. She didn't want to have this confrontation at Tillie's—though why she cared what the good citizens of Barton thought about her was beyond her comprehension.

The door opened and Jack stared at her; his eyes had a glazed look and she wondered if he was on something. He didn't speak, forcing her to take the offensive.

"What did you think?" she asked. "That I'd wake up, see you were gone, and just nonchalantly hop a plane back to LA?"

"You should have."

His voice was different now, in some way she couldn't pinpoint. He turned and walked away, leaving her at the door. She followed.

Everything in the formerly immaculate apartment was askew. The air was stale and smelled of cigarettes and cheap whiskey. There were dirty clothes lying across the unmade bed. His nice clothes from the Ritz-Carlton night were thrown haphazardly across the back of the sofa.

Jack looked worse than the apartment. He obviously hadn't shaved since she'd last seen him. His eyes were bloodshot. He was wearing khaki pants and a denim shirt, the latter unbuttoned and both as wrinkled as if he'd slept in them. Which couldn't be true, since he looked like he hadn't slept in a decade.

He picked up a pack of cigarettes from the desk, lit one, blew smoke toward the kitchen.

"Jack, the James Dean act is cute, but can we cut the—"

"Look, you knew who I was!" It was loud. Randa felt herself jump. "I didn't want to go in the first place!" he said. "It was your brainstorm!"

"Well, that night you seemed to think it was a good brainstorm," Randa offered feebly, trying to maintain what little composure she still possessed.

"Yeah? So what? When have you ever met a guy who complained about getting laid? You think that proves something? Is that your big accomplishment?"

Randa felt as if someone were scraping her throat with hot sandpaper. She didn't even try to speak.

He walked into the kitchen and dumped ashes in the sink. She watched and wondered what to do. He came back, looking no less angry. Stood and stared at her. She searched his eyes for any sign of compassion and found none.

"Randa, go home," he said. "You're all out of brothers." As soon as she could force her legs to move, she turned and left. He was standing in the same spot when she slammed the door.

TWO

Michael and Barbara had finished the first round of cleaning out Vincent's house by midafternoon. Barbara waited for the St. Vincent de Paul truck while Michael drove the forty-five minutes to the Jesuit villa with a large box of books that Vincent had asked be donated to the library there. Michael had a key to the villa and spent much of the way semi-praying he'd be able to drop them off without encountering Gabe Novak.

Michael turned down the long driveway, which was lined with enormous oak trees on either side, planted when the driveway was just a gravel-strewn path of red clay traveled only by horse and carriage. The villa itself was a beautiful Greek Revival antebellum plantation house, with large white columns and a porch surrounded by crape myrtle. Due north of Atlanta, it sat on an eleven-acre lake just off the Etowah River basin. It had been in shambles when Vincent had bought it with the intention of restoring it and donating it to the Society of Jesus to use as a villa, so that Michael and other Jesuits within driving distance could have it as a getaway. Vincent had done his usual immaculate job, but Michael had transferred to the New York province to take the job at the magazine, and hadn't seen the place in years.

He saw only one other car when he parked out front. The villa tended to stay empty during the weekdays, which was fine with Michael. He unlocked the door and stepped inside. The library was immediately on the left, an oak-paneled room with large curtained windows and three walls of bookshelves, floor to ceiling. On a coffee table in front of the sofa, a chess board had been set up. Someone was in the middle of a game. Had it been Gabe and Vincent?

Michael took the box of books to a window seat and set it down. He was debating leaving Gabe a note when, from behind him, a voice said, "Hi." He turned to find Gabe coming through the library door. Dressed in clerics, of course. Michael wondered if the guy *slept* in clerics.

"Oh. Hi. I didn't know you were here. I'm Michael Kinney; I'm Vincent Kinney's grandson."

Gabe nodded and extended his hand. "Gabe Novak."

"Yes, I know. I brought the books that Vincent wanted to donate to the library. I'm told he discussed it with you."

Gabe nodded. "I looked for you at the wake, but apparently you'd left for an emergency," he said. "I'm very sorry for your loss."

"I understand it was your loss, too," Michael said, and hoped there was no edge in his voice.

Gabe nodded. "I was very fortunate to spend time with him the last few months. He was one of a kind."

Michael decided to let that go. He nodded and refrained from comment, other than to tell Gabe he'd better be going. To his surprise and dismay, Gabe asked if he'd like to stay for a drink. Michael could think of little he would less rather do, and couldn't imagine why Gabe had offered, but he didn't want to seem like a jerk, so he accepted. Gabe grabbed a couple of glasses and a bottle of Maker's Mark and motioned for Michael to follow him out to the veranda. Michael tried to figure out how his affection for that particular spirit might have found its way into one of Vincent and Gabe's conversations. Maybe "Oh, you like bourbon? That might be the only thing that you and my grandson have in common."

"I'm sorry about missing the funeral," Gabe said as they sat. "I came down with this hell flu out of nowhere. It was gone the next morning, but the timing was lousy. I had planned to concelebrate, as I assume Tom told you."

Tom had not. Barbara must have passed on Michael's feelings about Novak and Tom had kept silent, assuming Michael wouldn't make a scene at the church. That was an incorrect assumption, but God had swooped in with a well-timed stomach flu. Everyone wins! With the exception of Novak, and Michael was sure he had offered it up for the souls in purgatory.

"So I hear you're in Barton," Gabe said.

Michael nodded. "Just for another month."

Gabe poured the bourbon into two glasses and handed one to Michael. Then he lifted his and said, "To Vincent." Michael could feel his teeth clench as their glasses clinked. As if this weren't bad enough, now the guy thought they'd bond over Vincent's ghost?

"Where to after that?" Gabe asked.

"You tell me," Michael said, tired of playing nice. "I'm not up on where they send out-of-favor Jesuits."

Gabe didn't flinch. "To the missions," he said. "If they just want you out of sight. If they want you dead, they'll send you to the Middle East."

"Have you been?"

Gabe nodded. "Couple of stints, but the terrorists disappointed them, so I ended up here."

They small-talked about Atlanta while Michael took the chance to study Gabe. He was smaller than Michael had imagined, but still a powerful presence, with the jaw of a Marine and unnervingly inscrutable eyes the color of a blue heron.

After ten minutes of polite but innocuous chatter, Michael excused himself to leave. Gabe walked him to the door and Michael had almost escaped when Gabe said, "Don't worry about the gulags. They don't send enlightened thinkers there. You'll be back in Manhattan by Christmas."

Really? You're going to throw that jab as I'm on my way out the door?

"Look. I know you and Vincent bonded because you're the priest he wanted *me* to be."

"He would have preferred that you be faithful to the Magisterium," Gabe corrected.

"Isn't that the same thing?"

"One is personal and the other is abstract."

"Semantics."

Gabe frowned. "Are we seriously doing 'Grandpa liked you best?'"

Michael wanted to slug the guy, but it was true. It really did boil down to that.

"You didn't really know Vincent," Michael said.

"And you don't really know me," Gabe fired back.

Michael had no response. "Thanks for the drink," he said, and walked quickly back to his car.

Michael ignored the ringing phone. It was the public line, anyway, and Father was supposed to have a buffer zone between himself and the mere mortals. He tried to remember if he'd seen Annie when he came in this morning. He'd had no fifteen-minute conversation, so he must not have.

He was going through the *L*s in the Barton phone book one more time, as if *Landry* might have been misfiled somehow. He couldn't imagine why else he was unable to find a *Jackson*, a *Jack*, or even a *J. Landry*. No one in a small hick town (not even the brother of a mass murderer) would have an unlisted number; it wasn't like a person could hide, even if he wanted to. Still, there was no *Landry*, and no amount of staring at the page was going to make one appear.

Realizing that Annie wasn't going to answer the phone, and that the person on the other end wasn't going to give up, he reluctantly lifted the receiver.

"Saint Bernadette's," he mumbled, hoping it was a wrong number.

"Michael?"

"Bob. Thank God. I've been trying to reach you."

"Yes, I know. What are you into?"

"I don't know exactly," Michael answered. "I think it's the same demon. Danny's. And I have reason to believe it's transgenerational." No need to tell him yet *whose* generations.

"Michael, do *not* go near that alone," Bob said.

"I know," Michael said. "That's why I called you. And it's not just that, Bob."

"What else?"

"It's me," Michael said in a low voice, as if he could keep himself from hearing it out loud. "There's something happening to me. It might be . . . infestation."

"What makes you think so—" More crackling, followed by a very loud snap. And then the line was dead. Michael hung up, then tried to get a dial tone to get Bob back. There was no dial tone. Only silence.

Annie entered the room with mail and set it on his desk.

"Annie, there's something wrong with the phone."

"Then you should call the phone company."

Michael ignored that. "Do you happen to know anyone in town named Jackson Landry?"

Dead silence as she stared at him.

"Annie?"

"Well, I don't know him. I know who he is. Why?"

"I need to talk to him about something and I don't know who he is."

"Yes, you do, Father."

"Excuse me?"

"I've seen you talking to him at the coffee shop. Because I was thinking I should tell you that you shouldn't do that. People will talk. It's bad enough being Catholic in this town."

"You've seen me talking to him? When?"

"At the coffee shop, Father. You know who he is. The one that always wears those blue-jean clothes and sits by himself at the counter." She lowered her voice. "He's the one whose brother killed all those people—"

The hermit? The hermit is Jackson Landry?

"—none of my business, but I think you should just leave him alone, like everybody else does. How do you know he won't kill somebody before it's over with? I don't know why he stays here. I wish he'd just move. I've got to go, I'm late for the hairdresser. Good-bye now," she said, and she was gone.

Well, here was another stellar development.

Excuse me, I know you hate my guts, but I'm actually your first cousin and we need to have a conversation about our Satanic heritage, because evidently Great-Grandpa Kinney put a curse on us. Has anything strange been happening to you lately?

The odor returned. It wasn't as fierce as before, and the air wasn't as heavy.

Maybe it's getting weaker. Maybe this whole thing will die if I just leave it alone.

The phone rang again. He picked it up, expecting to hear Bob's voice.

"Saint Bernadette's."

"*Salsipuedes.*" The demon's voice. He knew it now.

The familiar cackle, loud and long.

"If you have something to say to me, just say it!" The cackle faded out. The phone line popped and hissed, a sound that resembled static but wasn't.

"Michael . . ." the demon's voice whispered. Somehow hearing the vile thing use his name made it worse.

"What do you *want*?" Michael demanded.

"*Salsipuedes,*" it said, then cackled again. The line went dead.

Michael put the receiver down and sat. The smell remained, and he knew he was not alone.

Salsipuedes. It sounded like Spanish, but Michael didn't recognize the word.

Maybe it's not a word, Padre.

The voice again, but now it was in his head.

Michael fumed. This was all bad enough without having to play games. But demons loved games. Bob had told him that.

It's not a word? Then why is he saying it?

I didn't say it's not a word. I said maybe it's not a *word.*

Not *a* word. More than one word?

"*Salsipuedes,*" Michael said, out loud. "*Salsi puedes.*" Then he got it.

Sal si puedes.

Get out if you can.

The cackle filled the room again; rose, fell, and finally receded, its echo trailing it. Michael felt no relief in its retreat.

THREE

Randa found a pay phone right outside Tillie's Good Food Coffee Shop, affixed to the wall of the neighboring establishment, which billed itself as STEPHEN'S QUALITY GROCERY. Evidently there was some bad food in town that the local food merchants felt the need to distance themselves from. She dialed Delta's reservations number and booked the next flight to LA. It left in two hours. She could make it if she left now.

She bought a Coke from the vending machine outside Stephen's. It was lukewarm, but she didn't care. She was buying it mainly to hear the angry sound of the bottle sliding down the chute. She'd turned toward her car, thinking how glad she'd be to see Barton in her rearview mirror, when she saw Jack.

He was standing by her car, waiting for her. The cold anger from a few minutes ago was gone, as was the glazed look. He'd shaved and changed into a clean work shirt and painter's pants. He looked like the version of himself she'd fallen in love with, which made his presence all the more cloying.

"Hi," he said.

"Hi?" Seriously?

"You're in my way," Randa answered.

"I don't blame you for being angry."

"Well, that's very magnanimous of you. Move." She said it like she meant it, since she knew her façade was likely to crack at any moment.

"It's good to see you," he said.

What the hell are you talking about?

"Well, it's not good to see you and I have a plane to catch."

"I thought you'd gone back a couple of days ago."

"You thought, or you hoped?"

"Both."

She hadn't seen that one coming. "Excuse me?"

"Randa, I was just trying to protect you," he said.

"From what?"

He stepped closer to her and spoke quietly. "Look, let's face it. Whatever it is, it's in my blood. Everyone in my family goes insane, and the men go criminally insane. If *Cam* wasn't immune to it, I'm sure as hell not gonna be."

"Fine," Randa said. "So you stay here and rob liquor stores and I'll go back to LA. What's the problem?"

"I don't think you're hearing me," he said.

"I hear you. I also heard the part about you pretending to like me so you could get laid." She said it loud enough to be overheard. She could embarrass him if nothing else.

"What?" He sounded surprised.

"You heard me."

"Half the town heard you, but I don't know what you're talking about."

"I'm talking about 'Is that your big accomplishment?'" She did the best job she could of imitating him. "And 'Randa, go home. You're all out of brothers.'"

"I said that?"

"Half an hour ago, Jack. At your apartment. What the hell is your problem?"

"You came to my place? Today?"

"Jack, if you're going to blame amnesia for the ass you made of yourself, you should go all the way back. Tell me you don't remember the Ritz-Carlton, either."

"I remember that," he said. "But that's the last time I saw you, until now."

"Well, was that your evil twin I ran into at your apartment?"

"I didn't . . . you weren't . . . I was alone, and then I came to Tillie's to eat, and until I saw you on the phone, I thought you were in LA."

She looked at him. The confusion in his eyes was real.

"Jack—"

He cursed under his breath and rubbed his forehead.

"You really don't remember?"

He shook his head.

"How can that be?" she asked.

He mumbled something she couldn't understand, although she caught the last word.

"What about Tallen?"

Jack shook his head. "Go," he said. "You'll miss your plane."

He seemed to be totally disoriented.

"No. I can't believe I'm saying this, but I came here to help you. I'm not going home with you like this."

He looked at her; she could see his focus returning. "You came here to see your family," he said.

"No. That was a lie. And don't ask me to explain, because I don't understand what's happening to me any more than you understand what's happening to you."

That seemed to register. At least he couldn't find an immediate way to argue with it.

"Things have been happening that you haven't told me about, haven't they?" She didn't know how she knew that, but she would have bet family heirlooms on it.

He nodded. She took his arm. "Okay. Let's go sit down." He didn't offer any resistance as she led him into Tillie's.

They were greeted by the usual stares and whispers from the Tillie's regulars as they settled into the booth. Jack had regained his stoic mask and ordered a couple of Cokes as they sat.

"Will you please tell me what has been going on?"

"What I told you before. I've been having nightmares, I've been hearing voices and seeing things—"

"And now you're blacking out," Randa said.

"I don't know. Maybe it's schizophrenia . . ."

"I doubt it."

"Why?"

"You're way too old to be showing first signs of schizophrenia."

He smiled. "Oh really, Doctor?"

"Schizophrenia doesn't explain my conversation with your dead uncle."

"I told you, he's obviously not really dead. Or that wasn't him you talked to. You aren't going to start with the demon crap, are you?"

"Why are you so touchy about it?"

"Because there's no such thing as demons. That was just my mother's way of shirking responsibility."

"Oh? Does that mean *you're* responsible for what's happening to you?"

He started to answer, but was cut off by the appearance of the waitress and the Cokes. She plunked them down and was gone, along with Jack's inclination to speak, apparently. He sat in a mute funk.

"Jack, Cam knew what was happening to him," Randa said, trying another approach. "At the end, I mean. He had some weird reason for calling me the night he died, because we hadn't spoken to each other in a year. He could have called a lot of other people. But he said he had to talk to someone, and I was the only person he knew who might believe what he had to say. And then he said, 'I'm in trouble that I didn't even know existed.'"

"And then what? The demon took him over and he jumped out the window?"

"Doesn't it make sense?"

"No. Schizophrenia makes sense."

Randa fumed. "Jack, there are colleges with parapsychology departments. Duke has one. There are educated people who believe in this stuff enough to specialize in it."

"I can see why Cam thought you would believe it."

Randa noticed that Jack was watching a woman at the takeout counter. The woman, who looked like someone who had lived forty-some years the hard way, smiled and waved at him. He smiled and waved back.

"Friend of yours?" Randa asked, trying not to sound catty.

"Yes. I actually have a friend." He smiled at Randa. "You almost sound jealous."

"I almost am."

The woman at the counter picked up her takeout bag and started to leave. She mouthed something to Jack that Randa couldn't understand. He immediately looked pained. He nodded to the woman.

"Crap. I told her I'd come fix her gutters when it stopped raining and I forgot all about it."

"I'm sure she'll live," Randa said. Jack smiled at her, warmly.

"I like this," he said. "I haven't had anyone jealous over me in a long time."

"Well, good," Randa said, smiling. "Bask in it."

For a moment, Randa could almost imagine that they were a normal couple, doing the normal beginning-of-the-relationship dance. She felt comforted by the mundane thoughts of ex-girlfriends and leaky gutters. It was all so concrete and familiar. How could demons be lurking in a world where gutters needed mending?

She saw Jack's expression change again, his wall going back up. She followed his gaze and saw a man walking toward them. The man was about Jack's age, dressed in a plaid shirt and jeans. Staring intently at Jack.

Jack spoke before the other man had a chance. "Whatever it is, I don't want to hear it."

"Oh, I know. You've made that very clear."

"Apparently not clear enough," Jack said.

"May I sit?"

Randa slid over to give him room just as Jack said no. The man sat anyway.

"Look," the man said in a low voice, "before, I was trying to be friendly. Now we really have to talk." The man looked at Randa. "I'm Michael Kinney," he said.

"Randa Phillips," she said, shaking the hand he offered. His handshake was as firm as the look in his dark blue eyes.

"*Father* Kinney," Jack said pointedly. Now Randa heard a note of jealousy, and it amazed her. Almost as much as it amazed her that the guy sitting next to her was a priest. She was about to comment on the latter, but Father Kinney had already returned his attention to Jack.

"We should probably go somewhere private," he said. "This isn't something you'd want eavesdroppers to hear."

"There's nothing anybody can say about me that hasn't already been said."

The priest nodded, resigned to the fact. "Suit yourself," he said. He took a breath, then: "I know something that you don't know. About your family."

Jack stood up. "Now I *know* I don't want to hear it," he said. He looked at Randa.

"I'm going over to fix Cathy's gutters. I'll be back by dinner. You can wait at my place."

"Okay," she said, but he was gone before it was out of her mouth. She suddenly felt very self-conscious about sitting on the same side of the booth as the plain-clothed priest, but he stood before she had time to worry about it.

"Something about his family?" Randa prompted.

"Tell him that it's my family, too," he said. Before Randa could even take that in, he mumbled a perfunctory "Nice meeting you," and he was gone.

Randa felt the weight of every eye in the place. She watched through the window as the priest and Jack walked off in opposite directions. He had said "Michael Kinney." Was he really another Landry? And if he was, what would it mean? Could he help Jack with whatever was happening?

She kept her seat for a few more minutes, trying to understand why such a brief encounter had left her with such a huge sense of foreboding. It was like the low rumble at the beginning of an earthquake. A useless warning of something that is coming, but cannot be escaped.

FOUR

To hell with it, Michael thought. If the jackass didn't want help, so be it. He'd come home to a zillion phone messages, committee meetings, not to mention the ever-present plague of plumbing disasters. And while he'd been gone, apparently half the parish had suffered some major life crisis that needed immediate attention.

He made it through his eleven o'clock appointment only minimally distracted. A couple who wanted to get married on Valentine's Day, and were incensed to be told the church was booked. They'd already had their invitations printed. Michael tried to point out that since they had printed the invitations and booked the reception before checking on the availability of the church, maybe the three of them needed to discuss the order of their priorities. The couple wasn't interested in discussing anything except alternate places where Michael could perform the ceremony. They'd thought about a neighboring parish, but the priest there was old, and the bride thought Michael would look better in the pictures. Michael suggested they find another parish and ended the meeting.

After the couple, he returned phone calls, made appointments, and heard confessions for an hour and a half. It was all he could do to be fully present, as he doled out the Our Fathers and Hail Marys, and all-important absolution (*do I still believe in it?*), but he managed.

Back in his room, he played it all in his head one more time. He knew he couldn't forget about Jack; Jack's problems were attached to his. And given Jack's family history, there were potential innocent victims to consider. And then there was the fact that, for all intents and purposes, it was Vincent's deathbed request.

His throat constricted immediately when he thought of Vincent. He was simultaneously angry with his grandfather and sick with grief from the loss. He couldn't think of a thing he wouldn't trade to be able to talk to Vincent right now. To get the truth, if nothing else.

The truth. Even if he could get near it, he wasn't sure what that would accomplish. It would take more than knowledge to free him at this point.

Maybe Tom Graham was right. Maybe he *did* need four weeks in the woods with St. Ignatius. Time to recharge. Time to focus on something besides the darkness.

No. It's bigger than that.

That was what scared him the most. The fact that everything he was going through was bringing to the surface serious questions about his faith. The demon, whatever he was, was forcing him into a corner, where he had to look at things he'd shoved aside for too long.

Something about Evil. Something about all of it. The math had never added up for him. The Bible was lovely poetry, but the picture it painted was one of total chaos. A vengeful God, exasperated with His fallen children (who had fallen either by design or by design flaw, neither a comforting thought), patiently pleading with them while sending chastisements at regular intervals. Finally deciding the only way to redeem them was to send His son for them to torture and kill. Then He'd call it even. And for the rest of history, all anyone had to do was believe the fairy tale, and they'd be "saved."

It had never made any sense to Michael. He'd only been able to believe it by declaring it misinterpreted and incomplete. Basically, by believing the stuff he liked and concocting his own theories to fill in the gaps.

He poured himself a glass of bourbon, at the same time scolding himself for drinking so much lately. But what the hell else was he supposed to do? Sit calmly and wait for the next demonic attack?

Bob Curso suddenly came into his thoughts. Bob and his simple, black-and-white universe, where the Devil was bad and God was good and everyone got to decide whose team they wanted to play on.

To what end? What would the winner get? And why did the Devil waste his time in a battle that he surely knew he couldn't win? And why . . . and why . . . and why . . .

Michael found the number and dialed Bob's soup kitchen. He was amazed when the phone was answered on the third ring, and by a person with more than a passing knowledge of the English language. Michael asked for Bob.

"He's not here anymore."

"Excuse me?"

"He moved into a retirement home."

"Bob retired?"

"It was sudden. Health problems, I heard."

Michael took the number of the retirement home. When he tried it, he got the same static and disconnected lines as before. Exasperated, he sat down at the computer. He didn't have Bob's e-mail address, assuming Bob had one. But he could write a note and FedEx it, and maybe Bob would call him over the weekend and help him figure out what to do about Jack Landry.

Dear Bob,

I am so sorry to learn of your health problems. I can't imagine you in a retirement home; hopefully this is just a "time out" until you feel better.

Do you have a better phone at the new place? I really need your help on a case. Please call me.

Warm regards,
Michael

He proofed the note and printed it, then searched for a FedEx envelope while he was waiting. He realized how tightly he was wound when the sound of the printer made him jump. That was the main reason he wanted to talk to Bob, he knew. He was really getting sick of being in this thing by himself.

He filled out the address form, stuck it into the clear plastic pocket, and went to get the letter. He sat down at his desk to sign it. Something looked wrong. He squinted, then took his glasses off. It took him a moment to realize what the printed letter looked like; when he got it, it took his breath.

Dear Michael,

Sal si puedes. Sal si puedes. Sal si puedes. Sal si puedes. Sal si puedes. Sal si puedes. Sal si puedes. Sal si puedes. Sal si puedes. Sal si puedes. Sal si puedes. Sal si puedes. Sal si puedes. Sal si puedes. Sal si puedes. Sal si puedes. Sal si puedes. Sal si puedes.

The heavy presence had returned, along with the smell. Michael balled the letter up and threw it at the trash can. More angry now than frightened, he grabbed his jacket and wallet and stormed out of the room. He got into his car and took off. He headed north. He'd like to see how the damned thing planned to stop him from getting on a plane.

He landed at Newark just in time for the worst traffic; he called Bob's retirement home, managed to get through to the office and get directions. He rented a car and joined the gridlock.

Two hours later he arrived at the retirement home, which seemed a nice enough place. A two-story brick building, set off from the road in a small grove of trees. He got the usual "Yeah, sure you're a priest" looks from the staff until he flashed several IDs that began with "Archdiocese of . . ." He was led to Bob's room by a young priest who called Michael "Father" and treated him as if he'd be a resident there in less than five years. Seeing Bob's door ajar, Michael thanked the young twerp and sent him back whence he'd come.

Bob was sitting in his room with the drapes drawn. The only light came from a small lamp by the bed. Bob stared at the curtains blankly, as if they were open and he were gazing out the window. He didn't respond to Michael's slight rap on the door, so Michael stepped into the room.

"Are you growing mushrooms in here?"

Bob turned slowly toward the voice. Michael hoped his surprise didn't show. Bob looked years older than he had six months ago. He also looked as if he'd lost twenty pounds. His formerly round face was thin and hollow, and his formerly soulful eyes were lifeless. He stared blankly at Michael for a few seconds, then recognition set in and he offered a frail smile.

"Michael," he said, in an unsteady voice that should have belonged to an old man, "what are you doing here?"

"I was going to ask you the same thing."

"Sit down." Bob motioned to the bed and Michael sat. He hadn't expected a bear hug, but he was disappointed in Bob's detached reaction to his appearance. Then again, Bob seemed to be detached from the planet.

"How did you find me?" he asked.

"I called the mission and they told me. I hope you weren't hiding from me."

"No," Bob answered, as if it had been a serious question. "Not from you."

"How are you feeling?" Bob just shook his head. "The guy on the phone said you had a health problem."

"No," he said, quietly.

Michael waited. When it became clear Bob wasn't going to speak again, he pressed it.

"What, then?"

Bob looked at Michael. For a long time he didn't say anything. Then, softly: "I got into something that was over my head."

"A case?" Michael asked.

Bob nodded. "I told you to never try it alone. I should have taken my own advice."

"But you're okay?"

Bob smiled, a sad smile. "So they tell me. What about you? What have you gotten yourself into?"

Michael told him the entire story. Bob listened intently, with no verbal response, although his eyes widened at the part about Vincent's past, and again at *"sal si puedes."* When Michael was done, Bob spoke immediately.

"Leave it alone," he said. Michael looked at him, confused. "Michael, the thing I got into was just a more powerful demon than I could handle, and look at me. You're in deeper than I was. It's not after whoever happens to take it on. It's after *you.* And it's been waiting a long time."

Bob stopped, winded. He took a couple of breaths, wheezing as if he'd just climbed a long flight of stairs.

"That's why I was trying to call you," Michael said. "I wanted your help, but I'd settle for advice."

"I just gave you my advice."

"To run from it?"

Bob leaned forward. "Michael, this is probably the same demon that was in Danny."

Michael nodded. "That's what the demonologist said."

"Every time they win one, they get that much stronger. And you were no match for this one before."

"Well, what am I supposed to do? Vincent's family started all this. Now it's my debt."

"To hell with your debt. You're going to end up with a worse debt than you can imagine."

"Bob, it's not that easy. I'm not sure anyone else can get rid of this one."

"Then you have a big problem."

"How can I solve it?"

Bob thought about it for a second, then said, "Resign from the Jesuits and convert yourself back to Catholicism."

"That is not helpful," Michael said, bristling.

"Maybe not, but it's the truth."

Bob nodded, then closed his eyes and nodded off.

• • •

Michael could barely remember the way back to the city. Bob's appearance haunted him. His entire demeanor. It was so far from the Bob he'd last seen. How? And how had gentle ribbing about the Jesuits turned into a nasty dismissal of Michael's faith in its entirety?

What happened to him during that last exorcism?

Before the thought was fully formed, the first wave of nausea hit him. By the time he was halfway through the Lincoln Tunnel, it was all he could do to drive. He willed his way into Manhattan, half doubled over from the cramping in his stomach. The closest garage was five blocks from Tess's apartment, and he had to take a cab from there. He was in too much pain to walk.

The doorman, Deneb, recognized Michael and quickly opened the door for him. Michael walked past him and headed for the elevator.

"Hurry," Michael said.

Deneb followed without question. Closed the old elevator gate behind them and headed for the sixth floor.

"I'm not well," Michael managed to say.

"I can see that," Deneb answered in his thick Ukrainian accent. He opened the door again to let Michael out. "I should wait?"

Michael shook his head no. He knocked loudly on Tess's door, at the same time searching for his key. The door opened and he brushed by Tess.

"Michael?" she said, stunned to see him.

He was able to mumble "Bathroom" and headed for it, slamming the door behind him.

He made it without a second to spare, and was convinced he was going to throw up internal organs before it was over. It didn't make any sense, as he hadn't eaten anything all day, except for a bag of peanuts on the airplane.

He heard Tess outside the door.

"Michael? Are you okay?"

He leaned back against the wall. He knew he didn't have the strength to stand. "Yes," he called to her. He doubted it sounded convincing. "I'll be okay in a minute."

"All right," Tess said, obviously unconvinced. "What are you doing here?"

He didn't answer. As soon as he could stand, he turned on the shower, ditched his clothes, and got under the spray. The water felt cool against his skin and he realized he must have a fever.

In his head, the babel started again. First the demon's cackle, followed by what sounded like the soundtrack from the bar scene in *Star Wars*—garbled, unearthly voices with cocktail-party inflections. Over it, he could hear a voice similar to the demon's, only more effeminate, singing *"sal si puedes"* to the tune of some annoying kid's song. All of it was way more than his pounding head could stand.

Shut up. Just shut up!

Instead, it became louder. Michael thought he was going to have to scream.

Please. God . . . help . . . me . . .

A tune came to him; he didn't recognize it, but it was clear and lovely and he could hum it. He hummed with what little strength he had, and slowly the babel began to fade. So did the heaviness in the air.

He breathed a sigh of relief. He made the water cooler and let it fall over him until finally he felt some of his life returning.

By the time he got out and dried off, he felt light-years better. A bit dizzy, and certainly not strong, but he didn't feel sick anymore. He dried his hair with the towel, threw his shirt into Tess's hamper, and put his jeans back on. He found his toothbrush in the medicine cabinet and brushed his teeth until he couldn't taste anything but Crest. He looked at himself in the mirror. He was several shades paler than normal, and there were purple caverns under his eyes.

Dear God. This thing can do anything it wants to me, whenever it wants to. Wherever it wants to. How am I supposed to fight that?

Tess knocked again. "Michael?"

He opened the door.

"I guess it was something I ate," he lied. There was no reason to get her involved and worried. "Do I still have any shirts here?"

"I'll get you one," she said.

He followed her into the bedroom. She rummaged in the back of her closet and came out with a Fordham sweatshirt.

"So how's that for a romantic entrance?" he asked, pulling the sweatshirt on.

"The throwing up didn't bother me, but I can't deal with the fact that you sing the 'Kyrie' in the shower."

"What?"

"You heard me."

"I wasn't singing."

"Yes, you were. Maybe you do it unconsciously. In which case I might be able to live with it."

"You heard me singing?"

"Yes. You were singing the 'Kyrie,' to some tune I've never heard before."

"You heard actual words coming from me? Not humming, but actual words?"

"Yes, Michael. How else would I have known what you were singing?"

God. Was I singing without realizing it? Or was I humming with someone else who was singing, a voice I didn't even know I heard?

"I want to lie down for a while," he said, suddenly realizing how tired he was.

"You really don't look good. Maybe I should call a doctor . . ."

"No," he answered, too quickly. "I'll be okay."

"I'll get you a glass of ginger ale."

"Thanks."

As soon as she was gone, he lay down on her bed and pulled the comforter over himself, clothes and all. His teeth were chattering, and his muscles ached. He would have thought it was the flu, but he recognized it. It was the same way he'd felt on the train ride home from Danny Ingram's exorcism. It was that, only ten times worse.

". . . you were no match for this one before . . ."

Tess came in with the ginger ale and set it down on the nightstand. She sat on the bed beside him.

"Why are you in New York again?" she asked.

"Long story," he said. He was too tired to say more.

"Does it end with, 'and so I flew up here to tell my provincial that I'm resigning'?"

He tried to answer, but instead closed his eyes and surrendered to sleep.

The next time he opened his eyes, it was still dark. The digital clock said 3:47 and Tess was asleep beside him. He got up long enough to take his street clothes off, then slid back under the covers, pulled her into his fetal position, and fell asleep right away.

He came into the dream as if it had been going on without him. Joined himself in progress. He was in the meadow, sitting on the ground. The guy in the flannel shirt was sitting opposite him, leaning back against the same tree as before. His jeans-clad legs were stretched out in front of him, crossed at the ankles. His eyes seemed darker than before—more gray than blue. The look in them was the same. Steady. Calm. Uncompromising.

Michael was already talking when he became aware of being there. Somehow he fell into the flow of it.

"I know this is the thing," he said. "This is what I'm supposed to do. And Vincent set everything up so I could be near Jack. That's why he wanted me in Barton."

The guy in the flannel shirt nodded slightly but didn't speak. He was twirling a long piece of grass between his thumb and index finger. His skin was brown, as if from the sun. His hands were somehow sturdy and delicate at the same time. Michael had to work not to stare at them.

"So that's it?" Michael asked. "This is what my whole life has been building up to?"

"You're not happy about that."

It wasn't a statement or a question. More like "Admit it so we can get on with this conversation."

"Well . . . I'd just like to think I came to the planet for something more than to save someone else."

The guy looked down at the piece of grass in his hand. He had an odd look on his face, which made Michael realize what he'd just said, and to whom.

The guy smiled a little. "You'll forgive me if I don't get all choked up," he said.

Without warning, the guy stood up and walked away. Michael got up and followed him, eager to hear more. Suddenly, the meadow dissolved before his eyes; the guy went with it. Michael felt himself fall, then hit the ground running. He didn't know where he was or why he was running. He just ran. The terrain under his feet was hard and uneven, and there was a fog so thick he couldn't see anything around him. He caught a glimpse of something up ahead. A movement. A shadow. He ran faster, toward it. The fog grew thinner, and he could see the shadow more clearly. A person, moving ahead at a steady pace that seemed unhurried; yet running as fast as he could, Michael couldn't catch up. He didn't know why he felt so powerfully driven to run, except that everything in front of him felt safe.

The person up ahead stopped and turned, and now Michael could see him. It was the same guy. Dressed differently now, in something loose and light colored. He didn't smile this time. He had a stern look on his face. He motioned for Michael to follow him.

"I'm trying!" Michael called. "Slow down!"

The guy didn't answer; he turned and moved forward again, at the same steady pace that Michael couldn't keep up with.

Michael suddenly stopped, his heart pounding, as he realized he'd almost stepped off into a bottomless gorge. He regained his balance.

"Hey," he called to the guy. "Wait!"

He could see the figure in the fog up ahead. He watched it disappear.

Michael woke up shivering, but not from cold. He sat up. Looked around the room, as if he might see something. He felt consumed by a gut-wrenching emptiness. Tess lay beside him, breathing peacefully. No hallowed convictions tormenting her. No enigmatic messiah haunting her sleep.

FIVE

Jack opened his eyes and had no idea where he was. It was dark and cold and he was lying on the ground. He looked around. As his eyes began to focus, he could see he was surrounded by woods.

Oh, no. I did it again.

He sat up; pulled a couple of dead leaves off his face and threw them down. The night was quiet except for the sound of a train in the distance.

He smelled whiskey and looked down to see a pint bottle of Jack Daniel's on the ground beside him. It was empty. Trying to stand left him no doubt as to where the liquor had gone.

He steadied himself against a tree. He looked at his watch. It was nine thirty. Randa would be frantic. Either that, or on her way back to LA. Hell.

His jacket was a few feet away. He crawled to it, managed to get one arm in a sleeve on the third attempt, and left it at that.

He remembered sitting on Cathy's sofa, drinking a glass of sweet tea. He had finished the gutters and was in the process of telling her the Randa story. The last thing he remembered was Cathy going to answer the phone. It had given him an opportunity to look at his watch. It had been 5:35.

Where the hell have I been for four hours?

Where the hell was he now, for that matter? He surveyed the landscape, started to move slowly in the direction of the most light.

It didn't take him long to clear the trees, and then he realized where he was. He was in the woods just down the road from Cathy's. He could go back there and use the phone to call Randa. And maybe Cathy could shed some light on the missing block of time. Maybe she could do that while he worked on an explanation for why he smelled like a still.

The road was deserted, which made everything feel even creepier. He walked back to Cathy's as fast as his unsteady legs would carry him.

When he got within sight of her trailer, he froze. From the other side of the trailer, he could see the reflection of blue light, traveling in a circular pattern that was all too familiar.

He slowed down and edged closer. He made his way behind a dark trailer, then crept along the side of it until he had an unobstructed view of Cathy's.

His embryonic fears were instantly confirmed. Two cop cars and an ambulance were parked in front of Cathy's trailer. A cop standing in the front door of the trailer, barking at someone inside. A semicircle of neighbors had gathered around, standing behind a line of yellow police tape.

Jack's breath left him in one acidic rip.

Oh, no. Please God . . .

The cop in the doorway stepped aside to let two attendants bring a stretcher through the door.

Oh, God . . .

The body *(It has to be Cathy, there was no one else there.)* on the stretcher was covered with a blanket, but Jack couldn't see all of it. The cop was blocking Cathy's head.

Please be alive . . . How could I have hurt Cathy, even if I'm crazy how could I have hurt Cathy?

He heard a noise nearby, the static of a two-way radio. Cops in the woods. Searching for a suspect. Searching for him.

Maybe it wasn't me . . . Maybe it was someone else . . .

It was you. Don't be an idiot.

I don't know for sure.

You know who you are.

He saw the beam of a flashlight, far too close to him. Whether he had done it or not, a Landry lurking in the woods near a crime scene was all it would take for the sheriff to consider the case closed. He had to get the hell out of there.

He moved away from the sound of the radio, grateful for all the years he'd spent hunting, which had taught him as much as could be learned about moving through dead leaves with a minimum of noise, even given his current alcohol level. He also knew, from younger years, that the woods ran behind the Haskins' dairy farm and came out just north of town. If he could make it to the other side, he could make it home.

Home. And then what?

Worry about that when you get there.

He could hear the cops moving in his direction. They had the advantage of not needing to be quiet, so they could move at twice his speed. They'd be on him in a minute if he didn't do something.

He looked down at the ground. Found the right-sized rock. The moon gave him just enough light to see how to aim, though dodging the trees would have been a near-impossible task stone sober. He found the clearest spot, aimed, and sailed the rock directly in front of him. It cleared a good eighteen feet before hitting the trunk of an oak, but the sound was nebulous enough to be anything. He heard the feet and the radio noise begin to move toward it. He used the cops' footsteps to camouflage his own, and got away from them as quickly as he dared.

As had always been true in the course of Jack's criminal career, Barton's finest proved easy to elude. In ten minutes he had emerged on the other side of the woods. He waited until there were no cars coming, then trotted out to the road and picked up a normal pace.

All the while, he knew he was only buying time. Half the trailer court had seen him at Cathy's, he had no way to account for the hours since he'd left there, and his last name was Landry. The trial would probably take an hour. Not that it mattered. Whatever remained of his newfound will to live had disintegrated the second he'd seen Cathy on the stretcher. If she was alive, she'd wake up feeling hideously betrayed, as well she should. If she was dead, he didn't want to live anyway.

But he needed a chance to tell Randa what happened. He needed to tell her to leave quickly, before anyone knew she'd been at his place. She shouldn't even be alone in a room with him, but he had to warn her. And maybe he wanted a chance to say "I told you so." Hell if he knew. Not that it mattered. He was long past needing to examine the purity of his motives.

In his cloudy and grief-infested mind, he knew one thing. He was going to do what Tallen did. He wasn't going to argue when they came for him. He was going to shut his mouth, drop his appeals, and get this over with as fast as possible.

SIX

Randa stared at the clock and wondered what to do. By seven, she knew it was too dark for Jack to be fixing gutters, so she'd decided he must be on his way home. By eight, she'd decided he was dead, hit by a truck while walking in the dark; he was lying flattened on the highway somewhere, human roadkill. She was about to go and look for his remains when she heard him open the door.

"Where have you been?" she asked, instantly sounding like a nagging wife. He closed the door and locked it.

"Jack?"

He was pale and shaking. She went to him and when she hugged him, she could smell alcohol. He held her so tightly she thought he was going to bruise a rib.

"Jack, what is it?"

"Something happened," he said.

"What?"

He shook his head. "I don't know. I blacked out again. I woke up in the woods. When I went back to Cathy's, there was an ambulance—" He had tears in his eyes. "I think I hurt Cathy."

"Are you sure the ambulance was at her place?"

"Yes."

"Well, maybe she got sick—"

"No. There were cops everywhere."

He went and sat on the couch, put his head in his hands. "Oh, God. What if she's dead?"

Randa tried not to panic. Maybe he was mistaken. Maybe this was more of the same paranoia that had made him leave her at the Ritz-Carlton.

"Jack, do you know anyone who lives near Cathy?" He didn't answer. "Jack?"

He looked up. "The old lady who lives next door."

"Where's your phone book?" Randa asked.

"Closet. But I can't call—"

"I'll call. I won't mention you." She found the book. "What's her name?"

"Hardie. Mary, I think. Or Marie."

Randa searched. "There's a Martha Hardie on Chalk Level Road."

"That's it."

The old woman answered the phone on the first ring. Randa identified herself as a neighbor from across the street and asked what all the commotion was about.

"What did you say your name was?" the old woman asked.

"Randa."

"Amanda?"

"Yes."

"And you live across the street?"

"Well, up the street a little. In the . . . brick house."

"The one with the wagon wheel in the yard?"

"Yes."

"I thought that was Rufus Turner's house."

"No. He's next door," Randa said. Martha sounded too old to run across the street and find out Randa was lying. She looked at Jack and rolled her eyes at how long this was taking.

"Well, I hope you have your doors locked," Martha said. "Because they haven't caught whoever done it."

"Yes, I was trying to find out—"

"And I'm here by myself," Martha went on. "I called my son, but I guess he already left for work. His wife won't answer the phone at night because she knows it might be me and she's too stuck up to talk to me, ever since she started working for the school board. Jeanette Hardie. Do you know her? She used to be a Weatherford—"

"No, I don't know her. But—"

"She thinks I'm tryin' to move in with them, but I wouldn't ask them for a biscuit if I was at death's door starving—"

"Mrs. Hardie, I'm a friend of Cathy's and I need to know—"

"Poor Cathy, I told her last week to be careful because we haven't had nothing but problems since they built that apartment complex behind us, it's just full of lowlifes and I knew it was just a matter of time before something like this happened."

"Mrs. Hardie, is Cathy dead?"

Maybe the direct approach would work.

"Yes, she's dead. I thought you knew that."

Randa tried to keep it from registering on her face so Jack wouldn't know until she could tell him. Martha was still going.

"I know it's true because the policeman was Billy Thomas and I asked him and he said she'd been dead for a couple of hours when they found her. And I was sitting right here by myself, it could just as easily have been me . . ."

"Thank you. I have to go lock my doors now." Randa hung up, looked at Jack. She'd rather die than tell him, but no one was going to offer her the option.

"Cathy's dead?" he asked.

Randa nodded. "I'm sorry," she said.

Jack was quiet for a moment. Randa was about to go over and put her arms around him when he stood up. He walked to the door. He walked back to the sofa. He picked up a glass from the coffee table and hurled it against the wall.

"Goddammit!" he yelled.

"Jack, be quiet!" Randa grabbed his arm before he could throw anything else. "Jack! The last thing you need is the neighbors calling the cops."

He jerked his arm away. He sat on the sofa again, buried his face in his hands, and sobbed.

Randa went to sit beside him. She hugged him. He didn't respond, but he didn't knock her away, either.

"Jack?" She shook his shoulder gently. "Jack?"

He didn't answer. But then, she had no idea what she'd say if he did.

"It's okay." (It's not okay.)

"Don't take it so hard." (He killed a woman. He should take it hard.) "You weren't conscious, it isn't your fault." (So what? The fact that he wasn't conscious doesn't make Cathy any less dead.)

"Jack, you have to pull yourself together. We have to figure out what to do."

"There's nothing to do," he said.

"If the cops come—"

"I'll turn myself in."

"No, you will not! You don't even know if you did it."

Jack put his face in his hands again.

"Oh, God . . . How can this be happening?" His tone was plaintive, as if she might have an answer.

"What is the last thing you remember? Were you—"

Randa was interrupted abruptly by the sound of pounding on the door. She gasped.

Jack pulled the curtain back, just enough to see out. "Cops," he said.

"What do we do?" Randa asked.

"Let 'em in. What else are we gonna do?"

He reached to unlock the door. Randa took a deep breath and started to work on her lie.

SEVEN

Michael woke up. The nausea was gone. The dizziness was gone. The headache was gone. But the worst of it remained. The feeling of evil that seemed to taint everything around him, as if it were something he was causing instead of something he was caught up in against his will.

Tess was standing in the doorway, dressed for work, looking at him. He reached for his glasses so he could see her.

"Do you feel better?"

He nodded. "Physically," he said.

"What's wrong?"

He sat up. Waited a moment to make sure he wasn't dizzy. Most of his current fog was left over from the dream.

"What, Michael?"

"I don't know." He wanted to tell her. But he wasn't even sure how he'd describe it to himself. "I've been having these dreams that make me feel bad." It sounded sophomoric, but he couldn't think of a more sophisticated way to put it.

"What kind of dreams?" She came over and sat on the bed, appearing genuinely interested.

"I keep dreaming about this guy you think never existed." She didn't laugh, to his great relief.

"What about Him?"

Michael shook his head. "I don't know, exactly. It's not like I thought it would be. *He's* not who I thought He would be. But it's just a dream, right? No big deal."

"What's He like in the dream?"

He didn't know why she cared, but he welcomed the chance to talk about it. "Kind of . . . I don't know . . . it's not that He isn't warm, but there's . . . something else. No. I don't know. There's no word for it. It's like he wants something, and I don't know what it is."

She smiled. "Did you expect Him to have a sappy smile on His face and a robin on His finger? Because that's Saint Francis. People tend to get the two of them confused."

He knew she was trying to cheer him up. Somehow that annoyed him.

"Never mind. I shouldn't have mentioned it."

"I'm sorry. I can't joke about Jesus?"

He stood, looked at himself in the mirror, and instantly wished he hadn't. He took his glasses back off and laid them on the nightstand.

"You still haven't told me why you're here."

"I'm working on something."

"I mean why you're *here*, in my apartment."

"I wanted to see you."

"Why?"

He looked at her, puzzled.

"You said we were taking a break. Have you changed the rules?"

"I'm leaving. I just came for the meeting, now I'm going back to Atlanta."

"That isn't an answer."

"I don't know," he said. It was the only honest answer. "I'm in the middle of something and I can't think about us until it's over."

"What are you in the middle of?"

He wanted to tell her, but there was no point in it. They lived on separate planets, and on hers, everyone crawled out of the primordial ooze and evil meant refusing to recycle.

"I can't talk to you about it."

He saw her bristle at that.

"Why not?"

"Because it involves things you don't believe in." He was afraid that sounded harsh, so he added, "I'll tell you about it when it's over."

She nodded, letting it go, for now. She sat on the bed next to him and crossed a leg over his. Started to kiss his face.

"I didn't know how long you were going to sleep," she said. "I can undress and be late for work."

He wanted that. Badly. But he moved away from her, leaving her perplexed and frowning.

"I can't," he said.

"Why not? What time is your plane?"

"It's not the plane," he said. He went into the bathroom and closed the door behind him.

His plane was half an hour late getting into Atlanta, and Annie was leaving for her lunch break by the time he drove down to the rectory. She came to meet him as he was getting out of the car.

"I left your messages on your desk, Father," she said.

"Thanks." She was probably dying to know where he'd been, but she would just have to die.

"I guess you heard what happened to your friend," she said.

"What friend?"

"That Landry." She had a look on her face like she'd just gotten a call from Ed McMahon. "They arrested him for killing a woman out at that trailer court."

Michael felt himself go weak.

Oh, God . . .

"Are they sure he did it?"

She nodded. Lowered her voice. "They say he strangled her with a lamp cord."

Oh, Jesus . . . It's my fault, . . .

"Didn't I tell you?" Annie went on. "I knew it would happen sooner or later. At least this oughta get rid of him, and we'll be rid of the last of them . . ."

In his head, Michael could hear the sound of the demon's cackle. Sneering. Triumphant.

"Anyway, that's the news," Annie said. "Oh, and that plumber—"

Michael snapped. "Annie, tell him to get over here and do whatever the hell he wants to do and send me the bill. In the meantime, I don't want to hear another word about the piddlyshit plumbing problems!"

Annie had turned pale and could barely nod. He could still feel her wide-eyed stare as he turned away, and he was sure she was already planning her letter to the archbishop. He kept walking. Hell if he cared.

The police station was filled with stern faces, hushed tones, and self-satisfied looks. The Barton police department finally had a case worthy of its talent, and they were about to get rid of the final Landry, to boot. No one looked surprised to see Michael. They probably assumed the church had been vandalized again.

"Hi." A sheriff's deputy greeted him awkwardly. The Protestants knew they weren't supposed to call him Reverend and couldn't bring themselves to call him Father, so he was used to clumsy greetings.

"Is the sheriff here?" Michael asked.

"Yeah, but he's gonna be tied up for a while. Can I help you?"

"I want to talk to him about Jack Landry."

"Is that so?" the deputy asked, with no discernible attitude. "And why's that?"

"I think I might be able to help you guys out." Michael delivered it with subtext and a meaningful look, as if the implications were obvious.

Come on, Deputy, do the math. Every cop show in the history of television and a trillion B movies . . . Bad guy kills somebody, confesses to the priest . . . Priest has moral dilemma, finally goes to the cops, finds some ingenious way to divulge what he knows . . .

The deputy's face was blank for a second, then slowly brightened.

"Wait right here, Father," the deputy said. Evidently it was okay to address him as Father if he was going to be on their side. The deputy disappeared quickly down the hall.

The receptionist looked up from her desk and smiled at Michael, apparently thrilled and grateful that he'd brought a new dimension to the drama.

"Father?" The deputy was back, motioning for Michael to follow him. Michael was halfway down the hall when a door opened and the sheriff appeared, looking appropriately grim.

"Father, you wanted to see me?" Translated: "This better be damned good."

"Actually, Sheriff, I'd like to see Jack Landry."

"And why's that?"

"It's personal."

"Well, unless you're an alibi witness, personal's gonna have to wait."

"You aren't getting anything out of him. If you were, you'd be in a better mood." Michael moved on before the sheriff could decide on his level of anger. "I might be able to help you," he said.

"I doubt that. Even if he tells you he did it, you can't tell me."

"No, but I might be able to get him to talk to you."

"How are you gonna do that?"

"He trusts me," Michael lied.

The sheriff weighed it. He stared at the floor for a long moment. Michael got the feeling he was just waiting until enough time had passed that everyone would assume he'd reasoned it out in his head and decided that Michael had stumbled on a good idea.

"All right," he said. "I could use a break anyway." He led Michael back down the hall, to the door he'd come from.

"When was he arrested?" Michael asked.

"He's not under arrest," the sheriff said. "He's being held for questioning."

Michael nodded. Somehow he didn't think the Barton SWAT team was out combing the countryside for the real killer.

The woman who'd been with Jack at the coffee shop was sitting on a bench in the hallway. She looked exhausted and her eyes were swollen and red. She was justifiably puzzled to see Michael. He searched his mind for her name.

"What's going on?" she asked.

Before Michael could answer, she saw the sheriff reach for the doorknob.

"Hey, wait one minute. I've been asking you all night to let me go in there."

"Are you a priest?" the sheriff asked with a patronizing glare.

"No. I'm not male, either. What's the third strike against me? My California driver's license?"

"Look, ma'am," the sheriff said. "I don't—"

"Actually, I think it would be a good idea if—is it Randa?" She nodded; Michael went on: "—if Randa came in with me."

"All right, Father. You can have her. Just take her with you when you leave." The sheriff opened the door. "Y'all got fifteen minutes."

Michael wondered where that law was written, but didn't want to push his luck.

"Thank you."

Jack looked up as they came into the room. He didn't seem to have the energy to be surprised. He looked worn out and distraught. Randa hurried over and hugged him. Jack returned the hug, barely. His eyes were on Michael.

"Okay," Michael said, "you have three choices. You can hope they don't have enough to convict you, and if you're right, you can go free and then *kill* the next person who is standing there when you have an episode. Or you can let them lock you up and/or execute you for something you have no memory of doing. Or you can listen to me and do what I tell you to do."

"How do you know I don't remember it?" Jack asked, instantly defensive.

"Because, unlike you, I know what's happening to you."

"All right," Jack answered, annoyed. "What's happening to me?"

Michael thought for a second. He had to make it something Jack wouldn't immediately reject. Details.

"Your father was illegitimate, is that correct?"

"Yes."

"His mother was from a poor family. Itinerant workers. She left home when she was very young."

Jack nodded. "I don't know much about her, but that sounds right."

"Okay," Michael said. "Let me tell you a little about my family."

Randa broke in. "Do we really have time for this?"

"We have to have time," Michael said, and went on. "My parents died when I was a year old. I was raised by my grandfather. His name was Vincent Kinney."

"The architect?" Jack asked. It was Michael's turn to be surprised.

"I read," Jack explained.

"All right. But what you don't know is that Vincent is . . . was . . . the father of Will Landry."

Jack was clearly stunned. He stared at Michael in disbelief.

"You mean . . . your grandfather . . ." Randa looked at Jack, then back at Michael. "Your grandfather was also Jack's grandfather?"

Michael nodded.

"There's more," Michael said, "and it's not good. And it's going to sound insane." He thought for a second. There was no easy way to say it. "My great-grandfather—Vincent's father—was a Satanist. Apparently a pretty heavy-duty one, as these things go."

"Wait a minute," Randa said. "A *what*?"

"Believe me," Michael said, "I know how crazy it sounds. I could not say 'my great-grandfather was a Satanic high priest' with a straight face were it not true. My grandfather was raised in the cult . . . was a member of the cult until he was seventeen. They—" He took a breath, preparing himself. "The cult kidnapped a thirteen-year-old girl and . . . Vincent . . ." He stopped. He couldn't bring himself to say it. "Your father was conceived during a Black Mass. Ultimately, that's what is wrong with you, and that's what was wrong with your family."

"Let me see if I have this straight," Jack said. "You're saying this cult kidnapped my grandmother, and your grandfather impregnated her during some kind of a devil-worship ceremony, and that's how the world was graced with my father's presence?"

Michael winced at the harsh sound of the truth. "Yes," he said. "That's exactly what I'm saying. The cult planned to use the baby—your father—as a sacrifice to Satan. My . . . our . . . grandfather helped them escape."

"I hope you don't want me to thank you for that."

"I'm just trying to tell you what happened. I don't care what you thank or blame me or my grandfather for. None of that is important. You need to know this: that your father was a by-product of very dark circumstances, and you are now a victim of that."

"Jack's mother always thought there was a curse on the family," Randa said.

Michael nodded. "Jack's mother was right." He looked back at Jack. "The thing that is hounding you and taking you over and making you black out is an evil spirit. Summoned intentionally by my great-grandfather and ordered to destroy our bloodline."

He saw Jack roll his eyes.

"You know what? I think it's stupid, too!" It came out loud, and half an octave higher than his normal voice, but Michael couldn't help it. "I do this for a living and I can barely say the word 'demon' with a straight face. You know what else? This thing doesn't give a damn whether we believe in it or not. So much the better if we don't. No one will get in its way."

Randa shook her head. "It sounds so . . . I mean, I believe in Evil, but . . . demons?"

Michael nodded again. "I know." He could see a trace of belief in her eyes; he followed it. "Whether we're comfortable with it or not—whether we *believe* it or not—there really is a Devil. There really are demons. There really is some sort of war going on between forces of Good and Evil. All around us. All the time. Infecting our lives in ways we don't even dream of."

"I wish I *could* believe it," Jack said. "I'd love to blame everything I've ever done on the Devil."

"Well, you couldn't do that," Michael said.

"Why not? Isn't that what you're saying?"

"No. These things can't get in by themselves."

"What does that mean?" Randa asked.

"It means that somewhere along the way, Jack did something to accept its offer. He took some action, willingly, that unlocked the door."

Jack was staring at the table. Michael thought he saw Jack react, very subtly, to what Michael was saying. He had a feeling that whatever Jack had done, Jack knew what it was. There was no point in exploring it, though. It didn't matter anymore.

"Look, Jack, you don't have to believe it," Michael said. "You don't have to believe anything. Just let me do what needs to be done."

"What's that?" Randa asked.

"He needs an exorcism," Michael said.

Jack laughed sardonically. "Well, I saw the movie and it looked like a lot of fun, but I'm kind of tied up at the moment."

"What have you told the police?" Michael asked.

"The truth. I fixed Cathy's gutters, I woke up in the woods next to a mostly empty bottle of Jack Daniel's. I don't remember anything in between."

"Do they have anything? Witnesses? Evidence?"

Jack shook his head. "They haven't charged me yet, so probably not."

"I don't see what they could have," Randa said. "He admits to being in her trailer, so forensics won't prove anything."

"Okay," Michael said. "We have to get you out of here."

"And how are we supposed to do that?" Randa asked.

Michael had already been thinking about it. He remembered something Bob had said to him the day after Danny slashed his father's face.

"He could have passed a polygraph saying he didn't do it, because he *didn't do it."*

"Offer to take a polygraph," Michael said.

"He can't do that!" Randa said. "What if he actually did it?"

"I'm telling you, *Jack* didn't do it. He wasn't even there at the time."

Jack looked anything but convinced.

"Did you know this woman?" Michael asked. Jack winced and shut his eyes tight.

"Yeah," Jack finally said, in a barely audible voice.

"Were you angry with her about anything?"

"No," Jack said quickly. "Cathy was my . . ." He stopped. Took a breath. Tried again. "Cathy's the last person I'd ever want to hurt," he said, his voice trembling.

Randa put her arm around him. She had tears in her eyes.

"Jack," Michael said, "you have a right to save yourself."

"Yeah? And what will I have saved?"

"Your life."

"You've gotta do better than that," Jack said, and looked away.

Michael gave it a moment, then said, "This thing has already killed a lot of people whom I presume you loved. You're just spitting on their graves if you let it kill you, too." Michael left that hanging and tried another approach. "You know, you could have a life. You and Randa could have a life together. I know I just met her, but I'd be willing to bet it would never get boring." Randa smiled and looked embarrassed. "It's not too late. Get married. Get a house. Get a lawn mower. Have kids. Name them after your brothers." He saw Jack flinch at that. "Look, I don't care if you run away and join the circus. Just don't let this thing win."

"From where I'm sitting, it's already won," Jack said.

"I don't notice a noose around your neck."

"Stick around."

"Jack, take the polygraph," Michael said. "Don't tell them you don't remember. Tell them you didn't do it. And if you pass, then you'll know that I'm telling the truth."

"Don't you mean *when* I pass?"

"Yes. I do."

Jack looked at Randa. He reached up and brushed a tear off her cheek with his thumb.

"Jack, what could it hurt?" Randa asked. "If you flunk, they can't use it against you."

"I'm not sure it's flunking that he's afraid of," Michael said. He looked at Jack. "The real question is, do you have the guts to live, if you pass?" Jack didn't speak or look at Michael. Michael stood.

"I'll leave you guys alone," he said. Then, to Jack: "I don't know anything about this woman who died, but if she was your friend, I doubt she would want to be what made you finally give up your life."

Michael's footsteps on the tiled floor punctuated his exit. He reached the door and opened it.

"Michael?"

He stopped. Waited.

"Would you ask Barney Fife to have them send a polygraph examiner?"

Michael nodded. He left to find the sheriff, his feeling of relief completely eclipsed by a stronger feeling of dread.

EIGHT

Jack passed the polygraph. Apparently he passed it convincingly. Randa overheard the examiner tell the sheriff, "I'd be looking elsewhere." The sheriff was clearly unhappy—both that he hadn't solved his big murder case, and that he wasn't going to become the town hero for getting rid of the last Landry.

Even with the polygraph results, the sheriff kept them there for as long as he could, but time was running out and he had to let Jack go or charge him with something. Finally Michael got testy and asked if they were planning to charge Jack with felony gutter repair. Said he had a friend at the ACLU who'd be very interested to hear about it. At which point the sheriff got some religion; he grunted warnings about Jack staying close to home, and then he let them go.

Once they were outside, Michael wasted no time.

"We need someplace to do this. We can't do it at the boardinghouse or the rectory. We have to go someplace where the noise won't attract attention."

"What kind of noise?" Randa asked.

"Trust me," Michael said.

She supposed the answer was obvious. Demonic noise, whatever that meant. She told Michael about the farm. He nixed it.

"Too much evil in that place. It would have a home court advantage."

"Let me get this straight," Jack said, looking at Michael. "You're saying there's something in me . . . that my body is just a shell and I'm actually this invisible . . . thing . . . that lives in it? And I can be displaced by another invisible thing, which happens to be an evil thing . . . that wants to destroy me . . . and after it's done with me, it will go after you?"

Michael nodded. "Basically."

Jack shook his head. "Why?" he asked. "What's the point?"

"Nothing that I can explain to you quickly," Michael said.

"You want me to go along with this without understanding it?"

"Jack, if I came home and my house was on fire, I wouldn't stand on the lawn explaining to the firemen how I have all new wiring and batteries in the smoke detectors. I would help them put the fire out."

"How?" Jack asked. "By magic?"

Michael was getting impatient. "I guess so, from your point of view," he said. "Look, you just explained it yourself. It's a metaphysical problem. We have to fight it where it lives. If this doesn't work, you're welcome to come up with your own solution."

"He's right, Jack," Randa said. "Let's just do it."

Michael appeared to be deep in thought. "I have to figure out who can help me . . ."

She waited as he continued to think. For a moment he looked like he'd just smelled a bad odor. Then his face changed to something that looked like resignation.

"Okay," he said out loud.

"What?" Randa asked.

"Get in your car and follow me."

Michael took Jack in his car and headed north on I-75. Randa followed. They drove for almost an hour. Michael exited the interstate just north of Acworth and she followed him through winding country roads. It was just getting dark when he turned down a long driveway lined with huge live oak trees on either side. At the end of the drive, they came upon a large white antebellum house with a columned porch.

Okay. I'm going to an exorcism at Tara.

Michael waited for her by his car.

"You stay with Jack," he said. "He's been sleeping since we left Barton. I'll be as quick as I can be."

"Will I be safe?"

Michael thought about it.

"Okay. We'll all go."

As Randa went to wake Jack, she glanced back at Michael. He was staring at the house with a look of dread.

NINE

After half an hour of being grilled, Michael managed to convince Gabe to put Randa and Jack in adjoining rooms at the end of the hall so they could get some rest. Now the two priests sat in the dimly lit library, going over it all again.

"What makes you so sure it's demonic?" Gabe asked.

"Because of what I learned about Vincent's past. The family curse. Jack and I are the only ones left and we're the ones who are going through this insanity."

"That's not definitive."

"And because I feel it."

Gabe smiled. "Have you explained your 'feelings' to a psychiatrist?"

Michael looked down at his hands. How could he cut through this crap? He felt sure there was no time to waste.

"No," he admitted.

"I strongly suggest you start there," Gabe said. "And the diocese is going to require it anyway."

Michael shook his head. "Look, I don't expect you to understand feelings, since you don't have any, but I'm right about this."

"Maybe you are. But you need to go through the proper channels to find out."

Michael leaned down to look Gabe squarely in the eyes.

"I know there's a human being in there somewhere," Michael said, "and I really need to talk to him."

Gabe shrugged. "I'm listening."

"I tried the 'proper channels' last time. It took months, and in the end, we were denied permission anyway. And three people ended up dead because we wasted all that time. This . . . thing . . . that is attached to my bloodline, it doesn't just destroy the people it possesses. It takes out as many innocent bystanders as it can along the way. The body count is already high. If you don't help me, you *will* have blood on your hands, I promise you."

"This is not a minor favor you're asking."

"I know that."

"Okay, regarding *my* feelings? I feel like I don't want to go back to Syria."

"No one will know."

Gabe sighed; actually thought about it for a moment.

"Have you ever had any dealings with the demonic before?" Michael asked.

"Aside from my superiors, you mean?"

"The real thing," Michael specified.

To his surprise, Gabe nodded.

"I assisted in an exorcism. Once. A long time ago, in Baghdad. A fifteen-year-old girl who swore she was Ishtar."

"Did it end well?"

"Not for Ishtar," he said.

"So you know."

Gabe nodded somberly.

"Is that why you don't want to do it?"

"No. I told you the truth. I don't want to end up in trouble. As meaningless and unrewarding punitive jobs go, I actually like this one."

"You were ordained before 1972. So you were ordained an exorcist, just as I was."

"And if, like last time, my superior asked me to be involved in an exorcism, I would not hesitate. But that is not what is happening."

"We both know you have no respect for your superiors."

"Respect is irrelevant. I took a vow of obedience."

This was not going to work, Michael realized. He moved to the sofa and sat next to Gabe to underscore the importance of what he was about to reveal.

"You leave me no choice but to tell you the truth about Vincent, and it's not pretty."

Gabe nodded for Michael to continue, and he did. He spared no detail of the entire sordid mess. Gabe remained stoic, for the most part, but Michael noticed something shift in his eyes. By the time Michael was done, Gabe understood the full depth of Michael's request.

"I suspect," Michael concluded, "that Vincent asked me to bring those books here so that we would meet. I also suspect he didn't believe I could do this by myself."

Michael expected Gabe to concur, but he didn't. He remained quiet, thinking about it.

"I do realize what I'm asking of you," Michael said. It was true. He now knew well the weight of a broken vow. "But if no one has ordered you not to be involved, you have merely committed the sin of failing to ask permission. It's not the same thing."

"You're going to lecture *me* on obedience?" Gabe asked.

"You would hear a dying man's confession if you didn't have faculties to hear confessions in that diocese, wouldn't you? Because his soul would be at stake. How is this different?"

Gabe took it all in. Thought about it for a long moment.

"All right," he said quietly.

Without further comment, Gabe left the library and headed for the stairs.

"Where are you going?" Michael asked.

"To get ready," Gabe said, without looking back.

Gabe was waiting in the hallway, dressed in his cassock and a surplice, with a purple stole around his neck, when Michael came down the stairs. When Gabe handed him a stole, he kissed it and put it around his neck.

Gabe had prepared the room and Michael could see Jack already lying on the bed, arms and legs strapped to the mattress frame.

"I'm sorry about the straps," Michael said.

Jack shook his head. "Don't be. Make sure they're tight."

Michael looked at Randa. "Are you okay?"

Randa nodded. "Father Novak said I could stay."

"You don't have to."

"I want to," Randa said. "I'll stay out of your way, but I don't want to leave Jack."

Michael nodded. Out in the hallway, he could see Gabe motioning for him to come there. He excused himself.

"I want you to hear my confession," Gabe said, "and vice versa."

Oh, hell.

Of course Gabe was going to say that. Michael gave himself a mental kick for not anticipating it. Now what was he going to do?

They went to the library. Confession had never bothered Michael in the least, even if he knew the other priest. But he hadn't been since he'd met Tess. And the last person on earth he wanted to tell was the guy who was about to hear his confession.

Just do it. Leave Tess out.

That was it. He had no other choice. He'd deal with that later.

Once he'd made the decision, it was relatively painless. No surprises, except that Gabe actually admitted to pride. A sprinkling of sins against charity, some anger, some envy, the occasional impure thought. All routine stuff. Then Acts of Contrition, Hail Marys, absolutions, good to go.

Outside Jack's door, they ran through the plan like a rock band going through a set list. Holy water. Litany of the Saints. Our Father. Psalm Fifty-Three. Gospel readings. And then . . .

They began. Jack showed no reaction to the holy water. They knelt and began the Litany of Saints, which Gabe had insisted they chant in Latin, so Michael made him take the lead. He didn't mind. The chanting calmed him, and Gabe had a pleasant voice. But if his friends could see him now . . .

"*. . . Kyrie eleison . . . Spiritus Sancte Deus . . . Sancta Maria . . . Ora pro nobis . . .*"

The room remained calm through an hour of prayers. Jack kept his eyes closed and did not move. There was no smell, no heavy feeling, no voices in Michael's head. He began to doubt himself. He'd never seen any sign that Jack was possessed. He'd assumed it because of the blackouts Randa had described and the story of Vincent's demon. He was the one who had experienced the voices, the nausea, the presence. Maybe the wrong person was lying on the bed?

There was a rustle as Jack shifted his body weight to face the priests. His eyes were open now and, as Michael watched, his mouth twisted into a strange smile.

"You'll get your turn, Padre."

The putrid odor started to fill the room. Michael and Gabe exchanged a glance: an unspoken "Here we go." Michael continued the prayer.

"God of Heaven and Earth, God of the angels and archangels, God of the prophets and apostles, God of the martyrs and virgins—"

This prompted a howl of laughter that clearly did not belong to Jack. It was tangible. Michael could feel it on his skin. Randa was staring at Jack, wide-eyed.

"Virgins!" The demon laughed with delight. His eyes were fixed on Michael. "What do *you* know about virgins?" He laughed again, and then slowly turned his head toward Gabe.

"And what have we here? If it isn't the high priest Caiaphas."

Gabe didn't look up from his book. Michael picked up the prayer again and mumbled it to its conclusion.

"You're wasting your energy, Padre," the demon said, suddenly. "You can't put out the fire from inside the burning building."

"By the authority of Jesus, I command you," Michael said. "To what name will you answer?"

"You know my name," Jack said. He chuckled. "You need to learn your own name."

The air was heavy. It felt like a living thing. The odor had intensified; it smelled like an open garbage can on a hot summer day. Michael stopped and took a couple of slow breaths, trying to brace himself for the presence. Randa recoiled and steadied herself against a dresser. Gabe remained unfazed.

"*Mi casa es tu casa, Padre*," the demon said. "*Salsipuedes*."

"*Digame tu nombre*," Michael demanded.

"*No,*" Jack said, grinning.

"*Tu nombre*," Michael repeated.

"*No te acuerdas de mi*?" Jack asked, the grin widening.

"You will obey me," Michael said, "by the—" He stopped. The

pressure in the air had grown much worse in an instant, bearing down on him. A pain shot through his head. It took his breath and he couldn't speak. He shot a look at Gabe, who took the baton.

"Quod nomen est tibi?" Gabe asked the demon.

"Ana-Sin-Emid," the demon answered, laughing.

"Quod nomen est tibi?"

"Naramsin," the demon said, and then cackled again.

Michael had recovered enough to speak. "What was that?" he asked.

"Ancient Babylonian names. Ana-Sin-Emid means 'I trust in sin' and Naramsin means 'he who exalts sin.' He's playing with me."

Gabe returned his attention to the demon. *"Quod nomen est tibi?"*

The demon issued a deep-throated growl in Gabe's direction, followed by:

"Father Brilliance. Proud of that IQ, aren't you? So what? Every single thing He gave you is meaningless." He laughed heartily and then continued: "When you die, you will have had no effect on the world. The Jesuits did my work for me."

Without taking his eyes off Jack, Michael groped on the nightstand and found a crucifix. He grasped it tightly and held it up to face the demon.

"Quod nomen est tibi?" he demanded.

"Yes, I know. You can speak Latin, too."

A sound filled the room. A gruesome symphony—thousands of voices at once, all screaming in utter agony. Souls in complete despair. The demon was opening a window of their prison, allowing the sound and the feeling to reach out and grab all of them.

Michael lifted the crucifix and held it over Jack. He was trying to speak, but could not. Jack's smile turned into an equally hideous frown. He stared at the crucifix with a look of pure hatred. A low and inhuman groan came from somewhere deep in his throat. At the same time, something in the air broke loose, and the pain and the sounds started to fade. Soon they were gone entirely. The only sound in the room was that of Randa and the priests trying to catch their breath.

Suddenly the demon spoke again. "Put . . . it . . . down . . . you . . . bastard . . ."

The voice was different now. Grating. Each word seemed to take an enormous effort.

"He . . . doesn't . . . control . . . me . . ."

"He cast you and all like you into the pit," Michael said. "And by His power I command you to return."

"I . . . am . . . not . . . stained . . ." The demon's voice was getting stronger. ". . . by . . . his stinking blood."

"You are not *saved* by His blood," Michael said. The thing growled again.

"You don't know him!" the demon spat, his words now coming fast and sharp. *"You know lies! He was no one!"*

"Then why hate Him?"

"Because, you useless pig! He gets power from you brain-dead slime and your fairy tales! He had no power until you gave it to him! He was no one! You don't see the most obvious thing."

Michael didn't respond for a moment and Gabe jumped in.

"Lord, hear my prayer."

"And let my cry be heard by you."

"You weak shit!" the demon spat at Michael. "Your bread is bread and your wine is wine and nobody is going to save your ass! You're going to stand in front of the same wrath I did, and you're going to get the same amount of mercy!"

"Our Father," Gabe began, and Michael and Randa quickly joined in. When they finished, Gabe picked up the prayers again.

"God . . . it is an attribute of Yours to have mercy and to forgive . . . Hear our prayer, so that this servant of Yours—"

"You're not a skillful confessor, Father Holy Pants. Padre Pio would have known."

Gabe kept praying as Michael could feel his stomach constrict. He hadn't remembered that the demon would blurt out his unconfessed sins.

"He forgot to mention the leggy redhead in New York. He goes up there every other week for . . . spiritual direction."

Gabe stopped praying and looked at Michael.

Demons lie. Don't believe it.

Gabe knew. He might not be Padre Pio, but he'd looked up too quickly for Michael to lose his shocked expression. He handed his *Roman Ritual* to Randa.

"Hold my place," he said.

Jack's eyes were closed and he appeared to be asleep. Gabe headed into the hallway and Michael followed him, feeling like he was being called to the principal's office.

"You have a *girlfriend*?" Gabe barked.

"You're going to believe a demon?"

"Absolutely not," Gabe said. "I want to hear it from you."

Michael was trapped. To buy some time, he made his way to the library. Gabe followed on his heels.

"Yes," Michael said, figuring simplicity was his best defense.

"And you think you can confess, not mention the girlfriend, have me think I've absolved you, and then go exorcise a demon?"

"I don't want to make any major life decisions until this is over."

"You *already* made a major life decision that precludes this one. Are you deranged?"

"No. I'm counting on God to be more merciful than you."

"That's not mercy you're asking for; it's cheap grace. See Bonheoffer. There's a copy of *The Cost of Discipleship* in the library."

"Do you possess an ounce of compassion?"

"Michael, mercy is meaningless without justice. What you are doing is *lying* and inviting God *to share in your lie*. You're asking God to un-God Himself—to give up righteousness so as to approve of your moral cowardice!"

Michael knew, in some recess of his soul, that Gabe was right. But there was nothing he could do about it now, and they certainly couldn't stop in the middle of an exorcism.

"We have to get back—"

"No," Gabe said. "I'm not playing your game. Pick up the phone *now* and break up with her *now*, and mean it *now*, and *then* I'll absolve you and *then* we'll go back in there."

"I'm not going to break up with her on the phone."

It seemed like a no-brainer to Michael, but Gabe's face turned a darker shade of red.

"You're not an idiot. How can you believe in the Devil and think you won't end up in Hell for breaking a vow you made *to God*?"

"Gabe, you're a dinosaur," Michael bemoaned. "*No one* believes what you believe anymore."

"The truth doesn't become untrue because it's no longer popular!" Gabe snapped. "And the fact that it doesn't make any sense to you, or to me or to anyone else, is completely irrelevant to God."

Randa appeared in the doorway, for which Michael wanted to hug her.

"I'm sorry for interrupting," she said, "but he's asleep now."

"Good," Michael said. "We could all use a break."

They sat at the dining room table and picked at the pizza they'd ordered. No one was hungry but they knew they needed to keep up their strength. Gabe had barely spoken at all for the last hour. Thankfully Randa was taking up the slack, mostly with theological questions. Michael was sure his answers were driving Gabe insane.

"If God is so good," Randa asked, "why would He allow demons to exist? Or any evil, for that matter?"

"Ask him," Gabe said, nodding to Michael. "I'm not a sound bite guy."

"But you're the scholar," Michael said.

"Okay, Adam and Eve," Randa said. She looked at Gabe. "Explain to me how everyone on earth came from two people and we're all being punished because of an apple and a talking snake."

"For starters, in Hebrew the story is not about Adam and Eve but 'the man' and 'the woman.' Eve isn't named as such until the story is over and Adam is just 'the man' until chapter four. Secondly, the account is 'prephilosophical.' It wasn't written in the categories of Greek metaphysics, which didn't exist when it was written."

Randa put up a hand to stop him. "I'm not a scholar. Can you give it to me in crayon?"

Gabe tried again. "The story sets out the key points: that the human race has a single origin, divinely intended. That the man was endowed with rationality and free will, which he could have used righteously or unrighteously; that he used it unrighteously; that the consequences remain with us. It all sounds like bad Bronze Age mythology because the philosophical essay format had not been invented. And to dismiss it as 'mythic' is to make the same kind of mistake that a nine-year-old makes in criticizing the design of a chess set because *real* knights don't look like *that*. The Biblical account uses narrative categories to express distinctions of moral and metaphysical significance, rather than bio-anthropological generation."

"My head hurts," Randa said.

Michael had to admit to himself anyway that it was an impressive analogy.

"So if it's not meant to be taken literally, but it's also not meant to be taken as a myth, what does that leave?" Randa asked.

"The truth," Gabe said, without missing a beat. And then he busied himself with clearing the table. When he had gone into the kitchen, Michael smiled at Randa.

"He's what people call an 'old school' Jesuit. Luckily there aren't many left."

"Is the fact that you two hate each other going to make this fail?"

"No," Michael answered, though he knew it wasn't going to help.

Gabe returned from the kitchen just as they were interrupted by the sound of moaning coming from Jack's room.

"We should get back to it," Michael said.

"If you go back in there," Gabe said, "you deserve whatever happens to you." With that, he left the room.

"What is he talking about?" Randa asked Michael.

"Nothing relevant," Michael said.

"He's leaving? I thought there had to be two of you."

"He's just taking a break," Michael assured her. "We'll be okay."

Back in the room, they found Jack awake, but clearly not present. The demon glared at them, full of hate. The room was so cold they could see their breath, and filled with the now familiar rancid odor. Randa went to her corner. Michael picked up his stole, kissed it and put it around his neck, then picked up his book and found his place.

"I'll start where we left off," he told Randa, as if that made a difference to her.

"Alone again, Padre?" the demon asked with a sneering smile. Michael ignored him and resumed the prayers.

"You who made man in Your own image . . ."

"What are you going to do? Cast me out by boring me to death?"

"Look on this Your servant, Jackson Landry, who is assaulted by the cunning of the unclean spirit . . ."

"The primeval adversary," the demon said, mockingly. "The ancient Enemy of earth . . . Enemy of the faith . . . Enemy of the human race . . . Best Supporting Enemy in a Recurring Role . . . and let's not forget Most Likely to Succeed. Is this it? Is this the best you've got to throw at me? Name-calling by a fraud in a clown suit?"

Michael looked up. Weighed it. Anything the demon could be tricked into revealing about himself could be used to trap him later. It was worth the digression.

"Okay," Michael said. "Why don't *you* tell me who you are."

"You know who I am."

"I don't know your name."

"And you think I might be stupid enough to tell you?"

"Are you the only one?" Michael asked, trying a different approach.

"Oh, Padre. We are legion. You know that."

"Are you the only one possessing Jack?"

"It's all the same, you fool."

"What's the same?" Michael asked. He glanced at Randa. She was watching, riveted.

"Tell you what," said the demon. "You want to know who I am? Who *we* are? Why don't I give you *our* résumé?"

Something happened. It was as if Michael's mind suddenly became a projection screen and someone flipped a switch to roll the film. He was bombarded by a series of images. Pictures of horror and death. The nightly news without network mercy. He saw starving children with distended stomachs; skeletal bodies of AIDS victims; people hemorrhaging from the Ebola virus, their internal organs exploding like grenades. Natural disasters. Earthquakes, landslides, floods, fires, blizzards, droughts, hurricanes, tsunamis, tornadoes. Concentration camps: men lined up for the showers; children being wrenched from the arms of sobbing mothers and thrown against concrete walls. War-ravaged cities. Wailing children running naked through the shells of bombed-out buildings. Derailed freight cars spewing toxic fumes, poison gas in crowded subways, fourteen-year-olds with Uzis gunning each other down in the streets, suicide bombers driving cars full of dynamite into mosques, hypodermic needles washing up on pristine beaches, rescue dogs sniffing through the rubble of a daycare center that had been blown to bits by fertilizer and diesel fuel mixed with blind rage and raw hatred—the stench of death and destruction and waste and hopelessness. The putrid underbelly of God's allegedly glorious creation. Everything behind the façade.

And then the reel changed, and Michael began to see a montage of mankind's pitiful attempts at defense and protection. Labels on soup cans, airbags in cars, BABY ON BOARD signs, alarm systems, security gates, Mace canisters, the surgeon general's warnings, air-popped popcorn, turkey hot dogs, consumer reports, smoke detectors, antiradiation computer screens, earthquake kits, tornado warnings, flash-flood watches, iron lungs, organ transplants, bottled water, nonfat ice cream, rosaries hanging from rearview mirrors, plastic Jesuses on the dash . . .

Pathetic, Michael realized. *All our little safeguards and superstitions. Trying to fool ourselves into thinking we have any kind of control. We're the South in the Civil War—too proud to admit we are greatly outnumbered, poorly armed, and rapidly depleting our meager resources. Left with nothing but shame and humiliation, and the war-torn ruins of our souls.*

"Where's Jesus, Padre? Conjure Him up and let Him explain why I'm wrong."

"You're wrong because you don't know anything but lies," Michael said. It was a third-grade reflex. Nothing more.

"Who told you that? The Caped Crusader? Tell me, if God created everything, wouldn't that make *Him* the Father of All Lies?"

Before Michael could figure out how to answer, the demon was off on a new track.

"You want me to set you straight about Junior? It's a very simple story. He looked different. The whole world is in an uproar two thousand years later because he was taller than the average first-century

Palestinian Jew. Because his hair was lighter than everyone else's and his eyes were blue. A fluke of nature, like a white buffalo calf. It had to *mean* something. He looked different, so he had to be divine. If he'd been just another scruffy little Jew, no one would know his name by now."

"Did they kill Him for having blue eyes?"

"They killed him for being a self-righteous prick."

Don't listen. It's a lie.

"Is it, Padre? Then where is He? I'm here. You're here. Where's Superman?"

Michael opened his mouth to speak and realized he had nothing to say. Randa was staring at him, worried.

"In fact," the demon went on, "where has He been all these years? Where was He when your precious grandfather was raping a thirteen-year-old girl and she was screaming for His help? Where was He when your mother's brains were splattered all over Peachtree Street? Or when Tallen Landry used the Christmas Eve congregation for target practice?" He took a break to laugh, then went on. "I got one even better. Where was He the night you dumped Donna Padera?" He laughed. "You and your famous ego. You thought she was so upset because she couldn't stand the thought of living without you. You might have suspected something if you'd ever bothered to know her any better."

"What are you talking about?" Michael asked. How the hell had Donna Padera gotten into the act?

"Poor Donna. Your first victim. Believed everything you told her. Fine upstanding Catholic boy from a good home, with a rich and famous saint for a grandfather. If Michael Kinney said it wasn't a sin, then by God, it wasn't a sin. Let's see . . . first it wasn't a sin to jerk you off, because that wasn't really sex. Then it wasn't a sin for her to give you a blow job, because it wasn't a sin unless she could get pregnant from it. And then my favorite part. 'We might as well go all the way because if

God's going to be mad at us, He's already mad.'" He stopped to laugh. Then stopped laughing. "She didn't want to do any of it, but she wasn't about to lose her prize-catch rich Catholic boy. And you knew it. You used it. You used *her.* Now, tell me. How is that so different from what your grandfather did?"

Michael felt himself reeling. He'd been ready for attacks on his sex life, but it had never occurred to him the bastard would start with high school. He'd made a big mistake by talking to the demon in the first place. He'd broken the cardinal rule of exorcism, and now he was paying for it. He was no longer in control.

He opened the book again and looked for his place.

"Oh, no," the demon said. "We're not finished. You haven't told me where your friend was the night you dumped Donna. And I haven't told you why she was so upset that night. You're so vain, you thought it was about losing you."

Michael told himself not to listen to whatever lie the demon was in the process of making up.

"On the one hand, I was sorry to lose another generation of Kinneys to torment. On the other hand, you owed me a sacrifice."

What is he talking about?

"Your son," the demon said with a wide grin. "You dumped Donna the day she found out she was pregnant."

Michael stopped breathing.

That can't possibly be true.

"Oh, but I'm afraid it is. She didn't tell you because she didn't want to stand in the way of your hallowed calling. She spent a *lot* of time calling on His Majesty about it, but I guess He was too busy to weigh in." He chuckled. "So she did the easy thing and made it go away. She thought that would be the end of it. They always do."

Michael couldn't speak. He couldn't move.

"And where were you, for that matter?" He snarled. "Trotting off to show the world how holy you were. You're about as holy as I am. You're a murderer, from a long line of murderers! And you call *me* unclean? *You're* gonna cast *me* out? I've got a news bulletin for you about what's waiting for you on the other end of your leaky raft!"

Michael forced his legs to move and walked out of the room. Behind him, the demon was laughing hysterically.

He put the book down on a hall table. His hands were shaking. It couldn't be true. Donna would have told him. Surely she would have told him. He might not have ever been in love with her, but they'd always told each other everything. There was no way she wouldn't have told him.

Randa appeared behind him. "Michael?"

"I'm okay," he said. He took a deep breath. "I need a break. I need to go and do something. Why don't you try to rest, and I'll be back in a couple of hours."

"Okay," she said, clearly puzzled.

"Just don't talk to him. Go take a nap and leave him alone."

She nodded. He felt bad about leaving her, but he had to. He couldn't go on with this until he knew the truth.

TEN

Donna lived in College Park. He knew the house because Vincent had remodeled it, shortly after Donna had married the radiologist. He rang the doorbell and in a few seconds he heard footsteps. He dreaded this like nothing he'd ever dreaded, but it had to be done.

Donna opened the door. It took a moment for Michael's identity to register, probably because she'd never seen him in clerics. When she realized who it was, the smile left her face. She didn't speak.

"May I come in?" he asked.

"Why?

"I need to talk to you."

"I'm in the phone book," she said coldly.

"I didn't want to do this over the phone." Something flashed in her eyes and Michael felt it in his stomach.

Did that mean she knew why he was here? Did that mean it was true? She led him into the living room but didn't offer him a seat. The room was meticulously detailed with all of Vincent's finest touches, which made being there that much more difficult. The mahogany fireplace was lined with sienna tiles, hand-painted with troubadours on either side. The mantel was adorned with a collection of vases and an expensively framed picture of Donna's family. There were also framed photos of small children with Santa. Not what he needed to see right now.

"What is this about?" Donna asked. She was clearly uncomfortable. He knew of no easy way to get into it and wasn't in the mood to search for one.

"I need to know: Were you pregnant when we broke up?"

She looked away from him and brushed her bangs to the side, nervously. It took her a moment to speak.

"Who told you?" she asked, her voice trembling.

He didn't answer. Gave himself a minute to take it in. It didn't want to go in. He felt he might throw up.

"Why didn't you tell me?" he asked, finally.

"What would have been the point?"

"The point?" He forced himself to keep his voice down. "The point is that I had a right to know."

"Michael, why are you doing this? It was over thirty years ago."

Oh, dear God. It's all true.

"Why didn't you tell me? Even if it wasn't a big thing to you—"

"How the hell do you know what it was to me?" Donna half screamed. "You never knew who I was and you never gave a damn, as long as—" She stopped herself; she took a couple of breaths. Started again, slightly calmer. "What difference would it have made if I'd told you, Michael? You had big plans. What would you have done? Married me?"

He didn't answer. She knew the answer.

"All you would have done is what you're doing now. Barge in here on your morally superior high horse, judging *me*, like it wasn't your fault in the first place!"

She let him sit with it for a moment. She was right. It was entirely his fault, in more ways than one.

"I didn't see any point in both our lives being ruined," she said.

"Has your life been ruined?" he asked. He tried to make his voice inflectionless. He really wanted to know.

"You did something worse than ruin my life. You ruined me with God. The great irony." She was starting to cry.

"Donna, I think God knows who to blame," Michael said.

"I don't care who He blames!" she snapped. "All I know is, He punished me and He didn't punish you, and I can never forgive Him for that! And I guess He can't forgive me, either, because I sure as hell don't feel forgiven. Especially not with you standing in my living room out of nowhere in the middle of the night." It was his cue to leave, but he couldn't make himself move.

"There's nothing else to say about it. Now please leave before you wake up my family."

Michael nodded. He certainly didn't want to cause her any more pain than he already had. He walked toward the door. She didn't follow him. He stopped in the doorway.

"Donna . . . I'm really sorry," he said. "I would have been there for you, if you'd told me."

She looked at him, unimpressed. "No, you wouldn't have. And you're not going to use me now to ease your conscience."

It was as painful as she'd intended it to be. He left her standing in the living room, staring out the window at the rain.

He drove back to the villa as fast as he dared, given the weather and the condition of his head and heart.

Dear God . . . Dear God . . .

No prayer would form in his mind.

Why would God listen to you?

Back at the villa, Michael sat in the library and tried to pull himself together. He'd barely given Donna a thought after he'd dumped her. He'd been entirely focused on *his* future. And it had been the same way with Tess. He'd never thought about what *her* future might look like, if he left to marry her. That wasn't love, he now realized. And he knew what it was.

He sat for a few minutes, praying for the strength to do what he had to do. Then he picked up the phone and dialed.

Tess answered on the second ring.

"Hello?"

"It's me," he said.

"Hi, you!" She was in a great mood, which was only going to make it worse.

He sighed, still trying to find the words.

"Are you okay?" she asked.

"No," he said.

"Are you calling to break up with me?" Tess asked, her happy mood gone.

"Yes" was all Michael could say.

"You're breaking up with me over the phone?"

"It's complicated, but I can explain," Michael offered.

"Don't." The sound of the phone hanging up was like a slap across his face.

It took Michael a moment to hang up. He wanted to call her back immediately and try to make her feel better about it, but he knew he couldn't. He sat in the dark, aching for what he knew Tess was going through. And for Donna, and for sins upon sins. Lies, lust, fornication, broken vows, more lies, disobedience, pride, hatred . . .

And a dead child.

The thought was more than he could bear, and he broke down sobbing. Deep sobs that racked his body with a twisting pain and took every ounce of his breath. The weight of the grief crushed him.

The floor creaked and he opened his eyes to see Gabe standing there, purple stole in hand. Michael caught his breath and tried to reel himself back in. Gabe came over and sat on the ottoman in front of him. Donned the stole but didn't say anything. Waited.

Michael sat up, crossed himself, muttered a perfunctory "Bless me Father for I have sinned," and started spewing iniquities. The pain he had caused Tess, and Donna. The entire laundry list, ending with his murdered child. He wept with sorrow as his carefully orchestrated life lay in ruins before him.

"It's too much," Michael managed to say.

"You said you trusted God's mercy."

For having a lover, Michael thought. *Not for this.* And Gabe was right. He had *presumed* God's mercy. He hadn't asked for it.

Gabe leaned closer to him and spoke firmly. "Do you believe in the sacrament of reconciliation, Michael?" he asked.

Michael weighed it. If he didn't believe in it for himself, he couldn't believe in it for anyone else.

"Yes," he whispered.

He bowed his head and forced himself through an Act of Contrition.

". . . with the help of thy grace to sin no more and to avoid the near occasion of sin." And this time he meant it.

There was not a trace of smugness in Gabe's voice as he absolved Michael. The words washed over him and the weight that lifted was almost tangible, and Michael realized that a state of grace was a real thing.

Immediately there was a loud bang and a loathsome roar from down the hall.

"He didn't like that," Gabe said with a trace of a smile.

• • •

Back in the room, they found Randa quivering in a corner, terrified. The air was frigid and the presence heavy and overwhelming, and a foul stench permeated the air. There were two distinct voices coming from Jack. One maintained a low growl that never stopped. The other was Jack's voice, but with a ragged edge, as though he was getting over a bad cold.

Michael and Gabe were both gagging from the stench as they found their places in the *Roman Ritual*. Michael found his first, as Gabe barked, "Skip the preliminaries." Michael agreed. Things had ratcheted up intensely; there was no time to lose.

"I command you, unclean spirit, whoever you are, now attacking this servant of God—"

"He's *my* servant!" the thing bellowed.

"—by the mysteries of the incarnation, passion, resurrection, and ascension of our Lord—" Michael started to choke on the stench, but Gabe barely missed a beat.

"Christ, by the descent of the Holy Spirit—"

There was a loud explosion and the window blew out as if from a tornado. A huge wind swept through the room. With supernatural strength, Jack broke all the straps and stood up. At the same time, a lamp flew across the room like a missile. Its heavy brass bottom slammed squarely into Gabe's forehead, knocking him to the floor. Jack headed for the destroyed window and dove through it.

The wind was gone and the room was quiet. Michael knelt by Gabe, who was struggling to maintain consciousness.

"I'm okay," Gabe said. He tried to get to his feet but lost his balance and fell back to the ground.

"I have to go get him," Michael said.

"I'm going with you," Gabe said, groggily.

"I don't have time for you to recover. I'll lose him."

Gabe nodded. Michael turned to Randa, but she cut him off before he could speak.

"Don't even *try* to tell me to stay here."

Michael and Randa caught up with Jack, driving Randa's car, as he headed south on I-75. For a while they kept him in sight, but he was going too fast and they lost him.

"How are we going to know where he's going if we can't see him?"

Michael didn't know the answer to that.

Dear God, I can't fight him if I don't know where he is.

The silence did not surprise Michael. Seconds later, though, he was shocked to hear the demon's voice in his head, clear and loud.

"Este vez, Padre, nadie estará allí para atraparte."

It took Michael a little while to translate.

"This time . . . no one will be there . . . to catch you."

"I know where he's going," Michael said.

"How?" Randa asked.

He ignored her and drove.

Of course. It made perfect sense. The Winecoff, where he'd killed Michael's family. Where he had tried to kill Michael. He'd probably laughed that night, and sang his little "*salsipuedes*" song. Probably reveled in all the carnage, but he hadn't gotten the one thing he'd really wanted. He hadn't killed Michael. Vincent had been waiting to catch him.

Michael parked the car on a side street and led Randa up the street to the Winecoff. The glass doors to the lobby were covered with brown paper. Michael pushed them anyway. When they refused to budge, he looked around. On the other side of the building was the Chinese restaurant. Neon lights glowed in the window: DINE IN OR TAKE OUT and DELIVERY AVAILABLE, but the OPEN sign was not lit and the doors were locked. Michael motioned for Randa to follow him and ducked into the adjacent alley so they could check out the side of the building. From there, it was obvious how Jack had gained entry. One of the windows on the first floor had been smashed and was now open. Michael climbed through it and helped Randa in after him.

They ran into the lobby, where they made a beeline for the interior stairs. At the bottom of them, Michael stopped. "Okay," he said to Randa. "I need you to stay here—"

"I'm not—"

"Randa!" Michael raised his voice enough to shut her down. "This is going to take everything I've got. I *cannot* be worrying about you and your safety. You have to sit here, for Jack's sake if not for mine."

Randa sat. She pouted, but she sat.

"And Randa . . . Pray. You can believe it later. Just pray."

She nodded, and he left her and quickly climbed the stairs. He removed a plastic holy water bottle from his pocket as he went, like a cop taking his gun out of its holster.

By the time he hit the second landing, he knew he was right. He could feel the presence by the heaviness in the air and the heaviness in his soul. He had to stop on the third landing just to summon the strength to make it the rest of the way. The air was impossibly heavy and he was swallowed in a sudden onslaught of grief. The fire had started here, not more than twenty feet from where he was standing.

On the sixth-floor landing he was hit by another wave of grief, and this time it was paralyzing. Knowing its source gave him no power over it.

He sat on the stairs and cried. Sobbed. Deep, tight sobs that made his throat ache. His breath wouldn't come, and when it did, he started to cough and couldn't stop. When the coughing finally stopped, the sobbing started again. Everything inside him, body and soul, ached until he didn't think he could live through it.

God, why did You let them die? All those innocent people. Why did

You punish them for what Vincent did? Families, Christmas shopping. Fathers on business trips. A bunch of high school kids in town for the Junior Assembly . . . they were probably so excited to be here . . . their parents were probably thrilled for them to be staying at a big hotel in Atlanta, waiting for them to come home and tell their stories. And my family, completely ignorant of their maliciously summoned fate. Why, God? Where the hell were You?

No answer. Never any answer to the pain. Never any answer to anything. Just orders.

Pack. Move. Keep going.

Why? Why should I keep going?

He knew the answer to that. He picked himself up and started back up the stairs, counting the floors as he went. The stairs were lit only by what little light spilled through the dirty windows. The stairwell smelled strongly of urine. The paint on the walls had flaked off in sheets that had fallen to the floor and now crackled under Michael's feet. The paint on the handrail was peeling badly, too; it broke off in his hand, along with years' worth of dust. He kept moving. Reached the eleventh floor. He slowly stepped into the hall. Michael had spent countless hours over the years studying the floor plan of the building in Vincent's scrapbook, trying to figure out how his family could have escaped. He knew the suite of rooms where his family had died was on the other side of the building. He knew Jack was waiting.

He tightened his grip on the holy water, all the while thinking how stupid he was to consider it a defense.

Can't kill me. I've got holy water.

The hall was littered with food wrappers, old blankets, and other signs of the street people who called this hellhole home. The smell of urine was even stronger. Michael ignored it and made his way down the hall.

There were three rooms to the suite, and three doors. They were all closed. Michael chose the middle one, which led to the room that had been the parlor; it accessed both bedrooms. The bedroom doors were closed, too. Michael knew which room Jack was in: the one where his family had stayed that night. He took a moment to center himself.

The light from the hot stretch of Peachtree cast a blue glow into the room. The paint on the walls was peeling, not just in places, but everywhere. Michael looked out the window. What must it have been like? To sit here staring out at safety, at the world going about its business, while death moved rapidly closer?

Must have felt a lot like I feel right now.

He reached for the knob on the door to the corner room. Turned it. Pushed the door open slowly.

He saw Jack—or rather, the wretched thing that now controlled Jack—glaring at him with a repulsive smile on his miserable face.

"Well, look who's finally here. Did you have to run to New York first and screw your girlfriend?"

Michael felt himself cringe at the accusation, but forced himself to ignore it. He couldn't afford the distraction. Had to get his bearings. The room was small and hellish. Same peeling paint; same blue light from the street; same strange shadows. There was an odd metallic smell in the room that Michael recognized but couldn't place. Jack was standing in the corner, grinning mockingly at him.

Jesus, what now? Everything that hasn't fazed him before?

There was nothing else to do. Michael crossed himself.

"In the name of the Father, and of the Son . . ."

"Oh, no," the demon said. "No. We're not going to do the mumbo-jumbo again. And we need to clear up a few things about who's running the show."

Before Michael could wonder what he meant, it started again. His psyche was invaded by a sense of futility. Hopelessness. Pointlessness. The overwhelming impression that everything good and beautiful and holy was just a façade. Michael tried to fight it by conjuring up an image the demon couldn't defile.

A rose. It withers and dies and rots and stinks . . . A child. Who grows into an adult who lives a miserable, useless life full of pain and heartache, until gradually the body begins to break down at the same rate as the hope, and the dreams die and rot just like the body.

"Stop!" Michael yelled. The demon just laughed.

Michael could sense something changing. He began to feel dizzy. The air grew heavy and hot. The smell came back. The room started to spin. He felt the same pressure as before. The same pain shot through his head. He closed his eyes; it was all he could do not to scream. He could feel himself shaking, straining against the pain. It lasted for a full two minutes, and then it was gone, as suddenly as it had appeared.

The smell had changed. The rotten garbage smell was gone, replaced by a strong smell that Michael instantly recognized, from a lifelong fear.

Smoke.

He opened his eyes. The room was much darker, and full of smoke. The air was hot and thick. He dropped down and tried to crawl toward the window. He couldn't see anything through the smoke; didn't know where the window was. He moved in what he thought was the right direction.

He heard a sound he didn't recognize immediately. It seemed to fade into the room. As it got louder, he recognized it as a child crying.

A child? What child?

The smoke grew thinner and he could see the window. But there was something else. He squinted, tried to focus his smoke-filled eyes.

No. It can't be.

There were people by the window. Two women, one holding a toddler. Two men. All coughing, struggling to breathe. The women were crying. The child was crying.

No. He can't do this.

But obviously he could. Michael was back there. Or maybe the demon had just made it all materialize. It didn't matter.

A reenactment. Aren't they all the rage now?

Vincent. Michael's parents. His grandmother. Himself. He glanced out the window. There was no Ritz-Carlton. Somehow, he was back there. Being forced to live through it. Feel it. Smell it.

Michael tried closing his eyes, but the scene didn't disappear. If anything, it got clearer. There was nothing he could do but watch.

His father and Vincent were throwing a rope made of wet bedsheets out the window. The other end was tied to the bed frame. They tugged on it to make sure it was tight, then Vincent started down it.

"Send Claire down when I get to the ladder," Vincent said to Michael's father. Matthew nodded. The women were holding on to each other, crying. Laura was rocking Michael in her arms, trying to calm him. They all had to put their heads out the window to breathe, though the smoke-filled air outside wasn't much of an improvement.

Michael's father held the rope for extra security while Vincent climbed. The women watched out the window, their faces tense with fear.

Michael looked at his father. Matthew Kinney, standing there, alive. A man who'd never been anything but a question mark to Michael. Michael had never realized how young Matthew had been when he died. Ridiculously young. And handsome. He looked like a younger version of Vincent. He looked strong in body and spirit. Michael had never imagined his father as strong. He tried to move closer, to be closer to Matthew, but found he couldn't move at all.

"He made it," Matthew said, watching Vincent through the window. His voice was full of amazement. "We're going to make it."

The women were laughing through their tears. "Come on, Mother," he said to Claire. "There's no time to spare." He helped Claire through the window. "Don't look down," he said. "Use your feet to feel for windowsills." Claire nodded. Matthew kissed her on the forehead, and she started down the rope. She looked terrified, but she moved quickly. Matthew and Laura watched.

"You're doing fine," Matthew called. "You're almost there. A few more feet." He stopped to cough, and to take a breath.

"I can't believe it," Laura said, laughing, crying. "We're not going to die."

"Come on, let's get you down," Matthew said. "Give me Michael." Laura handed the child over to Matthew. She kissed them both.

"Don't drop him," she said, her eyes pleading.

"Laura, I'd die before I'd drop him," Matthew said. Michael felt a different kind of pain shoot through him. He could feel the love from this man he'd never known. The love that was about to be ripped away from him.

My God . . . don't make me live through this . . .

Why should He answer your prayer? He didn't answer theirs.

Laura climbed through the window and started down. Matthew watched her disappear. "You're doing great," Matthew said. "There's a windowsill about two feet below you. Just try to—" Matthew began to look concerned. He seemed to be listening to something Michael couldn't hear.

"No. You can hold on. You *can*, Laura. You *have* to! You're not slipping. No, you're *not*—"

He was cut off by the sound of a scream. "Laura!" Michael tried to yell, too, as if it could help. Nothing would come out of his mouth. And then he felt the spinning sensation again, and the pressure. The air around him changed, from searing heat to chilly, moist night air. New smells faded in. Pine trees. Candles. Smoke again, but not as strong. Some sweet smell he didn't recognize. Colors began to break through the darkness and a new scene appeared. Men in long black robes. A fire. Noises. Chants. Moans. Howls. The scene became clearer and Michael was surrounded by frenzied activity. He was in the middle of an orgy.

Opium. That smell is opium. How do I know that? Dear God, don't make me be here . . .

The men were all paired and grouped and their robes were open down the front and Michael refused to look at what was going on, but their faces were enough to tell him everything.

And then Michael saw Vincent.

Seventeen-year-old Vincent, but unmistakably Vincent just the same. On the altar in the middle of the circle. A young girl who must be Rebecca beneath him, terrified: screaming, crying, begging. Her pleas were useless, falling to the ground unheard. The look on Vincent's face dissolved any hope Michael had harbored. Vincent was enjoying the hell out of it.

The strange reality shifted and all the sounds faded except for Rebecca's screams and Vincent's heavy breathing . . . and then it all seemed to speed up and Michael felt himself caught in the frenzy . . . and then Vincent's breath became Michael's breath, and somehow Michael was suddenly seventeen again . . . not watching, he was actually back there . . . not in the woods . . . in Donna's basement on the sofa and she was under him and he could feel her mouth on his neck and their breaths rose and fell together and the frantic sounds he heard were his own and he could hear Donna calling his name and he didn't answer, didn't stop, didn't slow down and she called more insistently and she was pleading now (*"Michael, pull out! Michael!"*) and he didn't and he *could have*, but he didn't and then it was too late and he heard his own cry and then it became Vincent's and he was back in the woods and now it was Michael, not Vincent, who was on top of Rebecca and inside her as she screamed and her screams just excited him more and he could feel his body exploding with the pleasure of it as he gasped for breath and he could feel the heat of the ceremonial fire on his face and he could smell a mixture of booze and candle wax and semen and incense and somehow every smell seemed to wrap itself around him with slimy fingers and they wrenched the pleasure away and left a shell of self-loathing and then the scene changed again and he saw nothing but a flesh-colored blob . . . it started to take shape and it became a fetus, fully formed, totally human, sucking its thumb . . . and then a sound, a wailing that was coming from the baby, who was being pulled apart, limb by limb, by unseen hands . . . blood filled the screen of his mind, but not before he saw the pain and terror on the innocent face and he knew that the Satan worshipers had nothing to do with it . . . his baby, his fault, his selfishness, his crime . . . and the blood poured over him and he was covered in it and he could feel it hot and sticky and in a blinding flash he saw that he hadn't escaped the ghastly legacy at all . . . born of murderers, he was a murderer himself . . . his soul was blackened beyond repair, beyond redemption, and if there *was* a guy in a flannel shirt, He'd been finished with Michael for a long time, wouldn't hear him if he begged for mercy . . . the black hole in his soul was going to be Michael's home for the rest of eternity . . . he heard Donna's pleas again and Rebecca's screams and the baby's, and all the Landrys' and their victims' and the Ingrams' and the people's who died in the fire and all the screams reached a crescendo together . . . an ungodly sound . . . the sound of ruin and waste and destruction and hopelessness . . . He was the only person who could have made a dent in the agony and it was too late . . . He joined the scream and he screamed and screamed and finally realized he was back in the room . . . and the demon was howling with laughter.

"And you think a few words from your sanctimonious friend will save you from that?"

Michael was gasping, trying to get his breath back.

"Where's your hope now, Padre?" the demon asked. "Where's your savior?"

Not here . . . He's not here . . . It was just a dream . . . No Jesus, just an angry, vengeful God who has it in for me . . . I've been living a lie . . . My whole life is a lie . . .

Michael was crying. He forced himself to stop. Didn't want to give the demon the satisfaction of seeing it. He was standing in front of the window. He looked down at the street below.

This is what I could do. I could offer my life as a penance.

"Yes, you can," the demon said. "It's all you can do."

Would that repay the sacrifice stolen from Vincent's cult? Would that be the end of it?

The demon laughed. "Good, Padre. Now you're getting the hang of it."

The window suddenly slammed open. Michael looked at it. If he really believed that this would end it all, that the demon would leave and the trail of dead bodies would end . . .

You can't trust him. With you gone, he'll kill Randa and then Jack.

Michael put the window out of his mind and instead, he doused Jack with holy water in the shape of a cross. Jack yelled and recoiled as if he'd been scalded. Michael summoned words from the *Roman Ritual.*

"I command you, unclean spirit, whoever you are, along with all your minions—"

The demon filled the room with loud, maniacal laughter. When he could catch his breath, he said, "Let's revisit the window idea, shall we?"

Before Michael could wonder what he meant, there was a loud whooshing sound, and the entire side of the room burst into a wall of flames. They covered the door and quickly began to spread toward Michael.

Is this real?

The heat was certainly real, as was the smoke that was filling the room. Not in gray clouds, as before, but thick and black and acrid. In no time, Michael could barely breathe. He moved to the open window and stuck his head out to get fresh air.

"Now *you'll jump.*"

Michael could feel the intense heat of the flames as they moved quickly toward him.

He had lost. He could stay in the room and burn to death, or he could jump out the window and fall to his death like his parents before him. He made one last attempt at the *Roman Ritual*, in between coughs.

"I adjure you . . . every unclean spirt . . . every specter from Hell . . ."

The entire room filled with the sound of the demon's laughter, rising over the loud crackling of the flames. This had never worked, Michael thought. It was never going to work. There was nothing left but to choose his mode of death.

He decided on the window. At least he'd have fresh air on the way down. He quickly began the Act of Contrition as the flames roared closer.

"Oh, my God, I am heartily sorry . . ."

A thought struck him and he stopped.

Is this suicide?

"Go on, Padre," the demon said. "Speaking from experience, you don't want to burn."

Michael looked at the window. If jumping constituted suicide, the demon would get exactly what it wanted. This battle had never been about his *body*.

"If you want me out the window," Michael managed to cough out, "then push me."

For the first time Michael could see something different in those eyes. Disappointment? Trepidation?

Michael grabbed another breath from the window, then faced the demon again.

"It will not be my choice," he declared.

"We'll see."

The heat had become unbearable and the flames were right on him. Was there anything he could still do?

Pray.

He closed his eyes and tried to envision the cool shade of the pine tree and the guy in the flannel shirt. The picture appeared in his mind, as clear as a photograph. He felt the heat of the flames leave. He opened his eyes and the picture was real. The flannel shirt was gone, and the man standing before him was dressed in full regalia: flowing white robe with a bright red sash. A picture from somebody's grandmother's house.

"What can I do?" Michael pleaded.

"*You* can do nothing."

Michael suddenly remembered something Bob had said, before Danny's exorcism. *"Only God can save Danny. We're just the hired help."*

I can only do it through His *authority. And I have rejected every part of it that I don't like. Which means I have rejected it all. He either has all authority or He doesn't.*

He thought back to his ordination, when he had lain facedown on the floor in complete and utter submission. He immediately prostrated himself, arms out at his sides and face planted in the grass. He could feel and smell the ground under him.

"Please take me back."

He immediately felt a warmth rush over him. He looked up. The guy in the robe was once again the guy in the flannel shirt and he was smiling—beaming at Michael.

"Shall we?" he asked.

Before Michael could determine what he meant, the scene dissolved and Michael was back in the room, surrounded by flames, gasping for breath. The heat was brutal, but he was no longer afraid.

"Evil Spirit, in the name of Jesus Christ and by His authority, I command you to come out of him, return to the pit from which you were summoned, and return no more."

A horrible, brain-splitting howl filled the room. The demon was writhing, backing into the corner, battling an unseen enemy, putting up one last fight, and losing. When the howl finally ended, there was an enormous *boom*, and the fire was gone as if it had never been there. The room was a smoldering shell and the air was heavy with the smell of smoke and burnt wood. In the one unscathed corner, Jack collapsed to the floor, exhausted. He looked around, trying to get his bearings.

"It's over," Michael said. Jack stared at him, trying to take it in.

There were loud footsteps on the stairs, then Randa appeared at the door, gaping at the damage the fire had done.

"What happened?" she asked, but before Michael could answer, she had turned her attention to Jack.

"Jack?"

"It's okay," Michael told her. "It's over."

"Where am I?" Jack asked.

Randa ran to the corner and sank to the floor next to him. She took him into her arms.

"It doesn't matter," she said. "You're okay." She was crying as she said it. She buried her face in Jack's shoulder.

"Michael," Jack asked, "are you all right?"

Michael nodded. He looked out the window and took a deep breath.

Thank you.

It was well past midnight when Michael returned to the villa. He was surprised to find Gabe lying on the sofa in the library. There was a compress on his forehead and his eyes were closed. He opened an eye when he sensed Michael's presence.

Gabe sat up and Michael noticed the rosary in his hand. He also noticed he felt no irritation about it.

"Are you okay?" Michael asked.

"Of course," Gabe said. He put the rosary down on the coffee table.

"It's over," Michael said.

"Thank God."

"Amen," Michael replied. Now that his eyes had adjusted to the light, he could see a sizable knot above Gabe's left eye.

"Are you sure you're okay? You might have a concussion."

Gabe shrugged. "I boxed for six years. My head is used to concussions."

"Now I *know* you have one."

"I'll go to a doctor tomorrow," Gabe said, relenting, and then changed the subject. "Where are Jack and Randa?"

"I took them home. I tried to explain it all, but . . ."

"But?"

"What we believe is insane."

Gabe nodded. "That's why it takes guts to not give a damn what anyone thinks."

I want that, Michael thought. And then realized he was wishing to be more like Gabe.

"Does the piranha club need another member?"

Gabe smiled. "Come on in," he said. "The water's nasty, but you'll be fine."

ELEVEN

Jack was gone when Randa woke up. It was their second day back in Barton, and they had barely spoken in the last forty-eight hours. She didn't know what to make of it, except that they were both paralyzed by the giant *"What now?"* hanging over them.

She was on her second cup of coffee when the door opened and he entered. She watched in silence as he hung his jacket on the back of the desk chair and finally looked up to face her.

"Where've you been?" She tried not to sound accusatory, but was pretty sure she'd failed.

"Cathy's grave," he said, quietly.

"Was that a smart idea?"

"What do you mean?"

"The cops might have it staked out. I'm not sure what they'd make of you being there."

"I don't care what they make of it," he said. He didn't sound angry, or resigned. It was merely a statement. Before she had time to analyze it, he made it irrelevant with "I've been thinking."

Nothing good ever came from a conversation that started with "I've been thinking." Randa braced herself. "And?"

"We don't really know each other," he said. "And I don't know who I am, apart from . . ." He stopped. Neither of them had been willing, yet, to say the word "demon" without Michael in the room.

"It's a lot," Randa agreed. She'd been thinking, too. If she admitted she believed in a demon, wouldn't she then have to admit she believed in God?

"What we should do, if we're going to be adults about it, is return to our lives and figure it out independently."

He was right, Randa knew. Maybe, in a few years, they could get in touch and give it another shot. For now, everything was too close and too chaotic. Maybe Michael would spend some time with Jack and the two of them could figure out how to deal with the aftermath of . . . whatever. She was not really a part of this. She had interjected herself. It was time to go away and leave it to the people who were actually involved.

"Okay, then," she said. *You can do this. Don't fall apart.* "I'm going to go to the hotel and pack, Then I'll take a cab back to my rental car. . ."

She was half-waiting for him to stop her, but he was completely stoic.

She opened the door and he said nothing as she started out. Then, without even realizing what she was doing, she stepped back inside and slammed the door behind her.

"I *hate* this plan!" she barked at him.

"Oh?" he said.

"We're a couple. Even if we've only been one for a week. And after what we've been through, that week should count for three years. You don't get to unilaterally dictate the future."

Jack stared at her for a moment, then cracked a tiny smile. "I didn't say we had to do it. I just said it would be the 'adult thing' to do. You're the one heading out the door."

"Never mind that. What's Plan B?"

"It's your turn to have a plan."

"How about I stay here indefinitely and we figure out a better 'grown-up' plan?"

He laughed, then reached out and pulled her into his arms. They stood there for a long moment. Finally he spoke. "Your plan is better."

Was it? Randa wondered. There was no maturity to it. No logic. Only hope. But something had shifted, and hope no longer felt like a punishable offense.

ACKNOWLEDGMENTS

To all the people who were thanked in the 1996 edition of *Dark Debts*: you remain thanked, and just as enthusiastically, but for present purposes I am going to limit myself to the people who are specific to this version of the book. First on that list is my editor, Jon Karp, who has endured my lack of writing (for him, anyway) for decades and who said "yes" immediately when I approached him with the idea of a new version of my novel for its twentieth anniversary. That is the kind of support he has always shown for *Dark Debts*, since the day it first crossed his door. My second phone call was to my literary agent, Bennett Ashley, who was thrilled with the idea of another go at it, and once again kept me from doubting myself at every turn.

There are new priests to thank this time around, who have spent a lot of time over the years helping me dissect Catholicism and put it back together again, and it is because of them that I now have (in my humble opinion) a more mature understanding of my faith. They are: Fr. Sean Raftis, Fr. John Brown, S.J., and Fr. Christopher Gober. There is one more priest who has helped me more than words could adequately describe and to whom I owe a tremendous debt, both personally and professionally. He wishes to be thanked cryptically. There you go, Father. My friend Joe Garcia should also be thanked under this heading, even if he missed his calling. And thank you to my dear friends Barbara Nicolosi-Harrington and Norris Harrington, Steve Skojec, and the others (you know who you are) who are helping me survive the daily insanity of this age.

I have more family members to thank this time around: I am always grateful to Brian and Christine Walker, for taking me in as family when I showed up out of nowhere. I would never be able to accomplish anything without the love of my life, my husband Chris, taking up the slack and offering his much-valued (even if I don't always show it) opinions. Our son, Caleb, put up with a lot of being chased out of the room while I was working under a tight deadline. And, as my daughter Julianne Marie Bull would no doubt love to tell you, I ignored way too many of her phone calls from three thousand miles away, in order to get the book done on time.

I am grateful to everyone at Simon & Schuster for their hard work and the beautiful results. I spent the most time with Megan Hogan, publishing assistant, who is an incredibly patient and kind person. Laura Cherkas, my copy editor, did an amazing job. *Nothing* got by her. I am also grateful to: Cary Goldstein, VP and Director of Publicity; Anne Tate Pearce, publicist; Richard Rhorer, VP and Associate Publisher; Ebony LaDelle, Marketing Manager; Kristen Lemire, Managing Editor; Lisa Erwin, Senior Production Manager; Ciara Robinson, Senior Production Editor; Jackie Seow, VP and Executive Art Director; Alison Forner, Associate Art Director. I am often asked why writers need publishers in the year 2016. I offer this work as an answer.

And, one more time, I am grateful to my sister, writer extraordinaire Barbara Hall, for the day she said, "Just shut up and write the damned thing."

ABOUT THE AUTHOR

In her career as a writer, producer, and creative consultant, Karen Hall has worked on numerous series, including *M*A*S*H*, *Hill Street Blues*, *Moonlighting*, *Judging Amy*, *Northern Exposure*, and *The Good Wife*. She has received seven Emmy Award nominations, as well as the Humanitas Prize, the Women in Film Luminas Award, and the Writers Guild of America Award. Her first and only novel, *Dark Debts*, was a Book of the Month Club main selection when first published in 1996 and has been translated into French, German, and Japanese. She continues to work in show business. She is an adjunct professor at Appalachian State University. She and her husband own Black Bear Books, an independent bookstore in Boone, North Carolina.